A BALL OF FIRE

First published in 2008 by
Liberties Press
Guinness Enterprise Centre | Taylor's Lane | Dublin 8 | Ireland
www.LibertiesPress.com
General and sales enquiries: +353 (1) 415 1224 | peter@libertiespress.com
Editorial: +353 (1) 415 1287 | sean@libertiespress.com

Trade enquiries to CMD Distribution
55A Spruce Avenue | Stillorgan Industrial Park | Blackrock | County Dublin
Tel: +353 (1) 294 2560 | Fax: +353 (1) 294 2564

Distributed in the United States by
Dufour Editions
PO Box 7 | Chester Springs | Pennsylvania | 19425

and in Australia by
James Bennett Pty Limited | InBooks
3 Narabang Way | Belrose NSW 2085

Liberties Press is a member of Clé,
the Irish Book Publishers' Association.

Copyright © John Montague, 2008

The author has asserted his moral rights.

ISBN: 978–1–905483–45–7

2 4 6 8 10 9 7 5 3 1

A CIP record for this title is available from the British Library.

Set in Garamond
Cover design by Liam Furlong at space.ie
Internal design by Liberties Press
Printed by ScandBook

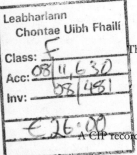

A BALL OF FIRE

COLLECTED STORIES

JOHN MONTAGUE

LIB
ERT
IES

To the memory of
Tim O'Keeffe,
an exemplar for all
gallant publishers

CONTENTS

THE ROAD ALSO TAKEN

I have always been drawn to the prose muse: how could I not be, reared amid the hills of Carleton's Clogher Valley, and attending the university of Joyce? So although poetry slowly took me over, I was fascinated by stories, especially those of the three O's (O'Flaherty, O'Faoláin, O'Connor), who charted the insular Ireland of their time. And then Ben Kiely, from my home county, beginning his career . . .

Joyce's near-perfect *Dubliners* haunted me, especially since I read it as a student in Dublin. But the real masters of the short story in English seemed to me D. H. Lawrence and William Faulkner. Lawrence has a wicked story where a collier comes to a mine owner's house with a message for a Mrs Montague, who opens the door stark naked, thinking it is her husband. This did not sound like my Ulster family!

And the burning, lava-like accumulation of Faulkner's prose led me to make an old-fashioned pilgrimage to his home place, Oxford, Mississippi. 'Bill' was away hunting, but his brother, John, a dapper little man wearing a pink button-down shirt, received us kindly, and, registering my stammer, remarked in his warm southern accent, 'You speak like our late King.'

I hammered together my first book of stories, *Death of a Chieftain*, in Paris, sometime after my first poetry collection, *Poisoned Lands*. It was the harsh period of the Algerian War, and in that fraught atmosphere I composed 'The Cry'. Although they came from the North, Ben Kiely and Brian Moore were dubious about the 'thinness' of the storyline, while *Les Lettres Nouvelles*, a leading French literary magazine, leaped at it. Considering it was written in 1962/3, it may now seem mildly prophetic.

Coming to the end of the book, I wanted to let loose, building a dream from memories of days at a hotel on the Isthmus of Tehauntepec, in southern Mexico. After all, a Sioux Indian from Rapid City had told me that Sitting Bull, like most famous people, had had an Irish grandmother, so why couldn't I let the balloon of my fantasy float?

In the 1970s I wrote few stories. I thought of a novel, but hadn't the time to develop it: some day soon I may reanimate the skeleton, although so far I only seem to be able to sustain a story to novella length. Yet poems kept coming, in the interstices of a busy teaching and family life, and what can one do if the Muse descends but be grateful? Approaching retirement, I felt I could kick up my heels a bit, and went back to an early manuscript, based on my 1950 *Wanderjahr*, which would become the erotic novella *The Lost Notebook*. But how explicit could I be? Contraception, abortion and divorce, sex in all its negative aspects, still preoccupied the Irish psyche. I chose to write as honestly – and graphically – as I could, and made sure that the Censorship Board and the Hierarchy received copies. No reaction, except that I got the first Hughes Award for Fiction.

I was also lucky with films, 'A Change of Management', scripted by Eugene McCable for RTÉ, and 'The Cry', scripted by Derek Mahon for the BBC. The latter created an uproar in the North, with protests by disbanded B-Specials. There were vague plans to film 'Death of a Chieftain' which never bore fruit, but the story was published in Mexico, where, to my amusement, it was recognised as a precursor of Magic Realism. After all, in its strange way, it was meant to suggest my solution to the Ulster Problem.

My first fiction editor was Timothy O'Keeffe, at MacGibbon & Kee. A highly generous man, he fostered both aspects of my writing, giving me an advance for two books of poems, *Poisoned Lands* and *A Chosen Light*, as well as for *Death of a Chieftain*. He also appointed me as a first reader, which gave me some influence on their list. His firm was duly absorbed by a larger outfit, but many years later Seamus Cashman of Wolfhound Press would reprint *Death of a Chieftain* and a new collection, *A Love Present*.

JOHN MONTAGUE
JULY 2008

PART I

1

THE LOST NOTEBOOK

If she does not come, my heart stands still:
Instead of summer, winter in a bound.
And if she comes, my golden girl,
Where do I stand? I die as well.

It was a makeshift notebook of the kind I am writing in now: small, neat, vellum finish; an ordinary writing pad of the kind one might buy in any shabby little street-corner stationer among the sweeties, perhaps with a wolfhound and round tower on its cover. I probably got it in Dublin before I left, but why I carried it with me through Europe that summer I don't really know; I was never one for writing home, though I probably managed an occasional note to stave off the anxiety of my elders, who had never travelled outside Ireland except via the emigrant boat, *ollagoaning*, lamenting all the way.

Besides, my wanderings were now accepted in the family with something near fatalism, as a youthful, probably pagan, ritual, leading me far from 'mother church, motherland and mother'. I do remember sending a triumphant postcard from Padua to my mother, who had a great devotion to St Anthony, among many other saints of course, and another from Assisi, Giotto's *St Francis Preaching to the Birds*. It was always my casuistical contention that Europe was packed with shrines, where the saints we heard of in church had lived and died, and now the half-century, 1950, had been proclaimed by the Pope himself as a Holy Year, *Anno Santo*, so that I could present myself as a pilgrim, ardent to reach the holy door.

It was also my twenty-first year, and in the absence of any official recognition of my coming of age, I had planned and was now giving myself a sort of *Wanderjahr*, to assuage the hunger for all sorts of experience which I felt lacking in my native land. It was a rhythm that had become part of my life: I would reach out as far as I could on the Continent, for as long as I could manage, and then return slowly, usually through repatriation, to Ireland. There I would manage to survive, buoyed up by all I had seen and heard, until I had to hit the road again. Years later, such escapes abroad would become part of ordinary Irish student life, but in my urgency I was something of a pioneer, a new kind of Hibernian savage, invading the Continent in search of art and love, *Peregrinus Hibernicus*, a horn-mad celibate with a bright red comb and a roving eye.

It was a different Europe, of course, not criss-crossed with charter planes, not crammed with package tours and student fares. Then you made your way slowly, wearily, by boat and bus and train, waking gradually to some new excitement, like walking out into the aquatic bustle of Venice from Santa Lucia Station. Or cycling through the French countryside, surprised by lines of vines, the thick rustling of maize, giant red tomatoes, a glowing Van Gogh field of *tournesols*. Or the straight line through Paris from the Gare du Nord to the Youth Hostel at Porte d'Orleans; it made my non-linear intelligence boggle. The fierce roar of the *Autoroute du Sud*, thronged with long-distance lorries and family cars, was still far away, in the crowded future.

I suppose I was planning to keep a Journal; Gide had just received the Nobel Prize and introspection was fashionable. But I did nothing as systematic as that, for now only fragments from that summer float up before me: a curious visit to the headquarters of the Soviet Zone in Vienna; a night sleeping in a field outside Bologna, waking wet with morning dew; a zealous perusal of the subtleties of Sienese Art, trying to distinguish between all that gold, those slanting eyes! Piecing the jigsaw, I realise that it was a bewildering but necessary summer of growth, a preparation for something unknown, some sensuous epiphany.

The first part takes place in Florence, *Firenze*, where I had dropped off again on my way back from Rome. Yes, I had made it to the Holy City, all the way down the spine of Italy from Venice, my beard now red and ragged, my arms stippled with freckles. And yes, I did visit the four Basilicas, and see the Pope being ferried on the *Sedia Gestatoria*. I was within spitting distance of the pale bespectacled Pacelli, *Pio Dodicesimo*, because I was there as part of an official delegation, the International Conference on Catholic Cinema, to give it its full, sonorous title.

That was because of my work as a film critic on *The Catholic Eagle* at home in Dublin. So I led a double life; nights in the youth hostel, a hectic barracks on the outskirts of Rome, where a late bus dropped me off in the evenings; days as a delegate at the conference, sporting my one suit for official meetings and receptions. A famous Irish actor was attending it also, using the forum as an excuse for a holiday. And he was very friendly to me, bringing me everywhere with him like a mascot, deferring to my unfledged but extreme opinions in literature and art, my wild plans. Together we gaped at the ceiling of the Sistine Chapel, loitered through the endless rooms of the Vatican Gallery. Then back to his central hotel in the evenings, where we had cherries soaked in red wine on the terrace. And if I was lucky he would bring me with him afterwards to a *trattoria*, my one meal of the day. Between the heat and the wine I barely made it back.

But let the journey curve back to Florence, through the white splendour of Rome's new railway station, after the conference was over, and my generous actor friend had flown away. I had stayed in a pilgrims' hostel on the way down, and been thrown out for returning late; I tried to explain to the priest in charge that I was trying to combine pilgrimage with sightseeing but the philistine refused to see my point. So this time I made my way to the youth hostel, another large, thronged, happy building. The night burned with light and voices until well after midnight. And during the day I continued my exploration of Florence, from Ghiberti's Baptistery doors to the Roman theatre at Fiesole, where I sat stunned in the afternoon sunlight.

My problem was time: three days was the limit in any hostel and, though I doubled it by hitchhiking to Siena and back, the time was approaching when I would have to leave. And I had only begun to understand the glory that was Florence! Earnest, intent, insufferable, I was determined to be an apostle of art, a martyr, if necessary, in the cause of beauty; but there seemed no way that I could simply stay on.

I shared the washing up with an English-speaking South African, who was also on his European year before he went home to take over the family business. He was stocky, neat and slow-spoken, but perhaps because we were opposites, we made a good enough team. He knew nothing about art, except that he should know about it, so he probed me for the little I had found out for myself, through a battered copy of an old-fashioned guidebook in my rucksack, which I promised to leave him. There was a Victorian earnestness about Pieter – he probably disapproved of all this paganism but it had to be seen.

So on my last morning he followed me through the city centre for a farewell look, and then bought me a light lunch, a *panino* and glass of wine, in a *trattoria*. We sat in the cool, listening to the rustle of the bead curtain as chatty Italians flowed in and out. All this richness and colour was about to leave my life; my rucksack was stowed under the table and I would shortly be tramping towards the station. I was sullen and down-in-the-mouth, a poor companion.

Sympathetic to my silence, he suggested that I should wait for the night train, and come with him to meet a strange young girl he had found himself beside in a queue at the American Express. 'Very strange,' he emphasised, in his clipped tones, under his little moustache. 'You know how Americans are,' he said, 'very green but very loud. But she did ask me round. God knows what for. Says she's a painter and I told her I'd met this young poet chap from Ireland. Like to know what you'd make of her. Really would.' He sounded uneasy, still terse but tense, for some reason. So instead of the afternoon train to Paris, or hitch-hiking on the dusty fringe of some high road, I found myself squatting on the stone floor of a small studio, at the feet of a young American girl. She was quite young, a little older than me, pretty but shameless by my provincial standards, as she twiddled her brightly painted toes right under our noses. Clearly my South African friend bored her, but she was lonely and wanted to speak English. I had never really known anyone like her, with a halter holding her overflowing breasts, and shorts riding carelessly high on tanned legs. Except that I had met her once before...

II

I had met her in the Uffizi Gallery. Since I didn't have enough money to eat at midday, I had taken to staying in a gallery through lunch-time, to avoid the sight of people eating; as well as to increase my knowledge of painting, of course. Trying to stave your hunger by staring at the details of master-works is an interesting exercise in mortification, especially in the heat of the day; what I had developed was a restless and ambulatory form of the siesta, like a mad monk on hunger-strike outside the door of a refectory. Down in the Piazza della Signora, happy tourists were tucking in, under gaily coloured awnings. If I looked that way, my eyes stuck out on stalks, so I stared at the paintings, as if through a magnifying glass.

On bad days, all still lifes were banned. Glorious pyramids of ruddy-cheeked fruit; vermilion cherries; green, black and purple grapes; soft furred peaches: on my imagination's palate they burst endlessly. Streams of juice ran down my chin, seeds stuck to be sucked in my teeth until in the intensity of my hallucination I ran from the room. Sticks of bread doubly disturbed me. Thank God I was in Florence and not in some Dutch museum, with rich rosy sides of beef, freshly hung game or venison, the saliva-raising sight of a Brueghel village feast, full bellies and distended codpieces, rich food and lusty love afterwards. The worst I had to face was Caravaggio's *Adolescent Bacchus*, his face already flushed with the wine fumes, a piled bowl of fruit before him to gorge on.

Sometimes I tried to assuage one hunger by another, spending a long time, for example, in the cool decorum of the Botticelli room. Venus rising from her half-shell, a strand of flaxen hair held demurely over her pudenda, her visage pensive; she was as mysterious and refreshing as an early morning by the sea. Luckily, I had not yet become an amateur of the oyster or *coquilles Saint Jacques* or that half shell might have been another source of temptation.

I was especially drawn to the room with the great Titians, large sensuous females at ease in their nudity, as leisurely and complete as domestic animals. The reclining *Venus of Urbino* also had a hand over her gently swelling belly to cover her thatch but the eye slid down that listless, boneless arm to join the fingers; it was a gently inviting slope, not a protective pudic gesture. And her soft, brown eyes and coiled auburn hair seemed to gather one into her rich nakedness, to lie beside her on that tousled linen bedspread where she had drowsed so long, be it only as the pampered lapdog curled beside her crossed calves.

But I would have to avoid even them if I had had no breakfast. The light-headedness of hunger can lead to extreme forms of lust, and sometimes I was less aware of the luminous Venetian tonality of the paintings, less inclined to compare them with Bellini and Giorgione in their use of colour, than overcome by their sulky physical presence. A scraggy frustrated Irish adolescent, I gaped at them hungrily, like the cats thrown in the Coliseum, and sometimes I could hardly hold myself back from leaping through the canvas to bite, even slice, a voluptuous golden haunch. Blake's 'lineaments of gratified desire', I thought, as my stomach growled. Would I ever know such satisfaction?

As I was gazing at them, I realised that someone was watching them and me. It was a young blonde with brown tanned skin and ice-blue eyes, like the corn maiden of some Northern tale. With her cascading hair, her slender but fullbreasted figure, she looked as if she had stepped down from the frame of a painting! She had a red belt drawn tightly around her waist and wore bright red slippers of a kind I had seen in the market behind the Duomo. They seemed to flicker back and forth under her light, long skirt, to match her impatience, as she sized me up before speaking: 'Gee, I wish I could lay on the paint like that,' she said in a nasal American voice, almost a whine. 'What's this guy's name again?'

Grateful for the excuse to show off my scant knowledge, I gabbled about Titian, *Tiziano Vecelli*, and his part in the Venetian High Renaissance. She listened with what I hoped was interest, contemplating me with her expressionless eyes. Then she turned on her heel and left with a parting shot that stung: 'Thanks for the lecture, Mick.' She made it sound like hick, an insult I knew from my reading. Was it so obvious that I was Irish, a gabbling Paddy? 'I have to run to American Express. See you around sometime, maybe.'

The last word was emphasised, *may-be* drawn out with scorn until it seemed to rhyme with *unlikely* or *not if I see you first, buddy*. So I had bored her. I watched her tight little bum swagger down the corridor away from me, the lift of each hip a gesture of disdain. Or so I thought, looking hopelessly after the first pretty girl I had spoken to in months...

And yet here I was speaking to her again, my head only a short distance from her warm brown legs and knees. And she was finding me amusing, or at least less boring than my South African friend, whom she

18

teased relentlessly. 'Are they really all like you down there? We've got Negroes, too, you know, but you sound like same fruity mixture of British stuck-up and Georgia cracker when you talk about them. Let 'em be, they can't be as bad as you sound. Bet your women like them – they got the old jelly roll.' And she waggled her bottom on the chair, above him.

Pieter did not know how to take her as she rambled on about race and colour and sex – I gathered she was from New York and had definite views about all three. For the moment, I decided to agree with her about them all, if it ensured my being close to her for even a little while longer. Maybe God will be good, I thought with a mixture of faith, hope, and lechery.

Pieter decided to master his irritation by showing that he did not take her seriously; she was too young. 'I think you are just a naughty girl,' he said indulgently, waving at her his imaginary swagger stick, a short ruler he had found on the floor near an easel. She went off into wild giggles.

'Don't you shake your little stick at me, Mr Man,' she said in what I recognised as a parody of a Southern accent. Then when he began to look not only puzzled, but angry: 'Haven't you read Freud, you nuthead? You're wagging that stick at me because you want to beat or fuck me, but you don't dare ask, do you, you silly racist prick?'

Raging, thin-lipped, my South African friend rose to go. He expected me to come with him, but I had been explaining to her earlier about having to leave the hostel. Watching me hesitate, she saw a chance to hurt him still more.

'Why don't you park your knapsack here? You look too young to be out but you can't be dumber than him. If you are, you can always just sleep on the floor for a few days.'

With a weak attempt at a chilly look, the South African left, and Wandy Lang and I stared at each other. That hot July night in Florence, I slept in her narrow bed, beneath her easel.

III

And spent the rest of the month in that cot, except when we quarrelled and I slept on the stone floor in my sleeping bag. A strange duel took place in that hot narrow cell, on the fourth floor of an old Florentine house: a duel of unequals. There was my timidity, so much a product of my time and place, our forgotten island off the broken coast of Europe, which had largely avoided the War. And her avid American greed for

experience, spoilt child of a rich but predatory world. We were both looking for something, but she expected it, I vainly hoped for it; the lately victorious and the colonial victim were bound to be at loggerheads.

She wouldn't help me, at first, during those long, hot nights; every
move was left to me. And my knowledge of female anatomy was restricted to picture-gazing: lacking sisters or adventurous girlfriends, I was a
typical product of an Irish clerical education, eager but ignorant.
Sometimes I made it to the magic centre, but often I fumbled, grappling
blindly in that airless tiny oven of a room, where our bodies stuck together like stamps. And every time I fell back, she made sure it hurt.

'I'm not going to help you. You're all that I hate, kids that are clumsy and stupid. Why should I show you the works, you little Irish Catholic
prick. Fuck you—'

At first, I tried to give some smart answer, like 'But that's just what I
want you to do.' But after tirades like these I usually lay awake; silent, hurt,
still hoping. And she would rise in the morning, blithe as if nothing had
happened. Then we would go to take a *caffe latte* together, inside the bead
curtain if it was too hot, on the sidewalk if there was a cool breeze. And
then we would begin our day together, which was usually easier than the
night, with her painting, and me trying to write.

And as the days passed, I began to hope against hope that I might be
able to please her. She was my meal ticket, of course, and the unsubtle art
of freeloading was one I had already learnt a little of in the drab school
of Dublin pub life in the late 1940s. But I also believed dimly in my mystic mission as a young poet, and around us lay all the ingredients for an
idyll. With that impossible mixture of hunger and idealism, I set out to
try and understand this ferocious young woman whom fate had flung
directly across my pilgrim path.

Wandy Lang was pretty, rich, but as wild and clawing as a lost alley
cat. She was not looking for the way out of an Irish Catholic childhood,
stumbling towards fulfilment, but seeking something thing that would
anneal, annul the empty ache that was already eating her. Somewhere
along the line, someone or something had hurt her, in a more drastic way
than all the pious regulations of my education. Or perhaps the combina-
tion of money and freedom that her background seemed to offer her was
only an illusion that left her still empty and angry. Whatever the reason,
she was trying to work it out, in her own strange way, far from her

20

compatriots, in a loneliness that somehow resembled my own intense, Quixotic quest.

Perhaps sex would help? She certainly seemed to have tried it, to judge by her wild language, her ceaseless use of words like prick and ass and cunt. In theory, I was all for calling a spade a bloody shovel, but to hear her pretty young mouth spew swearwords scandalised me; when she was angry it rang like a litany, a litany of desecration, of blasphemy, but also of loss and longing, if I had been able to hear its dark rhythms. But the bruised places in myself had still to unseal themselves, and I could not meet her pain with mine, although it was that hurt which called me to her.

But now her 'thing' was art. Her elder brother was a painter, whom she admired blindly, and wanted to emulate. Although, she emphasised, he would be disgusted if he knew she was daring to paint, herself. He had always discouraged her because he was a real painter, a serious painter, like Paul Klee, or 'Pete' Mondrian, who was the biggest modern painter, who had replaced nature. Did I know his tree series?

I had never heard of Mondrian, and I certainly couldn't judge the kind of painting Wandy was doing, carefully planned with an architecture of lines, constructed with the ruler the South African had waggled at her, and then intently filled-in squares, triangles and lozenges of colour. But she really worked: after breakfast, she set up her easel in the middle of the room to catch what little light came through our high window, and with bare midriff and loosely tied hair, she pointed herself at the canvas silently for hours. Heat flared up the Florentine sky, with its glimpses of red tiled roofs, the ochre façade of a high building. Her hair would tumble sweatily down, her forehead bead, until she unconsciously untied her blouse and stood bare-breasted before the canvas, like a defiant young Amazon. Now that I know more of painter and painting, I know that she was trying to imitate somebody, her brother probably, and his peers, in a pathetic parody of their intent professional preoccupation.

While she sweated before her easel, I tried to write poems. But it was too hot to concentrate properly and I was so obsessed with her presence before me in the small room that I could think only on one subject. Particularly when she stood naked to the waist before the easel, hair rippling down to her hips, oblivious of my surreptitious glances. I tried to write little poems about her, in praise of her unmarked young body, its mixture of sensuousness and childish boldness. They were Chinese lyrics, in the style of Pound, whose incarceration had made him an idol for the Irish young: a prisoner for the cause.

> Her blonde hair pours
> down her studded spine;
> bare to the waist,
> she stands, my girl.

Surrounded by the shy lasses of my country, I had touched, but rarely seen breasts. In Ireland, it was the blind leading the blind but with Wandy I could stare and stare endlessly, feasting my eyes on those mysterious forbidden globes before I began to try and net them in words.

> How warm her white breasts!
> Two bowls of cream with
> Her nipples, bright cherries.

Such naïve tenderness! But the ardour of that young man in the Florentine heat reaches out for my indulgence across several decades. We were a pair, a team in our blundering ambition: as she dragged her brush across an area of canvas, or peered before adding a touch of colour, I tried to study her as a painter might, my first life class – but a very modern one, for I was painting a standing nude who was trying to paint an abstract: a nearly Cubist vision of reality!

> As she works, she pouts.
> Her face is young, serious.
> Her eyes sharp blue.

And so forth. One day she looked over my shoulder. 'Hey there,' she exclaimed, 'you make me sound nice.' And she looked at me with warm, surprised eyes. Then she leaned over and gave me a quick kiss, the first she had ever given me in daylight.

From then on, the notebook followed us everywhere, to museums, restaurants, cafés, sometimes churches. She had taken to drawing in it; wild, impulsive scrawls to go with the poems. Clearly, I had found the way to her heart, for even in bed she began to ease up, relaxing her guard to the point where she seemed almost tender. And I was beginning to improve a little, learning how to please, to be a lover, although she was already so precocious that I lagged far behind, a blundering innocent, who had even to be taught how to kiss properly. She taught me other tricks, things that I only half-understood, bending her urgent young body like a bow, as she searched avidly for the next sensation; arching her spine, like a cat, in shudders of self-delight.

Somehow, desperately, I felt that this was wrong, that wild experiment should be the joyous fruit of love, not its budding point. But who was I to argue with her? She already knew so much more than I did about the mechanics of sex that our couplings were bound to seem clumsy and ludicrous, forcing her into the incongruous role of the older woman, the instructress of male naïveté. 'No, touch me here. Higher up. And keep that other hand down. And slowly, gently. Women like to be stroked.' Or, in another mood: 'Don't tell me you never did it like this! That's the best way to penetrate, to get it deep. Look at the animals; I thought you said you were brought up on a farm. Some cowboy you are!' And when I was spent, her hand or tongue would reach out, to revive me, rise me.

I did my best, or thought I did, to follow her urgent instructions. And she tried to control, restrain whatever irritation my incompetence caused her, compared to her previous male friends. Whoever had taught her the erotic arts had done it well, for there seemed to be little that she did not know: taking baths together like mad children, moving the bed until it was under the wall mirror, dancing together naked before we slid to the floor or bed. And for a while we seemed to enter into, at least hover near, the sweet conspiracy of lovers, although such words of endearment were not part of her harsh vocabulary. The widow next door, for instance, was shocked to discover that there was a young man staying with Wandy, a half-naked savage with red hair. Since we shared a lavatory on the landing it was difficult to avoid meeting, but she would lower her eyes when she saw us passing. And once when Wandy came to the door to kiss me, forgetting to cover her breasts, rather not bothering, the dark, startled Italian woman crossed herself several times, lifting the crucifix on her dark dress.

IV

To be twenty-one, to have a girlfriend – a mistress! – and to have the run of Florence; it seemed like the fulfilment of the dream that had lured me all the way from Ireland. I had padded dawn its narrow streets for more than a week before I met her and now she had given me a month's reprieve, with the added pleasure of being a guide to a beautiful young woman. For she seemed to have lived in Florence as if it were any flat

American city, seeing, sensing its quality without understanding it. She knew it was a place to be, but why wasn't clear to her. So the little I knew I lavished on her while I kept boning up in the British Institute library, to impress her, as I had tried that first time in the Uffizi. Laying my small treasures of knowledge before her like a faithful spaniel, I was often oblivious to the ironies of the situation, as when I introduced her to the Fra Angelicos in the Convent of San Marco.

The first time we got turned away because of the shorts and halter she was wearing. But we came back and in those cool cloisters shaded by flowerbeds and Lebanese cedars, we saw the fruits of the saintly painter's meditation, a guide to prayer, a fervent hymn to the glory of a Christian God. A long-fingered St Dominic clasping, embracing the Cross down which ran the ruby rivulets of Christ's passion, the delicate dialogue of the *Annunciation*, the blue of the Virgin's cloak and the multicoloured wings of the angel Gabriel, the rainbow-tinted dance of the Elect in his *Last Judgement*; I could not but hush before such feeling. These were not the gaudy repository images of my Ulster Catholic childhood – they seemed to breathe a mystical aroma, as light and radiant as the wing of a butterfly. Somewhere in me my fading belief stirred, the very faith I felt I had to disdain in order to live.

But for Wandy they were only pretty gewgaws, relics from a world long dead, inspired by emotions that no one would ever need again. Emerging from that rich silence she enquired plaintively: 'They're pretty colours, but why did he have to waste so much time painting virgins and saints and old stuff like that? We've left all that behind now. My brother says real painting should only be about itself.'

So I brought her to the Medici Palace, also built by Michelozzo. For me it was a Poundian paradigm of creative order, the walls where the Medici, those munificent Mafia, lived and lavished their wealth. They were all there in the ornate frescoes of Gozzoli, Emperors and Patriarchs invited from the East to join them in a stately procession through the landscape of Tuscany. It might be based on the Magi, but the emphasis was on earthly glory, clothes stiff with ornament, gloriously caparisoned horses. She looked for a long time at a handsome young man, astride a leopard.

'I like him,' she said, and when I explained that he was the brother of Lorenzo the Magnificent, she added: 'He's as pretty as my brother,' and smacked her lips.

She went silent at last in the Medici crypt before the unfinished tor-
sos of Michelangelo. She lingered before *Dusk* and *Dawn*, froze like a gun
dog before *Day*, fighting to free himself, large-muscled and intent, from
cloudy matter. But it was the graceful, sombre figure of *Night*, its large
breasts and bent head, with sad, brooding eyelids, which finally got to her.
'Jee-sus,' she exclaimed, 'I thought you said these were done by a man. He
must have been pretty lonely to feel like that. I didn't know you could get
that deep down chipping a stone. It's as bad as the blues.'

She tried to thank me, in her own way, for trying to show her so
much, for sharing. Day after day passed without a dispute, and in bed at
night she was, if not submissive, more subdued in her demands, less
insulting in her remarks on my performance. Something akin to peace
began to grow between us. Surprised by beauty daily, we made our fumbling efforts to create it ourselves, and afterwards we strolled by the Arno,
holding hands as the sun lit the red of the roofs, the intense yellow-brown
of the river.

On every walk we seemed to discover something, a lovely Venus in
the Boboli Gardens, *The Deposition of Christ from the Cross* by Pontormo, in
a church near the Ponte Vecchio. And if I didn't know about Mondrian,
I had heard of Masaccio, Big Tom, and led her to obscure churches where
the walls were covered with his work – Adam and Eve fleeing from paradise, his head bowed, her hands shading her body from a relentless red
angel. This time she did not complain about but admired the treatment
of the subject; after all, Florentine painting was a disciplined art, with the
kind of geometry of perspective that she was looking for in Modern Art:
colour called to colour, shape balanced shape.

From the blue and white cherubs of della Robbia to the flower-cov-
ered meadows of Botticelli's *Primavera*, I tried to offer it all to her, watching as she watched, ignorant but excited, a child gazing at a galaxy of dazzling stars. Back in the Botticelli room she danced for joy, like the three
Graces in their transparent veils, and when I told her that Venus rising
from her shell was Simonetta, the beloved of the young man riding the
Gozzoli leopard, she clapped her hands like someone listening to a nursery story for the first time. Especially when I added: 'She makes me think
a bit of you, when you look thoughtful, with your hair down.' And danced
for me again, shyly moving her lissom body to the inaudible rhythms of
the paintings. My heart was in my mouth as I watched, her graceful heel
and instep echoing the flaxen-haired Florentine beauties of the wall. And

then she bowed, and broke into a phrase of Italian I did not know: '*Mi piace molto ballare*', 'I really love to dance'.

When she had first come to Florence she had tried to learn Italian from a family to which she had an introduction, again arranged by her brother. Now she asked them if she could bring me along and told them proudly that I was a poet. With the deference of older Europeans to any mention of high art, I was received, scraggy, sweating in my single suit, as if I were the real thing, instead of a gaping novice.

Red wine flowed, *pastasciutta* and liquid syllables of Italian that sounded splendid even if I only dimly understood. And when our host began to quote Dante, with all the sonorous intimacy of a Florentine, I responded with Yeats, boom answering boom, like church bells ringing across the city. For the first time I heard those great lines describing the plight of the doomed lovers, Paolo and Francesca, their adulterous eyes meeting over a beloved book:

> When we read how a lover slaked his drouth
> upon those long desired lips, then he
> who never shall be taken from my side
>
> all trembling, kissed my ardent mouth.

and I countered with:

> Beloved, may your sleep be sound
> That have found it where you fed.

Our host's wife beamed. Wandy beamed. And when they wouldn't let us leave after lunch but ushered us for the siesta into a small white room with a real bed with laundered linen sheets, Wandy was beside herself with girlish delight. 'They must think we're married or engaged or something.' And she blushed. And in those cool white sheets we made love with no preconceptions, no inhibitions, sweetly, tenderly, turning to each other with muted cries of delight, nibbling and hugging like children before we started again, our lips still joined by a light skein of kisses. That afternoon was her richest gift to me, a glimpse of near ecstasy, of the sensuous fulfilment I longed for in my damp, distant island. And like all such moments it had a scent of permanence, a small addition to the sum of sweetness in the world. Finally she fell asleep, her blonde head resting on my numbed arm, in total ease.

In the crook of my arm
my love's head rests;
in each breath
I taste her trust.

V

That was our high point, the crest of the wave. But it couldn't last, it seems; we soon plunged down. Already that evening, as we stumbled home, she had begun to turn sour. Between the harmony of the afternoon and the airless heat of her little room, the dinginess of the narrow iron bed, was a distance she couldn't, wouldn't, cross. When she was in that mood she had to yield to every caprice, however hurtful. There is a certain kind of character that needs to strike out, to wound, and if the victim cares enough to complain, all the worse for them. I fought back at first, but when I found that not only was it useless but it made things much worse, I lapsed into stricken silence.

As she did also, except that she could dredge depths of melancholy, of sadness, that I had never seen in anyone before. As the heat grew daily, we took to going to a suburban swimming pool, to escape from the baking claustrophobia of her little studio. The pool was a gaudy, massive imitation of a Roman Baths, the kind of official architecture that flourished during the Mussolini period. Like most young Americans, Wandy Lang could swim like a fish, used to pools and swimming coaches from her infancy. And like most young Irishmen, I had not been properly taught, and floundered nervously at the shallow end, despising my own pale freckled skin.

And for most young Italians, the Baths was a theatre in which to strut, and show off their wares. They wore crotch-tight swimming trunks and as they looked at her they stroked themselves, openly. And she seemed to like it, to welcome it; there were very few other women present and she had their full attention, especially as she wore the first two-piece I had ever seen, exposing her acorn-brown navel, that cup from which I had newly learnt to drink. When she struck into the water they dipped and dived around her, like dolphins. And when she stretched down to cool, they paraded like distended fighting cocks; one could nearly smell the sperm. As I climbed gingerly in at the shallow end, to practise the breast stroke, they raced past, showering me with spray.

Humiliated, I sat with a towel around my burnt shoulders and tried to contemplate the water, as a kind of exercise. Water in swimming pools changes appearance more than in any other container. In a pool, water is controlled and its rhythms reflect not only the sky but, because of its transparency, the depth of the water as well. If the surface is almost still and there is a strong sun, a dancing line with all the colours of the spectrum will appear anywhere. I tried to share the intensity of my contemplation with Wandy, appealing to her pictorial sense, but she only grunted, as if I were a boring schoolboy, distracting her from the company of grown-ups. My appeal to our artistic comradeship was in vain.

One afternoon I could take no more, and tried to protest to Wandy, where she lay on the edge of the pool, holding her shoulders and breasts up to the sun, then untying her bikini halter to turn her breasts downwards. This move always delighted her audience, especially since she did it slowly, to let them feast their eyes on her body. I could neither stand nor understand it: I had begun to love that body, and that she should let them gape and slaver over it was beyond me.

'Shut up, you little puritan,' she snapped back at me. 'Just because you can't swim properly, you want everyone else to go round hunched up like a cripple. You Irish hate water and sun.' I tried to explain to her that, despite their preening and pushing, her admirers were as frustrated as any Irish provincial. The dark cloud of *la mamma*, as well as holy Mother Church, hung over the home; she was dealing with, teasing, regaling the most conventional males in Europe, with a double set of values – one for their own women, the other for whores and foreigners. Their only experience of sex, outside marriage, would be through the brothel, and there money ruled, especially since the dollars of the American army of occupation had ruined the trade. They were full of contempt for foreigners, especially women, on whom they would exact revenge for their humiliation in war. If she did let them near her, they would only despise and soon drop her.

I was brilliant, I thought, a week's bile exploding in a sermon that surprised even myself. Had the fury of Savonarola, as well as Fra Angelico, infected me after San Marco, where I had returned to visit his tiny cell and contemplate on my own? Certainly there was a stench of burning flesh in my speech, a furious rhetoric which wrapped up both her and them, my disappointment at her desertion, my jealousy of their sun-warmed maleness. But most of the information was not mine; I had collected it, unconsciously, from film after film, where the tension between the sexes in Italy inflamed the celluloid.

'So you think you know it all,' she said angrily, after we came plodding home from the pool, and began to pull off our heat-dampened clothes. She was sitting on the bed, half-naked, her skirt already shed to the floor, showing her warm gold thatch. 'Well, I've been fucking since I was fifteen.'

Silence.

'And when did you start?' She answered herself easily. 'You never did, did you? Boy, your country must be backward. You hardly even know where the cunt is. Well, take a good look at it now – for the last time.' And she lay back, provocatively spread-eagled on the bed, the pretty red shape of her sex, part wound, part flower, held open to me. But when I came forward to touch her, she jack-knifed up, laughing and jeering. 'You're not going to use me for your anatomy lesson, brother. If they didn't teach you anything about sex in your country, don't come crying to me. And don't try to tell me about men; I know. You're ashamed of your body; you can't talk. Before I met you, you didn't even know how to clean your foreskin, a real hillbilly. Christ, I don't know what they did to you in your silly schools, but your prick isn't part of you.'

She was right, of course; in school we wore shorts in the showers when we came to hose ourselves down after another sweaty, exhausting game of football, which seemed designed to drain us. And yearly we got a lecture on sex from a priest, his face brick-red with embarrassment as he tried to explain something that he barely knew about himself. Our information was garnered furtively, in dirty jokes and stories. Meanwhile the sap rose urgently, blindly, in our bodies, adolescents in the charge of celibates who were more scared than us of that pulsing power, the fermenting energy of sex that could not be denied, or channelled for long. But why did she have to mock me? Was I not more to be pitied than laughed at, to use our local Ulster expression? Between her early excess of knowledge and my ignorance was a gap that only goodwill could cross, and Wandy did not see why she should take charge of my re-education, any more than I was willing to accept her coarseness. Who had initiated her into sex, leaving her with such a mixture of avidity and terrible loneliness?

Meanwhile, we quarrelled, heat, anger, frustration crackling through that narrow room. After each attack, she tried to make it up to me, pleading silently, almost childishly, for forgiveness, in little ways that tore my heart. She would bring me a newspaper, for example, or an expensive book from one of the international bookshops. Or a brightly coloured pencil with a rubber on the top; a new fountain pen. But I wouldn't come to the pool again, determined not to be hurt by her, or those grinning young Italian males, shorts bulging like nets after a day's catch. I had had enough machismo to last me for a lifetime; instead, I trudged to the cool of the British Institute library, absorbing myself again in books, trying to blot out the images of longing and rage that surged in me. It was another version of my artistic hunger-strike and about as successful: a sex-starved bookworm, I could not, like the common or garden worm, split in two and have sex with my other half.

Suddenly a detail from Berenson's *Florentine Painters of the Renaissance* would come alive, and a slender, delicious young body would stand, not before me, but before a gaping crowd who devoured her with their eyes. Then I fled to poetry, laboriously trying to decipher the message of the *Duino Elegies*. But then Rilke would betray me, his spiritual search turned sensuous, and I would nearly weep with jealousy and desire, the words fading on the page before me. Where could I be safe from the fragrant, furious presence of that wild young woman whom I both adored and loathed? A raw little American bitch who could scarcely read – how had I allowed her to shred me apart like this when, a star student, I already knew so much more about everything than she did? Except sex; the sharp perfume of her young, hot body was in my nostrils, until, like a maddened monk plagued by noonday visions of lewdness, I neady swooned. I was in love with this terrible young woman, in love, maybe, with the idea that I had been sent to help her. But how? I struggled for some formula of acceptance, suitable for an Ulster ascetic, an Armagh anchorite.

When I wouldn't return to the pool, she organised a trip to the real sea, to Viareggio, perhaps because I said Rilke had once stayed there. And how sweetly careful her preparations were! She had a picnic basket, with a whole cooked chicken, a flask of wine, a good cheese and ripe fruit; just like any normal sweetheart, wife or mother, organising an outing with a loved one. We bathed, and lay under a parasol, and bathed again, running with linked hands into the waves. And to dance along the strand, that private intense dance of pleasure which I had not seen for a long time.

By the seashore
my love dances:
the waves press
to kiss her feet.

Phoebus Apollo,
the sun god,
the light bringer,
has blessed our feast.

But before we were bouncing back to Florence again by bus, her mood had already swung back to bitterness. There was a song she kept speaking of, a song of Billie Holiday; a name, like Mondrian, which I had never heard of in Ireland. It was 'Gloomy Sunday', and it was what she called blues, based on an old Hungarian tune, adapted by the doomed black singer. It had caused so many deaths, she said, that it was sometimes known as the Hungarian Suicide Song, and it was banned by some radio stations for its melancholy. If you listened carefully, you would realise that it was the lament of someone deep into drugs, for whom life was too much pain to sustain. And she told me of Lady's life, the heavy drugs, the brutal lovers; a black boyfriend of Wandy's claimed to have met her.

At this point, the seemingly endless cloud of our quarrels induced a kind of hallucinatory confusion. Did she possess some kind of radio or record player, an early portable phonograph? She certainly crooned the words to herself every evening in the hot darkness, as the light faded in the small, high window. I watched as the head I had tried to love sank lower and lower, drowning in a sadness, a thick, black gloom that resounded through those strange, husky tones, like the dark wax wasps exude:

Sunday is gloomy
My hours are slumberless.
Dearest, the shadows
I live with are numberless

Lulled by the spell of the song, she would topple slowly sideways to the floor, asleep. Above her was the easel she no longer used much; the few half-hearted attempts she had made recently reminded me of a pump or bucket trying to dredge from a long-dried well. Something was terribly

31

wrong, and I didn't know what to do about it. I was as unequipped as I had been at the pool to sound the depths to which she was sinking, to revive and rescue her.

> In the window
> daylight fails.
> My love's head
> also falls…
>
> The ochre shade
> of the walls
> fades; cracks
> on a grey rock.
>
> Love once
> lit the room,
> is there any
> way back?

VI

Towards the end of the month, her money began to run out. What were we to do? Half-heartedly, I offered to change my last traveller's cheque from Cook's, the one that was supposed to bring me to Paris. She shook my offer away, partly because she understood my reluctance only too well, and also because, perhaps, she wanted us to maintain our roles. It had to be her money, her flat, if she was to keep the upper hand in our relationship – to call the shots, as she coarsely said. 'I'm not going to raid the poorbox' was another mocking reply, when I tried again.

So I waited, using all my newly won training in restraint. After a day or so sucking oranges, propping her head with her fist in total, sulky silence, her features distorted, she seemed to come to some decision. She told me curtly to stick around, while she went to see the owner of the flat. She came back with him, and another, to my eyes, ancient Italian lizard, whom I had already seen in the Black Market when we went to change dollars. A typical *sensale*, behind his old-fashioned linen suit.

We sat talking for a while in pidgin English and then suddenly I felt as if there was a vacuum in the room. No one bothered to speak, all politeness was dropped as they stared at me, or rather right through me. Thick as a root, I finally still got the message. I went out and wandered the endless streets, raging. Even Florence couldn't please me: the statue of David seemed brazen, brutal, like the smirks of the young Italians on their farting motorcycles and lambrettas. At least I had a girl and didn't have to go to whores, as they did, or pester foreigners in the streets. Finally I decided to turn back: why had she driven me out for those repulsive old codgers, with their triumphant leers, like Rembrandt's *Susanna and the Elders*? Surely she would not let them touch her young beauty? I felt as protective as Galahad, as wrathful as Savonarola.

She was cleaning up the place when I got back. She had borrowed a broom from our surprised neighbour, and was wielding it well, with all our clothes, belongings, tidied into a corner, and the only carpet hanging through the small window. I came in slowly, spotted that my rucksack was still on its peg, and sat on the bed to be out of her way. It had been made, which was not usual, with the sheet tucked under the pillow.

'What happened?' I stammered finally, when she slowed down. She did not answer, so I waited until she sat down again, on the only place she could, on the bed next to me.

'What h-h-happened?' I tried again. 'I ought to know. I-I want to know what they did.'

She turned her face towards me, blank at first, that deliberate blankness I had come to know so well, which baffled and troubled me. Then a rising anger sharpened her features, made her blue eyes blaze.

'So you want to know, Mr Irishman, Mr James Joyce the Second, the budding poet. A little unwashed priestly prick is more like it. Well, you can hear my confession, you pious little bastard. They wanted to fuck me, the old farts, but they'd be too afraid, too afraid of heart attacks, too afraid of mama. So they just felt me up . . . '

Dumb, head down, angry at her, sad for her, ashamed of myself, I listened. There was no escape from, no recourse for, what I was hearing.

'Yeah, they felt me up, good and plenty. One stuck his fingers up, while the other mauled my breasts. Then they changed around, like a ball game. You're shocked, aren't you, little Mr Know-It-All from Nowheresville? Maybe I even liked it better than your fumbling. My nipples hardened, anyway.'

The anger was subsiding in her voice; that strange sadness again.

'The owner spotted that of course, and the bastard stopped. He said I was a bad girl and should be punished.'

At last I was indignant. 'Surely, you didn't let them?'

'Did I what? We needed the money, didn't we?' She turned to face me, on the bed.

'Yeah, I let them spank me a bit and tickle me with the ruler but the bruises won't show. And now we don't need to worry about the rent. And look under that pillow: we'll be able to eat out tonight.'

And so we did, splendidly, under a trellis lit with tiny coloured lanterns. We had melon and *prosciutto*, *bistecca alla fiorentina*, and pints of Chianti. As we made our way back she staggered; she had been talking volubly about her family, how her father didn't love her mother any more, and had been fucking around, of her admiration for her brother, 'who is going to be a great painter, you'll see', but was probably bent.

'But he has the prettiest boyfriends,' she said. 'I wish he'd pass them on to me. I wouldn't even mind climbing in with them: I love my brother, damn it. I hope he doesn't kill himself.'

As she cried out the last sentence people turned to look after us in the street. At first she didn't notice, launched into her monologue. 'But they don't want the kid sister. Only the old geezers come sniffing after me. Especially in Europe – everyone's so mixed-up over here.'

And then she saw the shock and amusement of the passers-by, who skirted us, as I propped her along: a drunken young girl was not a normal sight in Italy.

'Fucking Italians,' she screamed, turning to give them the finger. 'Why don't you go and get laid at home, you greaseballs. You fawning fuckers.'

There were two theatrically dressed *carabinieri* at the end of the street, and I didn't want them to spot her. I had already had some experience of the hatred Italian police could show for visitors who got out of hand; in every hostel there was someone who had a grim story. Besides, at long last here was a situation I was familiar with. I held her up as straight as I could, hauled her up the stairs, and when she lurched towards the bed I helped her to undress, the now-crumpled skirt and stockings she wore for special outings, to get into churches and restaurants, posing briefly as a modest American miss.

Slack and vulnerable she lay across the bed, drunken mirth slowly breaking down into something even deeper than her usual sadness. Desperation, perhaps?

34

'They'll be back, of course, the greasy bastards, old meat-balls. They know what I am, they know they can do anything with me. For them I'm just a little American whore. And maybe they're right. Anything goes—' She began to cry, a shallow stream that made her features ugly, nearly old. 'But you don't know who I am. And you never will.' And again she crooned:

> Sunday is gloom-y
> with shadows I spend it all.
> My heart and I
> have decided to end it all.

That night I tried to hold her gently, to console her, but she kept pushing my hands away, as if I were molesting her. 'Go away, go away,' she cried, from the depths of her offended youth. 'Leave my tits alone; they're mine, damn you, they're mine.' As she turned and moaned in the hot night, I lay awake beside her. I was at sea, out of my depth completely. I liked what I could understand of her, the childish eagerness when she saw something beautiful, clapping her hands before a Botticelli, doing her little dance when something I had written pleased her. But her other side frightened me. What she called my awkward body pulsed with need, and yes, I was ashamed of it, as I had been taught to be, in the gloomy corridors of school. 'Take your hands out of your pockets, boys!' rang out the Dean's reprimand. Or in the intimate dark of the confessional: 'Don't defile your body, the temple of the Holy Ghost.' But I was anxious to get rid of that shame, to be free. Until I was, I couldn't help her, and I was beginning to be afraid of her games, those emotional snakes and ladders that exhausted me.

That evening she had taken our notebook and scrawled furiously in it; what had she drawn? As she snored slightly into dawn, eyes and hair matted with tears and sweat, and the air cooled a little, I looked at the last pages. There was a scrawl of bodies, pricks and cunts coarsely entangled, in a blind ritual of defilement. She had given the sequence of squirming bodies a title which I could just make out: SEX IS SHIT.

VII

Next morning, I made my ultimate throw. Insular and ignorant I might be, but things were adding up even in my dim mind. And I was desperate for her goodwill. I went with my passport and last traveller's cheque to a bank and when she woke up (came to was more like it, rubbing blears from swollen eyes), a warm breakfast, *caffe latte* and fresh bread, was waiting.

She munched in silence and I let her be, knowing a little about the dull throb of a hangover. As she brushed the crumbs away, I ran the dishes under the sink, and then came over to stand by the bedside. She looked at me with a new, strange expression, a blend of pleading hangdog and weary defiance. I knelt by the bedside and took her lovely head in my hands. She began to weep again.

I slid in beside her, and parting the long matted coils of her hair, rocked her like a child, my hands around her shoulders. She still did not speak, and with slow hunger, my hands moved down towards the warm mounds of her breasts. As I grasped them, her tears began to flow down, thick and fast. As she cried and cried, I grew wilder, pinching the rising spikes of her nipples, drinking her tears like a lapdog. Then I drove my tongue into her mouth, tasting the coppery tang of stale wine.

At long last, the tables were turned. So often that month she had taunted and tormented me, for my awkwardness, for my smell even. 'You stink like a dog,' she would say, wrinkling her nose in mock disgust. 'Don't Irishmen know how to wash their groins?' Now, broken and uncertain, she lay at my mercy, accepting if not returning my hectic, blind advances as I forged and foraged my way. Most of what I did she had taught me herself, reluctantly; instead of the slow lingering lip kisses of Hollywood, the probing language of the tongue, moving from one orifice to another, the mouth, the navel, the soft nest of the quim.

At times during my apprenticeship she had frightened me with her intensity, reaching out for me again and again, where I lay weary and empty: 'Come on, little worm.' And when she had ruthlessly drained me, she thrust my head down between her thighs, rubbing my face against her warm, moist fur until I choked. Now I licked and drove like a madman, my whole body in a fury of sensual release; emotional revenge. She might not like it, but her body did, as whimpering she came, with harsh cries almost like pain, her body spread-eagled like a starfish, underneath mine.

But I still held my fire, hoarded my spunk, waiting by instinct for some last ritual of violation. She was so wide open now that I slid in and out of her, with a wet smack like a second kiss.

I stopped at one point, to find her eyes watching me, not bold any more, but the eyes of a frightened young girl, pleading for release, and I felt like a hunter, hovering near his prey. But I was still not satisfied: a mad energy of resentment burned in me, as though I were waging war against some ghostly antagonist who stood between us, that someone who had first discovered and used this body for his own purposes. Move by move, I was tracking him down, perhaps even becoming him, in order to displace, drive him away for ever; destroy him, if necessary.

Suddenly I flipped her over, and parted her legs. I mounted her, as she had taught me; she raised her buttocks obediently, a small hand reaching back to press my hangings. But instead of the usual entrance, her rosy cleft, I probed, then sank, like a bayonet, into the fold of her arse. Deep in her fundament I finally relaxed, and the seed poured. She cried out.

We lay side by side, in silence, afterwards. 'Is that what your brother did to you?' I asked at last.

She nodded, through tears.

'Then tell me about it,' I commanded.

VIII

As she talked, I saw a large house somewhere in the country, outside New York, perhaps Long Island or Connecticut, the kind of comfortable barn I had seen in so many films. Her father was away, most of the time, working on Wall Street; he took the commuter train from a nearby station, most mornings, and returned at cocktail time. It was the rhythm of her childhood: Mother fixing a pitcher of martinis before going to fetch Daddy at the station, when he had not rung to say that he was staying overnight in New York. It seemed a conventional picture, strange to me only in its assumption of continually replenished riches.

Then, in her early teens, her parents had begun to quarrel. She would waken to the sound of raised, angry voices, broken glass, and later, blows and cries. She knew her elder brother would be awake too, lying and listening, so one night, when she was tired crying alone, she tippytoed down to his room. He always slept naked and it was comforting to snuggle against his warm length, leaner but larger than her teddy bear. She came back the next night again, and they lay huddled together, listening to the warring voices below; clinging to each other like babes in the wood, as the tall trees lashed and roared.

Absorbed in their deadly fight, their parents noticed nothing. Then one night something happened; as she lay in her brother's arms, secure and warm from the frightening sounds, that senseless screeching, she felt his groin grow large and warm against hers. Silently, in the darkness, he began to move into her. She had played naughty games with high-school boys, her mouth sore from kisses, her neck and arms covered with lovebites. But this was in a different league: her brother was seven years older than her, and already a young adult, who had made his own sexual choices, sought his own world of escape.

Although he loved his sister, and tried to defend his mother, he had little or no sexual interest in women, was, indeed, already a practising homosexual. So while he showed her how it was done, and let her handle him, he did not care to satisfy the wild cravings he aroused, took pleasure, maybe, in thwarting them, preoccupied with his own revenges. Whatever he might do for her, it had to end with her sucking him or accepting to be buggered. It was what happened with his boyfriends, of course, but he also told her that it would keep her from getting pregnant.

For three years they had gone on like that, until their parents were separated, and the house was sold. By then she was eighteen, and although she dated boys at college, she found them too naïve to understand her needs; their pawings seemed grotesque. Her relationship with her brother still held her, a guilty secret, and she would slip away to see him, as often as she could. She loved him completely but when she stayed overnight in his studio loft in lower Manhattan, he would rarely sleep with her, although he was still glad to see her. Instead, he used her as bait to attract older men from Uptown, gallery owners, dealers and the like. He was determined to make a name for himself as a painter, and she was glad to be able to serve him, for she admired him completely; he was her lord and master. So sleeping with other men who could help him was a bit like sleeping with him; she would tell them about him and his work, sometimes pass them along, if he fancied them, as he did one marvellous black jazz musician. She would do anything for him as long as he would let her stay by his side. Their father paid for Art School and the rent of the loft but her brother hated him: he blamed him for the break-up and for their

38

mother's unhappiness and looked forward to when he could move away, make it on his own.

And he had, with a good first show, and a contract afterwards. But then something horrible had happened; usually his boyfriends had liked her, treated her like a mascot, and let her hang around, being helpful. It made a pathetic little scene, a young girl, sitting studiously beside her brother as he painted, waiting for him to throw a word her way, a stray among the fairies. There was a little blond boy from Cleveland, Ohio, however, who only pretended to be her friend, and schemed to get rid of her, tittle-tattling about things she had said and done. And when he moved in to live with her brother, she was not allowed to stay over at the flat, and even her visits became uncomfortable. He no longer needed her. One night he told her angrily that he didn't want to think about 'all that mess' any more – he had his own life.

Neither did she, after such pain, but she couldn't find a way back to where she should be. So she asked her father to send her to Europe; she didn't know how much he suspected about her goings-on but he had agreed, without conditions. He was worried about her not dating any more and hanging around so much with his pervert son. She didn't think he was as bad as her brother thought; he had a younger woman, and seemed quite contented. All he asked was a postcard now and then, and she had his number if anything happened to her.

But Europe hadn't worked. Everything and everybody seemed so poor, so desperate; many of them didn't wash properly, and there were no showers, or even proper baths. The little hotel she had stayed at in London had only one bath and you had to pay extra to use it; when all the machinery got working, it was like a steam engine. And English girls had dirt under their painted fingernails and didn't know how to lay on make-up properly; they applied it on what was left of yesterday's. And those funny Turkish toilets in France where you had to squat: it was kinda funny but after a while you felt hemmed in. And she never seemed to meet any-one young, though men followed her around everywhere, especially in Paris and Italy. As she blathered on about the shortcomings of the coun-tries I had just been travelling through, so excitedly, I kept pressing her for more details, for more clues.

Yes, she had had a few affairs, one with a rich creep in Milan – 'what else is there to do in that city? You can't eat the Last Supper every night!'

– another with a young sailor in Sicily. 'He was so good-looking, and knew how to move his body like a black boy does' – that made me squirm – 'but, boy, he was boring. He wanted to come back with me to America. Imagine bringing him home to Mother. He thought I was the girl equivalent of a GI meal ticket.' But in the end there was something about sex with men that had begun to disgust her: all that rooting around. I remembered the Irish street-corner description of sex – *getting your hole*.

She had been picked up by an older woman when she was in Rome and had spent some good weeks with her. There was something new and different about sleeping with a woman: they understood better what it was like to be a sexual victim, used and abused. And a woman understood another woman's body, whereas men were obsessed by their silly pricks, up and down, in and out. A skilful tongue could do just as much.

So much for *mise*, Mr Meself, Ireland's gift to womanhood, and future star of art and love. Whether she was at long last being honest or determined to get her own back, after what I had just done, or a mixture of both, was beyond me. I had travelled farther and faster in a single month than in many years of my previous existence, trying to keep up with this sexual meteor. From cunnilingus to incest and lesbian love; if I had been looking for experience, it had washed over me, nearly swamped me. We looked at each other warily, in silence. She had stopped crying.

IX

We didn't last long after that. An unfinished painting stood on the easel, with a dirty towel thrown over it. And I didn't try to make love to her any more – to bang, as she now crudely called it in our rare conversations. Even the weather had become murky with freakish storms that lit up our little window, high as in a prison cell. More often than not, I lay on the floor, coming awake to harsh flashes of lightning.

And the walls of that small stone-flagged room were beginning to feel like a prison, a narrow airless place from which I might never escape. In the end, I could take no more. Such brutal rhythms of aggression and affection were beyond me: I wanted love, yes, or at least mutual desire, but not humiliation again. I tried to explain what I felt to Wandy but she was lost in her strange torpor, a kind of pleasureless self-regard which a little Irish *schmuck* (another word she taught me) could not understand.

Neither of us talked much, neither of us wrote in the notebook. So I resolved to leave as I had originally planned. True to form, I borrowed money from her to pay for the train to Paris, although I saved part of it by hiding myself in the lavatory after the frontier, squatting determinedly while people pushed at the door. *Je suis malade, laissez-moi.* And I was.

We had a last meal, in our favourite neighbourhood restaurant. Obscurely honouring the occasion, I wore my only suit again, tie and drip-dry nylon shirt. We still didn't speak much, although it was good, especially the straw-covered bottle of Orvieto. 'Would you like another?' she asked timidly. 'I find it sometimes helps to be a little drunk on trains.' And she tried to smile, that wan aftertaste of shame and gentleness which had sometimes won me back.

Impressing myself at any rate, I did not accept. Instead, we had two *grappas*, those fiery liqueurs that stir the most sluggish tongue. It was our last hour together: she in her light-coloured skirt, high heels and silk stockings; I in my brown suit, almost like adults after what was, for me, at least, my first almost love affair. There was a girl awaiting my return to Ireland, but if I had failed in Florence, surrounded by warmth and beauty, would I not fail again in the dripping, claustrophobic melancholy of Dublin?

Perhaps sensing my mood, she made her last play. 'Look,' she said, 'it wasn't all that bad. I know I was tough on you but I can't help it: I'm not used to having a friend, a boy nearly my own age. I thought you just wanted to fuck me like all the others. And then drop me if the dollars dried up. Maybe you did too, a bit, but you did try to talk to me, and most of them don't. You're really the kind of pal I need, someone I can trust when I get so goddamn lonely. Maybe I could still find the way back, with your help. I was stupid and mean when I said you were awkward. You're really sensitive and sweet, a nice guy, if I'd given you more of a chance. I promise I won't spike you again, if you stay. I'll let you love me up, all you want, if you can just wait . . . '

It was, for her, a long speech. And I hesitated, for they were words I had longed to hear for some time. But now I didn't trust them, or myself, any more; the protective valves of the heart had closed, I had sealed myself away from her. Was it only selfishness and was I leaving her to drown? In Paris, the tribes were beginning to gather: Dónal who was hoping to re-meet the girl he had met on a train in Italy the previous year,

Richard, the young French writer I had met in Austria, and a host of others. We would dance at the Club Tabou and perhaps see Sartre sitting at a café terrace, Les Deux Magots or round the corner, at the Bonaparte. I could always ask her to come along: hadn't she met Gide briefly in Sicily? She might be waspish, but she was not stupid, and, besides, there would soon be another cheque coming from Daddy, which would certainly help matters.

I couldn't face it; I shrank from it. I imagined us all sitting at some place where the young met, like the cheaper Royal St Germain, across the way from Les Deux Magots and the Flore. Either she would turn on me in a tirade that would delight the more mocking of my friends or she would drop me for someone more exotic, certainly more expert, who took her fancy. Either way I would lose. I was already bruised enough almost to look forward to a period of loneliness.

My last glimpse was of her leaning against a pillar in that anonymous station. Above her head was a clock, and a sign: USCITA. She was not crying, she was not even looking, her face averted in what seemed to me now her habitual pose. It was my first adult farewell and it was a silent one. The train drew out of the station. She did not move, or wave.

> Little white flowers
> will never waken you;
> not when the black coach
> of Death has taken you.

XI

Where is she now? She may well be dead, for I can not easily imagine her settling down, submitting to the routines of marriage, however well cushioned. Or if married, there would be at least one divorce, with a sullen child, like herself, growing by her side. I can see no husband; perhaps a woman friend. Or did she, like Lady, find heavy lovers on her way into the netherworld?

I don't mean to sound hostile: I admired her wildcat ferocity, and honour her glooms which were, in many ways, more excessive than any I had met, nearer the suicidal. Born a generation later, she would probably have turned to drugs, the mixture of oblivion and release she so desperately craved. And she would have moved, pitched the ante higher and higher, graduating quickly from harmless pot to hash, from LSD to mescal, coke, or heroin. Horse, scat, angel dust, nose candy, smack, scag, shit, that was her kind of language and was it her fault that she was born too early to blast herself off through some Needle Park?

We never wrote to each other, for even if we had exchanged addresses what could we have said? It became a defensive fashion amongst us not to take Americans too seriously, GI geniuses and latter-day Daisy Millers on their predictable ego trips. But if I did not love her, I certainly tried to care for her, during our short summer together, for real as well as for mercenary reasons. And if she had found my gaucheness more tolerable, I might have leap-frogged over my bleak boyhood to maturity.

Paris brought other interests, a caravan of my contemporaries slowly moving through that astonishingly energetic post-war city, from the Mabillon to the Rhumerie Martiniquaise to the Bar Vert, dancing at night in the cellar of the Tabou, hoping for a sight of Juliette Greco. Some people were kind to me, some were not, but I lived on my own in a high room in the Rue de Rennes, trying to decipher *La Nausée* and modern French poetry, yet crying myself to sleep at night with visions of Wandy, hugging a pillow wet with semen and tears. The Director of the Catholic Cinema Office helped me to find odd jobs, and I sought out films in remote parts of the city, romantic films like *Les Visiteurs du Soir* of Marcel Carné, Gerard Philippe in *La Chartreuse du Parme*, burying my head in their beauty. Being systematic, making an inventory, has always been my remedy for dodging sorrow and loneliness.

My dearest friend, Dónal, was deeply in love with his French girl friend; they spent their days in bed, and emerged in the evening, rubbing their eyes like hibernating animals. To recover, they made romantic little trips to Paris suburbs like Robinson and Chantilly. Pleased for them, but profoundly envious, I kept away, padding through the city with my red beard, khaki battle jacket and slacks, like a lean monk. It was my second time in Paris and I was determined to hold out as long as I could, undistracted by sex, dreaming of future masterworks.

I wrote a long letter to Dublin, to be read with high amusement by one young poet to another. What a provincial pattern of malice we lived in, deriding the adventures of others in search of themselves! How could they know that a young American had just taken a lump out of me, and that I was still on the injury list? Yet in spite of myself, homesickness was growing and I trudged to the Irish Embassy to read the papers and scrounge a meal from a kindly Second Secretary. Malnutrition was beginning to wear me down: we discussed repatriation.

I was locked in, miserable, a strong dose of Wandy's anguish adding to my own, all the useless ache of being young, and Irish. Finally, there was nothing for it but the long journey home, across England, two boats and a train, never sleeping, always standing, until I saw the gulls creaking over Dublin Bay. And when I got back to my digs I came down with a painful and humiliating disease, *Epididymo orchitis*, a swollen testicle. I thought the worst, of course: was this Wandy's parting shot? A kindly specialist examined me on a bench in a lecture room in the College of Surgeons, and pronounced my malady the result of exhaustion. The medical students in my digs were delighted by this rare complaint and told all their contemporaries, who queued to see me. Up and down the stairs they clattered cheerfully, while our black-garbed mass-going landlady puzzled over my mysterious popularity. Disgusted, I charged a shilling a look, which they repaid with baleful prophecies.

'If you're not sterile you'll be stuck for the rest of your life, with one ball clanging your ankles. They'll call you Chief Hanging Ball: you'll see!'

For over a week I lay in bed with it resting on a little platform of elastoplast. Only my old girl friend couldn't come to see me but I was too embarrassed to face her anyway. I could barely speak and shuffled around, like a pariah dog, waiting for the day when I could put my library up, and start to write again, in a room of my own, neither home nor boarding house. I had stopped going to church, feeling no remorse, only longing after my summer adventures. A warm picture of Wandy in my wallet meant more to me than any ikon.

And the Notebook? It stayed at the bottom of my rucksack, except when I used some of the pages to write letters, begging usually. My eldest brother sent me a cheque, with no sermon attached, although in the first flare of fear at my malady, I claimed to have caught the pox. Finally I felt so low that I went home, to my mother's house, and inflicted my torpor on my family. The *weltschmerz* of my generation, those pestiferous post-war blues had caught up with me and I never lost a chance to cast a gloom over the proceedings. Which were, God knows, gloomy enough already, with the rain falling on the narrow streets, the one cinema, the parochial hall. Still, there was a place at the table, my old bedroom, and enough pocket money to go to a local dance, though at times I wondered if I was caught again, condemned forever to the pubs and the spuds, hemmed in by holiness. On nights when I had no excuse, I knelt down to join the Family Rosary, with its long trimmings for dead relatives. My knees ached when I rose but it had begun to seem normal to be uncomfortable again.

Someone asked me for a page of writing paper and I absentmindedly tore it out for them. I then left the pad lying around; not deliberately, I had just forgotten what unIrish material it contained. A big bookshelf had been bought at an auction and I arranged my books in it: Gide, Stendhal, Balzac, Montherlant, Mauriac, only the best! I was becoming intolerable, even to myself, lurching through the small town with my burden of suffering, like a provincial genius, coming home only to eat, or endlessly read, before I fell into my solitary, Wandy-haunted sleep. I woke to find the statue of the Sacred Heart in the corner staring at me; which was the real world?

I had long conversations with my mother which were like a parody of the end of Joyce's *Portrait*, with me mournfully pressing the case for freedom, and she arguing, with an equal measure of gloom, for orthodoxy, though she was still capable of a pretty good thrust. When I was deploying my favourite tactic of presenting France as the eldest daughter of the Catholic Church, she scoffed: 'Everyone knows the French have low morals.' I countered with Lourdes; and the absence of any authenticated visions of the Virgin in Ireland. One of the most recent attempts had been discredited as a homemade magic lantern show, and Virgin spotting, one of the favourite sports of the pious, had been discredited for a while. There was a time when she seemed to be flashing up and down the coast of Ireland, barren plateaux in Mayo, rocky inlets in Kerry, but never nesting, to bring lustre to Ireland.

'Why has France so many saints then, mother?' I asked, innocently cute. She swatted me with ease. 'Because they need them so much more than us, son.' Then, resting in bed with a mild autumn cold, she read one of the books from my library, attracted by the title, *Pity for Women*, by Henri Montherlant. Horrified, she turned to François Mauriac, whom I had extolled to her as a great Catholic novelist. The novel she fell on was one of his blackest, *Le Désert de l'Amour*, the desolation of carnal love. The morality was right up my mother's alley, but the details were not.

She was so upset by this exposure to normal French culture that she hightailed it to confession, and told the priest she had been reading dirty books. Learning that she had got them from her son's library, he reproved her for prying, with what seems to me still, for the times that were in it, the prevailing moral climate, a good answer.

'He probably needs them for his study, Mrs Mac . . . . A student must know all about human nature. But they could be dangerous for a quiet woman like yourself. Tell me, do you still have a subscription to *The Messenger of the Sacred Heart*?'

Coming from Father Gillfallen, whose annual sermon comparing sexual problems with the rules of his favourite game, golf, always packed the gallery, it was a good try. Some of his innocent injunctions had become legends among the cornerboys. 'It all depends on how you hold your hips, men. Too much wiggling is not wise, if you want a clean drive.' Or: 'Would you pick a ball up off the green when your opponent's attention was distracted? Of course you wouldn't but that's what an immodest touch is, stealing a march. You don't tap the ball into the hole because no one is looking! Respect the rules of the green and the game will take care of itself. And this French kissing; keep your tongue in your own mouth at all times. A dab on the lips is more than enough – like using the putter, gently does it. Just a flick.'

Then the Notebook disappeared. Even in my sluggish state I registered some alarm. To any member of my Ulster Catholic family it would almost certainly seem obscene, indeed, to most people in Ireland at that time, not to be unfair to my family, who were far more tolerant and aware than most. But the idea of it being read by the wrong person, by someone unsympathetic to the extreme feelings displayed in the commentary and the drawings, the scrawls of two young people so involved with each other, sometimes in anger, sometimes in pleasure, filled me with rage and dismay. Perhaps they would take it upon themselves righteously to destroy such a sinful document; that was my worst thought, some Manichaean dwelling upon Wandy's drawings with puritan horror.

A few days later the Notebook or writing pad reappeared but not where I had left it; by my bedside, on top of my Missal. Who had read it, or at least looked in it? My elder brothers? They didn't breathe a word. My uncle from Donegal, a sweet but innocent man, an ex-cleric and school-teacher with as gentle a nature as one could meet? A few drinks was the extent of his debauchery. Once I asked him about married sex, fascinated by the idea of a semi-permanent supply. 'Ah, sure you get fashed with that too,' and when I looked puzzled, added kindly 'Blow your bugle as long as you can. Marriage is the full stop.' And turned to talk of the All-Ireland Final, and the big Holy Year Cross they had raised over the town. 'You'll see it right over the Border,' he chuckled.

No one criticised me, no one chastised me, no one challenged me. And yet I felt haunted. Could someone have picked up such a document and left it down again without comment? Or somewhere in the heart of my family did someone care enough for me to contemplate what might seem to them the worst – *Com'on Baby, let's hit the sack* or *Let's stay home tonight and fuck* – and still love and cherish me enough to leave me alone? Perhaps it was my sainted mother, already thwarted by her adventures in *The Desert of Love*? It was a chastening thought – that night I dreamt of Wandy and awoke crying. I had glimpsed her, turning and twisting in a cage, a caught animal.

And I looked at the Notebook again. The poems were poor, I now knew, the lines derived from Pound or Patchen. But some of the drawings were quite good; what began as revolt, a girl child's swollen dream of sex, endless cunt and everlasting balls, had worn itself out quickly, becoming something else. What she had been trying to paint, in faithful imitation of Piet Mondrian and his disciple, her dominating brother, had nothing to do with her real self, which was wilder, more wilful, less perfect. In her scrawls, even the most obscene, there was a sense of hurt, an angry sharpness, something violated which was desperately trying to renew itself, a protest against that soiling by the world which is so much a part of growing up. And in some there was a reaching out towards ease, cartwheels of love, arms and legs linked warmly as in Indian sculpture.

Most people attain maturity within their society with some ease, a state towards which they have rightly aspired. But for others, however insatiable, even savage, their energy, all knowledge of the world is a kind of spoiling, an endless disappointment. Her drawings reflected that intense state, an angry disruption at being born into some place and time which could not immediately satisfy her excessive but genuine needs, as a woman, and as an artist.

And I was living proof of that constrictedness, alas. Perhaps I could have helped her; and myself at the same time if she had trusted me. Still, the idea that someone should look at our joint efforts with censorious eyes was almost a sacrilege. Love or lust, loathing or friendship, it was ours, a thrusting from our so differing worlds towards freedom, towards ease. What happened between us was a stumbling towards something without which two equal beings cannot survive, something called honesty. As I tidied the Notebook away carefully, I thought, perhaps next summer I might hoist my small sail again.

PART II

2

A LOVE PRESENT

Snobbery begins early. With my neat ankle socks over polished shoes, I was clearly intended to be a cut above the other boys in Garvaghey School, the sons of small farmers and farm labourers. After Easter, as the days grew longer, they came to school in their bare feet. In a few weeks their soles were as tough as the shoe leather they were saving, while in the evenings I still unpeeled sticky socks from soft, white feet.

My aunts wanted it that way: I bore my grandfather's name, and if the family fortunes had dwindled, some day everything might be restored to some mythical position which I couldn't yet understand. But how could they know that I wanted desperately to be like the others, to go slapping my bare feet down the Broad Road, and, joy of joys, to stick my toes in the tar which burst in small, black bubbles as the summer heat came? You cleansed it off with butter, mushy yellow on black, a glorious mixture, thick as axle grease.

And to run through the fields, like a hunter in an adventure story, without bruising a leaf, breaking a twig. Like Leatherstocking, or Fenimore Cooper's poor relation Altsheler, who wrote about the Mexican-American war, planting an early obsession. And, above all, Tarzan, Lord Greystoke with his Lady Jane, and pet Cheetah. What they all had in common was the call of the wild. Instead of town suits and ankle socks, I wanted to be clad in animal skins and leap from branch to branch in the forest. Clarke's Wood was a poor substitute for the steaming jungle but imagination could do a lot and I wonder what my aunts would have thought if confronted with me, stark naked, as I balanced in a tree above the river. I leaped from branch to branch, excited by the smell of leaves and peeling bark, the wind on my bare flesh, before dropping into the mud below. Then there was the chill of the stream to cool my excited flesh.

For I was not encouraged to play with the local boys, supposedly because they were too rough. I met them secretly though, admiring Gussie's ferret which climbed obediently up his arm, till it looked like a lady's long glove, of the kind I still found in our house, remnants of 'auld decency'. But the shriek of a rabbit seized by its needle teeth was not refined. Outside wilder life prevailed, setting gold loops of snares for rabbits, guddling trout by hand in rocky pools (I only gave up when bitten on the thumb by an eel), robbing orchards for green apples and gooseberries, stoning magpies. There the competition was to be as mustang wild as possible, not as good as gold. How sweet the little speckled trout tasted, roasted over a wood fire – firm-fleshed, fragrant, the taste of the forbidden.

And the rough games they played! If you didn't watch out, you would get pushed in the river, or in the nettles, or the oozing dunghill, a perfume hard to explain at home. Summer we roamed the hills, as far as Knockmany, or climbed into the mouldering mystery of a deserted house. We had a den among the hazels where we accumulated stolen goods: sweets I brought to curry favour, our first cigarettes, pictures of naked women from *Lilliput*. Rainy Sundays in winter, we sheltered in a barn, swapping dirty stories. Bulling a cow was a favourite game, large boy mounting smaller with a squeal of triumph. I did not join in but watched avidly; perhaps I hoped that I might be pulled in one day but they left me alone, as if, indeed, I was not quite one of them. Only when my father sent me a set of boxing gloves was I conscripted as an equal, though their styles were so ferocious that I was usually content to be referee. I can still see Gus charging in, a human juggernaut, oblivious to my deft flicks if he could only land one thunderbolt.

Boxing, leaping the river, playing ball in the Holm; I could present these as acceptable activities but I kept quiet about our other secret games, which so fascinated and repelled me. The only children I was officially allowed to play with were the Kellys down the road, who owned the new shop, which had largely replaced ours. They had a garden bordering the road, like us, and among the sweet peas and pansies I played with Mary, the eldest, and her puffy-faced brothers, all younger than me. Mary was demure and slender, with swinging pigtails, and perhaps because we were so often thrown together, I began to feel that I was in love with her, a pure devoted love like that inspired by a princess in one of the fairy stories we read together.

She had fair hair, a small mouth that pouted slightly, and light blue eyes, like the most innocent of dolls, or an angel bending its wings in the corner of the chapel. Was my love for her really that pure? Whatever I felt for her, she did not respond. I had to arrange games of hide-and-seek with her putty-faced younger brothers, so that I might find her, cowering in a corner of the garden, and throw my arms around her, crying 'Caught', as I inhaled the fresh smell of her skin, like wet, cut flowers. Or wrestle with the eldest, until he called for his sister's help, and we tumbled together on the lawn under the climbing sweet peas. Once I managed to kiss her, but she must have thought nothing of it, for she stood up and brushed her skirt as if nothing special had happened. There was nothing about her that I did not like; I was especially entranced by the twin trails of slime that so often descended from her slight nostrils. Unabashed, she poked out a tiny pink tongue and licked the snail tracks clean. Such is the power of love that I was fascinated by the sight of that silver syrup, sliding down towards those lips I coveted so much.

'Now, be good, children.' I hear the cry, and see myself and the little Kellys, listening to Uncle Mac on the BBC, from five to six in the evenings. The better-class children of Garvaghey, innocent as Ovaltine and arrowroot biscuits, while that unruly world roamed outside, full of the disgusting games I loathed and partly longed for. The next morning both worlds would meet on the school benches, hardly acknowledging each other. White ankle socks and swinging pigtails were small defence in the seething turmoil of a country school, with its rituals of defilement.

A favourite sport was spying on the girls' lavatory. The crudest way of doing this was peering through an open seat on the boys' side; there would be a rush to the look-up point, so to speak, when some poor girl went innocently in to pee, and the round, white moon of her leaking bottom was gloatingly described by the boy lucky enough to get his head down first. Because her house was so close, Mary never went to the school bog, and I tried not to, embarrassed by the smells, the sniggering prurience. But once Gus got me to climb on the wall that separated the two sections, where we were spotted by the senior mistress, a famous bee. She walloped my companion's thick skull with a giant blackboard ruler but let me off with a pointed reproof about letting down my family's good name.

'There's no excuse for you: you should know better than to behave like an animal.' There was a note of spite in her voice; she had once stayed in our house, and quarrelled with my younger aunt over something. I was thoroughly confused, by now, because Gus and I had become altar boys, patiently instructed by the priest with chalk diagrams on the school floor. The sweet, sickly smell of altar wine, the chink of the cruets, the locking and unlocking of the tabernacle, all that glorious ritual gave another, mysterious dimension to our lives. Should I confide to the priest in the confessional about our secret games, or would he find me unworthy to kneel on the cold marble of the altar? Gus had taken a swig of the altar wine and said it was great, but warned me against saying a word about our shenanigans to Father Cush.

'What we're doing is only natural. Don't you bring the cow to the bull, and haven't you watched the rooster light on the hens?'

Even grown-ups didn't seem exempt from the contradictory pangs of love. Our senior mistress was courting heavily with her future husband; 'lying in all the ditches of the country,' said my Aunt Winifred, in a rare burst of frigid malice. 'Not before the boy,' said Aunt Brigid, and gave me a sweet from the shop, before shooing me outdoors. Then one evening on the way home from school I stopped in to pray for my many sins before the altar where I served Mass on Sundays. Something in a side altar made me turn: our senior mistress was splayed, with spread-eagled, imploring arms, before the Twelfth Station, Christ Crucified. Her blonde hair flooded her shoulders, and she was sobbing; she did not notice me, so I tiptoed away, dumbfounded by such extravagance. She was beautiful, far more beautiful than my aunt; was she bad like me?

I spent only three years at Garvaghey School, and I cried when I was taken away, for at that age every detail is writ large: to change schools is to change worlds, and I was already attuned to the rules. I did not dare sit beside Mary at Garvaghey School but accepted the partners I was given, mainly girls, the mingling of the sexes seeming to be part of the policy of the school. There was a nice little Protestant girl I sat beside during drawing class but her nose was upturned, she wore glasses, and she was very serious.

While the senior girls blossomed out of reach: plump little Dympna MacGirr, who was supposed to be already courting, her sister Aileen, whose long hair flowed down her shoulders. One wet day, she stood by the school stove drying it; now and again she would shake out its fragrant coils, unaware of my silent adoration, only a desk away. It was as natural as a mare tossing her mane and, indeed, when one of our horses broke loose one evening as we were plodding home from school, I made a big show of taming the animal for her benefit. But when I found myself behind Aileen in Kelly's shop, I was tongue-tied.

Then the Schools Inspector called, and the prize children were put through their paces. On the junior side, Mary Kelly was to play Little Red Riding Hood and I was the Big Bad Wolf. I danced around her, licking my fangs, delighted with the idea of gobbling her up, neat bonnet, raffia basket and all. No matter if I got slain at the end by the clumsy hatchet of Gus; I had been seen by everyone holding Mary in my arms, and I rose from the dead to stand beside her at the end, while the whole school applauded.

But even amateur wolves fall sick and in my second year at Garvaghey School I came down with a bad cold that turned into a fever. I thrived on fantasy for a while; one of the older children had died that summer, a hefty girl who had spent the whole day in the unaccustomed heat of a blazing sun, and collapsed among the sheaves. We followed the coffin to the old graveyard, and for weeks afterwards we whispered about the mystery of death: bones, worms and ghosts, the terror of being buried alive. But after a few days, the novelty of dying died off; despite the books piled high on my eiderdown. I waited for one of my schoolfriends to come and visit me: I waited for Mary.

She didn't come, she didn't even send one of her awful brothers. And the boys across the way couldn't come; they weren't often in our house, though I slipped into theirs. By the end of the month I was allowed up part of the time, and was hungry for a visitor. It was then that my younger aunt came to announce that I had one, and that it was a girl. Pyjama warm, I hung over the banisters, hoping to greet Mary. But it wasn't her; it was someone else.

At the bottom of our class there was a heavy, nondescript girl from a small labourer's cottage back in the hills; I think her father was a road worker. I wasn't sure of her name because none of us spoke to her, neither the rough nor the politer children. It was Ellen, perhaps, and she had short cropped hair and large obedient eyes, like a waiting spaniel. She had shared a bench with me briefly and made some excuse to speak to me about all the books I read, but I brushed her off. Her plainness embarrassed me and, besides, the self-centredness of childhood does not easily allow for the simple fact that others may be feeling the same emotions as oneself, craving for friendship, for love, to escape from the loneliness, the confusion and fears of growing up.

But there she was in the front room of our house, speaking to my younger aunt, and showing her something, slowly and silently. I couldn't see what it was, through the rungs of the stairs, but it was bound to be something horrible, for her family had no money. What a pity it wasn't Mary of the swinging pigtails, with something bright and new from their shop! I would have raced down to see her; why hadn't she come?

My aunt climbed the stairs slowly to where I lay petulantly across the bed. She told me that a little schoolmate was waiting for me. A little schoolmate, a little playmate – how I loathed the expressions! I told her that I didn't know her, had never played with her, had hardly spoken to her, even when she sat beside me. She was dismal, a real ugly duckling.

'But won't you speak to her?' said my aunt gravely. 'She walked a long way, from Altcloghfin.'

'I don't know her. I don't want to know her.'

My aunt tried again, more slowly.

'But she brought you a present. She wanted to give you a present, she said, because you were away from school and she missed you, and heard that you were sick.'

'I don't want her old present.'

Through the banisters I could see the girl dully waiting – perhaps even hearing our conversation upstairs, if she dared eavesdrop. There was no way I could acknowledge her visit; it was too embarrassing: I would be a laughing stock with all sides for associating with someone like that, whom even the other girls shunned. She was too slow-witted to play most games, rapt in a kind of sleep-walking dream of her own, away from the brisk rattle of camogie sticks, or skipping.

'Tell her to go away. Tell her I'm still sick. I'm, I'm *contagious*!'

And so down she went, down the stairs, and I saw her speak to Ellen.

The little girl said nothing, but placed her present on the parlour table, then left. When my aunt turned from seeing her through the door, I saw something very strange: my aunt's head was bowed, as if she was praying, or crying. What under Heaven was wrong?

A safe time afterwards, I crept downstairs to inspect the object which had caused all the unpleasantness. It was a shoebox and in it lay a small, brittle, celluloid doll. Not a fancy doll, with long yellow eyelashes, which cried, or closed its eyes if it was laid down, like the big one her father had given Mary at Christmas. No, it was a frightful little object, like a juju from one of my adventure stories, made of some nasty pink material. It couldn't have cost more than a few shillings from some place like Woolworth's.

Was that all she could afford? In a corner of the box was a little note, badly spelt, which ran:

FOR MY SIC BOYFRIEND
THE DOLL I LUV

As I read it, each word, each laborious letter burnt with shame into my arrogant, precious little spirit. I had met true love, and because of the shabbiness of its dress, had spurned it from my door.

3

SUGARBUSH, I LOVE YOU SO

It was after Christmas in Tyrone and my pal Frank Carney said he would bring us all to the New Year's dance in Strabane. There was little Phil Barrell, who hated college boys like myself; there was Hughie the hairdresser, with his gleaming Brylcreemed hair, who was mad for the women, and kept touching himself absentmindedly; there was my boxing pal Gerry Cullen, whose proud boast was that he had double-jointed fists that he could crack like pistol shots. It was as unappetising a gang of louts or local scruff as our little town could manage, more like an invading party of Visigoths than a group of Catholic young men.

Among us, a rare enough occurrence, was a young girl home on her holidays from Scotland. I found myself talking to her as we drove slowly along the fogbound river. She had a job working in Glasgow as a clippie, or conductor, on one of the city buses, and was therefore better able to pay her way than any of us. She said very little on the drive up, probably intimidated by our boisterous bravado, our show of worldliness. And when I came to the dance hall I ignored her, eagerly casing the local talent, who had the advantage of living far from our home. After all, she was small, sturdy, freckled, not obviously pretty, and probably from the back-lane houses where my grandmother had once collected the rents, a member of a class I was not supposed to associate with, who had never progressed beyond primary school. Class was not something clearly defined in the country and the small towns, but it was very potent nonetheless, all the more so for being largely unspoken about: tuppence ha'penny looking down on tuppence.

Strabane that night did not seem to offer any answer to my vague romantic dreams; after the long slow drive beside the River Foyle, the dance itself was anticlimactic, the music tired, the girls listless. So I turned back before the intermission to give the young girl who had travelled with us a duty dance, a courtesy I did not always honour. To my surprise, it was more than a pleasure. Her body moulded sweetly into mine, as if we had been made for each other. I tried all my youthful masher's steps, so carefully learnt in Dublin, and she responded to them all. Usually when a dance ended, couples eased uneasily apart but she remained close to me, her arm round my shoulder, her breast and thigh warmly against mine, before we swung into the next dance. It was a hit tune of the period, which still sways in my mind: *Sugarbush, I love you so, I won't ever let you go.* By the time the intermission came, we were dancing cheek to cheek, and during the break she followed me outside.

The car was large, a hackney, and we settled into its back seat, snug as a double bed. The fog was still thick, with the street lamps burning through it. This time there was no calculation, no slow persuasion; she was just eager for sex. To my astonishment, I found myself doing naturally what I had spent so many hours dreaming of; entwined in easy ecstasy with a willing companion. I did not have to waste precious minutes on languorous Hollywood kisses – she knew what she wanted. Nor was there any need for the ritual fight through layers of clothing, as she loosened her skirt and bra to welcome me into the warm haven of her body. There was nothing extravagant or exaggerated about it, just natural desire naturally expressed; she wanted to go the whole way.

After our first bout, we sat talking and smoking Wild Woodbine cigarettes, like grown-ups, listening to the muffled music of the dance band, the Melody Aces. She told me that she had learnt a lot in Scotland, that the life on the buses was tough, but no tougher than at home, where her father had begun to bother her. The Scots were rough, but their hearts were easily touched. There was a kind of working-class solidarity of knowledge; the other girls on the buses taught her about contraception, the times of the month that were nearly safe, and where to go if things went wrong. She only had boys when she knew or thought things would

59

be all right, and I had been lucky enough to fall on that period. She was a bit shocked that a college boy like myself knew so little, but it did not prevent her drawing me back into another embrace. We managed to get back to the hall for the last round-up, but I did not dance with anyone else.

The atmosphere in the car on the way back was more than awkward. My pal the driver did not take sides; we were old hunting companions, and he was glad to see me looking so happy. But the others were very uneasy. Hughie the hairdresser shifted his hands in the darkness as the girl and I nestled together; it sounded as though he were masturbating, and yet he had barely spoken to her on the way up because in that infinitesimally graded class system of a social limbo like Fentown, he had mentally spurned her as being below even him, and therefore socially invisible. Little Phil was outraged, and kept muttering about how college boys thought they could get away with anything. Gerry Cullen was cracking his fists and announcing 'Good man, John' every time we kissed. That large black hackney, sailing along the fogbound river in the early morning, was as dense with class consciousness as a Proustian salon, but with everyone looking down, except the girl.

The car came to Fentown. Frank cheerfully asked me in to have a few slices of the big cooked Christmas ham, but I hesitated. The girl waited quietly behind me while Frank went in, and came out with a small parcel of sandwiches: 'I see what's on your minds, but I can't leave the car open all night, the old fellow would find out, and that would be the end of our wee excursions. I wish you luck, anyway,' he said, watching our disgruntled companions march off down the road. As he closed the door I thought furiously of the few possibilities we had. Our own side door was open, but we could shelter there only briefly, as our rustling might alert my family, and my new friend lived in the smallest of small houses, and probably slept with another member of the family, aunt or sister.

It was then I thought of Fentown's main claim to glory, the Horse Tram. This contraption was a two-storey carriage used to draw passengers from Fentown station to Fentown Junction one mile out along the tracks. It was the only one of its kind in Ireland, and indeed, as far as we were concerned, the world. It was old-fashioned, with well-cushioned seats and a curved wrought-iron rail leading to the balcony. Hand in hand, we found our way down to the station, and the empty tram. Side by side, we ate our sandwiches contentedly; then, spreading our overcoats like blankets, wrapped ourselves up on one of the benches, to resume where we had left off.

We were both young, full of ardour and energy, but although we went at it a long time, falling back only to start again, we eventually fell asleep in each other's arms. When we awoke there was a gentle swaying motion underneath us: it was morning, and the Fentown Horse Tram was on its way out to meet the first train from Enniskillen. In the early dawn, the driver had harnessed his horse with all the somnolence of habit, unaware that he was carrying people out to meet the train, since he had not seen us board. Sleepy, dishevelled, we prodded each other awake to watch the broad, thickly clothed back of the driver, with his cap like a policeman's uniform. At Fentown Junction he dismounted, and we sheltered in our corner to travel calmly back with the incoming voyagers a little later. Then we parted smartly, although I thought I saw someone watching from the far side of the street. Soon I was snug in my bed, under the Holy Pictures, as if I had never left it.

I slept through the late morning into the afternoon. I felt, or thought I felt, someone at the door, but the house in Fentown was slow to rise; my elder brothers usually lay late and long in bed. But this time I was out to rival them, pleasantly exhausted with the unexpected joys of lovemaking, and not hungry either because of the plentiful sandwiches, slabs of thick, pink, homecooked ham bordered with white fat and smelling of cloves, a kind offering from my friend Frank. So I descended into that lull between lunch and tea, said hello to my mother in the kitchen, and sauntered out into the twilight for a stroll to St Lawrence's Hall, to play a game of table tennis or billiards in the basement where the respectable young of the town met.

My red-headed middle brother was halfway through a game on one of the green billiard tables. I came over to watch and make encouraging noises, but got little change for my support. Indeed, he seemed almost hostile, and I began to have that vague feeling, which I remembered so well from school, that I had done something wrong, in some way I did not understand, offended against some code, offended against the immutable laws of society and God. I thought I had left all that behind when I went to college, but I could see from the snap in his eyes, and his bristling, laconic answers, that as far as he was concerned I had done something. Since he was the smoother of my brothers, a dancer famous for his skills from Belfast to Omagh, and a gambler who had often

borrowed from his baby brother, I looked up to him as someone sophis
ticated in the rules of our small society, who knew the score, so I waited
to walk home with him. He did not seem inclined to speak, but finally did.

'I hear you had a great time last night,' he said sharply.

It took me a while to answer. After all, it was only a few hours earli
er, and I was still warm from the experience, which I hoped to repeat as
soon as possible.

'I suppose you could call it that,' I said. 'I did meet a nice girl, and we
got along well.'

He emitted a peculiar sound, derisive, nearly a hoot. 'You know where
she comes from, don't you?' As if that explained everything.

I briefly tried my best. 'I think I do, but you know I don't know the
town very well. Besides, does it really matter? I thought she was a very
nice girl, and a pleasure to meet in a place like this.'

He turned to face me on the street, his jaw rigid with anger. 'Well, you
had better not meet her again. Don't even *you* know that you can't slut on
your own doorstep?'

How had he learnt? Probably from Phil Barrell, who had kept a jeal
ous watch during the night, probably masturbating at the thought of our
pleasure. Or had old Dick, the station guard, finally woken up to our pres
ence? He was a Protestant, as with almost all public jobs, and would prob
ably be glad to report any Papish misdemeanour. Anyway, someone had
told, and the damage was done: my brother had dropped the portcullis to
protect the morals of our home from any low-life adventure; I had
offended against the rules of society and family by having to do with a
girl from the wrong side of the tram tracks. I weighed her easy warmth
against such wrath, and, alas, gave in.

She sent some pencilled messages through her baby sister. I received
them at the door and then turned inside. I saw her once or twice on the
other side of the street, and she smiled at me and waved urgently, but I
passed heavily on. I did not have to suffer my own cowardice too long -
by the end of the holidays she had lifted anchor and sailed back to
Glasgow, her new and hopefully more generous home.

4

MOTHER SUPERIORS

Josie Mellon left the village early in the morning by the first train. The stationmaster was surprised to see her, dressed up to the nines, as he explained later to a large audience in the Dew Drop Inn. She wore a wide-brimmed floppy hat that might have belonged to a film star, an old-fashioned coat with padded shoulders, still crimped from its long wait in some cupboard or drawer, and a pair of platform shoes. In one hand she clutched a heavy snakeskin handbag, in the other her youngest daughter, startled and silent. Neither had ever been in the railway station before.

The journey to the county capital did not take long, the little train waving its plume of black smoke over the rushy fields. Brushing past the ticket barrier, Josie ignored the taxis, but marched her daughter on the inside, down towards the distant, spired centre of the town. Once or twice, people looked curiously at the pair, but, intent as a terrier, she ignored them also.

Josie halted before a pair of wrought-iron gates, carrying an elaborate inscription in blue lettering. A handyman working on a flowerbed looked up but did not move to help her as she lifted, pushed and pulled at the heavy gates. Finally she managed to open one, and she and her daughter set off up the gravelled drive.

It was a long walk for the child, especially as her mother kept tugging her by the hand. But there were bright flowerbeds and bushes to look at before they found themselves at the massive front door, to which, the child thought, everything seemed to lead, like an ogre's castle. There was a brass knocker, higher than her head, and after drawing a deep breath, her mother gave it a sudden, smart bang.

When the huge door opened, a starched figure, all black and white, or black up to the neck and then white above, looked questioningly down at the two strange waiting figures. But Josie did not falter.

'I want to see your boss,' she said in her sharp, nasal Ulster accent, 'I want the Mother Superior. As soon as you can, please.'

It was the nun's turn to look out of place, flustered almost. 'The Mother Superior,' she repeated, in a puzzled tone. 'Do you . . . ?' but she began to retreat before Josie's steady gaze and insistent demand.

'Aye, the Mother Superior, I need t'll see her,' said Josie, advancing. The nun backed, between two rows of religious pictures, down the bright corridor.

'I'll try and find Mother,' she flung back, 'but she is usually quite busy. You must wait where you are.'

The child found the size of the hall dazzling, like something out of a fairy tale, an empty ballroom in a palace. Everything was so clean and shining, and the holy pictures looked lovely, with pedestalled statues in the corners, big as in a church. And the black and white tiles looked as if you could slide on them; which she began to try. Her mother stood still, pointed, waiting.

The Mother Superior did not take long, bustling through a glass door, rosary beads rattling at her waist, to confront her unplanned visitor. She also was a smallish woman, face scrubbed clean as a new pin, except for the thin, dark shadow of a moustache. As the child sang, or skipped by herself in the unaccustomed spaces of the hall, the two women stood face-to-face, not speaking. The Mother Superior did not offer her hand, looking uneasily towards the door before she frostily enquired: 'You wished to see me?'

'Right, Sister,' said Josie, 'I do indeed. It's about me poor daughters.'

'About your daughters?' Puzzled, polite.

'Aye, I have five, you know. And I'd like you to take the two eldest.'

'Take them?'

'Aye, take them in here. Everyone speaks about the fine big place you've got and the great job you do. I'd like my two to become young ladies too, not like me.'

'And what do you do, Mrs . . . .'

'Josephine Mellon's the name, but they call me Josie, wee Josie – after me father, Big Joe. I was reared hard. Mammy and Daddy both died when I wasn't much more than a cutty. Da was in the Fusiliers and he had a pension but he drank it. I had no chance at all till the War came.'

The Mother Superior waited, at sea but casting desperately for a sign.

'You were in the War?' she managed, baffled. Who could this strange, scrawny little woman be, with her beady eyes, and old-fashioned finery, her funny clothes that smelt of the mothball?

'Ach no,' said her visitor, impatiently. 'Not officially. We'd be Nationalists, like yourself, I suppose: Da was only an accident, the only job he could find. But the Troops were very good to me. I'd known fellas before but never fellas like yon.'

The nun's face was a mask beneath which incredulity simmered.

'You know how it is, Sister, there's always a lot of lonely fellas in any town. But they have no money, our boys, only hit and run. Not like the Yanks, the doughboys, as they called them. They were wild kind.'

The little girl had temporarily exhausted the pleasures of sliding and then staring at a statue of the Immaculate Conception, blue-veiled on her polished pedestal. She came over and stood meekly near her mother, inspecting the strange, serious-looking lady talking to her, with her stiff, dark clothes and severe look. She touched the swinging Christ figure at the end of the Rosary with the tip of her finger, wonderingly.

'Stop, child. Biddy here's the youngest. I'd like to keep her with me till she grows up a bit. She's great wee company. But I'll send her along too if you treat the others well and give them the chance I never got. There's Teresa, and Bernie, and Maria and Agnes. I always tried to give them holy names, to call them after saints. Considering how they came into this world, it was the nearest to a good start I could give them.'

The Mother Superior's face coloured a little; could this be genuine piety or was she being mocked?

'And what does the father think?' she managed, eventually.

'God look to your wit, Sister. Which father? Two of them died in that dirty old war; poor boys, I often pray for them lying so far away from home, without maybe even a cross over them. And before the Yanks came there was one Englishman but he never wrote to me. I believe he was married. The last is Irish though, one of our own. I know her Daddy well.'

Slowly the Mother Superior mastered herself. All kinds of emotions, from indignation to pity, were running riot through her bloodstream. But how had this apparition, so shabby and out of place, yet so defiant, ever conceived the idea of coming to her, to the convent door?

'And who advised you to come here?'

'Everybody in the town told me, all the corner boys. They said you were great, and would surely understand my case. Go to the convent, they said, that's where they'll be sure to take you in.' She paused. 'I thought they were only having me on, like, but then I asked the Blessed Virgin. After all, she was a mother herself, like me, though she only had the one boy. And God knows, where we live in the Back Lane is not much better nor a stable.'

A bell rang and the Mother Superior looked down at her watch. Her whole face had flushed and her eyes no longer faced those of her visitor.

'I'm afraid I shall have to go now,' she said, ducking her forehead. 'But I'll see you out. Perhaps you'll leave your name and address so that I can look into your case, Mrs . . . .'

'Miss,' said Josie emphatically. 'I never caught one of them. Miss Josephine Mellon: everyone knows me.' Her hand fumbled for the door knob. 'I'm away now, anyway. We'll have to go straight back home. I have to make a bite to eat for the rest of them. You know how it is, at that age, you that have so many of them. Mouths gaping wide as scaldies. Come on, now, Biddy dear. I'll get someone to write to ye and then they can read me back the answer when it comes. Good day to you now, Ma'am. It was very kind of you to talk t'll us.'

The Mother Superior stood watching as the pair dwindled down the avenue. Little Brigid ran over to gaze at a flowerbed once and then looked expectantly over towards her mother, who called the child back just as she was bending down to pluck a blossom. Then they rounded the corner, out of sight, and in the distance was heard the insistent whistle of an approaching train.

5

THAT DARK ACCOMPLICE

The boys disliked him intensely, with his dark intolerant head, his way of walking as though contemptuous of stone and earth, they being merely the material on which he drew the unmistakable lines of his purpose and direction. 'No nonsense', the proud tilt of that head seemed to say from the start, and recognizing their master, as boys in a bulk nearly always do, they could still resent his mastery, as puppies resent sullenly the hand that makes them smart under the switch. Dislike? Was it anything as definite? Rather a vague resentment that forced its way towards expression through the long greyness of that Ulster winter term. Had you halted one of them, a shamefaced lad only broken to longers, dawdling by the ball-alley or kicking the scuffed grass of the Senior Ring slope with unpolished slackly tied shoes, and asked him, point blank 'Why?' he would have been startled and lost, with nothing to say for himself except to mutter rebelliously that the new Dean was 'a brute'.

Which seemed to mean, in fact, only that the new Dean knew how to handle them too, too well, and strode the dormitories punctually in the cold mornings as the electric buzzers clattered harshly against the wall, his high voice giving strength to the hated Latin greeting, 'Benedicamus Domino', the flexible cane twitching at his soutane's edge.

'Up, you sluggards! Little boys should be early birds. Come now, Johnson, don't fester in the bedclothes.' The cane rattled along the rails of the bed, flicked against thin legs dancing at a line of washbasins. 'Come now, boys, all together now –"Deo Gratias"!' Dodging on bare soles over scrubbed board, or tumbling from warm bedclothes, the boys mustered a weak, scattered reply: 'Deo Gratias'. O! he could handle them, reducing their boyish pride to little more than a scamper out of the way of a stick.

It wasn't only the cold mornings that gave them reason for hatred, but the hundred other deliberately irritating ways in which he proved his authority. Naturally an independent, highspirited man, he had spent his early priesthood in England where he quickly gained a reputation as a successful missioner and preacher. Then, one day, he found himself transferred from the pulpit and placed among schoolboys, unable to relax his trained arrogance, his emphatic rhetorical gestures, and too far from boyhood to appreciate its special gauche tenderness. Even his speech seemed alien, brusque and clear-cut, the exact opposite of the slurred speech of the boys and the other local priests, snuffling over Greek texts in Ulster accents and making pawky jokes that endeared them to successive generations of pupils. 'Corny', 'Chappie', 'Dusty'; those were nicknames that testified to familiarity, even love, but all they could think to call him, reaching out vainly for some image to equal their dislike, was 'Death's Head' or 'Hatchet'. 'He's a brute', and with that recognition, humanity, for them, dropped from his shoulders; he became someone who struck, and must in turn be struck, the problem being where or when or with what concerted violence.

In one small incident or another, he came to sense their hatred, but remained unperturbed; indeed, he seemed almost amused by it, as though waiting to pounce with joy on the first reflex of insubordination. It became his custom to speak to them on every possible occasion, after prayers, in the still moment before Grace, from his dais in the study hall above their sullen heads. His vibrant tones rebuked, lectured, played with them, sent them running out with a kindly general pat of dismissal. Under the substance of his words, the breaking of some minor rule, the loss of rosary beads in the grounds, or the 'slovenly disgusting' habit of sticking hands to the wrist into tattered pockets, ran a nervous note of triumph that seemed to recognize the silent war declared against him, even to defy it. 'Try it, you little fools,' it seemed to say. 'I'll soon show you how to handle a pack of grimy schoolboys.' Yet, steadily they sensed in him, somewhere and not explicit, a weakness, a febrile excess of emotion that might, for all his outward show and insistence, leave him helpless in some extraordinary situation.

II

One Friday evening, Benediction ending with the Divine Praises and the restless chink of the thurible in an altar server's hand, four boys, older than the rest, left the school chapel early, tiptoeing down the aisle with lowered heads and out onto the yard between the lavatory and the concrete air-raid shelters. They stood, rubbing their thighs nervously, looking across at the lit glass of the chapel windows, all opaque save one where a Virgin's dark blue head curved tenderly over the slight cube of the Child's body.

'Much time left?' asked one. 'A few minutes.'

'Maybe we've time for a fag. I'm nearly dead for the want of one,' said the third, gesturing towards the lavatory door.

The boys generally smoked in the damp lavatory, twenty yards or so from the back of the sacristy, passing the butts under the wooden partitions or pretending to stand at the urinal where the tepid water gushed and leaked. At a moment's notice the hot end would hiss into the water, or turn alive against the palm as the hurrying Dean peered and prodded under the doors, or turned out the pockets of malingerers. 'Pah, this place reeks of smoke, stinks of it.' The cane would grate across the glass in the top half of a lavatory door, while inside a frightened boy cowered among white tiles, a cigarette dead under his foot, braces dangling down his back.

'Better not. He'll be here any minute now, and we're to give the word to start.'

'Shush! There's the first touch of the Adoremus.'

Inside the chapel, the congregation of boys rose for the last hymn, singing loudly and unevenly, and then subsided into their seats. Some craned rudely around to watch the priests rising from their prie-dieus: old Father Keane was, as usual, the last to leave, lifting his lame leg outwards and shuffling towards the door. Others prayed with averted heads, making a cage of their hands. On the high-altar the server dowsed the last candlelight and the nave of the chapel was heavy with incense and smoke from the fuming wicks. Restless with the thought of some strange excitement, the boys waited as the head-prefect went over to lock back the swinging doors. Then they came in a rush.

Supper always followed Friday Benediction, the refectory only thirty feet away, with rickety wooden stairs up to it, the space between like a platform onto which the boys poured. This evening they were unusually silent; the four boys who had been waiting outside the chapel now appeared a little way apart, up the corridor, lounging with their backsides against the wall, eyes alert. At the far end they saw the Dean approaching, a tall figure with billowing soutane, carrying himself proudly as if bearing the Sacrament. 'Right, boys, let him have it!' they called. Turning their faces to the wall, everyone booed, dragging air into distended mouths, and forcing it out through tightened twisted lips. Boo-o-o-o.

Half-way down the hall he stopped, head flinching backwards as though from a sudden blow across the mouth. Watching intently, Tony Johnson, one of the four ringleaders, cried in excited confirmation: 'We have him, he's yellow.' The long harsh sound became stronger, gathering into itself all the suppressed vindictiveness of months and seeming to fill the area around the chapel door with the palpable presence of hatred.

Then, regaining confidence, the Dean began to walk forward, but his eyes shielded slightly, his body in the exaggerated posture of a man under stress. The crowd opened before him. As the last students, timid boys with Holy Water damp on their foreheads, came pushing their way through the chapel door, having deliberately lingered to escape any possible punishment, he reached the foot of the stairs, and sprang into the refectory, two steps at a time. There was a moment of doubt and delay; the booing subsided: there were whispers of 'What'll we do now?' The bigger boys gave the lead, climbing after him into the barn-like refectory, filing according to age and class among the oilclothed tables, with their regular mounds of loaf bread, white damp plates with a print of butter on each, and exactly arranged rows of chairs. There was the usual silence for Grace, all facing towards the end of the hall, where, directly over the Dean's bent head, the crucifix hung like a twisted root on the yellow wall. 'Bless us, Lord, and these thy gifts…' the voice was steady but the hands perhaps a little too tightly joined. Chairs scraped on the linoleum as the boys settled into their places.

Any ordinary evening, after the hush of Grace, conversation broke out immediately, almost like an explosion. Now there was silence, dead, utter silence, as though someone had given a signal, or everyone been struck dumb. The white-aproned country maids, grinning good-naturedly as they carted the big blue and red teapots to each table, looked around with surprise, hearing nothing but the rattle of knives, the chink of cups, the bodily shifting necessary in the sharing out of the tiers of white sliced bread: in the space above the moving hands and heads and the white

70

cloth of the table covers, the air seemed to thicken with expectancy, as though every breath was being held too long, and the damp walls sweated.

A quarter of an hour passed without break. The meal was nearly over and the Dean had done nothing yet, fidgeting slightly before the dais, playing with the sleeves of his soutane, brushing them, looking at the chalk-smeared elbows. At the Senior tables the boys kept glowering around anxiously, hoping that he would do or say something, while the little boys shifted on their seats with half-frightened excitement. He gave no hint of his feelings, however, appearing to turn the incident slowly over in his mind, meditating some unusual form of retaliation.

The boys began to feel uneasy; perhaps, after all, their action had been too hasty, presenting him only with a new cause for amusement? The unnatural atmosphere of silence, in a place which usually resounded with laughter and squabbling voices, strained their nerves to a jagged pitch. Perhaps indeed their action had been foolish, a glancing ugly blow that left him unharmed and put them even more at his mercy than before. The very silence they had created cut them off from further action, and his acceptance of it seemed to say with a shrug: 'All right, if that's the way you want it, then all the better for me. You can keep your silence to the crack of doom for all I care. You're only depriving yourselves.'

Suddenly, every startled eye upon him, the Dean began to walk up and down between the tables, his rubber soles squealing softly on the linoleum. Slowly at first, a thinking pace, with the head down; and then, as resolution formed, more swiftly. The nervous lengthy stride, parallel to the listening tables, now had its usual impulsive rhythm, the rhythm of a man whose mind was made up, who was confident he could master the situation. As he took a corner with almost theatrical swiftness and firmness, the soutane belling out like a skirt round his ankles, someone tittered. His head went up, with a sharp decisive movement. Far down, at one of the Junior tables, a boy sniggered helplessly into his teacup.

'You down there, O'Rourke. Was that you?'

He came hurrying towards the boy, now blubbering with fear and hysterical laughter.

'Was it you, I say? Have you no manners at all, man? Can't you speak up?'

'Yes, Father.'

'So it was!' Arms folded, he stood at the edge of the table. 'That's a pretty thing for a boy of your age to be at – sniggering behind backs like a schoolgirl. It's a pity we can't get you something better to do than that, isn't it?'

'Yes, Father.'

'Well, I know something that'll fit you better than sniggering. Do you see that book up there?' He pointed towards the dais for reading during meals, usual only during Lent. 'You can go up there and keep us all edified with *The Lives of the Saints*.'

'Yes, Father.'

'I suppose you can read' – the voice came down low and sarcastic – 'and you all want to keep silence anyway, so here's something to keep your little minds busy.'

The boy rose and scuttled towards the reading dais, the whole school watching him with stunned curiosity, while he searched eagerly for support in every face. Propped up high over all the wondering heads, a minute sulky figure, his ears red at the edges as though the flesh had been smartly slapped, his hands frantically turning the leaves, while a leaflet fell, swirling, to the floor:

'Hurry up, man, don't be so clumsy. You've got an audience, you know. We're all dying to hear you.'

'Where, Father?'

'Anywhere. We're waiting.'

'The life of the saintly Vicaire d'Arcueil teaches us this lesson: that the true way of sanctity lies in an infinite gentleness and patience with all human follies, all human wickedness. We must expel from our rebellious hearts every taint of self before we can hope to see God. As a seminarian, he was ridiculed for his ignorance of Latin, his peasant clumsiness. As a sanctified priest, he was mocked by his parishioners, who found him naïve . . . .'

The Dean was enjoying his part now, playing it to perfection, almost a Mephistopheles in dark deliberate position, mouth tilted and sardonic, foot tip-tapping restlessly as he leaned back at an angle against the food-presses, under the crucifix. A kind of grim contentment arched his eyebrows; he seemed to savour every mispronunciation with intense interest, gloating over every slur and stutter – and there were many, the boy on the reading dais stopping and starting, squirming and shifting – till he could no longer contain his great mirth.

'Good Lord, man, higher.'

'And yet for the forty years of his ministry, he moved through the parish of Arcueil like a ministering angel...'

'Louder, boy, louder. Is that the best you can do? Is there a stone in your throat, or were you never taught to read?'

'Please, Father, there are too many big words,' the boy wailed, his fingers hot and fumbling the pages, his timid eyes pleading for release. O'Rourke was an awkward lout at any time, the kind of boy who, through sheer lack of even the most ordinary schoolboy cunning, was always caught out in mischief, or found himself left behind to bear the blame after his more cute companions had skipped aside. And yet nothing pleased him more than to be thought daring and impudent, scuttling around the edge of a crowd with a vehement conspiratorial air or trying to catch the limelight in class by loud words and laughs. Knowing his victim of old, the Dean now played him with all the nervous mockery he could command, goading the boy till he stammered like an idiot.

'Open your mouth, man. Wider!'

'This humble man had learnt the ways of charity, that sweet radiance of the Christian soul which is our best weapon against evil. Conceit, egotism, pride, all the diverse and unsuspected ways of selfishness were alien to him; as though by dint of prayer he had driven that dark accomplice forever from his bosom...'

'*Booosom.* Is that the best you can do?' the Dean intoned down his nose, making the word sound as broad as a snore. Driven past all enduring, O'Rourke collapsed into a flood of tears, weeping with great ugly shudders, as though the breath was tearing out the softer part of his throat. The Dean looked stunned; a faintly comic amazement made his mouth gape open like a fish. From every corner of the refectory, low but insistent, a growing undertone to the boy's abandoned sobbing, came again the sound of booing.

'Leave him alone,' someone called, 'leave him alone.'

The Dean pulled himself up as though trying to escape the accusing sound, as though suddenly very weary.

'Boys,' he began uncertainly, striving to get away into some kind of speech that might right the balance, administer remorse. 'Boys, you have done something this day which I had not expected of you and which I will not forget for a long time to come. I have tried to keep silent, to pass the matter off as a joke, but if you are not careful it will go too far, and I will be compelled to put the whole matter in other hands.'

'Boys,' groaned a wag sepulchrally, from a corner. The whole school laughed madly, beating the spoons against the cups, the plates against the wood, jangling the gross enamel teapots. Above the tintinnabulation, his voice strove to be heard, no longer exact and peremptory, but high and nervous, falteringly demanding an audience.

'You are too young perhaps to know what duty means. You do not know how hard it has been for me to play this unpleasant role of Dean. But since it is my duty, I have tried to do it well, though it is the last thing I would have chosen for myself. I'm not good-tempered, perhaps – I may have seemed unduly harsh to you – and I may have made mistakes – but I have tried to be conscientious. Do you think I like to be shut up with schoolboys day after day, watching their every whim?'

At first they listened, struck by a note of sincerity in his voice; then, ceasing to understand, recognized only the familiar smoothness, the intellectual fibre of the words that was so hateful to them. As they began again their systematic interruption, he lost all self-control and began to rail blindly.

'You have chosen to show your hatred for me in the only way you know – that of booing. It is entirely typical. But I'm not afraid to face it, I can tell you. I can take it. You might have scared someone else with your Nazi hysterics, but I can take it.'

His own image, no longer proud and disdainful, but crushed and reduced, returned to him openly from every grinning, gesticulating face. Seized by something like the impersonal frenzy of the hunting pack, no longer single ordinary boys, hiding their hatred behind barred fingers, they rocked back and forward in moaning laughter, hooting and cawing and quacking.

'I can take it, boys,' squeaked someone in a high feminine voice.

The Dean's face flushed and for a moment he seemed to resist the temptation to lift the cane and plough madly among the tables, striking everyone indiscriminately. But he would have had to flail half the school and the big boys might easily have struck back, made reckless by their hatred and conscious of their advantage in numbers. The dangerous aloofness which had been his power was now swept away from him; he was no longer a priest or a person in authority, but merely someone who had humbled and hurt another past enduring.

Almost crying, he tried to raise his voice above the noise: 'Do you know what you have done? Is there no limit for you at all? Boo me if you like, it makes no difference now. But tonight you have booed me, a priest, before the very chapel door. You didn't think of that, did you? No one can forgive you for that, neither I nor anyone else.'

There was a sudden silence. He had played his last, best, and forgotten card, facing their monstrous grinning abandon with his outraged cloth. This was an appeal none of the boys had anticipated, a transference of their insult to the person of Christ himself. And in a moment they knew it was false, that he had only thought of it as a weapon to protect his injured egotism.

'You might have chosen some more suitable place for your hoodlum demonstrations. Has education taught you nothing better than that?' Refreshed, he felt the silence, guessed that his words had shocked them back to their senses, restored his shrunken image. 'Imagine, for a group of boys from good Catholic homes…'

At one of the three Senior tables, someone belched: a deliberate vulgar sound. The school shrieked with merriment. The sound was repeated on thick burbling lips, from every table in the hall. The Dean stumbled in his words as though shot; he fumbled and lost the thread of his argument and then let his head slip into his hands, seeking darkness in the warm shelter of his palms.

The head-prefect rose hurriedly and said Grace. The Dean did not look up, though it was normally he who announced the end of a meal.

'We give thee thanks, O Almighty God…'

Quietly and in perfect order the boys filed out between the tables. The winter mist had filled the corners of the large refectory windows, making them look like show cases. Going out, one or two boys looked closely at the Dean, without sympathy but with a detached curiosity. He was weeping silently. He looked like a man either drunk or sick, his back humped and his shoulders slack as though props had been taken away and the cloth sagged without support. 'Go away,' he said, without raising his head. 'Can't you go away!' The last clumped down the stairs, leaving the Dean alone, except for the boy on the dais who had stopped whimpering to watch him. 'Go away,' he said, sensing somebody still near. O'Rourke rose and scuttled towards the door.

Outside the evening was cold, softly growing darker, the ball-alleys a great grey bulk without separate outline. In the town below, the lights were coming on, vague points against the winter mist. The damp air was threatening; another night of rain would drown the playing fields and turn the slopes into a sea of mud. Already, around the Senior Ring, moist drops hung like grain from the naked branches.

The boys scattered with wild and joyous cries.

6

A Prize Giving

When the doorbell began to sound frantically around six o'clock, Mike Byrne knew it must be his niece, Samantha, come to fetch him. And there she was at the door, sporting a miniskirt lurid as her painted eyelids. Beside her was a student, a Trinity student to judge by his scarf, who was clutching her hand. They were both drunk, he realised, had spent the afternoon trailing through the new desert of Dublin Central, from oasis to oasis, the Bailey, Davy Byrne's, the long barn of the College Mooney outside the side gate. But what were they going to do with the swaying student? He could hardly bring him to the Prize Giving at the Convent of the Holy Lamb, the main event of the evening that he and his niece were due to attend, she as a past pupil, he as their annual guest speaker, brought by her at the special request of the nuns.

Giggling, she lurched past him into the darkness of the hallway.

'This is Daniel,' she said. 'He's a philosophy student and he seems to want to go to bed with me.'

He received the information with the mixture of interest and disapproval that seemed appropriate to an uncle greeting a favourite but wayward niece. She clutched his coat, and as he leaned forward to support her, he could catch the sweetish smell of gin and tonic off her breath.

'How are we going to get rid of Dan?' she wailed, and let her head sag on his chest.

It took him one minute flat – years of broadcasting had taught him how to act quickly when the warning light glowed. He hardly remembered what he'd said but soon he was closing the door firmly behind young Daniel, or Dan. Then he hustled Samantha, or Sam, up the stairs, though at the second landing she nearly toppled back into his arms again. When they reached his rooms at the top of the building he stretched her out on a sofa, then hurried off to prepare a makeshift sandwich to sober her up quickly. She had probably not eaten at lunchtime, a cup of coffee, perhaps, in some greasy spoon, before herself and Dan hurried back to hold hands in a dim, smoky pub corner.

When he came back with it on a tray, she was fast asleep and snoring. Mouth wide open, long, damp hair straggling; it was hardly the picture of the perfect past pupil to present to Mother Superior in an hour or two. There was only one thing left to do. He ran a full basin of cold water and half-helped, half-ran Samantha into the bathroom. Then down with her face right into the full basin, glug, glug, glug.

She rose, spluttering and angry. 'W-w-what,' she gurgled and gargled and gagged as he thrust her relentlessly down again. Finally he let her stand upright and confront herself, flushed and bedraggled, still bleary-eyed, in the big bathroom mirror.

'Jesus!' she cried. 'Is that how I look? The nuns will be horrified.' And she began to wipe off her trails of mascara.

While she tidied herself up, he made sandwiches for both of them. Moving around his trim bachelor kitchen he noticed that there were still several fingers of whiskey left in the Jameson bottle. There would hardly be much to drink at a convent do, he reflected – just a preliminary snort of sherry, or some other genteel drink, like ginger wine, and then the easily exhausted pleasure of the water jug on the podium.

Besides, despite all his professional aplomb, he was beginning to feel a little rattled. He looked through the window to where a gantry swung over a new hideous building, a bank probably, dwarfing old Dublin. God knows how chilly some of those convent parlours and presbyteries could be, and Samantha would be immediately noticeable, stinking like a little distillery. And if there was anything that made him ache for a drink, it was moral disapproval, disguised as good behaviour. He had first one drink, and then another, to steady his nerves, as he changed into a sober, well-cut suit, and tie, subdued in colour. By the time he was ready, Samantha was too, with face done and clothing straightened, the little snack she had

78

eaten already absorbing the outer layer of her drunkenness. However, she did still look, if not quite tipsy, tiddly, and after he had called for a taxi he had another quick snort himself, to catch up a little. When the second ring came to the front door, the bottle was empty.

*

The new and fashionable Convent of the Holy Lamb was at a polite distance outside Dublin, and the road ran through a pleasant wooded park, designated as a Green Belt. Samantha nodded most of the way, although once she started awake from her daze and fumbled wildly for her handbag. 'Mother of God,' she wailed, 'how will I face Reverend Mother?' and began to dab wildly at her damp face again.

'You'll be grand,' he said flatly, and soon they were swinging through the great iron gates of the convent. A late Georgian manor, whose last owner now lurked in a small flat in Cannes, it had taken on a faintly military air, like a civilian fortress, under its new dispensation. What a strange paradox that the religious had taken over the homes of many of the dilapidated gentry, scrubbing away the scents of sin with their prayers, banishing the flowers of evil with innocence and incense. There was an obscure form of historical justice in the change, Mike Byrne thought as the taxi crunched the gravel before the front door.

As he was paying off the driver, he heard a clumping noise behind him. In clambering out of the taxi, Samantha had tripped and tangled her long coat, and was sprawled on the gravel, displaying a considerable extent of leg. And someone was tackling the forbidding entrance door of the convent, which might gape open at any moment, like a portcullis.

For the second time that evening, he leaped into action. Thrusting a few notes into the driver's hand, he turned to haul Samantha up, and managed to have her nearly upright as two nuns came floating through the door. But he was also dusting her down, with the other hand, so that it looked as if he was embracing her. Or so he feared as he wheeled her smart around to face the advancing nuns, who were dipping and ducking towards them, with welcoming cries, like amorous penguins.

'Agnes, Agnes, my child, how lovely to see you! And you've brought your famous uncle, after all. How nice of you, and how fine and well you're looking…'

They were wafted indoors, in a welter of incomplete greetings.

'You forgot to tell me to hide my mini-skirt with my coat,'

Samantha/Agnes hissed as they stumbled along the antiseptic corridors.

'Holy Virgin,' invoked Mike, raising his eyes to heaven – only to be confronted with one! Blue, mild, and smiling, Mary trod the serpent down gently with her slipper as the cortège passed underneath towards, presumably, the convent parlour.

They halted before a large oaken door. Sister Mary and Sister Agathon – or so they had introduced themselves since Samantha was too embarrassed to do more than gulp – led the way in, clucking pleasantly. The room was wide and empty, except for the inevitable holy pictures and a large polished table with a set of accompanying high-backed chairs, guaranteed to stiffen any spine. But there were two ample armchairs beside the empty fireplace, and into them he and Samantha sank, grateful but by now decidedly uneasy. Sister Mary had disappeared again and Sister Agathon was on the floor, kneeling before a side cabinet.

'Do you think they're going to leave us here, high and dry?' he queried, apprehensively, surveying the black rump of Sister Agathon.

'We're going to get some tea, God help us,' whimpered Samantha. 'Tea and bloody digestive biscuits. I told you it was going to be deadly.'

Sister Agathon, emerging backwards from the cabinet, gave a wave of victory, like a bear discovering honey in a tree. She was clutching something, a shining silver salver.

'I knew we had one!', she said triumphantly. And then: 'But where are the nuts?' She dived into the cupboard again, a foraging squirrel this time, and was still absorbed in her search when the door opened and Sister Mary came back in, smiling.

She had a bottle in either hand, holding them out before her, by the neck, like a wine merchant in an off-licence. But by the shape of the bottles it was whiskey, not wine, and behind her flowed a whole troupe of nuns, large and small, old and young, and all of them beaming. With glinting glasses and laundered cheeks they reminded him of a flotilla of ships, and not old-fashioned sailing ships, but trim coiled yachts, enlivening the sea with contrast and colour and movement:

Sister Aquinas – Sister Maria Dolorosa – Sister Immaculata – Sister Attracta – Sister Francis Borgia – Sister Augustine – Sister Ignatius – Sister Mary Alacoque – Sister Scholastica – Sister Perpetua.

Mike and Samantha shook their proffered hands, smiled back into their delighted faces and then settled back into their leather chairs while the nuns swirled expectantly around. They did not have long to wait, for

80

Sisters Mary and Agathon were busy as barmaids. The salver was now graced with the two open bottles of whiskey and not only one but several packets of nuts and cocktail scraps. Sister Agathon had foraged well: even to someone used to receptions, like himself, it was a fair do. And Sister Mary had a lethal hand with the whiskey, the water just squeaking in at the top of the glass, as an afterthought; Mike found himself sucking in the meniscus. Soon they were all gabbling away happily, lapping the amber liquid.

'You see,' said Sister Agathon, 'we were going to have tea but Mother Superior phoned to say that she was on her way over. It seems she's a great fan of yours, as indeed we all are. So we decided to have a reception afterwards, and warm up with a quiet drink first. I hope you don't mind.'

He glanced over at his niece, Samantha alias Agnes; no, it was the other way round: he had just got used to her new name for her new self, since she had gone to college. She was babbling away with a whole group of nuns, so intently that her skirt was riding up her ripe thighs. Apart from the nuns' habits they look like girl friends gossiping in a lounge bar, thick as thieves. What could they be gostering about? She was certainly not explaining to them, as she had to him recently, that she could no long bear the name Agnes because of its religious implications. He didn't get much time to speculate because his own entourage was going strong, brimming with surprisingly informed questions, and never letting his glass level sink for a minute.

It was about the fifth whiskey, he thought afterwards, when Mother Superior arrived. She was lugging a side of smoked salmon and, between herself and the two younger Sisters riding shotgun with her, the larger part of a crate of wine. He stood up and made a clumsy attempt to bow slowly, but she brushed away his formality by raising the glass of whiskey she had been given as she put down her offerings.

'To a splendid prize giving,' she said, and clinked her glass against his. 'It was so nice of you to come. And little Agnes,' she turned her formidable but friendly glance on his niece. 'My, she has grown. She is no longer our little lamb; that was her nickname here, you know, *agneau*, a little lamb of God, she spent so much time in the chapel. I'm sure that's changed; did she ever tell you she once thought of joining us?'

Mike Byrne nearly choked on his whiskey; this was the first time he had ever heard of a lamb being let out of the bag! He was going to deny all knowledge when he caught the imploring eyes of his niece and nodded instead. 'Of course,' he muttered. and accepted the fresh whiskey that flooded into his glass. Several more drinks down, he began to panic. The conversation was fascinating but was he ever going to meet the convent girls, the ostensible object of his visit?

Finally the Mother Superior seemed to give an invisible signal and they trooped out in a long procession towards the study hall. And just as he was beginning to worry about the embarrassing side-effects of such a torrent of drink, Sisters Mary and Agathon appeared at his side, like two bodyguards.

'You might need to pay a little visit here, first. Father Flynn always goes in before Mass.'

Here was a discreet toilet up a side passage, probably close to the chapel. Everything was bright and clean, and he was unburdening himself with relief when he remembered that the two nuns were only a few feet away in the corridor, within earshot of his waterworks. His flood had been splashing so merrily that it sounded more like a horse than a human. He tried to modulate the volume but he was still tipsy enough to forget where he was and emerge, adjusting his fly, as though he were in some grotty pub. But if the nuns saw or heard anything they gave no sign but shepherded him towards his destination, still chatting warmly.

Propped up high on a dais at the end of the hall, with the décor of the school play behind him, and flanked by smiling nuns, he discharged his prize-giving duties with automatic professional skill. Mother Superior began with a short eulogy of his works and pomps, describing him as a social catalyst, one of the first to try to compel the Irish to take a hard look at themselves. Was he a Catholic catalyst, he wondered facetiously, or a Protestant catalyst? But he did manage to weave a few pointed references to modern problems, like birth control, and contraception, into his general encomium of youth. Things had changed in Ireland, he said, but between liberty and licence there was a delicate balance, which their training here would help them to discern. There would be difficulties, because I was still an island of belief set in a sea of secularism, but things had relaxed, and freedom was far better than old-fashioned frustration. What else could he say, looking out on a wave of young faces, eager, laughing, and sometimes surprisingly pretty? But pace themselves, he suggested: life was a marvellous gift but to enjoy it properly one must show one's gratitude.

Altogether pretty painless, he felt; the sound of polite clapping filled the hall, as each successful candidate came tripping up for her prize. The only times he felt uneasy were when a particular fulsome remark seemed to get confused with a hiccup, and afterwards when, trying to adjust his seat, it nearly disappeared off the platform. He clutched for the table to right himself, and it also began to teeter. Luckily no one seemed to notice, and as he stepped carefully down, Mother Superior took his arm contentedly.

'Well done,' she said. 'You gave them something to think about. And now we can relax.'

And what had they been doing before, he wondered, as with a firm hand Mother Superior piloted him away, to the renewed sound of clapping. He had never seen so many young girls in his life, dividing like the Red Sea before him. And they were smiling, perfectly at ease in their setting. Where was the grim Ireland of his youth; indeed, where were the chilly nuns of yesteryear? Even Samantha seemed to be out of touch, so the change must have happened recently, or she had succumbed to the usual anti-clerical cliché, and remembered only the bad about her boarding-school days.

He was happily planning a programme on the Modern Nun when he was ushered back into the convent parlour again. Somebody had been at work, for it was transformed – as well as the smoked salmon, now tastefully sliced and displayed, there was a fine large bird, a roast tom turkey with its cooked leg cocked in the air. The wine bottles were lined up ready for battle, red on the right, white on the left, with what was left of the whiskey in the front. Had they really drunk that much? There were only a few glasses left in each bottle, and by the same token it seemed as if the wine would soon suffer a similar fate as it was splashed into thin-stemmed glasses.

Plate on his knees, glass in hand, he found himself rattling away with Mother Superior as if they had always known each other. The most impressive thing was that the conversation was not restricted in any way; she had spent a long term in the mother house in Paris, and spoke of things, Irish and otherwise, with the frank interest of a cosmopolitan, or at least someone who had lived in the wide world. She did speak of declining vocations but also of Women's Liberation; what did he think of it?

Before he could gather his thoughts, she gave him her own strong opinion – she found it had been too long delayed and consequently a

A BALL OF FIRE

shade strident. But there still were areas left untouched – priests, for instance, were never mentioned. And yet they were the ultimate citadel of Irish male chauvinism, masculine dodos who expected nuns to lay a boiled egg every time they appeared, in their lone majesty. Father Flynn always brought his underwear with him when he came to say Mass, as if the convent were a laundry. And he hung around afterwards, wolfing down a big fry.

And many Irish women had mistakenly given this kind of treatment to their sons, ignorant gulpins who sat at the top of the table, waiting to be served. This priestly syndrome had spoiled many Irish men forever, waiting for women to dance attendance on them. Not only could they not handle a washing machine, they could hardly boil a kettle. And if they were so inert about such everyday details, so deliberately helpless, what must they be like in bed? She knew it was not a nun's place to speculate, but she thought the pleasure quotient must not be high. To think of her little charges (all of whom now received instruction in anatomy) in their clumsy, ignorant hands, made her blood boil.

Mike Byrne lay back, roaring with laughter. This handsome, civilised, humorous woman was a terror when she got going; he loved her ferocity. It was the best sport he had had in a long time; instead of tea and biscuits in a chilly parlour, here he was pleasantly fluthered and blessed amongst women. What further surprise did the evening hold?

It came soon enough. The oaken door opened and a last nun came sailing in, an old nun, as old as the hills. And she sailed straight towards him, with, to his astonishment, open arms. 'Mikko,' she said, using the childhood diminutive, 'I bet you don't remember me from Adam.'

Mike Byrne rose hesitantly from the depths of his armchair. Clearly the scene had been set for some kind of exchange, for all the other nuns went silent, waiting with interest to see what happened. Either the old girl was dotty – but how could she have known his nickname? – or she had been bragging of knowing him at some time in the past. But when and where? He knew his hair was already grey and there was a middle-aged paunch growing, despite the Canadian exercises, but she must be fifteen or twenty years older than him. All his professional muscles began to flex, reluctantly forcing themselves through a cloud of alcohol; it was part of his job never to forget a face. Abundant grey hair, with some flecks of red, a broad, still freckled face, a familiar accent; not nasal Dublin, not a Western lilt, but vowels flattened by a pleasant drawl. Ah, yes…

84

In his memory's eye he saw a farmhouse in the Irish midlands, beside a broad lake. He went there every year for summer holidays and he and his cousins could borrow a boat to go fishing or swimming. It was a lonely spot, but in some way charmed; the swans would come drifting in to beg for bread beside the little jetty where boats rode. He had sat there late in the evening, listening to a stocky young woman, the eldest daughter of the house, as she told him of her plans for the future, her secret wish to become a nun. Even if she had wanted it, marriage was out of the question; there was hardly a man left in the area: except for a few heavy farmers, they had all emigrated. The little village was closing down; the anvil of the blacksmith would never ring again, after he left down his hammer. In all the emptiness, this accelerating change, she saw only one constant: the love of God. She had decided to dedicate herself to Him, and the small boy was very impressed as she told him shyly of her wish. She had come home obediently from the convent, when her mother died, to help look after the younger children, but when they were fully fledged she would go to speak to her father again…

'Mary Reilly!' he said – and they collapsed into each other's arms – after forty years. Whatever test, or contest, was involved, they had both passed it, for when he turned, all the nuns were up and smiling. The evening had come to its natural end, or climax, as, with an odd combination of personal warmth and ritual politeness, the nuns came up to embrace him. Mother Superior was first, of course, saluting him warmly on both cheeks, *à la française*. Sisterly hug or polite peck, they all had their say, after which he and Agnes were shepherded to a waiting car. His last image was of them crowded on the steps before that same great door, waving their arms like wings.

On the way home, the headlights of the taxi illuminating the startling green of the early summer leaves, he lay back in his seat, wondering. If he ever tried to tell the story of this evening, who would believe him? Indeed, did he believe it himself? A whole evening spent getting riotously drunk with nuns, ending up with his being kissed by an entire convent? Content and sleepy, he decided that maybe it had never happened, that it was all some kind of waking dream. He looked over at his niece; she had fallen asleep, or passed out again, a smile of total contentment on her young face. Dream or not, she clearly did not wish to wake from it, and he could hardly blame her, for neither did he.

PART III

7

THE PARISH OF THE DEAD

'That's the last time you'll see your aunt!'

Down the hill towards the chapel came four black horses, black plumes on the two foremost, nodding like shakos. And behind them was the hearse, an oblong of polished wood, with glass sides which exposed the black solemnity of the coffin, draped with artificial flowers. On the coachman's seat perched a familiar figure, the handyman of the local undertaker, magnificently metamorphosed in frock coat and tall hat, gripping varnished reins. Behind the hearse came the mourners, relations first, discreetly silent, and then the double line of well-wishers, appearing gradually over the brow of the hill like the unwinding spool of a film. As the funeral crossed mountain roads that morning from the neighbouring valley where the dead woman had lived, the line had grown, men emerging from house or field to swell the slow-moving, quiet-talking column.

'It's a bloody big funeral, isn't it?'

'It's always big when they have to bring them to the home graveyard. One townland travels with the corpse and one meets it. They have the wake and we have the funeral.'

'We'll get paid well this morning, anyway!'

'Shut up, Stumpy; after all, it's Johnson's aunt!'

Side by side on the sacristy wall they watched, four altar boys in skimpy white surplices fringed with lace, and black soutanes which hung down against the concrete. Behind them the bulk of the post-Emancipation chapel loomed up, a barn-like building of the same pebble-dashed stone as the wall, laid out in the rough form of a cross, with a steeple over the intersection, directly above the altar, and a bell-tower near the door. Without particular distinction of feature, it yet dispensed a certain dignity, a matter of silence and shade, as though the centred reveries of a whole countryside had created a patina of peace and longing to cover its inoffensive bleakness. And around the chapel lay graves, protective railings tangled in rank grass headstones obscured by moss and snail trails of damp; Lynch, Mellon, Carney, Kelly, Johnson, Tague, Donaghy: a whole parish lay under the clay. Only a few yards from where the boys sat, under the imitation Celtic cross of the Johnson plot, was a newly opened grave, a pile of bones and rotting coffin wood placed neatly to one side, and a shovel projecting from the mound of wet clay with the incongruous assertive gaiety of a flagpole.

'Death's very odd, isn't it? You never knew they were living until they die, and then you can hardly remember them.'

'What'll you remember about your aunt, Johnson?'

Before he had time to answer, a door opened behind them and the sacristan's head peered out.

'Boys,' he called, 'the priest's ready.'

Dropping to the ground, the boys raced to the sacristy where the priest, his robing completed, was arranging the chalice. The covering of the chalice was black and his vestments were black with a silver cross on the shoulders. As the boys filed out onto the altar, two before and two after the priest, John Johnson was still wondering what he would remember about his aunt, for whom this Mass of the Dead was being offered. She was the first of his relations to die, but already she seemed to have shrunk to little more than a presence, with that lean benevolence so typical of the women in his family, a tall bony figure who proffered apples or oranges, and caressed him, without asking where he had been or with whom, inextricable already from the gaunt figures that remained, grouped in mourning, on the front benches of this draughty chapel. As the slow tolling of the bell gathered the last of the people, the boy reflected that one thing that certainly distinguished her, for him, was the day he brought news of her illness, the day of her death.

II

All that afternoon the boy came running, running across the dusty mountain road that linked the townlands. A man working among the potato drills, a stooped figure against a background of blue sky as in a religious painting, raised his head to call: 'Where do you think you're going?' But his voice died away as the boy came under the silencing shadows of trees, and down into the hollow of the road. Then a horse, cropping the rough grass at the edge, threw up a frightened head, thrust out its great slovenly underlip, and backed wildly against the ditch. His breath harsh in his lungs, the boy drove his feet onwards with the hammered reiteration on his tongue, *Hurry, hurry, hurry.*

He passed a line of tiny County Council cottages, with window-boxes shining unexpectedly against dirty whitewashed walls. A greyhound, sniffing hungrily at the doorstep of the last, raised its pointed snout as he jogged past, and then came flying out, elongated and loping, to wander a few yards at his side and then drop back.

'O Mary, Mother of God,' he prayed, for the first time in his life feeling the words rise with real intent and urgency, rather than the accepted ritual. 'O Mary, Mother of God, let me be in time.'

He passed the last farm – a long low series of buildings, the farmhouse with greening thatch and a half-door on which a chicken roosted, the outhouses roofed with corrugated zinc and with no doors at all – and came over the brow of the hill and down onto the smooth surface of the main country road.

Elated but breathless, he halted when he came to the house. In the afternoon sunlight its long slanted roof seemed dull and unprotected, its windows facing the road like blank eyes, lit only by the occasional reflection of passing cars. Once there had been trees and outbuildings, but year by year they had fallen away, leaving the outlines of the house more exposed. As he stood, seeking to regain his breath and fumbling for the right way to convey his message, he seemed to sense the sadness of the house, from which a large family had scattered, leaving only a few survivors who gradually let the place shrink to the extent of their needs. And to this sadness, he must now add. He saw his Aunt Mary, a tall woman with loose white hair and a straggling apron, lost as always in reverie or prayer, come through the door and walk absentmindedly across his path. She was carrying a pair of hedge-clippers, and proceeded to fix the loose tendrils of a rosebush so that they hung in a pattern over the painted wooden gate leading into the farmyard.

'Aunt Mary!' he called urgently.

She turned, hearing his voice, with the puzzled uncertainty of someone already slightly deaf, and then stood, clippers in one hand, the steel points jabbing downwards, the other hand raised towards her face in an involuntary gesture of amazement at his sweat-coarsened features, dust-white shoes, and tousled hair.

'Goodness, John,' she said vaguely, 'where did you come from?'

He did not know what to say, but stood looking at her, uneasily.

'Did your father send you?'

'No,' he said, scuffing the ground with the side of his shoe.

'Your mother, then? Is there anything wrong?'

'No, it wasn't her.'

'What is it then?'

Gathering courage, he blurted: 'I've come from Aunt Margaret's. There may be something wrong with her.'

Startled, she motioned him indoors. 'Come inside and tell us about it. Martha's making tea, and you'll be able to get your breath back.'

In the dark kitchen, before the fireplace where a large black pot swung from a soot-covered crook, he found the atmosphere of intimacy he needed to speak. He sat on a sagging armchair and watched the expression change on the faces of his aunts as he explained his errand, like cloud succeeding light on an upland field.

'Some of the children going past told me Aunt Margaret wanted to see me and when I came up to the house, Uncle Malachy was leaving in the lorry for the doctor. So I went up to the room and there she was lying and when she heard me, she rose in bed and she looked very strange. She asked me to come over and see if Mary could come. And there was such a look on her face that I didn't stop running until I'm here.'

But Mary did not go after all. There was too much for her to do at home. So Martha set out, with a stick in her hand and a mongrel dog at her heels, to take the short cut across the mountains and down into the valley where the few houses of the neighbouring townland squatted along the banks of a bog-brown river. John stayed on at the house, bringing the cattle in for milking and then driving them out again into cool evening fields. Then he herded the drowsily squawking hens into their house for the night. As he moved around the farmyard in the summer twilight, hearing the rattle of buckets and the warm sound of calves shifting in an outhouse, he gradually lost his sense of strain and bewilderment, hardly even remembering the news he had brought just a few hours before. Only when he joined his aunt to say the rosary did it all come back; the words seemed to mean so much more than usual, his aunt giving them the weight and colouring of her own sorrow, as she knelt with her white hair spread on her shoulders. Was it true that she had heard the banshee when his Uncle John, the eldest son of the family, had died in America? There were pictures of him upstairs, posed photographs in the style of the 1920s, in which he looked large and clear-eyed as an ox; Uncle John had played the fiddle and liked to drink, that was all the boy knew of him. When she came to the family prayers, his aunt added one for a special intention, which he knew to be Margaret's health. Then, shaking holy water around his shoulders and giving him a lighted candle, she told him to go to bed.

His sleep was fitful and unhappy; the memories of the day took on a new shape, grotesque and terrible. He was running on a dusty road and something was following him, filling the sky above his head, blotting out the sun. He looked up, thinking it might be only a rain cloud, but as he watched, it began to take shape, the shape of a carriage with horses travelling at a reckless speed. The horses were black, the carriage was black, but the great iron-rimmed wheels made no noise as it sped past him. He woke, crying out, to see the morning light on the bedroom wall, the emerging shape of the washstand, the tossed bedclothes. During the night, news of Margaret's death had come. The funeral would be the following day.

III

After the last gospel, the priest turned to the sacristy to remove his vestments, and emerged again in soutane and surplice, followed by the head altar boy with a collection box. It was the time for Offerings, a tradition which still survived in a few Northern parishes, whereby relations and neighbours showed their respect by contributing money in proportion to the closeness of their tie with the dead person. Since the lump sum (often as large as £50 to £100) fell to the priest saying the Mass, there was always a good deal of grumbling about the practice, and comparisons were made with more enlightened parishes where the Offerings had been stopped.

But the people of Altnagore were secretly entranced by the slow ritual, beginning with the relatives (Thomas Johnson, One Pound! Mary Johnson, One Pound!) through the local merchants and strong farmers (James Devlin, Ten Shillings! Frank Mulgrew, Ten Shillings!) down to distant acquaintances and farm labourers (Dan MacNulty, Five Shillings! James Carty, Half a Crown!) It was an expression of hierarchy, fatalistically accepted, but also something more – a form of propitiation, a tribute by the parish of the living to the parish of the dead to which they in turn would belong. Even the few Protestants came to pay their respects, filing sheepishly into the back of the chapel just as the Mass ended, in time to join the slow procession to the altar rails, their abrupt, biblical Scottish and North-country names blending for once with those of their neighbours (Sarah Wilson, Half a Crown! William Clemens, Half a Crown! Isaac MacLean, Half a Crown!)

Today it was a big Offerings, since two areas of the parish were involved and the Johnson family were known in the district. Presided over by the priest and one of the chief mourners, the long line of people many in their working clothes, wound up and down the aisle. The chief mourner was the boy's uncle, Malachy Gorman, Margaret's husband. Properly sombre in an old-fashioned high collar with a flowing silk tie Uncle Malachy nevertheless looked a bit strange, disquieting. It was not the colour of his suit – he generally wore black in any case – but its cut he looked jaunty, almost dapper, like a dummy in a draper's window. He might have taken the same pose on his wedding day. And there was his expression: it was not that he did not look sad like the others, but that he looked almost contented in his sadness, taking misfortune not as a blow in the dark, but as the confirmation of his views about life. Like a seal in water, like a lark in the air, Malachy Gorman visibly revelled in his position of chief mourner. In many ways, the boy thought, the most extraordinary thing about his aunt had been her choice of husband. Now that the tie between him and the Johnson family was broken, he would probably not see Uncle Malachy very much in the future, but he would certainly remember him.

IV

It was not that his family had ever said anything in his hearing about Uncle Malachy; it was an uneasiness he sensed, rather than a definite objection. They were glad his Aunt Margaret had finally married, but they seemed to feel that she could have done better than Malachy Gorman, especially after waiting so long. Nor was it an act of desperation on her part, watching her thirties fall away; Aunt Margaret presented the same plain, lean, smiling face to the world, whether wedded or single: She seemed encased in effortless good humour. As the youngest of a large family she had received, despite the early death of her parents; more affection than most, and she saw no reason not to return the kindness. She had taken Malachy Gorman as she had taken everything else that came her way, good or ill, vaguely regarding this, her first and last proposal, as part of God's inscrutable will, part of an inevitable pattern of good.

It was not even that her husband was a 'traveller' – the local euphemistic description of a man who traded in everything from hens to old clothes to scrap iron – that troubled the family; it was rather something in his character, something exaggerated and unreal. He was monumentally gruesome. Tall, thin, lantern-jawed (but the lantern gave no light, only the blue-dark shadow of stubble), he always dressed in a black suit, with fraying cuffs, and a worn, shiny green bowler hat. Even his eyes were dark: magnificently black-irised like sloes, they gazed with voluptuous bleakness into a devastated world…

And yet it was this melancholy which made him so successful a businessman in his own peculiar line. He toured the countryside in a black Ford lorry with rattling mudguards, calling at every house and cottage. 'Any old hens today, Ma'am?' he would say, leaning his dark jaw over the half-door. He had a regular litany of dead objects which he intoned in a harsh singsong: 'Any old clothes, any old metal, any old buckets or bedsteads?' And the woman of the house would invariably rise, even if she was in the middle of a meal, and bring him around where the hens scratched in the casual dirt of the farmyard, among old tyres and upturned buckets. By the time she returned, the dinner might have gone cold on the table, the pot on the fire boiled over, the cat tumbled the cold crocks of milk in the dairy, but the woman would hardly notice.

For the secret of Malachy Gorman's success was his ability, as the country called it, 'to sup sorrow with a long spoon'. In him the hard-pressed farmer's wife met a real companion in misery – one who would make no attempt to raise but weigh the scales still further. Others might bring gossip or, as in the case of the doctor, a professional breeziness as a right of entrance; he responded to her long-hoarded melancholy with the professional attention of a priest bending over in the darkness of the confessional. As they moved around farmyard and outhouses, slowly and deliberately as a cortege, he would listen attentively to the long catalogue of tribulations and trials, aches and ailments, and then dextrously interpose his comment: 'Ah, yes, I know exactly how you feel, ma'am. My own cousin James had the same pain for a long time. It took him one day during the harvesting; he was nearly doubled up with the dint of it. Just below the kidneys it was. He was in bed for a month and the worst of the year, too, when all the help was needed. The wife herself had to go out to work in the fields and while she was away the cows broke into MacMahon's field and ruined their udders on the barbed wire.'

As he spoke, his gimlet eye continued to survey the landscape, estimating the amount of salvageable iron in a discarded plough, the suspicious limp of a rooster, its horny leg roughly bound with a cloth. Then, suddenly, he saw what he wanted and bent quickly down to grab some hen with trailing wings or droopy wattle. Held aloft, it squawked miserably, terror battling listlessness for a moment in its white-bleared eye, a thin stream of excrement jetting from its tail. 'That one's in a bad way, Ma'am. I'd better take it off your hands before it falls apart. You'll never see another egg from that girl, not if you live till Doomsday.'

And the hen went to join a squawking assembly in a dung-soaked cage at the back of the lorry, together with a piece of old iron and a broken bedstead with sagging metal springs. When the farmyard had been gutted of everything redundant, decayed, and discarded, the lorry moved out onto the road again, top-heavy and rattling. A week later, the hens, clipped, cleaned and briefly rejuvenated by a special diet (corn soaked lightly in whiskey, some said) and with brightly coloured strings on their legs, were dispatched to Belfast on an evening train to be sold as young juicy pullets for officers' tables. The mattress was gutted for its feathers, which were in great demand for making fleece-lined jackets for the invasion army now gathering in Ulster and remote parts of Britain. Scrap metal was also scarce; a German soldier, falling in a ditch in Normandy, would never know that, owing to Malachy Gorman's ingenuity, his life had been taken by a piece of Maggie Devlin's bedstead in the shape of a bullet. (As for Maggie Devlin, had she known the chain of cause and effect, she would have prayed for the poor man all her life.) The remains, a soaked and ripped mattress cover, a crazy tangle of wire and springs, fragments of rotting wood, went to swell the great mound of rubbish that gradually rose behind Malachy Gorman's house, dwarfing it like a pyramid.

So engrossed did he appear in his sombre but highly rewarding task, that people had been very surprised when Malachy married; one did not associate him with such ideals of happiness. But Margaret Gorman, née Johnson, seemed quite contented with her new position: she worked on with quiet and diligence as she had done all her life until, bearing out her husband's view of life, she died, in her third year of marriage, after a brief illness. Happiness, in the ordinary sense, did not seem to be Malachy Gorman's destiny.

V

After the funeral there was the ceremonial breakfast; funerals, like weddings, brought together relatives and friends. There was his father, Thomas Johnson, restless as he watched yet another good harvest-day squander its sunlight outside the window. There was Uncle Francis, who had given up farming to keep a pub in Clogher; prematurely grey, he spoke little, but whistled continually through his teeth. There was Cousin Michael, now a parish priest in a small town in Armagh, the orchard county; he generally brought the children apples – Beauty of Bath and Bramley seedling – but not today. And there were his aunts: the married like Frances and Brigid, who had come with their husbands, one a schoolmaster from Cork, the other a cattle dealer from Westmeath; the unmarried, like Mary and Martha, who still lived in the house where they had been born, and Aunt Lucy, who was in a convent in Newry and was also called Sister Bernadette.

At first, everyone seemed uneasy, as though chilled by the long morning at the funeral and in the chapel, and by the sensation of returning, through a receding mechanism of time, to the place in which most of them had been brought up. Perspectives of childhood mocked them at every turn. Above their heads was a blackened bullet-hole where Michael Johnson, wrestling with the boy's father for possession of the rifle, accidentally fired a shot through the roof. For days the family had lived in fear in case the shot had been heard and the illegal possession of the rifle discovered. There was a picture of their father, a great white beard clouding on his chin, and their mother, a plain woman, tightly corseted. Almost involuntarily their eyes rested on these things, though without attempting to share a melancholy which each probably thought was restricted to himself.

Only the children were obviously excited, scurrying from room to room, watching the chicken and the ham being prepared, smelling the strange tang of whiskey in the air. And slowly conversation sprang up to remarks about the funeral, souvenirs of the dead woman, each memory rounded off with a dying fall: 'I never dreamt she'd go so quick!' It was stimulated still further by the bustling arrival of a group of latecomers. James Gormley, the undertaker, restless and dapper, his narrow breast encircled by an elaborate gold chain, moved from group to group, announcing briskly: 'It was a great Offering. Margaret Gorman was a highly regarded woman.' The parish priest, Father Donnelly, an enormous mottled frog of a man, eased himself with accustomed sobriety into the sombre pool of the conversation: 'Margaret Gorman was a fine woman I only hope we all have as holy and happy an end as Margaret Gorman.'

Gradually, as whiskey and companionship warmed them, the conversation widened. There was even subdued laughter. Father Donnelly told how, at a clerical conference recently, anxious to leave early, he looked for his hat, only to be confronted with an avalanche of similar black hats. One priest, however, had anticipated the problem – the lining of a hat he picked up contained the legend in large letters: LEAVE IT ALONE, DAMN YOU, IT'S NOT YOURS. Taking courage from the priest's example, the schoolmaster from Cork gave a colourful account of a recent election in his county, where the candidates had come to blows. ''Twas as good as a hurling final,' he ended, with a smack of the lips. Everyone laughed.

That was only one side of the room, however. On the other side, the boy saw his aunts sitting in a sad row, like hens sheltering from the rain, their eyes glazed with memory. And before them stood Malachy Gorman, a glass of mineral water in his hand. His head, unaccustomedly bare, showed a bald patch on the crown, bleak as a soft-shelled egg. And above the clink of glasses and the increasingly robust laughter the boy heard his voice: 'I knew it could never last. We were doing too well. Only last Easter, Margaret said that now we were making more money than we ever had, we should build a new wing to the house. The war was very good to us, you know. But I knew it couldn't last. And then I was driving over the Hill Road one evening. I saw a hearse coming towards me, it was travelling at a great rate and just as I was wondering what poor soul i could be, I saw there was no coachman in the box. Mother of God, said I, and I blessed myself as it passed, without the creak of a wheel. And when I looked after, it was gone, not a thing in sight down the whole stretch. And I knew then something was going to happen. We were doing too well.'

In the clucked but unsurprised assent of women's voices the boy remembered and recognised his dream. Now that he had come to know death, such dreams might recur, hints of that mortality he shared with everyone in the room. But he hoped he wouldn't be frightened by them. For some people, he would discover, death, contemplated too long and too lovingly, became almost a reason for existence; although they sometimes consoled others, they ended by becoming monstrous figures themselves, almost comic in their obsession. Hearing the boy behind him, Malachy Gorman turned, showing a smile as brief and purposefully bright as the cutting blade of a MacCormick reaper. The boy smiled uneasily in return. Then he turned away, reluctantly, to the other side of the room, where his father was calling him.

8

ABOVE BOARD

When my cousin Agnes came up from the South for the summer holidays I suddenly became very popular. She was at a convent school, but in her sixteenth year she had sprouted, with all the signs of young womanhood. I was uneasy about the change, which I dimly understood; after all, I had known the precocious girls of Glencull School, but that sort of thing was not discussed in our house, and to have a sleepwalking young beauty under our own roof was something new.

It also changed our relationship. She and her younger brother were my best friends, but her change made him very angry: he hissed at her at every meal and silently kicked her under the table. The older people ate at another table, when they were together at our house, and her older brothers ignored the drama as beneath them, which it was. Sometimes I got a hefty kick on the shin myself when young Seán missed his target.

Meanwhile she drew near to me, as if she needed me, which was very flattering. She came with me to drive the cows to the mountain pastures in the morning, leaving a sulking Seán behind. And then we would strike out into the high bog, cart tracks sunk so deep that you were invisible between the high banks, the mystery of MacCrystal's Glen with its twisted thorns and banks of prickly yellow whin. Sometimes we stopped for a rest, and we would share a bar of chocolate, which I had saved from my wartime rations for her. We sat side by side on a spread raincoat, talking, usually about love, whom we would meet; and marry, of course.

100

She had already introduced this theme, a year earlier, when I went South. I had got off the bus in Longford, and begun to haul my suitcase towards her home, but there was no sign of her, although she was supposed to meet me with her bicycle. Finally Agnes appeared, dusting her skirt, and wheeled the bicycle from a gateway. She had used the excuse of meeting me to spend an hour with a young clerk from the town, called 'Tosh' Ryan. She showed me his letters, four or five scrawled pages, full of vague compliments. She said they might help me if I was in love, to know how to write to please girls, but I was sure I could do better. 'Bosh' Ryan seemed a better name for his style!

Another swain was introduced to me, a turf driver from Castle-pollard. He came rattling past the door every day, lashing the poor donkey to give some impression of speed. We met him in the snug of a public house once. He bought me a lemonade while he drank a pint, and Agnes and he stared at each other. He had reddish-brown crinkly hair hanging over his eyes in a quiff, which he kept smoothing back. I thought he looked terribly vulgar, no class, but I sipped my free lemonade and said nothing.

I doubt if much happened on these meetings; kissing, cuddling, and muffled endearments from love stories were all that were permitted to the better-class, convent-bred girl. I was more afraid for my cousin in my own home area, where I knew the score and she didn't. Whatever about fancy letters from town clerks, I knew what the boys around Garvaghey were thinking – hadn't we played under Rarogan Hill, making drawings of women in the sand? Every copy of *Lilliput*, with its pictures of naked women tastefully posed between sailing swans and ripening fruit, was devoured with an avidity we rarely brought to our lessons.

So when big Shamus Lynch began to lumber behind us as we drove out the cows, I managed to drive him away. Big Shamus had a dull square face and a dogged manner, with the leglifting attitudes of a canine in heat. But, despite a head crammed with bad thoughts, he was bashful, so I just told him I would tell his mother on him. She was the rival of my Aunt Brigid for holiness in the parish, kneeling long after everyone had left the chapel, praying and sighing to herself: 'Mother of Jesus, help us'. As well she might sigh, since she was so pregnant at her wedding that she gave birth to big Shamus on the side of the road on her way home from the feast.

101

Or so I heard. You must understand that I was not part of all this interest in sex, except as a bystander. My maiden aunts never mentioned it, and I knew that I would be going to a better school, maybe even to become a priest! No one knew about my secret yearnings to be as bad as the boldest of them. If that was what was wanted, of course: my real inclination was towards chivalry but it didn't seem the way love was practised in my home territory.

So I didn't want that sort of game associated with my lovely cousin upon whom, in return for her confidences, I began to lavish my longings. We took long walks; heads together, we read the same books, from Zane Grey to Leslie Charteris.

I saw myself as a knight who would stand guard over her, come what may. The expeditions I planned, to the pictures in Omagh, or a climb to some secret place, were partly invented to please her; poor Seán tried to tag along, but soon dropped away when we barely spoke to him, or walked too fast for his shorter stride.

The last intruder I had to drive off was Austin, a foxy-haired young fellow a few years older than myself, who knew more than was good for him, and who had already boasted about having got the knickers off several girls. Since my cousin Agnes had arrived he had become very friendly with me, by the way, but I could see his play coming.

One afternoon he came down towards us, whistling, as we were starting to drive out the cows. Luckily, his father called him away, but a few days afterwards he slithered down a hedge so abruptly that he startled one of the cows, who shot off through a gap in the hedge. He shot off after it, but the damage was done: he had presented himself more as a rustler than a useful cowhand. I was able to go on calmly pursuing my conversation with Agnes, who steadfastly ignored him, having already been fed scarifying reports from me about his grossness.

We were using each other, I suppose: I was acting as a shield for her, and she flattered me by showing so much attention to a youngster like myself, whom the older girls ignored. And slowly I fell in love with my sense of her; not the breasts and thighs I and the other boys discussed hungrily, but a real young woman who asked me to sit beside her on the edge of her blue school raincoat, shared my chocolate, accepted my sweets, and let her long, dark, fragrant hair fall across my face.

It was summer, of course, and what few flowers we knew were in blossom. The foxglove thrust its red fingers at us on the way to the

102

upland pastures, and irises showed their yellow flags in bottom meadows. There were more intimate sights: the minute blue of forget-me-not, the daisy's tiny heart, a shock of bluebells sheltering under a tree. We were not strong on flowers, but their perfume mingled with our wanderings, and in the high bog, as the wind combed the heather, there was a constant, sweet scent, a silent sound of heatherbells. We found blaeberries or fraughans, the blue berry of the bogs, which we smeared on each other's faces, laughing all the while. We were discovering a little about life at the same time as nature herself was coming alive; although we carefully said nothing about our feelings for each other, it was a sweet exchange.

Then one admirer made an outflanking move. He was Manus Donnelly, the young shopboy from the local grocer's. A sheepish young fellow with flaxen hair, he had not attracted my attention much since he didn't play football for the Garvaghey team. His only claim to fame so far was that he had cut the top off his finger with the new Berkel bacon slicer; I was in the shop at the time and saw him holding up the reddening finger in surprise. Then he touched it and the nail fell off, onto the counter, before the waiting customers. Mrs Lynch fainted and Manus himself had to be helped away, before the doctor came.

That a fool like that should be wooing my beautiful cousin seemed ludicrous to me, but she appeared to like it. He seemed reluctant to make direct moves, though we spent longer and longer in the shop over some simple message or other. I fumed as he fumbled for topics of conversation: how could anyone stand those long silences? Agnes did not seem to mind, ready to wait as the Calor-gas lamp hissed and other customers came and went.

Then he devised a Trojan Horse, which brought him right inside our house. I don't know if my aunts or her parents were aware of the interest that Agnes was causing: the way boys gaped through the window, came into the post office to buy stamps for non-existent letters, or waited on the roadside to greet us as we went forth on some simple errand – going to the well, or fetching the cows. But then Pa Doherty arrived one night for a card game, with young Manus in tow.

Cards are, or were, a bit like religion in the countryside: you had to welcome the players who chose your house. And Uncle John loved cards, in a mild sort of way, a vice I had never suspected him of. Even my aunts would join in, grumpily at first, because visitors meant a disturbance of the household routine, and making tea for everyone; but they also liked the bit of drama. Bit, indeed, because it was one of the slowest and simplest games in the world: twenty-five for a penny. That it was not being played for purely gambling motives didn't seem to cross their minds, though the obsessions of Pa Doherty were well documented.

Pa, Or Pa-trick, lived opposite the church, with his two scraggy spinster sisters. He was a not-so-spry bachelor in his early sixties, a long drip of a man with a straggly moustache, like Mr Gump in my American funny papers. But he had a thing about women, in a harmless sort of way; one was always hearing that Pa was visiting with some new Dulcinea, usually a middle-aged woman whose brothers had suddenly died, leaving her in charge. He was also to be seen at the corner as the school scattered; he never offered sweets to little girls, but he looked sweetly at them. That this wizened rooster should dare to dream, even daydream, of my cousin was something monstrous to me. I joined in the card games from evil motives, whenever I was allowed, hoping to cheat the lovelorn. For he and Manus spent more time looking at Agnes than at the black and red of their playing cards. It made me rage to intercept their lovesick glances as they played wrong cards, missing suits or tricks because they were thinking only of one thing.

After they had been there several weeks in a row, even my elders began to feel the game pall. There was no sharpness in it and it was clear that young Manus was losing part of his salary every evening, playing as if he were sleepwalking. No matter how small the stakes, they added up, and the winners felt abashed at taking such easy pickings, whatever the reason. Besides, people were beginning to talk, and we became dimly aware that somehow or other it had to stop.

So what I decided to do to bring them to their senses was not punished as it might otherwise have been. Time after time, when a card was dropped, a bright red heart or a dark cluster of clubs, I dived in search of it, still small enough to go down inside the forest of legs and retrieve the missing rectangle of cardboard. I got to know that strange world down there, under the table: the solid knees of my Uncle John, the skinny ones of Pa Doherty, the flannels of Manus Donnelly, the demure convent-pleated skirt of my cousin, the longer, warm aprons of my aunts, like Indian tents.

A few times, when I slid down quickly, I noticed that something was going on. Pa Doherty's knee would abruptly withdraw from near that of my cousin, or I would find Manus's foot out of its shoe, and wandering, also in the vicinity of Agnes. I decided to do something about it, in that strange half-lit world of knees and legs and ankles. One night when I was down I tied the shoeless foot of Manus to the nudging knee of Pa Doherty, using a length of string I had smuggled down with me.

The result was spectacular enough to satisfy any of my fictional heroes. Pa put down his pipe, which issued clouds of acrid grey smoke, and decided to cross his legs, to bring him luck perhaps. The border twine – I had not stinted in my subterranean operation – lifted the foot of Manus which landed in the lap of Agnes. She rose with a modest expostulation and the table rose with her, or rather tilted. Seeing her rise, Pa also rose, like a true gentleman, and the deck of cards slid into Aunt Mary's lap, Kings, Queens, Jacks and all, to be followed slowly, the table now bounding and bucking as though possessed, by the teapot, which disappeared with a slow and stately motion over the edge, onto Uncle John's trousers. He was a quiet man by nature, but the roar he let out as the scalding contents of the big teapot – it had just been wet for the nightcap – landed across his fork would have done justice to Coote's bull.

The great thing was that through hauling and pulling, the string broke, and no one ever really knew what had happened. I slid down under the table like lightning to untie the remaining knots and slip the evidence into my pocket, or up my gansey, whichever was quicker. The wreckage I confronted when I came up was very satisfactory: everyone wore a startled and strained air, as if they had swallowed a hedgehog. The parents of Agnes were not overly protective but they had realised that in some way their daughter was in danger, and that even a senior citizen like Pa was not above suspicion. As for young Manus, he was beetroot with embarrassment and loss.

Nothing was formally said, but they never came back. I was sorry for Manus: although I could not bear his lovelorn, gawky looks, he was less menacing than some of my cousin's suitors, but there was something pathetic about him wooing a serious girl, someone so foolish that he could cut off his finger with a bacon slicer! He had taken to wearing a little red sheath over it, which made people ask about it so that he could bare the stump to admiring eyes. But it didn't sound like bravery to me – he was far from the front line when he got that wound. As for Pa Doherty, he had brought out all the amorous bigot in me. He was a gentle soul, gentle to the point of simple-mindedness, and whatever feeling he may have had about girls during his younger days had been strangled by his situation. He was, in effect, married to his sisters, two renowned churchgoers, and already fulfilling that mystic role of being 'the man about the house'. I can see him now, leaning over the gatepost as school broke. Were his watery blue eyes and drooping moustaches moist with lust, as he gazed at the young MacGirrs and Johnsons and Kavanaghs? I doubt it: looking at them, deep down in him, his distant youth stirred, like a fish lost in a pool who had once heard tell of the ocean.

9

THE NEW ENAMEL BUCKET

When John Rooney left his home to go to the fair in Moorhill he meant to be back early. It was spring and there was a lot to be done, from ploughing late fields to sowing early ones. Besides, he had to do all the work now himself: his father was too old to do more than complain, watching behind the window-blind all day to see that his son did not slacken, or hobbling along the margin of a field to judge if the furrows were straight. Indeed, as John rose to lift his cap from a nail, his father glared at him: 'What do you want to go hightailing to town for anyway?' he said peevishly. 'Do you think the fair won't get on without you? Nothing but outings for the young nowadays: fit you better to stay at home.' And as he passed through the scullery door, his mother called after him, raising her head from the bucket of hen's meat she was preparing: 'Mind, now, don't make your stay too long.'

He got his bicycle, an ancient Raleigh with truncheon handlebars, from the turf shed, where it was propped up against an old spraying barrel. A flock of chickens scattered from under his feet as he mounted with a slow but stately movement. Moorhill was only a few miles away, first down the lane and then along the country road which ran towards Enniskillen. He took the lane slowly, for the surface was uneven: now and again one of the wheels hopped and bumped on a big stone and he cursed under his breath. At last he swung out, with relief, onto the tarred surface of the main road, and began pedalling vigorously towards town.

John Rooney was in his early thirties, a little over six foot in height, with large hands, weak blue eyes, and a long nose. He always wore a cap, with the peak pulled rakishly over one eye, in imitation of a Gaelic footballer he had once seen, famous for his burly viciousness. But in reality he was a quiet, gentle person, passive by nature: 'John Rooney's a good sort,' people said, without enthusiasm, as though speaking of some placid cow or sheep. As he cycled, he observed with interest the land on either side, the chug of a Ford tractor crossing a headland, crows converging on the steely-black of a new furrow, beneath the dark line where the heather began, like the fringe of a scalp. In former times, the Black Mountain district had been known for its highwaymen, outlawed Catholics whose farms had been seized, but there was nothing to remind one of that today. It was a fresh, sunny morning and, though the land was neither rich nor particularly well-tended (the upland fields tough and sapless, the lower meadows damp with the drainage of the mountain), everything seemed pleasantly relevant: birds darted in the spring hedgerows and the freewheel of his bicycle sang on the gentle descent of the mountain road.

As he approached Moorhill, he began to overtake knots of cattle being driven to the fair. Most of the men were from his own area, dressed in the half-style of towngoing attire, a good coat worn with overalls or other working clothes. He nodded to them soberly as he passed, a swift sideways dip of the head indicating recognition and greeting. Among them was his nearest neighbour, Willy Boyle, or 'Long Willy' as the countryside called him, with cheerful misanthropy, because he was only five foot in height. Willy was driving two heifers in front of him, shouting energetically as he thumped their backs with a sally rod: 'Up there, you bastards, yup there.'

John Rooney had never been a close friend of Willy's but he believed in being a good neighbour, so he drew in to accompany him, letting his legs dangle from the pedals.

''Lo, Willy.'

''Lo, John, how's the farm? For the fair?'

'Might stay an hour or so. You should do well with them beasts.'

'I could do well and I could do nothing at all. Depends on the bloody dealers!'

'Them's good animals, though. If the one on the outside takes after her mother, she'll be a great wee milker.'

The cow in question, a sleek brown polly with soft white markings, like splashes of paint, made a sudden dart for an open gap. As Willy rushed after it with violent oaths, John Rooney drove his bicycle forward, interposing the front wheel to block the heifer's path.

'In the nick. I'll be moving on now, Willy.'

'Abyssinia, John.'

'See you, Willy.'

*

Moorhill consisted of one long main street, originally used as the fairground, and a rabbit warren of side streets, where cottages crumbled into sad disorder. Seen from the narrow-gauge railway, or the lofty new bypass of the main road, it gave an impression of extreme bleakness: the huddled grey backs of the houses, festooned with piping, looked mortuary. In the border area of Ulster, cut off from its natural southern hinterland, there were generally two sorts of towns: the surviving and the slack. But Moorhill was more than slack, it was stagnant, which was partly responsible for its peculiar reputation among its neighbours. 'I was never married,' people would say with relish at the mention of its name, 'but I was twice in Moorhill.'

There had only been one attempt at an industry within living memory: the stump of a dead linen mill dominated the centre of the town like a funeral monument. Under the system of social relief developed by His Majesty's post-war government, extreme poverty had passed, but there was still an aura of raffishness, a down-at-heel quality about Moorhill. The town remained sharply divided between the middle-class (professional people, merchants, publicans), whose main income came from the countryside, and the unemployed, whose quarrels received vivid reports in the rather biased local paper produced in the county seat, twenty miles away. Of late, there had been some agitation to improve the housing, but the town's reputation, and the consequent uneasy belligerence of its supporters, had prevented much progress: it still remained, according to a county councillor, 'one of the dirtiest wee towns in the North of Ireland'. He was referring to the plumbing and was lobbying for its improvement, but when he next passed through Moorhill his remark was remembered: he found a dead dog and a brimming household utensil in the back seat of his parked car. In its fiercely defensive patriotism, Moorhill found it hard to distinguish friend from foe.

*

John Rooney drove his bicycle slowly up Main Street until he reached the embattled virgin of the Boer War Monument. On one side of the street was a bar, The Mountain Rest, which belonged to a family which had originally come from Black Mountain; it was there John generally left his bicycle. He wheeled it down the piss-sour entry into an old shed and then came through the back door of the house into the bar. He ordered a bottle of stout and stood drinking near the window, through which he was able to see the early business of the fair, a cart passing with a load of pigs, an old clothes man setting up his stall. Now and again he turned to speak to the barman, a lean young fellow in a spotted sportshirt.

'How'd your bitch do in the trials?'

'You never saw anything like it. She ate the track.'

'If she hits that form in Belfast you'll be all right.'

'I'll be made.'

'Is she as good a goer as Moorhill Lass?'

Moorhill Lass was a famous greyhound, bred by the same man, which had reached the final of the Balmoral Cup only a few years before. Its prowess had already passed into local mythology and various forms of foul play on the part of the city people were held responsible for its downfall.

'She sights the hare better, a better starter, like. You should see her shoot from that trap, man, like a bloody bullet. But she's bad on the bends, comes too wide. And she's very easy upset, finicky, you know. The least wee thing puts her off her food.'

'It's the breeding makes them nervous.'

There was silence for a few moments. John gazed deeply through the window and the barman busied himself behind the counter, arranging empties.

'Are you for buying, the day?' the barman asked finally, for civility's sake.

'Naw. No grazing left. But I still like to come in for a look round me.'

'Nothing like a fair,' said the barman, without conviction: he obviously regarded the countryside as an inexplicable hangover from the days before the invention of the internal combustion engine.

'People say the move to the Commons has spoiled it.'

'Ah, I dunno, we do the same business only later and longer.'

110

'Well, good-bye now.'

'Maybe you'll be by again.'

'Hardly. There's a lot to be done at home and I can't stay more than an hour or so.'

'Good luck, anyway.'

As John Rooney passed out through the door, the barman reached for his glass and rinsed it under the tap. Countrymen were all right, but God, some of them were a fearful drag. If his bitch won, maybe he should move to Belfast and get a job in a really flash bar, with a lounge and all the latest: his mother could easily do without him for a while. Then he could take out that big blonde he had met in the Club Orchid: she had headlights on her like a Transport lorry. She might get more than she expected, and better than she thought, if his boat came in. Through the window he saw a group crossing the street towards The Mountain Rest: business was slow but it was beginning.

*

The hands of the courthouse clock registered midday as John Rooney walked down the street towards the Commons, the large stretch of waste-land between the cinema and the railway yard, which had recently been taken over as a fairground. The fair was now in full session: cattle bawled mournfully and pigs raced squealing around wooden pens, where buyers leaned ceremoniously over to inspect them, scratching their scaly backs with ashplants. A sow and her litter lay exposed in the crate of a cart, the piglets burrowing with blind fury into the pink recumbent body of their mother: now and again, one tottered to its feet and rooted for a better position. Children out for their play-hour darted through the pens and the carts, and around the great wheels of the cattle lorries. From a public house near the fairground came the nasal twang of a ballad singer.

John pushed his way through the throng, halting every now and then to appraise a beast, or watch a bargain being made. Within a ring of onlookers, two men faced each other, hats pulled low, ashplants stuck under their armpits like swagger sticks. The object of their contest, a large heifer, stood sullenly between them, swishing its tail over its fly-spotted flanks. Then, a third man broke through the spectators with massive authority, just as the prospective buyer was turning away in an elaborate mime of disgust. Seizing a hand of each man he brought them together in a reluctant banging of palms: 'Now, John Kelly, you and Jimmy

Drummond are both decent men; you wouldn't let a few pennies stand between you. Split the differ and the bargain's made: are you game, Kelly?'

John Rooney savoured the scene with deep satisfaction. The ritual of bargaining always gave him great pleasure, although it was on the way out, now that the cattle dealers had become so strong, smooth middle-men who went from fair to fair and knew the ways of the world, how to keep prices down, where and when to ship. And the move to the Commons had taken away a good deal of the interest of the fair, though people said it might end well if the cattle-marts took over. But hand to hand bargaining was what John Rooney knew best, secret ploys and approaches passed on to him by his father while he was still a gaping boy. It was one of the reasons why he had come to the fair, that and the vague urge for a little company after the lonely weeks working in the mountain fields. But today he wished to remain uninvolved; whenever he was asked to give his judgement on an animal, he was careful to speak only in platitudes, and if anyone tried to enmesh him as mediator to complete a noisy deal, he managed to escape. 'Not today, James,' or 'I have to be going soon,' accompanied by elaborate shrugs of self-deprecation, butting his cap sideways at the air: 'Naw, naw, not now.'

But the lowing of the cattle, the strong sour reek of dung and old clothes, so many familiar sights and sounds soothed him, like a drug. Meeting a neighbour from Black Mountain, they would fall into an attitude of interest like two crows on a paling wire. The sun had begun to move down the sky before he finally turned to leave the fairground. As he plodded reluctantly up Main Street, he heard somebody calling him: 'Hello there, John Rooney, you long streak of misery, you.' It was Willy Boyle, his hat set back on his tiny head at a jaunty angle, his face lit with excitement and compulsive goodwill. He saluted John in a derisive whine:

'Lord, some people are in the tearing hurry! Are you going to walk right past a neighbour and not ask him if he had a mouth on him at all?'

'Hello, there, Willy. I was just heading home.'

'What hell hurry's on you? Sure it's only a while since you passed me on the Black Mountain road. It's long till bedtime.'

'I have to be home,' said John uneasily, but his companion was not even listening.

'Do you know how much I got for them?' he said excitedly, digging a bundle of notes from his pocket. 'Go on, guess.' But before John could hazard a figure, he blurted out his news: 'Sixty pound … and I declare to God me only counting on fifty.'

'You had luck the day all right,' said John, eyeing the bundle of notes under his nose with appropriate approval.

'I had the luck all right,' said Willy, grudgingly, 'but I had something more important than luck: a good sharp eye in me head. Come in to Donnelly's now to christen this handful, and I'll tell you the whole story.'

John Rooney looked at the little man with vague apprehension. His eyes were slightly red-rimmed and he spoke very rapidly: it was obvious that he already had a few drinks in him and was ready for more. He had a new bucket looped over his arm, a white enamel bucket of the kind used in the country for carrying spring water: it gave him a slightly gipsy look.

'Honestly, Willy, I'd rather not. I told them at home I'd be back to do a bit of ploughing before evening.'

'Ach, hold your horses, man. One drink won't harm you. Sure I have to get home myself, and I have more to carry than you.' He tapped the wad of notes significantly. 'Come on, now, and stop dragging. Isn't it a terrible thing when your own countryman won't drink good fortune with you and you have to spend your money on strangers?'

Reluctantly, John surrendered: an appeal to local patriotism was too final to reject. He did not object to drinking with the little man, but Boyle had the reputation of being troublesome when he had drink taken. Yet if he only stayed for a round or two there would be no harm done and he would still be home in time for a late dinner.

'OK, Willy, just the one for old time's sake and to christen your bargain.'

'That's the man. You can take me home with you when you're going and we'll both be the one road. Right?'

*

By evening the main street was quiet, the few clothes dealers dismantling their stalls, an occasional straggle of cattle passing through on their way home, unsold. 'There's old Clemens driving home his three stirks,' said Willy Boyle, looking through the window of the public house. 'God, but they're the right hungry creatures. You'd think they never saw a pick of grass in their born days.'

113

'They're not too fat, indeed.'

'Fat! Ye could nearly walk through them. If he wasn't too bloody mean to feed them he'd have done better today. But they were always a close pack in Castleisland anyway.'

'Easy on,' whispered John Rooney into Willy's ear. 'There's a neighbour of Clemens, Big Tom Jackson, over there drinking in the corner.'

'What do I care about Tom Jackson,' said Willy, pushing John's hand away. 'Do you think I give one damn. I was only saying what everyone knows, that Clemens's cattle are no bloody good.'

'All right, Willy, you're right enough. Drink up your stout and we'll be going.'

'Going me ass. There's time for a few yet. And if you don't have the money, I'm the boy can do the trick.'

Staggering slightly on his pigeon-frail legs, Willy Boyle reached into his inside pocket and drew out the soiled bundle of banknotes. He waved them at arm's length above his head, like a victorious boxer posing for applause.

'Do you see that, men? You never saw a Boyle yet without money to stand his turn.'

The group of men in the corner, towards whom Willy Boyle was ostentatiously addressing his remarks, were from the rich farming district of Castleisland, on the far side of Black Mountain, towards Lough Erne. Large-headed, colonial, calm as the plump animals they bred, the Castleisland men chewed the cud of their conversation, without paying much attention to the other people in the pub, although once or twice Tom Jackson gave Willy a sharp, half-amused glance. Their indifference angered the little man, who was now pretty far gone, and spoiling for a fight. In their refusal to take him seriously, he scented their poor opinion of him, as though he were no more than a bluebottle buzzing in the window. He struck the counter with his fist, making the glasses jump.

'I'm fit to buy a drink with any man here. Isn't that right, barman?' he queried, shoving his face, with its uneasy ferret's eyes, fiercely forward. 'What hell pub are we in, anyway?'

Since their meeting at three o'clock, he and John Rooney had been in several, beginning with the one nearest the fairground, and then working their way up the street in illogical order, from the Dew Drop Inn, to the Corner House, to the Sunshine Bar, until they reached the one where John had left his bicycle, The Mountain Rest. There they had been for

114

over an hour, during which time John had made many proposals to leave for home. Willy, who was now at the stage when he spilled half his drink in raising it to his mouth, was still determined, as he said (with a leer towards the corner to stress his mocking use of the old Orangeman's war-cry) to move 'not an inch'. John was relatively sober, most of his energy being taken up, not with drinking, but with trying to keep the little man out of rows; but the noise, the lack of food and the anxiety were beginning to tell on him: his head felt heavy and his eyes ached with smoke. He made another appeal, *sotto voce*.

'Right now, Willy, drink up and we'll hit the road. I'd like to see you bring that wad home safe, as well as yourself.'

'Ah, damn your drink up. Won't we be at home for the rest of our lives. Home was never like this.'

'I know all that, Willy, but there's some boys about this town would skin you as fast as look at you.'

John Rooney looked anxiously around him as he spoke, to see if his remark had been overheard. In his triumphal progress up the street, Willy had accumulated quite a few hangers-on, whose eyes glistened at the sight of his much waved bundle of banknotes. For one of the characteristics of Moorhill was the number of 'gentlemen of leisure' it supported: stray unemployed in whom the pristine loss of pride at being without steady work or craft had been perverted into a systematic delight in living on their wits. The dole gave them barely enough to live on, but nothing to fill their empty hours. Generally, they were to be seen against the court-house wall, where their shoulders had traced a wavering line of grime. But they could smell free drink as bees smell honey from one side of a field to another, and their system of communication was highly developed. The leader was big Andy Cleggan, who wore a raft-like straw hat from which ribbons dangled. As a boy he had been clever beyond the average, and his fond parents had sent him to college, hoping to turn him into a white-collar worker; but he fell promptly to the bottom of every job and by the time he had decided to reform, it was already too late. He had lost his last job, driving an oil tanker, three years before, when he crashed into a tree outside Lisburn. Beside him was Jimmy the Jail, whose thirst derived from the dimly remembered horrors of the Flanders campaign. A stonemason, from a long line of stonemasons, he had emerged shell-shocked and spent, with shaking hands. When his pension was done, he would take to drinking methylated spirits or turpentine; his pockets were littered with tiny bottles, sold illegally for a shilling or two, which gave off a sickly sweet odour. He had even been known, in extremis, to drink boot polish: long periods in jail, sewing mail bags, had not eased his longing for oblivion, in whatever form. There was 'Dandy' MacHugh, who dressed carefully in a natty grey suiting, indeterminate in age, but with razor-edge creases, brown brogues with a Celtic design toecap, and a checked golfer's cap. There was a clothes salesman called Black Barney, whose speech was so slurred as to be almost meaningless: he wore a bright red shirt, a tattered black hat and army surplus fatigues, part of his stock in trade. His face was a fiery claret, under the chalky white of his albino eyelashes, the inverted source of his nickname. In their instinctive and terrifying war against life, as presented to them in Moorhill, every means was fair, only a victim – for money or amusement, or both – necessary. Although they did not say much, sinking their noses luxuriously into their stout glasses, they registered with disapproval John's insistence.

'What do you mean, Rooney? Aren't we among friends?'

'That's right,' said Andy Cleggan graciously. 'Willy Boyle was always a decent man. I always said that. Isn't that right, boys?'

'Right. Willy Boyle is the heart of corn.'

Leaning on the counter, the barman watched them with growing distaste. He had planned to leave for half an hour or so about this time, to catch a meal, and, more important, 'to feed his greyhound which was probably slavering for its bit of steak. But he was troubled by the rancour in the air, the obscure quarrelsomeness of Willy: if anything happened, his mother wouldn't be able to handle it. A fair was good for trade, but countrymen were hard to get rid of: unused to drink, they lay around all evening gabbing, the porter going sour in their bellies. And that crew Willy Boyle was playing Pied Piper to, they could drink an iron lung apiece, but they were also damned dangerous. If only one could find a way of selling drink without having to put up with the kind of people that bought it: they would never tolerate goings-on like that in Belfast.

Willy Boyle solved his problem for him. At intervals during the afternoon, he had suddenly remembered his enamel bucket and searched for it frantically, accusing everyone until it was found. Looking for a reason to reassert himself, the bucket came to his mind once more, and he began to look for it wildly. 'Where in hell's that bucket? If any of those Castleisland whures...' His attendants searched for it with assiduous servility and discovered it sitting on a case of empties near the entrance

116

to the kitchen. Andy Cleggan passed it to him, reverently. Enraged by such promptness, Willy let it fall slapbang on the floor.

'Are you calling calves, Willy?' said one man in the corner, civilly. He was a fair-haired Presbyterian, called George Booth, with the rather attractive slow smile of someone at ease with himself and the world.

'It's good I have them to call anyway, and don't plan to buy other people's,' snarled Willy. This was meant to be a hit at Booth who had sold one of his farms and was rumoured to be moving into town to set up as a dealer. Since the Booths had been strong farmers in the Castleisland district since Plantation times, the move was regarded, on both sides, as a failure to maintain tradition.

'Mind your tongue, there,' warned Tom Jackson, 'or there's some as will mind it for you.'

Willy laid down his glass slowly and, teetering back towards the wall, squared himself into what he considered a fighting position, left hand thrust forward, right poised behind his head in menace. John Rooney hovered around him like a distracted mother-hen.

'I won't take lip from any dirty get of a Protestant, anyway,' said Willy, glaring at the other end of the bar.

In the commotion that followed, everyone participated, in hot confusion. Booth, Jackson and the others rose from their seats and plunged vaguely towards Willy, to be halted by the imploring gestures of John Rooney: 'Never mind him, now, he's drunk and he doesn't mean a word of it.'

'Maybe you'd like a touch yourself,' said Tom Jackson, brandishing a knobbly fist.

Behind John Rooney, Andy Cleggan and his associates formed a wavering second line of defence: 'Easy on, now, men, easy on.' In the background Willy Boyle danced in dervish rage, daring all to come. The two groups swayed back and forwards, voices heavy with drink, until, whipping off his apron, the barman came around hurriedly to separate them.

'Come on now Willy,' he said, pointedly, 'you'll have to go. There's no room for that kind of chat here.'

'What chat?' said Willy, sullenly. 'It was them started it.'

'You'll have to go now, Willy, and that's flat,' said the barman, with the double authority of a sober man and a property-holder on whose premises a misdemeanour has been committed. 'I won't stand for that class of mischief-making.' He grasped Willy by the collar.

'Come on, Willy,' said John Rooney, seeing his chance.

'That's right,' said Andy Cleggan, with lofty decision. 'Come on, Willy, we will not stay where we are not wanted.'

His companions agreed, with pleasing unanimity, that they would not stay where anyone of their number was not wanted.

Mollified, Willy led his troop towards the door, with the air of a betrayed but undefeated general. 'It'll be a long time,' he said bitterly, with his head still inside, 'before I darken this door again.'

'Good riddance,' said the barman, as the door banged behind them.

*

In the middle of Main Street, the group assembled in glum silence. It was twilight now, and the lights from shop-windows and doors threw butter-yellow rectangles on the pavement. Outside the garageman's concrete of the town cinema a queue was forming, country lads in belted overcoats, shuffling large feet. The drink sour in his stomach, his head throbbing in the cool air, John Rooney reflected sadly that it was the first time he had ever been thrown out of a pub: The Mountain Rest into the bargain. If his father heard of it, he would kick up holy murder: he had always given his patronage to The Mountain Rest and regarded it as a 'good country pub'. Maybe he should wait a while, until he sobered up, before going home. The busy millrace of the normal life of the street made him realize how far gone he was: he swayed slightly on his feet.

'What'll we do now?' said Willy Boyle, doubtfully.

There was a pause and then Andy Cleggan cleared his throat. 'What about going down to the Glory Hole for a wee sup before you go?' he said, with anxious heartiness.

'They mightn't let us in,' said Willy Boyle. A policeman passed, pushing a bicycle, his cape black as a bat, his Sten gun gleaming. He looked curiously at the group in the middle of the street. 'They mightn't let us in when we have drink taken elsewhere. It's getting late, you know.'

'Yer all right,' said Dandy MacHugh. 'There's no keeping out or putting out down there. You'll be welcome.'

'Better not,' said John Rooney, in half-hearted protest.

'Come on,' said Willy, decisively.

*

118

The Glory Hole, otherwise known as the Dead End, was the most notorious pub in Moorhill, spoken of by the matrons of the town as though it were an antechamber of hell. It belonged to a bachelor called 'Sheriff' MacNab, who, though he lived over the pub, had never been known to drink himself, preferring poker and 'the nags'. Formerly a coachhouse, it had, as the saying goes, seen better days, but its gaunt façade, distempered a bilious yellow, was still impressive. It stood directly in front of the old Protestant graveyard; emerging on a moonlit night to relieve a full bladder, one was confronted by ranks of tombstones on the hill opposite: an accusing army of puritan dead. It was reputed for its bad drink, served at all hours of the day and night, despite the vigilance of the Royal Ulster Constabulary. It was even more reputed for the curious things that happened there, especially to strangers who fell into the cunning hands of its clientele. A commercial traveller from Enniskillen, a dignified, moustachioed gentleman of the old school, had woken to find himself stark naked in the town river. A hardboiled sergeant of the WAAFs had found her underwear flying from the top of the War Memorial. It was the operational headquarters of Andy CIeggan and his friends, who, when God was good, ended the night in a drunken stupor in one of the straw-filled outhouses. Its real name, executed in straggly Gothic letters over the door, was the Moorhill Arms, and it was, in its way, the most lively place in Moorhill.

As they trooped into the low-ceilinged room, John Rooney trailing behind, they were greeted enthusiastically. The thin middle-aged man behind the bar raised his palm in a salute, Indian-style.

'Well, if it isn't long Willy Boyle, the terror of the prairies, and his side-kick Big John Rooney, the fastest plough alive. Howdy, partners. Tie your hosses to the hitching-post and name your poison!'

Willy Boyle blinked. He was suspicious and a little awed by the fluency of the greeting; but it seemed friendly, particularly after his ejection from The Mountain Rest. He felt suddenly generous.

'Whiskey for all,' he declared.

'Better stick to the stout,' advised John Rooney.

'Firewater for five,' said the man behind the bar, reaching for a bottle of MacDimnocks Special Scotch Whisky and measuring out five halves swiftly, below counter level. 'And how is life in the prairie these days? Any Indians? Any Sioux smoke-signals betokening death to the white man?' He pushed a glass across to Willy. 'Any Blackfeet squaws?'

'Damn the one,' said Willy fervently. MacNab was obviously a wee bit touched, but he was a friendly man, unlike some he could name. And he wasn't too far wrong about the women. 'Spoken like a true cowboy. A man's best friend is his horse. Isn't that right, Andy?'

'Willy Boyle,' said Andy CIeggan, heavily, 'is no common cowpoke. He is the best rancher south of the Sperrins. He drove a herd to town today the like of which was never seen on the old Chisholm Trail, let alone the wide ranges of Black Mountain and Castleisland.'

'They were damned good cattle, all right,' agreed Willy, happily. 'And I made a damned good deal. Another round there, men.'

*

Three hours later Willy Boyle was explaining, for the tenth time, to a large and steadily growing audience, first, how he had triumphed in his bargain and then, how he had given the Castleisland men their comeuppance. His speech was nearly as incomprehensible as that of Black Barney: he left sentences trailing in mid-air, ran words wildly into each other; sometimes, he would stand for a moment or two in baffled silence, as though he had lost something, peering intently down the well of his consciousness. Finding nothing, but painfully aware of some lack of coherence, he would cover the transition with oaths and imprecations.

'I showed them, the bastards, I showed them, didn't I, damn them?'

'You did indeed,' said Andy Cleggan, draping an enormous arm over Willy's tiny shoulders, and belching warmly. 'You're a murderous man when you start, Willy Boyle. We were all afraid of what you might take into your head to do.'

'I wouldn't like to face you, Long Willy,' said 'Gentleman' Jim Brady, winking at the audience. The 'Gentleman', Andy Cleggan's closest·crony, was a local strong man, famous for his double-jointed fists, which, for the price of a drink, he could make crack like pistol-shots. Although never properly trained, he had fought briefly as an amateur with the local Don Bosco club, smothering the majority of his opponents by the unprincipled violence of his attacks, until a more experienced referee had spotted his repertoire of rabbit and kidney punches.

'He'd be dangerous, all right,' everyone agreed, admiringly.

Everyone, that is, except Jimmy the Jail, who had achieved the oblivion he sought, his grizzled poll sunk on a barrel-head, and John Rooney, who sat beside him, in a waking doze, his eyes glazed, his body slumping forward every now and then, like a badly filled sack.

'But a generous man withal,' said Andy, raising what Sheriff MacNab called his sombrero, with a fine gesture. 'No kindlier friend.'

'Generish,' agreed Black Barney, his red shirt open to the navel, his eyes wild under his tattered black hat.

'No truer friend,' said Dandy MacHugh.

Puzzled but pleased, Willy made a gallant attempt to acknowledge this recognition of his merits. 'All friends here,' he said, and then paused. 'Set them up again, Sheriff.' He rummaged in his pockets and produced a diminished bundle of notes which he placed on the counter. 'All friends here,' he muttered briefly again, and then closed his eyes, and shuddered, as another bout of nausea passed swiftly over him, like a large green wave over a very small boat.

*

Whose idea the football match was would be hard to say. It was an hour after closing time and they were still drinking behind closed shutters, by the light of a candle behind the bar and the minute glow of a red Sacred Heart lamp from the kitchen. It was probably big Andy, who had reached the stage where he showed everyone the medal he had received as a minor footballer, twenty years before. As he held the tiny silver-plated disc aloft, his eyes became moist with fond memory. 'I was ten stone then, and as fit as a fiddle,' he said sadly, as though speaking of the dead. Or it may have been Gentleman Jim, who had been describing a game the previous Sunday, between Moorhill Gaels and Fentown Pearses. In his eagerness to demonstrate the winning goal, he had taken Black Barney's hat (the head it covered had long lost any sense, not merely of ownership, but of reality), rolled and tied it into a ball, and placed it carefully on the floor in front of him. With a neat swipe of the instep, the professional's penalty kick, he sent it flying past Andy Cleggan. 'Up Moorhill!' he roared. 'Offside!' roared Big Andy, confusing his codes.

Befuddled but eager, the drinkers plunged into the fray. At first, there were the semblance of sides. Willy Boyle was appointed captain of the Fentown team, but since he had been sick only an hour before, the position was titular. Gentleman Jim was, therefore, Acting Captain, Andy Cleggan opposing him; the goalposts were stout bottles. But in the poorly lit pub, the small black hat was almost indistinguishable; body crashed into body in confusion. Placing his head well down, Andy

Cleggan ploughed through the room like a rogue elephant. 'Moorhill abu!' he roared, but as he poised for a kick at goal he found that the hat had disappeared, and only a piece of white string remained.

After a brief moment it was found, wedged under a door, and disintegrated into flitters. 'We need something easier to see,' said Andy, with keen disappointment. Referee Dandy MacHugh, resourceful and dapper, appeared carrying a large white object and placed it down before Andy. 'There you are,' he said, 'a new Croke Park pigskin.' Andy drew back his boot and sent the enamel bucket sailing through the air to land with a smack in the lap of John Rooney. With a start, Rooney awoke, and shot to his feet, sending the bucket clanging to the floor again.

The effect produced by the bucket, the kick and fall following each other in the darkened room like claps of thunder, was instantaneous. James MacNab shot from behind the bar into the centre of the group: 'Now, men, you'll have to go. Fun's fun, but a noise like that will bring the police down on us like a ton of bricks.' Willy Boyle, who was dully aware that there was something wrong and resented the sudden shift of attention from himself that the football match had produced, suddenly recognized his bucket. 'Jesus,' he said, with a squeal of rage, 'you curse of God whures, you've ruined my good bucket.' He bent down to cradle it in his arms: a shower of enamel drifted to the floor like flakes of snow. Shock, and an empty stomach, combined to produce a sudden, chilled sobriety: 'Where are the sponging bastards?' he said, bitterly, looking around the room. Andy Cleggan, Gentleman Jim Brady and Dandy MacHugh were nowhere to be seen: neither was John Rooney.

When the bucket had landed in his lap, bringing him sharply awake, John Rooney did not know where he was. The smoke-filled room, the swaying bodies: it was like a nightmare, and for a moment he wondered if he was dead and lost for ever. Then he remembered, shame and pain mounting in his skull and a retching spasm in the stomach, and his first thought was to escape in the night air.

It was raining slightly, a light damp rain that was like a blessing on the drum tap in his temples. A full white moon occupied the sky. He saw the yard stretching down towards the river, the shapes of the bottling shed, the old barn, a heeled-up cart like a gallows. He picked his way, gingerly, over the bright stones of the yard to a darkened corner. On the slope opposite, the gravestones of the old Protestant cemetery rode the night like the white sails of sailing ships in a long forgotten school book.

Protestants, he reflected as he peed, were a funny class of people: they didn't believe in Purgatory, for example. But then, how did you know what Purgatory was like, anyway? Then, there was this history business: one minute they were Irish, and the next they were English, whichever suited them. Why couldn't they just forget the past and then, maybe, we could all live together as neighbours, happily ever after? There was no point in stirring up bad blood the way Willy Boyle did; live and let live was what he felt, whoever was wrong, and the more credit if you forgave your oppressor. The calm, perfect night filled him with mild benevolence.

As he was buttoning his trousers he heard, as in a dream, voices behind him, quarrelling voices.

'No point in going back now.'

'That bloody bucket put the kibosh on it. Why the hell couldn't you leave it alone ?'

'Why did you suggest the game, you stupid cur?'

'It wasn't my idea. It was your big brain thought it up.'

'A good night ruined.'

'Who's that galoot standing over there, listening to us ?'

'That's that Rooney. If he'd had his way, there would have been no night at all. Yapping for his home all day like a child.'

'Dirty spoilsport. Will I get him ?'

'No bloody harm.'

As the first blow struck him, sharply, in the back of the neck, below the ear, John Rooney turned, astonishment and shock lengthening his features. 'We're all friends, here, men,' he said, with obscure conviction. The next blow caught him full on the mouth and he staggered backwards. Just as he was wondering what to say or do, all the gravestones in the Protestant cemetery began to topple in on him, avengingly.

*

Willy Boyle poised for a last diatribe at the back door of the pub. 'Easy now, Willy,' said James MacNab, 'or you'll bring the police down on top of us.'

'Right good lesson for you if I did,' shrilled Willy. 'And the rest of that pack too. Not a dacent man among them.' And then, a thought striking him, 'Where's John Rooney?'

'He went home,' said a voice from the shadows, behind the publican's shoulder.

'He did not,' said Willy vehemently. 'John Rooney would never leave a man the way you would.'

'Maybe he'll come back in a minute or two. Hold your horses and we'll have a quiet drink and wait for him.'

'He's hereabouts somewhere,' said Willy Boyle, 'and wherever the hell he is, I'll find him. I won't leave this town the night without him.'

A search party, led (reluctantly) by MacNab and (militantly) by Willy, probed the length of the yard. In the bottling shed, stumbling over a forest of empty bottles, they heard something moving and flashed a match on it. It was a mouse, which regarded them for a moment with beady, unfrightened eyes, and then scuttled away. Knee-deep in moonlight, figures swayed drunkenly, like bathers in a long stretch of surf, poking in the nettle-wild remains of a coachshed, examining with a desperate summoning of interest a sagging clothes-line, a discarded outdoor wooden closet. But it was Willy Boyle who finally found John Rooney where he had been thrown, at the base of the triangle of the uptilted cart. His face was badly cut, with a gash across the forehead. As Willy, calling for help, knelt at his side, his left eye opened, and he regarded Willy briefly, then spat out a particle of tooth and a dark gobbet of blood.

'I meant no harm,' he muttered thickly.

'Of course you didn't,' said Willy, in deep misery.

James MacNab came hurrying down the yard, carrying a bucket of water in one hand, and a sponge in the other: he passed them both to Willy. As the enamel flashed, milk-white in the pale clarity of the moonlight, a thought seemed to stir in John Rooney's mind, like a fish turning in deep water.

'Did you get your bucket, Willy?' he whispered through broken lips.

Willy held the bucket out, at arm's length. There was evidently a small hole in the side, for a thin stream of water trickled onto their clothes.

'The only clean thing in this town,' he said, with defiant bitterness. Then he began to swab away the blood from his friend's face. His hands were still awkward, and he fumbled.

'Up Moorhill,' said John Rooney, wincing as the sponge touched his eye.

'Up Moorhill,' agreed Willy Boyle, bleakly.

10

THE CRY

Finally he rose to go to bed. His father had shuffled off a few minutes before and his mother was busy preparing a hot-water bottle, moving, frail as a ghost, through the tiny kitchen. Seeing her white hair, the mother-of-pearl rosary beads dangling from her apron pocket, the bunny rabbit slippers, he felt guilt at keeping her up so late. But he came home so seldom now that he was out of the rhythm of the household and tried to do only what pleased them. And sitting with their big Coronation mugs of cocoa, they had drunk in his presence so greedily that he felt compelled to talk and talk. Mostly of things they had never seen: of travelling in Europe, of what it was like to work on a big newspaper, of the great freedom of living in London. This last had troubled his father very much, centuries of republicanism stirring in his blood.

'What do you mean, son, freedom?'

'I mean, Father, nobody interferes with you. What you do is your own business, provided you cause no trouble.'

Seeing the perplexity in his father's face, he tried to explain in local terms. 'Nobody on *The Tocsin*, for instance, would dream of asking if you were Catholic or Protestant – at least not the way they do here. If they did ask, it would be because they were genuinely interested.'

'Then can you explain, son, why England has the reputation she has abroad? Didn't she interfere with freedom everywhere she went, from Africa to the North here?'

'That's not the real England, Father; that's the government and the ruling class. The real Englishman is not like that at all; he stands for individual liberty, live and let live. You should hear them in Hyde Park!'

'I must never have met a real Englishman then,' said his father, obstinately. His face had gone brick-red and his nostrils twitched, showing spikes of white hair. With his bald round head and bright eyes he looked like Chad in the war-time cartoon, peering over a wall, but it was anger, not humorous resignation, he registered.

'Maybe,' said his mother timidly, 'they're all right when they're at home.'

And there the matter rested. His father had always been violently anti-English: he remembered him saying that he would be glad to live on bread and water for the rest of his life if he could see England brought to her knees. And the struggle there had been when he had first announced his intention of trying to break into newspaper work in London! Dublin would have been all right, or America, where his father had spent ten years as a cook in a big hotel before coming home to marry and settle in the little newsagency business. But England! Religious and political prejudice fused to create his father's image of it as the ultimate evil. And something in his father's harshness called out to him: during his adolescence, he had contacted the local branch of the IRA and tried to join. They (rather he, a lean melancholy egg-packer called Sheridan who had the reputation of being a machine-gunner in the force) had told him to report for a meeting, but when the time came, he had funked it, saying that he had to go away.

And so, Peter changed the conversation. He spoke of shows he had seen, the big American musicals, the Bolshoi and Royal Ballets. But his father still seemed restless: once he saw him glance mournfully across at his mother and wondered what he had said wrong. Her eyes glinted with pleasure as he described a Charity (tactfully amended from Command) Performance, with all the stars arriving in their glittering gowns.

'Oh, that must have been lovely,' she said, with placid yearning.

It was only when he was climbing the stairs that he realized what his father's glance had meant. 'Good night, now, son, and don't forget to say your prayers,' his mother called after him. That was it; because of his visit, they had not said the regular family rosary, waiting for him to remember and suggest it. How could he explain that he had never seen anyone in England say the rosary, except two Irish lads in his first digs in Camden

Town, who had embarrassed everyone by kneeling down at their bedside and saying it aloud in Irish. English Catholics did not believe in loading themselves down with inessentials. But if he had begun to explain all that, they would have jumped to the conclusion that he had lost his faith completely. Religion and politics he should try to leave alone for the short time he was home.

*

The room was on the top floor, that front bedroom in which he had always slept. The top sheet was turned down, with the same inviting neatness, the blue eiderdown was the same, even the yellow chamber pot beneath the bed. Over the fireplace was the familiar picture of Our Lady of Perpetual Succour, an angular Madonna cradling a solemn-faced Child, a slipper dangling from his chubby foot. Opposite it, on the wall over the bed, was a Victorian sampler, worked by his grandmother as a young girl: THERE IS NO FUN LIKE WORK.

It was all so unchanged that it was almost terrifying, like being confronted with the ghost of his younger self. He heard his father moving in the next room, shifting and sighing. Taking off his clothes, Peter knelt down in his pyjamas for a few moments at the bedside; he hoped the old man would hear the murmur and guess what it was. Then he wandered round the room for something to read.

Spurning *The Wolfe Tone Annual* and *With God on the Amazon* on the dressing table, he discovered a soot-stained copy of the *Ulster Nationalist* which had obviously been taken from the grate to make room for the electric fire; this he carried triumphantly to bed.

The editorial spoke with dignified bitterness of the continued discrimination against Catholics in the North of Ireland in jobs and housing. Facts were given and, in spite of the tedious familiarity of the subject, Peter felt his anger rise at such pointless injustice. He turned the page quickly to the Court Proceedings:

UNITED NATIONS FOR MOORHILL?

Moorhill Court was taken up on Wednesday with a lengthy hearing of a civil summons for alleged abusive language and assault.

Giving evidence, James MacKennie, Craigavon Terrace, said that Miss Phyllis Murphy had thrown a bucket of water over him as he was passing on his bicycle. Cross-examined witness admitted that he had spoken sharply to Miss Murphy but he had not threatened, as she said, 'to do her'. He admitted borrowing 5/- from Miss Murphy 'to cure a headache'. His solicitor, Mr John Kennedy, said that his client was a veteran of the First World War and had a disability pension. It was true he had been in jail several times, but he was very well thought of in the community.

The defendant, Miss Phyllis Murphy, said that James MacKennie was a well known pest, and besides 'he had been coming over dirty talk'. She denied throwing water over him and said he had had been making so many 'old faces' that he had driven over the bucket of water. She denied saying she hoped 'that would make him laugh the other side of his Orange face'.

In giving his decision, the R.M. said it was a difficult case to disentangle but he felt both parties were to blame and he therefore bound them over to keep the peace for a year. It was a pity, now that people were trying to outlaw war, to find neighbours disagreeing; maybe he should ask the United Nations to come to Moorhill ... (laughter in court).

Peter Douglas read on with delighted horror. For the first time since he had returned, he felt at ease; he threw the paper on the floor, and turned contentedly over to sleep. Somewhere downstairs, the cuckoo clock he had brought his mother was sounding.

II

Some time later, he came suddenly awake to a sound of shouting. He listened carefully, but it could not have come from the next room. Perhaps it was his mother; no, it was too strong, a man's voice. It came from down in the street, but not directly underneath; he sat bolt upright in bed and turned his head towards the window. Yes, there it was again, clearer, and he sounded as if he were in pain.

'O, Jesus, sir, O Jesus, it hurts.'

Maybe somebody had been taken ill suddenly and they were carrying him to the ambulance? Or a fire: he remembered the night, years before, when old Carolan had been carried out of his house by the firemen, screaming like a stuck pig, rags of cloth still smouldering upon his legs. But who was the man in the street talking to, whom was he calling sir?

'O, Jesus, sir, don't touch me again.'

128

All across the town lights were beginning to come on; the shadowy figure of a woman, wrapped in a dressing-gown, appeared at the window directly opposite; only something unusual could sanction such loose behaviour in Moorhill. Maybe it was a fight? Then, with a cold rush of certainty, Peter Douglas knew what it was: it was someone being beaten up by the police.

'O, God, sir, don't hit me again.'

The voice was high and pleading. Then, there was a scuffle of feet and the sound of a blow, a sharp crack, like a stone on wood. Throwing back the bedclothes, Peter ran to the window and craned out his head. At the bottom of the street, he saw a knot of people. One of them was kneeling on the ground, his shape circled by the light of a torch held by one of the bulky cape-clad figures surrounding him. In the windows above, shadows moved, silent, watching.

'Come on to the barracks now and quit your shouting,' said an impatient voice.

'Oh no, sir, I can't, I'm nearly killed. Somebody help me, for God's sake, please.'

Again the voice was abject, but at a muttered order the torch was extinguished and the four figures closed in on the kneeling man. Was no one going to protest, none of those darkly brooding presences? Peter Douglas opened his mouth to shout, but he was forestalled. A door opened behind the men, letting out a shaft of light. He heard a sharp, educated voice:

'What in blazes do you thugs think you are doing? Leave the man alone.'

One of the four policemen turned, switching his torch directly into the face of the speaker.

'Keep your bloody nose out of it, will ye? Do you want to get a touch too?'

He heard further muttering and then a door slammed angrily. The four figures seized their victim, who now hung like a sack between them, and half-walked, half-ran him down the street towards the barracks. There were no further cries, only the drag of boots on the pavement, an occasional groan and (as the barrack door opened and shut behind them) a gathering silence. One by one the lights went out over the town. Peter Douglas was one of the last to leave, his eyes sore (he had left his glasses on the bedside table) from straining after any further movement. As he climbed into bed again, he heard the cuckoo clock, Cuckoo, Cuckoo, Cuckoo.

III

When he came down to breakfast next morning, after a short and troubled sleep, he found his father waiting impatiently for him. Generally, he was in the shop by this time, but it was his mother's voice he heard, dealing with an early customer : 'Yes, Mrs Wilson, nice weather indeed, for the time of year…' And it was his father who prepared the meal, cornflakes, tea and toast, bacon sizzling fragrantly in the pan. It was clear he had something on his mind; Peter felt as suspiciously certain as a prisoner who finds his warder suddenly affable.

'You're pretty lively this morning, aren't you?' he said, digging into the cornflakes.

His father did not reply, fussing around the stove with plates and cloths until, triumphantly, he placed a full plate of bacon, eggs and sausages before his son.

'The old man can do it yet,' he said. Then he sat at the end of the table and watched his son eat, nervously, with an urban lack of zest.

'They don't seem to have much appetite in England, anyway,' he said, 'whatever else they have.' And then, without further preamble: 'Did you hear what happened last night?'

'I did,' said his son, briefly. 'Did you?'

'I only heard the tail-end of it, but I heard them all talking this morning.'

'What did they say?'

'They said the B-Specials beat up a young man called Ferguson, whom they accused of being in the IRA.'

'Was he?'

'Sure how would I know? Most people say not, a harmless lad that was courting his girl on the bridge, without minding anyone.'

'Then why did they attack him ?'

'Why do you think? You know bloody well those boys don't need a reason for beating up one of our sort.'

'Maybe he had papers on him, or an explosive. After all, there's been a lot of trouble lately.'

In the preceding months, the IRA campaign against the North had been revived. It was the same sad old story: barracks, customs huts blown up, and police patrols ambushed. Several men had been killed on both sides, and the police force had been augmented, even in relatively quiet areas like Moorhill, which, though predominantly Catholic, was too far from the border for a raiding party to risk. A hut at the end of the town had gone on fire one night, but it turned out to be some children playing a prank.

'Damn the explosive he had with him, except,' his father smiled thinly, 'you count the girl. But those bloody B-Specials are so anxious to prove their importance, strutting around the town with their wee guns. Besides, they're shitting their britches with fear and mad to get their own back.'

'I see.' Peter forbore from pointing out that some of these motives were mutually exclusive, recognizing his father's mood only too well. He poured a last cup of tea.

'Well, what are you going to do about it?' said his father fiercely.

'What do you mean, what am I going to do?'

'You were talking last night about Englishmen and freedom. Well there's an example of your English freedom, and a fine sight it is. What are you going to do about it?'

'What do you want me to do? Look for a gun?' he said sardonically.

'You could do worse. But your sort would faint at the sight of one.'

Peter flared. 'Would we, indeed? Well, maybe we've seen too many, handled by the wrong people.'

'What the hell are you going to fight them with, then?' his father snorted. 'A pen-nib? A typewriter? A fat lot of use that would be against a Sten-gun.'

'It might be of more use than you think. Moral protest is always best, as Gandhi showed. But they did not teach you that in Ballykinlar.'

'Moral protest, me granny. How are you going to bring moral protest to bear on bucks like that? Force only recognizes greater force.'

Peter Douglas rose and, placing his back against the rail of the stove, looked down at his father. The dark-blue pouches under his eyes, gorged with blood, the right arm raised as though to thump the table in affirmation: he could have been cast in bronze as The Patriot. His own limp ease, the horn-rimmed glasses, the scarf tucked in neatly at the throat of his sports-shirt, the pointed black Italian shoes – everything represented a reaction against this old fire-eater who had dominated his childhood like a thundercloud. But now he felt no fear of him, only a calm certainty of his own position.

'You know well, Father, in your heart of hearts, that violence is the wrong way. Now you ask me what I can do. Well, in this specific case, I can do more than you or a whole regiment of the IRA. I can write an article in *The Tocsin* which will expose the whole thing. Good, decent – yes, English – people will read it and be ashamed of what is being done in their name. Questions will be asked, maybe in Parliament, if not this time, then the next. And gradually, if they are shown the enormity of what they are doing, the ruling classes of Ulster will come to their senses. One cannot hope to survive in the twentieth century on the strength of a few outdated shibboleths: prejudice always breeds violence.'

His father was silent, whether impressed or not, Peter could not say. Then, rising to clear away the breakfast things, he said: 'You'll do that then. You'll write the article.'

'I will.'

His father smiled, cunningly. 'Well, at least I got you to do something. You haven't completely lost your Ulster spirit yet.'

*

Peter's first task was to collect the information. He began to move around the town, listening to conversations in shop and pub. At first he drew a blank; seeing him enter with his pale look, his city air, the men at the bar went silent or whispered among themselves. When they had established his identity ('Oh you're James Douglas's boy,' a double recognition of family and religion flooding across the face) they spoke again, angrily.

'Oh, the black boys gave him a good going over, like,' said one man with a knowing wink and nod. 'You don't get off lightly when you're in their hands.'

'Is he badly hurt?' asked Peter.

'Now I couldn't tell you that exactly, but the doctor was with him this morning. They say he has a broken arm, anyway.'

'I heerd he had two broken ribs and stetches in his head forby.'

'Oh, they gave him the stick all right.'

'You'll get no fair deal from the likes of them.'

'They're black as can be.'

But when Peter asked what was going to be done by way of protest, they looked at him bleakly, shaking their heads.

'Sure you know it's no bloody use,' said one, hopelessly.

'You'd be a marked man from that day out,' said another.

'Sure you know the black boys have it all sewn up,' said a third, joining the litany of defeat.

Their passivity only heightened Peter's resolution, the only thing troubling him being the lack of specific detail. Very few people seemed even to know the boy, who lived far out, in the Black Mountain district. And those who did did not always approve of him; they said he was very 'close' and used to hang around the juke-box in Higgins's Cafe. Yet they were all agreed on the wanton brutality of the beating, though the majority confessed to having been too far away to see much.

The source for the earlier part of the story was the girl, but she had run away when the struggle started and her father had forbidden her to leave the house. Since the man whom Peter had seen rebuking the police was the schoolmaster, he would not be home until evening and the nearest to an eye-witness he could find was the owner of the Dew Drop Inn. He and his wife slept in a room overlooking the street, exactly where the worst of the struggle had taken part. Yes they had struck him a lot, he told Peter, but he had heard one of them say: 'To be sure and hit him round the body, it leaves less mark.'

'There should be a boycott against them bucks,' concluded the publican, grimly.

In The Mountain Rest, however, Peter found the town clerk calmly drinking a large whiskey. Tall, with a drooping sandy moustache, he had served in an artillery regiment during the Normandy campaign and the boyish vigour with which he propounded atheism in a community highly given to religious hypocrisy had always amused Peter. The clerk thought that what had happened the previous night was a storm in a tea-cup. The boy had been looking for trouble and the only mistake was that the police had not acted promptly enough. 'The only thing to do with a gulderer like that is to hit him on the head with a mallet: that puts a stop to the squealing!'

No one spoke. Gulping down his lager, Peter left: it was time to start his article.

*

It is depressing to encounter violence again, its familiar pattern of fear and impotence. The first time I met it was in New York: a huddle of boys under a street lamp and then the single figure staggering backwards, hands to his side, while the others fled. My first impulse was to help but a firm hand held me back. By the time the ambulance arrived, the boy was dead.

That is the classic scene of urban violence; the spectator is absolved in the sheer remoteness of the action. It is not quite so scenic when it happens among people one knows. Recently I returned to the small town in the North of Ireland…

Well, it was a beginning at least; a little academic in its irony, and the 'philosophical' lead-in would probably have to be scrapped; but still, a beginning. It would improve when he got down to the actual incident: should he begin with a description of the town to give the background, or should he just plunge in? And there would have to be interviews with the police especially – not used to being taken up, they would probably condemn themselves out of their own mouths.

As Peter hesitated, he heard someone enter the bedroom where he was sitting, his typewriter propped on a suitcase in front of him. It was his mother; she had a brightly fringed shawl around her shoulders and she was carrying a hot-water bottle. This she inserted into the bed, with great ostentation.

'I thought I'd put it in early this evening, and have the bed warm for you. It was pretty sharp last night.'

Peter waited impatiently for her to leave, but as she delayed, rearranging the sheet several times, it became obvious that the hot-water bottle was only an excuse.

'I see you're writing,' she said at last.

'Yes.'

'Is it about last night ?'

'More or less.'

'I suppose it was him put you up to it.' She always referred to his father in this semi-abstract way, as if he were not so much her husband as someone who had been wished on her years ago, a regrettable but unchanging feature of the household.

'More or less. But I would probably have done it myself in any case.'

'Do you think it's a sensible thing to do?'

'How do you mean, sensible? One can't let things like that pass without protest.'

She looked at him in silence for a few moments and then, placing her hands on her hips, said: 'You're much better out of it. You'll only make trouble for all of us.'

'That's not what Father thinks.'

'I don't care what he thinks. I've lived with that man, God knows, for over thirty years and I still don't understand him. I think he never grew up.' She offered the last sentence with a grimace of half-amused resignation.

'But I agree with him in this case.'

'Oh, it's easy for you. You don't live here all the year round. That thing you're writing will create bad blood. I've seen too much fighting between neighbours in this town already.'

'But, Mother, you used to be a great rebel!'

His father had often told, with great amusement, how she had been arrested for singing 'The Soldiers' Song' on the beach at Warrenpoint; she had picked off the policeman's hat with her parasol and thrown it into the bathing pool. This incident was known in the family as Susie's fight for Irish Freedom.

'I've seen too much of it,' she said, flatly. 'My brothers fought for Irish independence and where did it get them? They're both in Australia now, couldn't get jobs in their own country. Look at you: when you want a job you have to go to England.'

'But I'm only writing an article, Mother, not taking up a gun.'

'It's all the same tune. Sour grapes and bad blood. It's me and him will have to live here if that thing appears, not you. Come down to your tea and leave that contraption alone.' She gestured towards the typewriter as if it were accursed.

Peter rose reluctantly. Despite her frail body, her china-pale complexion, her great doll's eyes, she had the will of a dragon. During the next few days, mysterious references to this article would crop up again and again in her conversation, references designed to make his father and himself feel uneasy, like guilty schoolboys.

'But surely you don't approve of what they did?' he said.

'Approve of them, of course I don't. They're a bad lot.' Muttering, she disappeared into the kitchen, to reappear with an egg-whisk and a bowl of eggs. 'But we have to live with them,' she announced, driving the egg-whisk into the eggs like an electric drill. 'Why else did God put them there?'

IV

One must distinguish between the Royal Ulster Constabulary and the familiar English 'bobby'. The Ulster police are the only ordinary police, in these islands, to carry revolvers; during times of Emergency, they are armed with Sten-guns. Add to that 12,000 B-Specials and you have all the elements of a police state – not in Spain or South Africa, but in the British Isles. Such measures are not, as is argued, preventive, but the symptoms of political disease.

Police! Peter Douglas never knew a moment when he had not feared and detested them. It was partly his father's example: walking with him through the town, as a child, or on the way out to the chapel, he would feel him stiffen when a black uniform came in sight. If a constable, new to the place, dared salute him, he would gaze through him with a contemptuous eye. It was also the uniform; the stifling black of the heavy serge, the great belt, above all the dark bulk of the holster riding the hip: the archetypal insignia of brutality and repression. There was one, in particular, who was known as 'the storm-trooper': a massive ex-commando, he strode around the town with a black police dog padding at his heels. He had long left the district, but for Peter Douglas, he had become the symbol of all the bitterness of his native province, patrolling for ever the lanes of Ulster, as dark and predatory as the beast at his side.

And then there were the Special police, young locals, issued with rifles and Sten-guns, and handsomely paid for night duty. The first time Peter had seen them he was about ten years old, cycling home one warm summer evening from his uncle's house in Altnagore. There were about thirty, drilling before a tin-roofed Orange Lodge. Although he knew most of them, local Protestants whom he had met in shop or street, or in whose farmhouses he had been, they ignored him, gazing bleakly forward. Three nights later, they had stopped him and his father at a street corner and, pretending not to recognize them, held them up for nearly half an hour.

Darkly unjust these memories might be, Peter Douglas reflected as he walked down the street, but the events of the previous night seemed to bear them out. From Higgins's Café came a gush of light and music, the harsh sound of a pop-record. Under the circle of a streetlight stood the diminutive figure of Joe Doom, the village idiot, eating from one of his

136

tin cans. A group of children surrounded him, but they shrank back into the dark as Peter passed.

Outside the barracks itself, on a hillock at the end of the town, there appeared to be an unusual amount of activity. There was a Land-Rover, containing several police, drawn up in front, together with a long black car the wireless antennae and the dark glittering body of which unmistakably proclaimed a squad car. The barracks was a large building, painted in panels of white outlined with black; without the blue police sign over the door, it might have been a doctor's or a company director's house in some comfortable English suburb. But, surrounded on every side by great rolls of barbed wire and with a sandbag blockhouse, from the slit of which protruded a machine-gun, it looked like a fortress, the headquarters of the Gauleiter in an occupied town. As he came up the path, he saw a flash of movement in the blockhouse; he was being kept under cover.

'Is the Sergeant in?' Peter asked. And then, irritably: 'For God's sake, put that thing down. I live up the street.'

'What do ye want with him?' A young constable emerged, the Sten-gun dangling on his arm, insubstantial in its menace as a Meccano toy.

'I'd like to interview him. I'm a journalist and I work for a paper in England. I'd like to discuss the incident last night with him.'

'You're a journalist,' said the constable, with an intonation of flat incredulity. 'In England?'

'Yes, and I'd like to see the Sergeant, please.'

There was a moment's silence, while the policeman looked at him, his eyes pale blue and vacant in a dead-white face, emphasized by the black peak of the cap. Then he turned and motioned Peter to follow him into the day-room.

There were five men in the room, two local policemen whom he vaguely recognized, two rather sulky-looking B-Specials and a fifth, who, by his bearing, tailored uniform with Sam Browne belt and polished leggings, seemed to be a superior officer. They looked surprised to see Peter.

'There's a man here, Sergeant,' said the Constable, addressing one of the local policemen, 'says he's a journalist. He works for some paper, in England.'

The Sergeant came forward, slowly. 'You're Mr Douglas's son, aren't you?' he asked, with a mixture of civility and doubt.

'Yes, Sergeant, I am. I work for a paper in England and I'm home on a short holiday. I'd like to get a few facts from you about the incident last night.'

'Last night?' The Sergeant looked in vague desperation towards the well-dressed officer.

'Which paper do you work for ?' said the latter in a crisp voice. As he spoke, he came forward to face Peter as if by his presence hoping to subdue the intruder. It was the unmistakable voice of authority, British and chilling, as level in tone as a BBC announcer's.

Peter explained, politely.

'Yes, I see,' said the officer, noncommittally. 'I think I know the paper.' Then, to the Sergeant: 'Don't you think we should bring Mr Douglas into another room, Knowles?'

As Peter followed Sergeant Knowles into a large room at the back of the barracks, a thought struck him.

'That's the County Inspector, isn't it?'

'It is indeed,' said the Sergeant. He looked as if he wanted to say more but thought better of it, poking the fire for an instant in an aimless way, before leaving the room. So that was it: they were definitely troubled about the incident last night and the County Inspector had come down in person to investigate. He was on the right track after all.

The Inspector entered the room briskly a few moments later. Planting himself luxuriously in front of the fire, he turned to Peter with a bright energetic smile. Thin hair brushed back above his ears, a long oval face with neatly divided moustache, lean-bridged nose and almost slanted eyes, he was decidedly handsome, a man born and used to command.

'Well, now, Mr Douglas, it's not often we get one of you chaps knocking around this part of the country. Sorry I can't offer you a drink, but I doubt if the facilities of the barracks are supposed to rise to that.' He laughed briefly. 'You're a local man, I take it.'

'Yes,' said Peter. The bright offensiveness of the man's tone angered, but also cowed him, so that, almost against his will, he found himself volunteering further information. 'But I went to school in Laganbridge.'

'Oh,' said the Inspector with interest, sensing common ground. 'Went to school there myself. The Kings, I suppose.'

'No,' said Peter shortly. Then – incredulity merging into satisfaction at the unexpected trap into which the Inspector had fallen, deceived by the British sound of Douglas and the fact that *The Tocsin* was a London paper – he added, 'St Kieran's.'

It was like confessing, Peter thought with a smile, to an unrecon-
structed Southerner that though one looked quite normal, one really was
a Negro. The Kings was one of the most famous Protestant schools in
the North of Ireland, a Georgian nursery for cricketers, colonial admin-
istrators, gaitered bishops and even (as though to demonstrate its all-
round ability) a distinguished literary critic. On the hill opposite, sheltering under the great bulk of the post-Emancipation cathedral, was the
diocesan seminary of St Kieran's where the sons of strong Catholic farmers, publicans and merchants studied, mainly for the priesthood.

'Oh.' The Chief Inspector paused, visibly taken aback. Then, with a
gallant return to self-possession: 'Used to know your Bishop a bit. Nice
old chap. Don't fancy his taste in sherry much, though.'

'His sherry?' echoed Peter in amazement.

'Myas.' The way he pronounced it, with a prefatory hum and a hissing follow-through, it could have been anything from 'my arse' to 'my
ears'. 'Gets his shipped direct from Spain; our boys see it through the
Customs for him. Bit dry. Prefer Bristol Cream myself.'

If such a man thought about Nationalists at all, it was probably as
some obscure form of trouble-making minority; he did not mind contact
with them providing it took place on the highest level, a maharajah or a
bishop, or some complaisant highly placed native official. And why
should he change? Convinced of his tolerance, assured of his position
within the framework of Queen and Country, he would probably end his
days in honourable retirement with a minor decoration in the Honours
List.

'My bishops are on chessboards,' Peter said curtly.

He might have saved his breath, the irony of his remark falling like a
paper dart from that unruffled brow. The Inspector had already moved
on.

'Well,' he said, 'about that little matter you mentioned. Don't think
there's much in it for a fellow like you. Pretty small beer after all. Some
young thug cheeked our boys and they took him in for a few hours to
cool off. Released him in the morning. Routine affair.'

'After beating him up on the way,' Peter said, stubbornly.

'Oh, I wouldn't say that,' said the Inspector, judiciously. 'He did resist
arrest after all, so they had to help him along a bit. May have got a few
scratches, but that would be the height of it.'

'Enough to put him in a hospital bed.'

'Oh, you heard that, did you ?' the Inspector said with interest. 'Well, well, it's wonderful how rumours get round, though I'm afraid you won't find much substance in that one. Chap kept complaining so we called the doctor. He couldn't find much wrong with him but, just to be on the safe side, he sent him down to the County for an X-ray. Released in a few hours, right as rain. Mother came to bring him home.'

'So you mean it was all nothing?' asked Peter, incredulously.

'Pretty well.'

'But the noise woke up the whole town.'

The Inspector laughed dryly. 'Yes, that was rather a nuisance. Chap was a bit of an exhibitionist. Roared like a bull, boys said, every time they laid a finger on him. Pretty cute trick when you come to think of it.'

'Trick?' Peter stared at the bland face opposite him. But he found neither deception nor doubt in the Inspector's level gaze.

'Yes, a trick. Can't be up to some of these fellows. Bit of a Teddy boy by all accounts, likes to show he's not afraid of the police. But I think he realizes he went a bit too far last night, made a fool of himself.' The Inspector rubbed his hands together in a gesture of satisfied dismissal. 'Well, there you are, there's the whole little story. Sorry I can't provide something more juicy for you. I know what you Johnnies like. Perhaps next time.'

Stunned, Peter followed him along the corridor and out through the door. He was halfway up Main Street before he realized that the IRA had not even been mentioned.

*

'So that's what he said to you,' said the schoolmaster admiringly. Peter had called on him on his way home and they had crossed the street to the nearest pub, the Dew Drop Inn.

'Yes. I'm afraid I was so taken aback I couldn't think of anything to say. I mean, it all sounded so plausible; maybe the man was telling the truth.'

'Still, that doesn't explain why he called upon me.'

'Oh, did he, indeed?' breathed Peter.

'Yes, when I drove in from school, there was His Nibs waiting in the parlour. Said he often heard my brother who works in the County Health Office speak of me and thought he should drop by. Then, cool as you please, mentioned the business last night and said I would be glad to hear

140

it had all been a misunderstanding. They had given the boy a good talking to and sent him home. There was no further reason for me to be troubled in any way. Special Constable Robson was sorry for what he had said to me, but it was all in the heat of the moment and meant nothing.'

'So they were troubled…And what did you say?'

'What could I say? I just smiled back and said I accepted Robson's apologies and was glad to hear the boy was all right. I work here you know and so – as he delicately pointed out – does my brother. Besides' – he blinked nervously and hunched his narrow raincoated shoulders forward – 'I've been thinking the matter over and it seems to me we're not on very safe ground.'

'What do you mean? Surely a civilized man cannot let someone be beaten up under his eyes without protesting.'

'In an ordinary case, no. But the boy doesn't seem to have been badly hurt and we wouldn't be able to prove anything definite. We'd only be playing into their hands by showing ourselves as trouble-makers.'

Peter was silent for a moment, sipping his Tuborg. 'That's more or less what my mother says,' he said eventually, 'but not my father.'

'Your father, if you don't mind me saying so, is nearly as thick as an Orangeman in his own way. His kind of talk may be fair enough in Dáil Éireann, but as you know yourself, it cuts very little ice here. After all, even if we did get a United Ireland we would still have to live with them, so we'd better start now. And you must admit the police in the North have had a pretty rough time lately. If this was the twenties, there'd be a lot of dead Teagues around.'

'So you think I should drop the article I'm doing?'

'Oh, I don't know, that depends. Why don't you go and see the boy before deciding? After all, he was the one who was beaten up.'

The owner of the Dew Drop Inn peered hurriedly round the door. 'Come on, gentlemen, please,' he said. 'It's half an hour after the time already.' As they passed through the kitchen on their way out, a group of men were on their way in. They were the B-Specials Peter had seen at the barracks. 'Good night now, Mr Concannon, good night, Mr Douglas,' the owner said as he shepherded them through the door. Then he turned to greet his new customers.

V

'That must be it,' said James Douglas, craning across the shoulder of the hackney cab driver. For ten minutes or so, ever since they had left the main road, they had been bumping along a narrow country lane. At first there were signs of habitation, but as they wound their way up the mountainside, first the houses and then the trees began to fall away, long stretches of melancholy bog opening up on either side. At last, just as the gravel surface of the lane began to merge into the muddy ruts of a cart track, they caught sight of a small cottage. Whitewashed, with a greening thatched roof, it stood on a mound, without any shelter or protection from the wind except a rough fence, hammered out of old tar-barrels. Against the wall, its front wheel almost blocking the half-door, was a battered racing bicycle, painted a bright red.

'That's it, right enough,' said the driver. 'Any bids?'

'It looks bleak all right,' said Peter.

'Hungry's the word,' said the driver cheerfully, as he applied the hand brake.

'Do you want me to come with you ?' his father asked, looking at Peter doubtfully. All the way to Black Mountain he had been humming to himself, in evident satisfaction, but the sight of the cottage seemed to have unnerved him.

'No,' said Peter shortly. 'I'll go myself.'

The swaying progress of the car up the lane had already attracted attention: a brown and white mongrel dog came racing down to greet it, and the startled face of a woman flashed briefly at one of the two small windows. As Peter descended from the car, his thin shoes sinking in the mud of the yard, the dog plunged towards him.

'Down, Flo, down.' A woman of about fifty, wearing a shapeless red jumper and a pair of thongless man's boots, appeared in the doorway. She stood, drying her hands in the corner of her discoloured apron, and waiting for Peter to speak.

'Does Michael Ferguson live here?'

A look of dismay, animal, uncomprehending, passed over her face. 'God protect us,' she muttered, 'more trouble.' Then, turning towards the door: 'He's in there, if you want him.'

After the light of the mountainside, the interior of the cottage seemed dim as a cave. A crumbling turf-fire threw a fitful smoky light

142

over the hunched-up figure of an old man, who looked up as the intruder entered and then, with a noisy scraping of his stool, turned away. Beside the kettle in the ashes lay a sick chicken, its scrawny red head projecting from a cocoon of flannel. The other side of the room was taken up by a cupboard and a bed upon which a young man was lying. There was a bandage around his forehead.

'Can't you rise, at least, when someone comes to see you?' said the woman, gruffly.

The young man raised himself stiffly from the bed. He was about twenty, tall and rather well-built with broad shoulders. He wore an imitation leather jacket, heavy with metal buckles and clasps. It rode high above his waist, exposing a torn khaki shirt. This was stuffed loosely into a pair of threadbare jeans, supported by a studded leather belt with a horseshoe buckle. The outfit was completed by bright blue and red-ribbed socks above the black heaviness of farm boots.

'Are you police?' His eyes, close-set in a face heavily blotched with acne, avoided Peter's; he could have been speaking to the dog which by now whined and twined around his legs.

Peter explained as best he could. In his nervousness, he found himself using words that, by the puzzled expression in their faces, he knew they could not understand, so he repeated his story several times. 'I want to help, you see,' he ended.

'I don't think I can do much for you, mister,' the boy said at last.

'What do you mean, you can't do much for me? That's not the point at all. I want to do something for you. I want to write an article that will expose the way you have been treated by the police. You don't mean to say you haven't been beaten up?'

From the hearth behind came an unexpected sound as the old man swivelled on his stool. His eyes, small and red-rimmed as a turkey cock's, were bright with venom, and as he spoke a streak of spittle ran down the front of his collarless shirt.

'If he'd stayed home with his mother the way a dacent-rared boy should, not a hate would have happened him. But nothing for it nowadays but running off to the pictures and the music boxes. He deserved all he got, and not half good enough for him.'

The boy's face flushed, but he remained silent. Instead, his mother spoke for him.

'To tell the truth, sir, we'd as lief the matter was forgotten. It would be better for all of us, like.'

'That's right, sir. The way it is, I wouldn't make too much of it, sir.'

So there it was, plain as a pikestaff. The police had spoken not merely to the boy, but also to the mother. They were quite prepared for the boy's sake and the sake of his parents that the matter should be overlooked; in their magnanimity, they had probably provided transport, an impossible expense, otherwise, for people in their position. Whatever redress Peter could offer, whatever hope or help would mean nothing compared to their unspecified but real threats. He would never know the truth of the incident, now: whether the boy had connections with the IRA, whether he had provoked the police; whether even, his – Peter's – interpretation of their silence was correct. Between their helplessness and his freedom lay an unbridgeable gulf and, with a despairing gesture, he turned to leave. The boy and his mother accompanied him; the former, despite half-hearted attempts to conceal it, had a distinct limp.

'I'm sorry I can't help you now, sir,' he said. His voice, though flat in tone, sounded almost kindly. As he bent his head under the door, Peter noticed that, above the bandage, his hair was plastered back in two oily swathes, like the wings of a duck.

As the hackney lurched down the mountainside, Peter and his father were both silent. A storm cloud was gathering over the valley, dark as a shawl. Only the driver seemed in a jaunty mood, as he expanded on the history of the Fergusons for their benefit.

'He's not a bad lad that, you know,' he said reflectively, 'rough and all as he is. The two other boys, cute enough, sloped off to England. He was in Barnsley too, but he came back when the old man had the operation. There's many wouldn't do it.'

It was only when they had reached home that James Douglas spoke, climbing laboriously through the door his son was holding for him, onto the kerb.

'Are you still going to write that article?' he asked apprehensively, peering into Peter's face.

Peter looked at him for a moment, as though in calculation.

'I don't really know,' he said.

…There is a way of dealing with such incidents of course, familiar to every colonial officer from Ulster to Rhodesia. The charge is dropped or minimized, the too zealous police or soldiers reprimanded, any public fuss avoided. Perhaps as the authorities claim, it is the best way in the end. But one is left wondering in how many small Ulster towns such things are happening, at this moment, *in your name*.

After his return, Peter had gone straight to his bedroom to continue the article, with little success. He could not even decide, staring blankly at the paragraph he had just written, whether to give it up or not: he could get a beginning and an end, but the whole thing did not cohere into the outcry, logical but passionate, for which he had been hoping. He rose to pace the room; finally, he found himself at the window, vacantly looking out down Main Street, as he had done on that first night.

It had been raining heavily for an hour or so, but now it was clearing. On the rim of the sky, just to the west of the town, a watery sun was breaking through grey clouds. Soft, almost a dawn light, it shone on the town, making the long line of the main street, from the Old Tower to the War Memorial and beyond to the railway station, seem washed and clear.

There it was, his home town, laid out before him, bright in every detail. He knew every corner of it, had gone to school in that low concrete building, run his sleigh down that hill, had even, later, brought his first girl down the darkness of that entry. He knew every house and nearly everybody in them. One did not like or dislike this place: such emotions were irrelevant, it was a part of one's life, and therefore inescapable. Yet all through his final year at school his only thought had been to escape; the narrowness of the life, the hidden bitterness of political feeling had suddenly seemed like the regime of a prison. The Irish were supposed to be a gay race, but there was something in these people, a harsh urge to reduce the human situation to its barest essentials, which frightened him. It was years before he had felt able to come back, sufficiently secure in his own beliefs to be able to survive the hostility their ways seemed to radiate.

But did that strength now give him the right to sit in judgement, particularly where an incident like this was concerned? Already, only two days afterwards, indignation had died down in the town. Was it fear or an effort to foster that goodwill which people like his mother thought was the only solution? Or mere passivity, the product of a commercial spirit which saw everyone as a potential customer? Whatever destiny lay in these grey walls, they might surely be left to work out on their own, two peoples linked and locked for eternity.

As he looked over the town, sober with self-judgement, suddenly from out of a laneway, as though propelled, shot a dwarflike figure. His clothes were of various colours, and he wore a tattered cap pulled squarely over his ears. One foot was bare, the other encased in an elderly boot. Around his waist hung a bandolier of tin-cans. Peter recognized him almost at once: it was Joe Doom, the village idiot. He lived in a tiny house on his own, at the end of the town, begging pennies from passers-by, stewing scraps in his tin cans. The people teased him, fed him, tolerated him, with a charity older than state institutions, and in return, his antics, the gargles and lapses of logic which were his sole method of speech, amused them. Now he looked wildly around, at the sky, at the watery sun, at the light shining on the fronts of the houses. Then, as though focusing, he saw Peter at the window above him. Their eyes met for a moment and something like triumph entered Joe Doom's. He fumbled frantically behind his back, the line of cans shaking, and produced a piece of white cardboard. With a quick glance behind him towards the entry, as though for confirmation, he held it high above his head, so that Peter – or anyone else in the street who was watching – could read. In large crude letters, like strokes of charcoal, it spelt

```
Nosy Parker
Go  home
```

11

THE ROAD AHEAD

We met halfway down where the steep hill used to be. He was on his way up, pushing a bicycle, I was walking down. The traffic had been so heavy that I had taken the mountain lane (the old grass-grown detour farmers used when driving their cattle to the fair) and was only now re-emerging onto the bright macadam. The new road was lined, for the sake of visibility, with a white stone border, and it was just inside that he was walking, with the bicycle wheels over the edge.

We saw each other at a distance, and had time to prepare our responses, though now and again cars came whipping past to obscure the view. I had not expected him to recognize me, but he did, stopping when we came abreast, on different sides of the road.

'Hello there,' he called expectantly.

There was no point in trying to talk so far apart so I waited for a moment until the traffic eased, and then sprinted across. 'Hello, yourself,' I said.

He stood looking at me, with his elbow propped on the worn heart shape of the bicycle saddle. The left eye was as bad as ever, watery and unfocused, with (if you could look closely without flinching) the eyeball lying in its cradle of pale blood. He had got it working with barbed wire, and it had never been looked after. It gave him a baleful look which he was not above exploiting; like the cripple who offers his maimed right hand only to friends, he would watch steadily, daring you to drop your gaze.

'There's a queer change,' he said, indicating the road.

Just then a Ford Consul and Vauxhall Cresta came around the corner, locked in speed. We watched them meet the slight incline of the hill, without checking, and then zoom past. The Consul, which was on the inside, was so close to the shoulder of the road that it sent up a shower of pebbles that rang on the bicycle frame. But it did not yield, and we watched them disappear into the distance, like two runners between the narrowing white tapes of the stone border.

'Aye, there's a change,' I said.

We remained in restful silence, looking at each other (with the half-smile of people exchanging common, but unstated memories) for a minute or two. Then he shifted and I saw it was time to speak again.

'Still you take the bicycle,' I ventured.

'It's better than nothing for them that's poor.' Then he grinned. 'But they got me in the end.'

'How so?'

'I was coming by MacCrystals, pushing hard to get a bit of a run up the hill. Not that there's much of a slope now, but if you have the habit...' He paused.

'Well ?'

'There was a bus behind me, one of those big city double-deckers they use now to bring the schoolchildren home. That was bad enough but then (you can see nearly half a mile now, you know) a big brute of a CALCO oil tanker came sailing over the crest. The bus nearly had me in the ditch as it was, but when I saw the other buck, I said to myself, John Mooney, you should know when you're beat. I declare to God a midge couldna passed between them.'

Though he made light of it, I saw that the incident had depressed him, and hastened to add an interested comment. 'It reminds me of the war.'

'How, like?'

'You remember when the American troops were training here, and used to stage manoeuvres? I came out of school one day, and found a whole armoured column on the road: one of the Shermans went over the ditch around here. We had to go home round the lane, just as I did today. I suppose you might say that the war never ended here!'

But he was in no mood for my pompous theories, and stood looking at the road.

'Do you know what it is,' he said suddenly. 'I'm often sorry I didn't go 'way, like yourself. As it is, I don't know sometimes whether I'm here, or someplace else. Only last night, when I was coming back from Donnelly's after a few drinks, I declare to my God, I got lost...' There was such a depth of terror in the one good eye that all I could do was change the subject.

'Is that MacCrystals you mentioned the people who have the shop?' Not that I didn't remember it well; it was halfway on my three-mile walk from school, and we would stop to buy lollipops. Or drink from the clear spring that ran under the elm tree at the other side of the road.

'They sell the odd sweetie,' he said indifferently.

We stood side by side, looking at the landscape. Something curious about the quality of the silence struck me: I could not hear a single bird. There were no hedgerows any more, they had been bulldozed to level the ditch on either side, and lengthen the view. So there was nothing between us and the small, damp fields but the metal fence, supported every now and then by concrete posts, inset with cat's-eye reflectors.

'Did you have a drink at the spring?' I tried again.

'Spring!' he said incredulously. 'God look to your wit; sure they scared the water back into the ground again!'

The phrase seemed to please him, for he laughed shortly, and changed the subject.

'Do you know MacNeils?' he demanded, naming another shop about three miles down the road.

'Why?'

'It's up for auction.'

I waited, to see his face turn directly towards me again. I had never noticed before the contrast between the bad eye, and the hesitant, almost tremulous mouth below, like a mournful horse.

'Do you know why that house fell?'

'Why?'

'There was a beggar woman by the name of Meanens lived in a wee hut on that land; she had a coupla weans and some say old MacNeil himself fathered the last. But there was one winter so hard that even the river froze; she came down to the shop every day, looking for scraps, until they had to drive her away. And when they refused her, she stood on the hill, with her children around her, and took the rosary beads from her pocket…'

It is Christmas. On a white hill, a ragged Snow Queen stands, a child at her breast, a dog at her heels. Below lie the few houses of the village, mysterious as a crystal ball, under the drifting snow. She takes from her apron a bag of Fox's Glacier Mints, and a pair of horn rosary beads to which a sweet paper clings. She begins to intone.

Down in the village shop, the light of the Calor gas lamp shines on ruddy flitches of bacon, crusty soda farls, and Tate and Lyles fine powdered sugar. As the grocer fills brown paper bags, he talks to his customers, and laughs the laugh of the well-fed. He is a small man, clad in a brown dustcoat: there is a white pollen of flour on his eyelashes. Little busy bee, he seems oblivious of his danger: only the collie dog lying with crossed paws at the door scents something, and rises, hackles bristling before the supernatural.

'And from that day to this there has been a curse on that place.'

Giddy with nausea, I wrench myself back to consciousness; who have I been talking to, and where? Luckily, a rattling lorry is drawing up: I recognize the contractor who lives across from us. That house also had a bad name, a tubercular family having wasted in it. For years it stood deserted, except for the cattle that sheltered in the kitchen or the bats that looped through the empty windows. Now he has rebuilt the grey walls, and is flattening the field before the house to make an avenue. He is offering us both a lift; I help my companion to put his bicycle in the back, where it rests with the front wheel lightly spinning.

'You're not coming,' he says, with one foot on the running board.

'I'll go on ahead yet.'

'Take care of yourself,' the one good eye winks ferociously through the rectangle of the window.

One hundred yards further down the hill, I reach the spring. It is true that they have done something to it: the tree is gone, and a white concrete wall has been constructed, to support the empty space of the ditch. But there is a kind of porthole, through which a trickle is coming. I kneel down, on one knee, to put my hands under it. How strange that a spring should flow opposite a house called MacCrystals, a sign of that magic congruence which rules so many aspects of life…

It took nearly five minutes for the cup of my palms to fill. Then I bent my head, and took an expectant gulp. It tasted sour, brackish, as though strained through metal. Turning my hands over slowly, I let it drain to the ground.

12

OFF THE PAGE

A lecture engagement brought Seán up from Dublin on the train, a bit dismayed to find that it was no longer the smooth Enterprise Express he remembered, which linked the two capital cities of the two parts of Ireland twice a day. The train had a kind of tattered wartime look and there was a bomb scare beyond Dundalk, near the Border.

After the train had been searched, he wandered towards the dining car. Waiting for someone to come to take his order, he pondered over the paradox that there seemed to be two menus, one the familiar overpriced one of CIE, the other announcing an Ulster Fry. That stirred a pleasant memory from his graduate student days in the North – fat slices of fried potato cake flanking back rashers – but he found out when the attendant came that he could have that only on the way down, not up, when CIÉ was in charge. Seán gave in with bad grace, especially as the alternative menu card had not been cleared away, thus arousing false hopes of getting into the old atmosphere. And in any case he was not sure that the attendant was right; in his experience, most minor officials managed to get everything arseways, or baw-wise, to use a Northernism. But by now the train was pulling through the Gap of the North, and the South Armagh Hills always stirred him: there was something timeless about them, a stony patience that made factionalism seem absurd. But what was that hovering near the summit, above the Hag's Lake, dipping and rising?

He recognised with distaste the flickering hornet shape of an Army heli-copter.

Seán had to run the gauntlet of the bar on the way back; it had opened again, just after the Border. He was surprised but pleased to be hailed, not once, but twice. A stray Englishman who had heard him lec-ture at Cambridge on the Eighteenth Century; an in-law he had not seen for years. It was an unusual haul and Seán thoroughly enjoyed himself, with the Black Bush flowing; the Englishman doted on Ireland, and the Southern relative was planning to buy a house in Belfast, since both his daughters were studying there. So a pleasant wrangle ensued, spoiled only when another attendant refused to accept the Englishman's Irish money, now that they were across the Border. They settled it among themselves, with grace and good humour, and a good few rounds later, they were entering the outskirts of Belfast.

They shared a taxi to the centre of the city but there Seán's good humour soon soured. How had he become so out of touch that he had not realised that there was a new station, replacing the gaunt but familiar shape of Victoria Street? Thank God the Ulster Bus Depot was still there at least; he would be able to get rid of his baggage. But the Baggage Department was closed and he stood baffled in the middle of the hall, with one hand growing longer than the other, his overnight bag and brief-case feeling as if they were loaded with stones. He had been looking for-ward to a few hours on his own in Belfast before he joined his colleagues at the university; that was why he had chosen the earlier train, but the pos-sibilities for pleasant reminiscence seemed to be evaporating fast.

The little hotel opposite the station, for instance, where he had often stayed on his way through; the rooms were makeshift but the night porter was most accommodating: it had been a favourite after-hours watering hole for all sides, but now it was gone, gone completely, a waste ground. He had stayed in the Crown once, a feat since its rooms were as dilapi-dated as its front was magnificent. He had a consoling conversation with one of the barmen there about old times. No, they no longer sold Single X, the old flat porter with the cheesy taste, but the pint was good, slow-ly pulled with its clerical collar of creamy froth. And the chat around him was much the same: Belfast working class intent on the Sports Page ('I don't think the fukken dog will fukken win' or 'The odds are too fukken high', the same familiar adjective applied to greyhounds, boxing, soccer as if they were all the fukken same). Two or three still wore dunchers, flat working-class cloth caps.

There was a sprinkling of middle-class types and the Bar Menu seemed to have become a shade classy: wine could be bought by the glass, hardly a beverage favoured by either Shankill or Falls. And did the windows not look a little different? The barman told him that some had had to be replaced, after a bomb blast; a reprisal, he said, looking around carefully, but not by the side you'd expect. The jacks was unchanged, though, and he watered the intricate art nouveau patterns of the rose porcelain with pleasure, after his first pint. When the barman brought him his second drink to one of the wooden booths, opulent in its carving as a medieval confessional, with griffins and other strange, fantastic animals interlaced, he explained his problem with his luggage.

'Ah, sure you can leave them with me, behind the bar. By the looks of you, there's nothing more dangerous than a few books in them. But don't take too long: I go off duty at six, for me tea, and the next man mightn't know what the hell they were.'

And so Seán got his walk through central Belfast, at last. He had never really liked the city in the way he loved the melancholy of Georgian Dublin; it was, after all, a typical mid-nineteenth-century British industrial city, which had largely lost its link with the country around it, now often suburban, like Bangor and Lisburn. But he had grown used to it during his year as a graduate student, spending afternoons sitting at a desk in the Linen Hall Library, raising his head from some rare book to stare at the pseudo-classical weight of the City Hall. Both were still there and he wandered up Royal Avenue, a bit disconcerted to find the Bank Buildings open, but Robinson and Cleaver closed. This sudden shuddering gear-change of emotions was disturbing: people were indeed shopping in the city centre but they had to pass through checkpoints manned by black-clad officials. Hadn't there been a bookshop there, or had he only dreamt it? And a hotel – he felt disorientated, only half-knowing where he was; the only thriving industry seemed to be security systems, advertised on every second door and window. Chubb Alarms, Shorrock, Modern Alarms, Guard Dogs, Control Zone – it was a new bleak form of semiotics that flustered him. There were two sets of taxis, both black, but he didn't know which queue to join, so he decided to hoof it to the university, picking up his gear along the way.

*

The lecture went well, Seán thought. As usual, it took him a while to warm up himself and his audience, to slide back into the Eighteenth Century until it was no longer history but the real choices of real people, some of whom had lived in their home area, like Thomas Russell, arrested in his own Linen Hall Library. To illustrate a point about historical change, he mentioned his walk through Belfast, how it had moved and saddened him to see so many of the landmarks he had known as a student obliterated. What would the United Irishmen think of the New Ireland, North and South? It was not the vision they had campaigned and sometimes died for; he hoped that a small flame of tolerance and intelligence still flickered in some hearts. One of the ironies of the present bombing campaign was that it meant that people were destroying their own childhood memories. He sensed a slight unease in his audience at this divagation, so he moved back to his analysis of the ideas of the Enlightenment, the way they had influenced America as well as France. As he came to a graceful halt, gathering his papers, there was a steady ripple of applause. History was great stuff to discuss, when it was at a safe distance. The chairman said a few words and then they surged quietly to the bar, across the street in a private club.

He was halfway through his first drink when he felt a tap on his shoulder. It was so light that he ignored it at first until it became more insistent. Turning, he saw a face he recognised, the once-familiar face of someone he had been at school with, but now sharpened, shadowed by age. A determined, almost hard face, and not smiling.

'Why, hello, Danny Cowan,' he said. 'Nice to see you again.'

Danny nodded, but he did not seem interested in the courtesies or in the people who were swirling around – teachers, officials, a handful of students.

'I want to talk to *you*.' The 'you' was emphasised.

'But you are talking to me,' laughed Seán.

The other made a dismissive gesture. 'Not with shites like these around.'

Seán went silent, surprised. 'What about tomorrow then?' he said at last. 'You can call for me at the staff club, surely?'

'Now. I need to speak to you now.'

Seán looked around at the crowd. They seemed happy enough, and he had spoken to the few graduate students. Still, it would be impolite to desert his hosts. 'How long will it take?'

'Not long. Only a brief minute.' Or had he heard 'briefing'?

'Will you drop me back before this place closes?'

'Aye.'

He excused himself to the chairman of the meeting and a few other staff members. They looked curiously at Danny but when he said 'school-friend', they nodded. 'We'll hold the fort for you here. Get back before the well runs dry, though.'

On the drive through a darkened Belfast Seán sought for some common subject of conversation. But his companion was laconic, brusque to the point of unpleasantness. Danny had married a good-looking girl, he remembered, also militant when she was at the university. They had both been involved in protests, some of them leading to jail terms. But he had not been heard of in recent years, since the bombing campaign began.

They were stopped at two roadblocks, but Danny handled the soldiers with almost contemptuous ease as they poked their heads into the car. Once, as a Gloucester was leaning his rifle on the slope to probe in the back of the car, Danny pushed the weapon aside and held the few objects up for inspection: a rag doll and a box of pamphlets.

'Did no one teach you how to handle a rifle properly? It is not a broom handle you're holding, you fool. And you might take one of those away with you to read instead of your gutter press: you might learn why you are over here.'

The soldier started but seemed to accept the rebuke. Afterwards, Seán realied why – he was responding to a tone of voice, the crispness of someone of the officer class addressing a common soldier.

'That was a good trick', he said admiringly as they moved again through the darkness. But his companion did not seem to understand, or even care, what he meant. Sandy Row, Grosvenor Road, the Royal Hospital, barbed wire, bombed or blackened buildings, the grim décor of a wartime town seemed to go with his silence. There was only an occasional shaft of light with pub windows glinting through heavy shutters. Now it was a poorer district, with identical redbrick houses, little hutches where the Catholic working class bred, survived, clawing out a living. Even in the night-time there was a sense of desperation, cramped lives behind net curtains; a few yards away a wall was raised to cut off this area from a similar Protestant one – a building-block version of the Berlin Wall, a sectarian Lilliput.

But the house they finally stopped before, much further on, was quite respectable, a semi-detached with a garage, and a pocket-handkerchief lawn. 'Edenview' it was called, he saw in the car's headlights, but when he made an appropriate laughing comment there was no response; any attempt to lighten the proceedings was, it seemed, out of place. At the door his tall wife (Eve?) appeared, and he found her as pleasant-looking as he had remembered but, like her husband, much more tense, harsh almost. Was this the inevitable erosion of feeling caused by living in such an atmosphere?

After a few ritual greetings, she disappeared into the kitchen, and he was left alone with Danny. Seán looked expectantly around but there was no drinks cupboard. They sat opposite each other in identical armchairs – part of a wedding suite? – for several minutes, but nothing was said. There were a few wedding pictures, a library which seemed to be largely political, and a copy of the 1916 Proclamation over the fireplace. Then the tea trolley was wheeled in, china teacups and a jug of the same design, an already segmented sponge cake and biscuits. As his wife dispensed the little cups of tea, Danny cleared his throat:

'You should never say that.'

Seán left it for a while, balancing his tea carefully, before he answered. 'What?' he said, then, 'I gave an hour's lecture.'

The silence was flinty. He tried again, with teasing humour this time. 'Come on, Danny, I didn't know you were a student of the Enlightenment.' Again, silence, until Danny's wife edged forwards on her chair. 'Was the lecture on lighting?' Both men sniggered, in an embarrassed way. Then, just as Seán began to fear that he was stuck forever in this ice-pack of parlour politeness, Danny leaned forward again, shifting his hams. Whatever about the hungry streets they had passed through, neither Danny nor his wife looked starved – maybe protest could also be a paying proposition.

'You know well what I mean. The remark about Belfast.'

'What remark?' was Seán's first reaction but, as he ran the tape of his lecture back swiftly through his head, he thought he remembered some chance remark, a throwaway comment before he warmed up, or a way of filling in a silence when the current of attention flickered.

'About it being destroyed.'

156

'But it is being destroyed. And rebuilt. And presumably will be destroyed again. Modern terrorism is a bit like the medieval plague – it comes back.'

'That's not the point, smart aleck.'

'Then what is the point? Urban violence has a self-perpetuating quality.'

Despite himself, Seán had begun to feel that not only was he under cross-examination, but that he was, in some sense, to blame for the situation. Otherwise, why should he be trying to justify himself? 'What point?' he repeated again, sharply. 'Come clean, brother,' mockingly. Cowan leaned forward again, and launched into a speech, almost a tirade. At first, Seán wanted to protest, to respond, to discuss, but the man's tone, his chill and relentless intensity, precluded it. His message was simple enough: consciously or not, Seán had said something from a public platform that should not be said and he should never say it again, in his puff.

'You said you felt sorry to see the city so torn and destroyed. That you had known it as a student and that despite its lack of obvious beauty, it meant something to you. Let me tell you that no one, but no one, in this part of the city cares a flying fuck if the whole place was bombed, broken, blasted to hell. You saw those small streets we came through: all that City Hall represents to them is repression, endless repression, dole queues and undying bigotry. So people died for the Crown; more than half of them were from these small streets: they didn't have a choice. Look at the names of the places they live in, old Empire battles, Balaclava Street, Bombay Street, Crimea Street. So for some simpleton like yourself to suggest that this hellhole ever had any good reason to exist is sentimental shite and you know it. You and your history – it's phoney liberals like you fuck things up: you're so unaware that you don't even know that the first sectarian campaign was organised by the British, using the UFF, four hundred dead and tortured. Then when they had started the old hatred machine again, the sappers sealed the sides off, with that Wall you saw. You and your history – you can't see it when it hits you between the two eyes.'

The diatribe was impressive, but Seán was not content to let it pour over him – somewhere, he felt, there was a right response. 'But surely memory. Feelings. Emotional deposits over the years. Family.'

'Fuck memory. You sound like Edmund Burke flashing his sword for

Marie Antoinette against the French Revolution. All the memories any-one from our side has of this city is dirt, darkness and pain. If a bomb wiped out Royal Avenue and stopped the Albert Clock, I'd howl with joy, not weep crocodile tears about old times. John Betjeman's Victorian City is the nearest thing to a gulag the West has to offer, from the prison ships in Belfast Lough to Castlereagh. So shut your educated mouth when it comes to serious subjects: closet philosophers the lot of you – toilet, more like!'

Seán remained silent. He was used to academic malice but this was on a more desperate level. He remembered a moon-faced colleague, a moth-er's pet if ever there was one, who seemed to thrive on spite. Someone's book linking the Viking Period and violence in modern Ireland was men-tioned and his only comment was 'putrid'. Asked playfully to develop this theme, he had only responded obstinately: 'I mean putrid. Old shite with hairs on it.' Seán had shuddered at the vindictiveness, wondered also at his own naïveté. If the intolerable situation dragged on, they would all become mutants; certainly that one was on the way: the combination of peculiar looks and Ulster's plight already made him look malign as a gar-goyle. And now the anal fixation again, a reversion to the war cries of the nursery floor. He couldn't even be sure that Cowan was really angry – he had never once raised his voice, just stared steadily at him with something like indifferent scorn. He ended as he began: menacingly.

'So never say that again from a public platform in this city, *in your life*.'

This time Seán understood what he meant. He rose to leave.

'You'll drop me back, as you promised?'

Cowan nodded and his wife went off to put on her coat. They all three drove in silence back through the now nearly lightless city and Seán did not ask them into the club bar. There the hardy annuals were in ses-sion, and Seán was greeted warmly on all sides, with no 'what kept you?' The bartender, an ex-serviceman who had fought in the desert, and claimed to have driven Monty, pushed a double Bush to him, with a wink, the drinker's conspiracy against seriousness.

'On the house, Doctor,' he said. 'You're the excuse for this badness.'

Seán laughed relievedly. It was good to be back among friends, he thought, but then had he not been with a friend? His head hurt a little and he felt squeamish as he looked around the comfortable surroundings, the affable sound of voices raised in friendly dispute or banter, the sudden normality; there did not seem to be a shitehawk in sight, eager to play the game of Gut the Visitor. But then the Cowans had looked normal, so the cosiness of this ultimate watering hole might be another mirage. As the full effect of what he had heard that evening came back to him, he excused himself, and hurried to the Gents.

The naked neon over the washbasins seemed unusually harsh, garish: he felt as if he had just been on an all-night flight and had been abruptly woken. It glittered like a spotlight off the tiled floor, making him feel sick, or worse: maybe at this very moment some poor bastard was being interrogated somewhere else in the city. But before he could even work out what was wrong with him he found himself looking at his own strained face in the mirror. How could he guess how he would look if he lived in this taut climate? Much of what Cowan had said rang true, though such weasel venom was beyond him. All tenderness, all gentleness, was ruled out, all cosy exchange. Yet there was something admirable in this flinty obduracy, like the determination of cave people. Perhaps he needed to be shaken out of his academic reflexes, his incipient pomposity? So history had come off the page and he did not know what to say or do about it; there was no way he could explain what had happened to his waiting hosts, or anyone else. Bracing his hands on either side of the washbasin, he leaned his head over and began to retch. Half-digested biscuits, sponge cake and brown tea spilled out of his mouth in a dirty stream. He wiped his face clean and headed back towards the warmth of the bar, and that full glass.

Part IV

13

THE LETTERS

That special silence of Sundays. All the family have gone to Mass. I listen to their steps fade down the road. There are no lorries on Sunday, so sounds are clearer: I can hear the crows in Lynch's plantation, the cows on the hill behind the house lowing to each other occasionally between mouthfuls of grass (there might be one looking the bull), the hens in the backyard, ceaselessly chatting about nothing, except one announcing the arrival of an egg. And my aunts' voices dimming down the hill, every second fainter, as though down a well.

*

When Aunt Brigid entered the bedroom, I groaned and turned my face to the wall.

'My stomach is hurting,' I said, and managed a realistic hacking cough. I didn't want to go to Mass; I liked the flowers on the altar, the bright vestments, but it seemed to go on forever. I would read the little bit there was in the Missal, or play with my beads, but there was always time left over, and shifting and staring at other people was supposed to be bad, especially when God was looking. And today was late Mass when Father Cush preached a long sermon till everyone's knuckles were raw with cold. He had been to Rome last Easter and could not stop talking about his visit: 'as many statues as people'.

So I groaned again, my face buried in the bedclothes. Aunt Brigid left the room and came hurrying back with a glass of white, foaming liquid. It tasted nasty but it was all in a good cause, so I drank it down while she watched me anxiously.

'It must have been a cold he caught,' I heard her telling Aunt Freda in the kitchen downstairs afterwards. 'He'd better stay in bed a while till it clears. These cold mornings…'

Freda grunted doubtfully, but she didn't bother to climb the stairs and inspect me herself, as she might have done if it had been a schoolday. I had never dared to stay away from Mass before.

*

So at long last I was alone in the still-warm bed, which was far nicer than kneeling stiffly on a wooden bench, or fidgeting as Father Cush droned on. But in a few minutes I would be leaving this warmth in order to creak along the corridor, then down the stairs. Because the real reason for my staying at home lay in a cupboard in the kitchen, a book that my cousin Kevin had left behind. I had watched him reading it while he was holidaying with us; had found it once, lying face upwards on a chair, when he had gone for a walk as far as Clarke's, the Protestant farm up the road. There he would play the mouth organ, running up and down the keyboard with his head cocked sideways while the whole family and their farmhands gaped at such light-hearted skills.

SEXTON BLAKE AND THE PEARL OF INDIA, sang the tall letters on the cover. And underneath, in red, the subtitle screamed: *Our Famous Detective Fights the Devotees of the Goddess Kali – Another Thugee Mystery.* In the accompanying drawing a tall pale man in tropical clothes was being strangled slowly with a cord by a small brown man perched like a monkey on his back. And above them shone a milky pearl, lighting the forehead of a mysterious lady with long dark hair and angry liquid eyes. How lovely she looked and yet how strange and violent the scene beneath her – at which she was smiling like the Virgin Mary. I needed badly to discover what it was all about.

When Kevin left, at the end of his holiday, I hovered around to watch him pack. He wrapped his mouth organ carefully inside his pyjamas but he left the precious book behind. 'Perhaps Johnny would like that,' I heard him say, 'though it might be a bit old for him.'

Aunt Freda looked at the cover dubiously, and turned it over.

'I'll put it away for him,' she said noncommittally; 'he has some comics at the moment.'

And I watched her pack it away at the back of the top left-hand drawer of the cupboard, the one where all the photographs and letters concerning family business were kept. Why was she putting it there, and how could they talk as if I was not present? I was sitting at the big table by the window, drawing with a crayon, and I heard and saw everything.

So, in a way, the book was already mine, or would be, and I was not committing a sin, I told the Infant of Prague on the bedroom table as I got up. And yet here I was tiptoeing like an Indian along the corridor, under the large smiling photograph of Uncle John, who had owned this house but died in America. Houses where people used to live are mysterious, and these empty rooms were peopled only when my cousins came to stay. But a whole family had lived in them, not only my uncle and father, but also my grandfather, whose old Bible, large as a flagstone, was in the smoky dark room over the fireplace. There was also a book about the American Civil War, full of illustrations showing bearded men in slouch hats carrying long rifles, or setting up their tents around a campfire. A famous photographer had taken them, sometimes endangering his life. There were no photographs of my father.

Each one of the stairs had a different squeak as I descended. Under the linoleum were copies of old papers which I had helped Aunt Freda to put down, so that we would have the pleasure of reading them in years to come. The death of President Douglas Hyde was described in one, an All-Ireland Football Final in another. And now I was in the silence of the kitchen, with the great black crook swinging over the fire, carrying its burden of black pots and thick-bellied kettles. They were planning to replace it with a stove but I loved the open fire where I could sit watching the flames as I dressed in the morning.

The cupboard drawer was too high for me to examine properly, so I took the stool from the fire to enable me to look into it. There were several prayerbooks at the front and a wallet of photographs, most of which I had already seen. They were usually taken in the summer when my cousins were up from the South and we went for a holiday to the seaside at Bundoran. And there was the Sexton Blake mystery, a thin volume, neatly tucked in behind the photographs.

As I pulled it out, I saw that there was a bundle of letters behind; an elastic band held them together. I could see from their length and colour that they were foreign; the first one carried what I recognised as an American stamp, with their president's head – FDR, was he called? The handwriting looked familiar; could it be my father's? I had so few letters from him, and yet I was always longing for one of those blue envelopes with the big stamps. They were the only proof I had that I existed in the mind of a man I barely remembered seeing.

Now and again, dreamlike fragments of that American past rose in my memory. Wearing earmuffs against the tingling cold of a New York winter. Placing pennies on the shining trolley tracks. The tenement roofs of Brooklyn where one could play, peering down at the people far below: feeling small, I clung to the chimney stacks. A wooden Indian with head-dress and tomahawk in the door of the movie theatre where we went to see Mickey Mouse. He was scampering across the screen, squealing, while Minnie clattered after him in her big clogs. But there were less pleasant memories as well: the wearing heat of summer, with water hydrants spouting in the street; the sound of voices raised in anger. Surely it would be right to have a look at the letters and find out a little more than my stray memories? I rolled back the band and opened the first thin sheet of what was not my father's writing but a large fair hand like I now learnt at Garvaghey School.

> You asked me how things are going between 'the couple', I wish you hadn't because I'd rather not think about the whole thing. You know I don't think much of him and events have borne me out. After she came out with the two boys he pulled up his socks and got a job in a grocery business but lost it because of some carelessness. They have a flat in a very rough neighbourhood and seem to quarrel all the time, since he is at home. He comes over to me looking for help but what can I do? He is my own brother but if I can work and drink, why not him?

I stood trembling on the bare flagstones. It was not an ordinary cold I felt but something new to me, a kind of weakening terror. Was this the way grown-ups thought and spoke about each other? The oleographs of St Francis looked down at me from the wall, a tiny army of robins and sparrows around his sandalled feet. A legend of pure love, Father Cush called him. I took out the next letter in the series, looked at the thin light page.

> I gave Jim a job last week and we are all keeping our fingers crossed. You know the old story about the rat in the cheeseshop? Well, the point

is that the poor rat set out to eat the lot and got so sick after the first day that he gave up cheese forever.

So I hope that working in a speakeasy will make him see what drink can do to people. I certainly wish it would do the same for me, though since I have to keep things going, I keep my head pretty steady. Strange how these years have been so good for me when bad for most people. I fell on my feet in New York doing what our father disapproved of back home, making poteen, that is.

It's illegal here, too, but the boys on the beat are mostly Irish and they turn a blind eye. They call it 'hooch', and do it differently than back home. We distil it in the bath, which is always full. So we have to go next door to McGarrity's to wash, which the children find funny. They are living near me now on the top floor. I forgot to say that the reason I gave him the job is that she's pregnant again, a get-together after one of their quarrels, I suppose.

The sprawling signature read JOHN and was followed by a lengthy PS.

If she weren't so hard on him I think he might hold out better. But they squabble like tinkers, and she is much sharper than him, dainty though she seems. The last time shse was banging him around the head with a saucepan – it was a daft scene – shouting: 'You're no good, like the rest of your family.' When she caught sight of me she had the good grace to go red with embarrassment. She told me – privately as she says – that she married the wrong brother. And I must say that when she's angry she looks pretty with her big blue eyes, and her hair astray. But I find women more trouble than they are worth, though not you two, of course, sisters are different.

The baby is due next February, I think.

Like a stunned calf, I fumbled through the little packet, to open the very last one: the date was several years later, 1932.

I hope you won the law case about the right-of-way to the bog on the top mountain. Anything to do with the law is always so tricky, though I think I got the details right on the map I drew for you. It was quite uncanny to sit here trying to get the details of bogroads, gates, and the length of bog banks right, over here in Brooklyn. I couldn't help wishing I was up on Knockmany Hill, that cool wind on my face. Shall I never see Tyrone again?

I regret to say that I have bad news to report from here. She is sick again and in fact has not been really well since the birth. I must say Jim

167

is marvellous with the baby. To see him crooning to it (he still sings quite well) makes me like him all over again. As its godfather I am concerned about it and wonder what will happen to this new John 'Junior' as they say here.

I do my best for them but I have not been feeling myself lately, and there are plans to change the drink laws which would close down my business. I told him that if anything happened to me he should think about sending them all home again.

Finally I understood, standing there with the letters in my hand. I felt the harshness of that lost Brooklyn world again. My stomach began to heave with small, dry sobs, and I felt cold again, colder than I had ever been. But there wasn't that much time, and things had to be tidied up. Still queasy, but determined, I began to rearrange the letters, one after the other, according to their postmarks, and snapped the rubber band around them before slipping them back, behind the lurid cover of the Sexton Blake, which I now did not care if I ever read.

*

Across the creaking house then, past my Uncle John's photograph, past the Infant of Prague, I crept, back to bed. I was still shivering but eventually I fell, or cried myself, asleep.

That special silence of Sundays.

I awoke to footsteps coming back up the broad road. The sound of voices, without hearing words, meaningless as gulls crying over fresh ploughland. Gravel grating underfoot, a key grating in the door. I heard my older aunt's anxious voice in the hallway. 'I hope the boy's all right. Maybe it wasn't wise to leave him alone.'

14

THE LIMITS OF INNOCENCE

It was his especial pride that he was always the first, and sometimes the only one, to answer in class. Auburn-haired and inquisitive, he gathered knowledge without difficulty, passing from class to class as though school were only another sort of game. Standing in a sullen line by the blackboard, the country children swung their heads in bewilderment as the agile little schoolmaster questioned and abruptly demanded: 'The Black Country, where is it? What is Sheffield famous for? The chief industries of Belfast? The chief rivers of Spain?'

Then, meeting no answer, the schoolteacher turned: 'Surely somebody knows! You, Leo Donaghy, what are the chief rivers of Spain?'

'The Douro, the Tagus, the Ebro, the Guadiana and Guadalquivir.'

In his mind's eye he saw five silver rivers race across a rocky tableland, and wondered why anyone should find history or geography difficult when they presented such strange and exciting images of places unseen, as in a story-book. And yet, for the other children, school was only a form of unsunned prison, a dumbfounding purgatory from which they gladly escaped in the end to the relatively simple work of the fields. The country people marvelled at his alertness, saying, 'He's a bright lad, that', though half-convinced from their own experience that such learning was only a useless burden, to be shed when one left school to toil and moil long days on the cramped stubborn fields of a hill farm. 'It's grand to be a scholar if you're going to be a clergyman or a schoolmaster, but what use is it herding cows, or driving a plough?' was their attitude, dutifully passed on to their children, to the total exasperation of the master.

Nevertheless, they had a great respect for intelligence, a bright transitory ornament, and in school Leo found himself called again and again to help others avoid punishment, especially when the schoolmaster was in an angry mood.

*

He did not know, then, when he noticed her first, a large torpid girl standing on the line with the third class, her head bent, her fingers fumbling on a jotter with a stub of gnawed pencil.

Concentrating on his work, following the squeak of chalk outlining a problem on the blackboard, he had little time for anything else, until one day when she leant across his shoulder to copy the answer to a sum, and he felt the fragrance of her arms, the peach-like bloom of her cheek touching his, ever so slightly. He felt puzzled, and could not remember what to do next in his work; it seemed pointless to him. It was early spring, with flowers bursting into colour on the contrary rock garden; he was moved by her presence as though by a breath of warm air flowing into the schoolroom through an open window.

From that day forward, he watched her, quietly, and without being noticed, hardly even realising his own absorption. She was a year older than he was, though in a lower class. Tall, his own height, her brown hair hung limply down her back in pigtails. Her temples were rounded, and in the slight warm dent between them stray hairs glinted. She moved slowly as though in a constant dream, and even when the schoolmaster questioned her, she answered with the disinterest of a sleepwalker.

'You, Sally Hanlon, do you know?'

'What, sir?'

'Did you hear the question or were you sleeping?'

'No, sir.'

'Do you ever do any work at all?'

'Yes, sir.'

Then he saw her cherry red palms tilted for the cane, coming down sharply on the long fingers. She never cried, but wrung her hands mechanically, as though washing them, or pressed them against the cool stuff of her dress. The schoolmaster seemed to have some special reason for disliking her; he punished her so often that her hands showed welts where the blood had clotted. The boy wondered why anyone should wish to hurt someone so beautiful; it seemed like a sacrilege. He offered to help her, with some humility, hardly knowing how to speak to her, or what about.

'It's easy. Honest it is, I'll show you.'

She smiled back at him as he babbled in his efforts to explain. She had a self-absorbed smile that bent the corners of her lips and made shadows around her brown eyes.

In the playground at midday she stood apart from the other girls, hardly bothering to join in the shrill camogie game waged on the patch of ground before the school. They, in turn, resented her quiet, watchful air, the fact that companionship hardly seemed necessary to her. It was as though she was waiting for something; he did not know what.

A certain unspoken intimacy grew up between them. Although she was in a class below him, they shared certain lessons; by accident he found himself placed in the desk directly in front of her. She said little, but now and again she bent over his shoulder, so that he could feel the slight pressure of her breast, and the subtle lightness of her breath.

That whole spring he worked harder than ever; he was preparing for a scholarship examination that would take him away from the valley. But though he had very few hours to himself, he was completely happy, in a wild and exhilarating way that he had never known before. After working all evening he would walk across the fields, delighting in the smell of rain on the hawthorn hedges, the damp musk of leaves and ferns in a corner of a ditch. All these sights and sounds, sharp and releasing on the senses as physical pain, were somehow mingled for him with the knowledge of her working behind him daily in school. His days were dictated by a new rhythm: the knowledge and adoration of beauty.

*

He spoke to her only once outside class, lacking both courage and opportunity. It was the following autumn; there was a choir practice in the chapel in preparation for October devotions, and he took a shortcut down by the river. He saw her coming, a brown beret on her hair, the slender legs moving under a brown coat. He hardly knew what to say to her, she seemed so assured and self-contained. With great nervousness he spoke of the day in school.

'He was very cross today.'

She looked at him; her dark steady gaze made his face redden.

'Why is he so angry with you?'

She thought deeply, eyes on the ground. 'I never have time to do my exercises.'

'Why don't you? I always do. I could help you.'

'I think they're silly, and besides I haven't time.'

He was silent, not understanding very well. 'Do you have to work so hard at horne?'

'I'm always out late,' she said, with a curious shyness as though confiding an important secret. 'And he knows that.'

'And how does he know?'

She was silent. He pretended to know the mystery which kept her from staying in the house and working. His face was tense with the effort of sympathy, for he realised that she must have something very important to occupy her all the evenings, something more important than a childish thing like housework, and something certainly which he for all his supposed brightness could not easily understand. It was part of the mystery of her loneliness in school, the heady perfume of her body, the vicious way in which the schoolmaster showed his dislike and the girls pointed their gossiping, jealous fingers.

'I'll do your homework for you if you like,' he said gallantly.

She did not bother to answer, but walked closely beside him, so that he was almost drunk with the warmth of her presence. Across the river lay a football field; a few boys were punting around a heavy ball, and there came an occasional shout. The river gurgled quietly over silvered stones, and in the shadowy half silence of the autumn evening, with the smell of dead leaves and bark in the air, he could hear her soft breathing. Crossing the bridge halfway down the path their bodies touched. Suddenly bold, he took her hand.

'That's very nice of you,' she said.

'What?'

'To try to help me. But I don't mind being slapped.'

Her fingertips were warm and she moved them against his with a delicate circular movement that made his palm itch, until he felt himself crushing her hand without restraint.

'O-oh,' she said, wincing,

'Did I hurt you?'

172

They stood facing each other at the curve in the path, hidden from the main road and the chapel, under a high elm tree.

'No,' she whispered. Again, their bodies touched, and he saw the lovely head within reach of his fingertips. She leant forward and he felt his arms around her, and for a strange moment they stood, hearing a bird cry above their heads in the elm tree.

'*Silly Billy kissing Nelly.*'

Four small children, two boys and two girls, were dancing at the end of the path, calling and chanting.

'*Silly Billy kisses Nelly.*'

Abashed, they separated, and hurried on; there was a slight blush on her cheeks, but their fingers were laced.

As he sang in the choir that evening, and all the evenings of the following October, the young voices rising in the cold roof of the chapel, he thought of her, and when the incense fumed across the rails at Benediction, he could think only of her image, and not of the coloured statue of the Virgin before the altar. Joining in the Litany of the Divine Praises and the sequence of adoration in the words of the Litany to the Blessed Virgin, it was as if he prayed to her, seeing her move, young and warm-bodied, in the background of his mind.

Again and again, at home or in school, he tasted that single kiss on his lips – the warm tenderness of it, which his physical innocence worshipped like the receiving of a sacrament. Though he continued to watch her in class, and occasionally saw her impassive gaze answer his, they never spoke alone again; walking home in the evenings he heard the boys joking about her, with a strange laughter that he could not understand. Once one of them came over to him, with an air of coarse excitement.

'Weren't you seen with Sally Hanlon down by the Waterside Road?'

'What do you mean?'

The boys laughed and leaped wildly, flinging their school-bags in the air.

'Was it good?'

'What do you mean?'

They hooted, and he turned his head away, keeping his bewilderment and doubt to himself. But he could not help overhearing their stories, coloured with loud and awkward oaths.

'And there they were stretched out in the feckin' grass, and his leg over hers like a bull trying to mount a cow...'

173

Another time, in the boarding house of the schoolmaster, where he sometimes called in the evenings for special scholarship lessons, he heard someone say: 'That one. No wonder she hasn't time for school. She takes all her lessons in the dark.'

*

The months passed slowly, with autumn merging into the frostbright days of winter, when the birds were quiet and the bare thorn hedges crisp with rime. It was his last year in the school, and the thought of going away filled him with a certain melancholy.

Before Christmas there was the bustle of preparing the annual school concert, organised by the teachers with the help of the parish priest. As head of the senior class he was to assist in producing a short play. Shy himself, he yet knew exactly what others should do when they took the stage. He coached them with a firmness and certainty that surprised even himself.

When the night came, the two cloakrooms, which had been changed into dressing rooms, were full of excited children; the costumes for the play had arrived only that morning by bus, and there were 'Ooh's of wonder as the glittering dresses and soldiers' uniforms were drawn out.

He had been deputed to act as steward, and in his new suit and white collar he felt rather important, ushering people to their seats, or rushing to the door of one of the dressing rooms.

'Hurry up there. We've no time. The priest's here.'

When the concert began, he watched from a side doorway. The first part of the programme consisted of children singing, mainly to please their parents, who formed the bulk of the audience. The play made up the second half. During the interval he felt very restless and nervous. Now that the green makeshift curtains were about to open, and knowing that she was to play the part of the fairy godmother in the first act, he felt afraid in case anything should go wrong.

When she appeared on the stage, only for a brief moment, gliding mysteriously from the wings in order to grant the wishes of a sleeping child, he saw that her hair had been loosened from the pigtails, and fell around her shoulders in a great mass. She had a circlet on her head, with a single star shining in the front. As the curtain came down on the first act, he moved towards the girls' dressing room, hardly conscious of what he was doing. He knocked on the door, gently. There was no answer.

Entering, he saw her standing before a mirror, hair still loose, flowing down her back. She turned in surprise, and he saw that her dress had been unbuttoned from the shoulders down; he could see, peeping above the thin white undergarment, the tops of her breasts.

On the stage a bell rang sharply for the beginning of the second act. She adjusted her dress with a quick movement, and came towards him. 'Could we go out for a while?' he stammered. The request seemed idiotic but she did not appear to mind. He caught her hand and, with a quick look round to see if anyone was watching, they ran out through the door into the school playground. The sharp iron railings on the top of the wall and the worn stone of the playground patch shone under moonlight.

'Look up,' she said.

The cold procession of the northern lights filled a part of sky. He looked for a while and then said: 'I prefer looking at you.'

She laughed at his earnestness. He could see her body moving under the transparent shimmering dress of the fairy godmother, as though even such delicate stuff hindered her natural freedom. She continued to look upwards, as if willing to lose herself for the moment in watching the glittering immensities of the night sky.

'Come on,' he said.

'Where?'

'I have an idea.'

Filled with an extraordinary spirit of adventure, he took her hand, moving towards the dark shrubbery which grew on the hillock surrounding the school. This sandy contorted patch, where bushes and shrubs dug their twisted roots into the earth, was part of the playground, and even during the daytime a dark and dew-damp underworld, with secret hiding places, long grasses where the children searched for pignuts or, in winter, slopes for sliding. A thorn tree sent drops of moisture tingling down the backs of their necks.

'Where are we going?'

'Anywhere. Are you afraid?'

She pressed slightly against him but did not answer.

'Come on. We can see the school from the top.' He pulled her by the hand as high as they could go, laughing as they tumbled over the roots that sprawled like snakes across the path. He held a swinging briar aside to prevent her dress from being torn, until, parting the screen of heavy leaves, they fought their heads clear of the sour-sweet-smelling tunnels of the shrubbery. Below them the school lay, a good deal smaller now in its miniature valley, with moonlight on the tiles of the roof and lamplight pouring from all the windows.

They stood together watching. The night smell, compounded of leaves and earth, was dense in his nostrils; in some way it reminded him of the girl at his side.

'Are you sure they won't miss us?'

'We've lots of time. They haven't even ended yet, and then they'll have to clear up.'

'Look, there's the Parochial House.'

The large yellow-brick house of the parish priest lay on the other side of the slope. The top of the hillock marked the boundary of the school playground; beyond a barbed-wire fence lay the grounds of the house, with mist swirling over the shadowy mass of a plantation. There was a rigidly enforced rule that none of the children ever crossed into these fields to play or even to chase a lost ball.

'Could we cross it?'

'We daren't,' she said.

In his nervous way he was more urgent and daring than she. He pushed through the strands of wire in a flash, and then held them apart for her to follow. She climbed cautiously through, lifting her dress with one hand. For a second he saw the white flesh above her knee exposed.

'Hurry up.'

Then they were both through, and ran breathless away from the fence through the wet high grass. She was laughing and he pretended to chase her, until they found themselves on the other side of the field where the outskirts of the pine plantation cast an aromatic shadow, and the giant trees strode away, ghostlike and glittering, into the darkness towards the river.

A frog ran with electric leaps through the grass. She screamed slightly and stumbled, falling to her knees. He bent down beside her.

'Are you hurt?' he asked tenderly.

He touched her shoulders with his hands, gently and yet with great excitement. He knelt down beside her and kissed her, feeling her breast against his, soft against firm.

'You shouldn't do that,' she said softly.

'I can't help it. You're so beautiful.'

She hid her head, turning it slightly away from his.

176

'You shouldn't say things like that. Nobody ever does.'

'But it's true.'

He touched the frail mist of hair above her ears. He was most afraid to touch the rippling lustrous mass of hair; it was if he would lose his wrists in it. A sheep came stumbling towards them where they lay on the grass. It sniffed suspiciously, then took to its heels.

'Look,' she said, laughing. 'Aren't sheep silly?'

He made as if to kiss her again.

'Behave yourself.'

There was a note in her voice that he had never heard before, as though she were pretending to be an adult, and yet was half-ashamed of the pretence. Suddenly she pulled his head down towards hers again, shifting her body so that it touched his full-length. A shudder of feeling passed through him, so intense that he did not know whether it was good or evil, pain or ecstasy.

'Bad boy,' she whispered. 'What were you doing in the dressing room?'

He was apologetic. 'Honestly, I'm sorry.'

She laughed. 'Am I so ugly then?'

'Oh Lord, no!' he said, in a hushed voice as though speaking of something sacred. His innocent awareness, nearer to adoration than love, must have touched her; the harsh uncertainty left her voice.

'You're so funny,' she said. 'And really nice.'

'Am I?' he asked with surprise. He didn't know whether to be pleased or not.

'You are,' she said. 'I wish others were as kind as you.' She spoke as though trying to release some sorrow that he could not understand.

He moved his fingers around the column of her throat, touching the front of her dress. It was still partly open; in her hurry she had left the top undone.

'You'll catch cold,' he said.

'Button it for me.'

His hands moved over the substance of the dress, searching for the buttons. He felt her tense, her shoulders tighten, as he fumbled, conscious of the small mounds of the twin breasts under the cloth. Raising her shoulders with a slight moan, she reached down, shrugging back the dress and the thin undergarment until the upper part of her body lay bare on the grass. In silent wonder he touched the flesh of her side, pale as buttermilk, with the veins delicately blue under the skin. It was the first time he had seen the body of a girl even partly naked. With sudden heat and daring he touched her breasts. His hands, moving over the skin, had learnt a new and secret tenderness, as though the nerves under the finger-tips were bare. The crisp nipples arched under his touch like tiny spikes. He almost swooned with excitement and terror.

They lay in the grass without moving for a few minutes. A star disintegrated in an arc down the sky. Her body was motionless under his now quiet, caressing touch. He half-closed his eyes, feeling the rhythmic movement of her torso beneath his hands, smelling the acrid fragrance of her hair against his mouth. The side of his face was growing wet with dew.

'We'd better go,' she said suddenly, sitting up. Her voice was soft and she looked more openly at him. He helped her to her feet and she stood combing her hair.

'Where's the band?'

He found it lying in the grass, the cheap crinkled star winking up at him. He helped her to pull it down upon her forehead, and drew a few scattered twigs from her hair. Then he took her hand.

'Come on,' she said.

Hand in hand, they walked across the field, away from the smell and shadow of the pines. They scrambled through the barbed-wire fence and stood again on the crest of the hillock looking down at the school. The lights were still on; the concert was only ending. She kicked a tuft of grass, moodily. The tip of her shoe was wet and gleaming.

'Do you like me still?' she asked.

'I love you,' he said. He had never used the word before, but he was sure he knew what it meant.

They moved downwards through the dank windings of the shrubbery. Stones slid under their feet, and with her moist palm in his, the boy felt no longer doubtful. He whistled lightly with assurance and joy. The steam of their breaths mingled in a loose skein on the night air. He had come to understand something of mystery, and yet, miraculously, it remained mystery for him still.

1952

15

THE OKLAHOMA KID

It was my Cowboy period. On the fringe of the newly ploughed field behind the house I practised my draw, with two sticks peeled and whittled to revolver shape. There was the simple hip draw, like Buck Jones, thumbs resting on the belt, fingers crisply spread, like eagle's talons. Then, as your opponent moved (batted an eye nervously, before slapping leather), the releasing plunge downward to action. A double explosion – Bang, Bang! and a thistle fell dead, in the full pride of its pale, prickly life. The daisies shook their sunbonnet heads in dismay while all other thistles moved (despite their roots) a step backwards: the Oklahoma Kid was in charge.

Then there was the border cross draw, hands flat across the stomach, relaxed but dangerous as serpents. A cow moved its flank to shudder off a fly and the serpents uncoiled. Twin mouths of flame flickered in the air, gunsmoke and cordite (I did not know they were irreconcilable) drifting across the spring grass.

Tim, our farm horse, watched me, a green scum of grass on his protruding lower lip and wedge-shaped teeth. I renamed him Thunder and rode to town, his flanks glistening with sweat, his glove-deep nostrils pulsing as he heaved for breath. Unconcerned, he lashed his tail, dropped his head to lip in a daisy, and I saw the harness marks on his neck, the sagging belly roped with veins, and felt oddly ashamed. A smell of clover, the drone of a bee away into silence, and the prairies of my imagination –

long grass of Wyoming, red-rock mesa of Arizona – dwindled to a boy in dungarees standing in a field in County Tyrone; Northern Ireland to some, Ulster to others. Hearing my aunt call, I raced in, tamely: someone was looking for me in the shop.

*

Every day, the country people came down the mountain roads to our house. Some came punctually to collect their pensions, for it was a sub-post office, and one of my aunts was postmistress. White-haired, gaunt as a rake, she stood in her little office among the weighing scales and postal regulations, indicating where X his or her mark should go. Others came to buy odds and ends, liquorice allsorts, Paris buns, MacLean's Headache Powders, from what had been, in my grandfather's time, a flourishing shop and to which they were still attached by vague strands of loyalty. One family came – one or other of seven identical children, lugging a basket as big as himself across the fields because they had quarrelled with the new grocer, an entirely new and more up-to-date business, half a mile down the road.

These were the usual callers, bound by no regulations (though the post-office was supposed to close at 3 PM) save weather and the rhythm of work on the land. A dry day in winter, a wet in summer presented equal opportunities but, generally, they preferred to come at twilight, thus saving labour and light. Which is why I remember the shop as a scene by La Tour, the people standing well back in the shadows, my aunt's white head bent close to a grease-spattered candle, a smell of damp clothes, bread, cream of tartar, pervasive as the smell of paint in a studio. They loved her, unjudging audience of all their troubles, but they wore her out.

During the winter, we had another group of callers: those who came to borrow books. For our house was also a branch of the Tyrone County (Carnegie) Library and my other aunt was Honorary Librarian. As she was often occupied around the farm, I was consulted as Deputy Librarian. Already, at ten, I was a formidable bookworm, imagination sprouting in isolation like one of those sickly potato stalks one finds in cellars. A hundred books came each quarter, arranged in wooden cases with hasps like pirate trunks. Sixty fiction, twenty juvenile and twenty general knowledge and by the end of a month I would be familiar with the contents of some and the titles of all, and be able to advise with authority. Ranged on the half-empty shelves, they soon smelt like all the other

180

commodities, faintly sweet and musty, with patterns of damp on the bindings.

The main demand was for fiction. At school, few of the older children read, plunging directly into the work of the farm when they came home. So the Juveniles lay unused except for my predatory dismissal. And General Knowledge meant little to the people of the district, speculative only about local things. Even books on farming, with their background of hops, cider and Harvest Festivals, seemed far removed from life on the soggy hill-farms of Tyrone. So it was fiction they sought, to fill the long hours of the winter nights. And fiction consisted of only two kinds, Love Stories and Cowboys.

The Love Stories were my aunt's domain. A reader herself, she sampled them before passing them on, and not merely for pleasure. Many of the farmers' wives read, but the most voracious were two large ladies, one seventy and one fifty, one single and one married, alike only in their unslakeable thirst for that mysterious thing called Romance. If my aunt was out, she would have left a selection aside, which I would pass over the counter, primed for the moral discussion which seemed inextricable from Love Stories.

'Is there any Love in it?' they asked, peering at the title doubtfully in the poor light. Ruby M. Ayres, Isobel C. Clarke, Annie S. Swan, Ethel M. Dell – how I remember those romantic-sounding names! And the titles, *A Stranger to Paradise*, *The Primrose Path*, *An Open Heart*, wicket gates to a world where slender, flowering English girls called Penelope or Millicent awaited the dreamlike destiny of love. No one found it strange that, like the books on farming, they should always deal with settings completely foreign to us: books were like that, a province of the unreal.

'Your aunt said the last was good, but there was damn all love in it.'

'There's plenty this time,' I said, hedging furiously.

'Is it good love or the other sort?'

'The other sort', that vice to which love-stories were prone, was beyond me, but I could parrot a testimony. With childish cunning I saw that what they deplored, they secretly coveted: the questioning was a necessary moral front.

'It's mostly good,' I said, 'but there's a doubtful bit at the end.'

When the choice came to be made, however, the questionable book generally went into the basket, joining the Inglis Pan loaf, the pot of Richhill jam, the Andrew's Liver Salts. I had no illusions about love stories: in any case, I was delighted to be accepted in complicity in an adult mystery. But my capacity to corrupt was limited: the really questionable books, the ones entirely devoted to love of the wrong sort, had already been locked away by my far-seeing aunt.

*

With the Cowboy stories I came into my own. I had only recently graduated from Juveniles (the face of the prince suddenly shaded by a sombrero, the witch changing her broomstick for a rustler's pinto) and for a time the charm of mere killing was enough. But I was in search of more than the elementary violence of the Wild West Club, and when I discovered my first Zane Grey, I knew I was in for a long ride. It was *Riders of the Purple Sage*, and when the boulder rolled down, sealing off the Mormon family in the valley, I trembled with excitement. I asked Mr Ferguson, the post-van driver, who spent the day in a little hut at the end of our turf shed (it was the end of his thirty-mile run) before driving back in the afternoon to head-office, whether Zane Grey had written many books. He said that he had seen in the paper once that Zane Grey was a woman and that she had written over a hundred books, many of them posthumous. This information puzzled but pleased me: a hundred books would take a long time to read.

I can see now that the hallucinatory hold these stories gained on me was because I connected them with a mysterious previous life. Every six months or so, Mr Ferguson brought long blue envelopes bearing flamboyant stamps to remind me that I had an existence elsewhere in the mind of a father, who had sent me back, during the Depression, to the only place where he had been happy. How was I to know that Arizona was nearly a continent away from Bushwick Avenue, Brooklyn, where only cigarstore Indians were to be seen, and that in fostering my dream I was cancelling that of my father?

*

My circle of fellow-readers was small but intense. Besides Mr Ferguson (who hardly qualified since I saw him only on Saturdays when I was free from school), there was a dark-jowled young man called Dan Lynch, who lived with his mother and sister on one of the most remote farms under the shadow of Coal Hill. With his hat crushed on his head, he would swing in onto the gravel before the house and leap from his bicycle as

182

though from a lathered horse. Henry Anderson, on the other hand, was a gaunt Presbyterian farmer who demanded my advice gravely before making his choice. If Dan was the typical hard-jawed cowboy, Henry Anderson was the Mormon preacher or sheriff; just, severe, taciturn. When he gave back the book, it was generally wrapped in a page from *The Farmer and Stockbreeder* upon which he had laboriously noted the words he could not understand. Hugh Kelly, who drove Gormley's lorry around the back lanes, made a fourth. There were others, like John Mooney, our serving man, who read an occasional book, but these were the cream of the outfit.

To these rather quiet, hard-working men, my childish insistence was at first strange, then amusing. Cowboy stories had been for them a recreation after a hard day's work, but I demanded more. Before passing out a book I would give a judgement and expect one in return. If there were too many people in the house, we talked by the roadside, turning over pages by the light of a hissing carbide bicycle lamp. The incongruity of the scene did not strike us: briefly we shared the illusion of a wider world, with electric storms crackling over the prairies, stampeding the wild horses. Was that the sound of hooves on the Belfast road?

One thing did trouble me, although I was afraid to speak of it. We were all agreed that Zane Grey was the best. Although Clarence Mulford and W. C. Tuttle were also good, they lacked the authentic detail of *Wildfire* and *West of the Pecos*. But there was such a lot about women in some of Zane Grey (perhaps he was one after all?) who were often discovered without their denim shirts, a warm flush mantling neck and bosom. This was all right if the hero was involved, because he had the shyness of chivalry, but when, in one story, a vicious outlaw kept a woman chained in a cave, I was dismayed: the Cowboy stories seemed to be following the Love stories. That the scene filled me with a new feeling, at once hot and guilty, dismayed me even more: was I turning outlaw? I finally showed the book to my aunt who took a brief glance at it and put it away, without comment. But what was so fascinating about naked women? Whipping my imaginary mustang as I drove the cows home from the hill pastures in the evening, I wished I knew the answer.

My great sadness, however, was that, as the winter ended, the work of the fields slowly reclaimed my cowboy friends. First it was the ploughing. Coming home from school, I would see another field opened and wave to a figure on a headland, turning with his team. Then, as the days lengthened, there was the sowing; when the oats were in, I would be staying at home a few days to help with the cutting and planting of the seed potatoes. In the meantime, people read still, but more slowly, taking as much as a month to finish a book. Soon they would stop reading altogether.

It was then that I heard about the film. Someone had seen in the local market town a poster announcing the coming of *The Greatest Cowboy Film of All Time – The Oklahoma Kid*. I had been to a few films (each year a visiting priest showed slides of Mission work on a sheet in the local hall) but this was different, and not to be missed. After dinner, I ran out to bring the news to my fellow-readers where they were working in the fields. Henry Anderson was gathering dried potato stalks and burning them by the riverside.

'What do you think we should do?' I asked.

He threw another gripful of stalks on the pyre, which fumed a grey-black smoke.

'I'll have to talk to the others,' he said, slowly. 'But if it is as good as you say, I think we should go.'

Several nights later, at the end of the week, we met at the crossroads to discuss the situation. Henry, as the eldest, led the conversation, proposing that we should club together and hire Gormley's hackney.

'How much would that be?' asked Dan Lynch anxiously.

'Gormley generally charges two quid for the run, but he'd give it to me for less,' said Hugh, with an expert's smooth knowledge. 'Not counting the cub here, that makes about ten shillings a skull.'

Although the sum was far beyond my savings, I was decided not to relinquish my equality.

'I'll pay for myself,' I said, with defiance.

'If the nadger pays, that makes a four-way split; are you game?'

We all looked at Dan. Despite his habitual cheerfulness, everyone knew that he found it a hard struggle to support his mother and sister on the tiny farm and that he rarely had pocket money, even for cigarettes. Nevertheless we could not offer him a loan, however well meant, because it would indicate that we knew his plight, and reticence in money matters was one of the facts of the countryside.

'If you can find a fifth man,' Dan said finally, 'I'm game.'

For the following week, we talked of little or nothing but the film. According to Hugh Kelly, the principal part was taken by an actor who had been a cowboy himself, and the whole thing would be authentic, down to the last cowclap. Even the taciturnity of Henry Anderson dissolved before such golden possibilities: 'It might be a real good night,' he said. As for myself, I rehearsed the scene daily after school in the fields behind the house. It would be the first time I had ever gone to town, on my own account, without a watchful relative.

It was not until the evening we left that I learned who was to be the extra man. They had canvassed several people, including casual readers like John Mooney, but all said they had neither money nor time for such a foolish jaunt at a busy time of year. There was one man in the parish, however, who was well known never to refuse the chance of an outing, however long or for whatever purpose. In despair, therefore, they asked Papa (short for Peter Anthony) Cummins.

Papa was a smallish, rather dusty-looking man who always sported a green hat with a large chicken feather stuck under the band; together with his mottled complexion, it made him look an ageing Indian brave. This, however, was the only relevant thing about him, from our point of view, because he openly scorned books, all the more so since his wife was one of the two romance addicts. His chosen activities were card-playing – he was a deadly hand at twenty-five, the favourite game in the district, and above all, talking. From morning till night his flow of chatter went on, ceaseless and indiscriminate as a river, down which floated anything, dead dogs, cornstalks, old turds. Seeing him approach, people doubled on their tracks, disappeared under bridges, vanished in a cloud of pipesmoke, but he was still there when they reappeared, a bucket or spade tucked jauntily under his arm, his nasal voice grinding away at their wits.

My own uneasiness where Papa was concerned was simple: his outspokenness troubled me. Generally, country people never talked much about themselves. But Papa recognized none of this reticence, speaking of his wife, for instance, as casually as though she were something he had picked up at the Hiring Fair. His conversation was spiked with jokes and innuendoes, which by the subdued guffaws that greeted them, I guessed to be somehow connected with the Love stories. My prudish altar-boy's soul was both fascinated and revolted.

But there was a further reason. As I grew older, the strangeness of my situation troubled me increasingly: not only could I not remember my life in America, but I could even hardly remember my father. With the indifference of the hardworked, my aunts did not speak much of the past and failed to understand my secret pleas for information. My main hope lay then in what casual knowledge I could find. Patiently as an archaeologist, I reconstituted the past from old books and photographs and the rambling conversation of the older men in the parish. The image of my father I got was vague but flattering, that of a red-haired young man who sang occasionally at dances and was a demon for practical jokes. Only Papa among the men of my father's generation refused to answer my questions and I sensed he disapproved. Once when someone, in the way of adults, placed his hand on my head and asked what I was going to be when I grew up, he rounded sharply, before I could speak, and said with a rough emphasis I have never forgotten: 'He'll probably be a blackguard, like his father before him.'

*

At the crossroads, that evening, Papa was the first to arrive. Typically enough, he had not changed, his hands stuck in the pockets of his overalls, a newly cut ash plant under one armpit. The others had washed after coming in from the fields, their faces shone a scrubbed red and they had on soft Sunday shoes. When Hugh appeared with the car, his arm dangling self-consciously through the driver's window, the group was complete. It was a big Vauxhall and we all piled in, Papa in front and the three of us in the back.

The whole journey was dominated by the whine of Papa's voice. Henry and Dan sat on either side of me, their hands square on their knees. It had been a damp day and the landscape had that stereoscopic brightness that sometimes comes after rain, or just before twilight. On either side, men were still working in the fields. My companions should have been delighted with this chance to observe the methods and progress of others, but they seemed stricken with self-consciousness. Only Papa kept his eyes open, delivering a running commentary as we passed: 'That's good even ploughing now,' or, 'The man drove that furrow should be shot.'

Outside Laganbridge, where the river curled under a grey bridge, there was one field sloping directly into the sun, in which the green shoots of an early crop were just beginning to appear. A sight like this was so rare that I expected a comment, but all my companions did, when Papa drew their attention to it, was to knead their caps slowly, nodding assent to his admiring 'There's a right snappy farmer for you!' What was wrong with them, and why were things not going as I had expected?

Soon we were at the outskirts of the town, the wealthy well-tended grounds of large private houses, the golf-course with its striding pylons. Laganbridge, a sturdy market centre with about eight thousand population, was ten miles or so from my home. I was brought to it twice or three times a year on shopping expeditions, and its main street, dominated by the Courthouse and the War Memorial, was my only real image of urban life. As we turned in the Belfast road, I felt a familiar excitement, all the sharper because I was now entering for the first time as an equal among adults. There was the long low shape of the County Library, the centre from which all our books came. Above it appeared the twin-spired silhouette of the Diocesan Cathedral, with the college in its shadow to which I might be going in a year or two. All these details seemed to fuse into a mysterious and seductive whole, promising something subtly different from the pace of the farm. My awareness of Papa's presence diminished: the *Oklahoma Kid* was finally coming to town.

There was a further dimension to this new and potent image: the town was nervous with change. This was spring 1940, and through Main Street paraded a detachment of British soldiers. We stopped the car at the foot of the courthouse to let them pass. First came a tall man wearing a busby and leopard skin, his eyes fixed fiercely ahead, runnels of sweat coursing down his jaw. Then drummers, left legs dragging with the weight of their instruments, upon which they gave an occasional marching pace rattle. Then pipers, in kilt and cloak, with white mouth-pieces resting on their shoulders. Behind was the rank and file, in sober khaki, polished boots clattering, arms rising and falling like puppets. Under the sand-bagged courthouse they marched, out the Barracks Road, and in the distance we heard the band strike up again at the drum-major's harsh command. Its sudden flourish sent a shiver down my spine.

We were not the only ones to have stopped to watch. Along the pavement was a thin line of people, still in attitudes of listening. Some seemed countrymen, like ourselves, their inexperience betrayed by their weighty pose. A few customers had emerged from shops, packages in hand; there were even one or two shopkeepers, wearing their white aprons. But most of the onlookers were girls, of every shape, size and age, their eyes bright, their lips wounded with lipstick.

'There's no shortage of women about here,' said Papa, appreciatively, looking around him.

In order to be in time for the film, we had agreed that it was better not to eat at home but to have something in town. After a hurried fish-and-chips in Danielli's, we made our way towards the cinema – it was the smallest of the three in town – which lay through a maze of side-streets. Our pace was slow, because the pavements were clogged with people. At first, we took for granted that they were shoppers, but, as we elbowed our way in single file, it gradually dawned on us that they were mainly soldiers. Of various ranks and regiments (thick serge of the Inniskillings, black berets of the tank corps, even blue of the RAF), they pushed their way along, obviously at ease and at home. And when we finally got to the cinema, we found them again, a large queue of fighting men and their girls, stretching straight down the street and round the corner. Five sheepish Oklahoma Kids come to a twentieth-century town, we stood looking on: there was not the remotest hope of getting in.

*

It was as we were making our way despondently back to the car that Hugh suggested that perhaps we would have a chance of getting into the new cinema. This magnificent building, a concrete palace called the Coliseum, stood right in the centre of Main Street, between Littlewood's and Woolworth's. Ordinarily, it would never have occurred to us to try such a place, which had the reputation of being very expensive, and was frequented mainly by townspeople. There was added reason for suspicion which my companions understood but I did not. Run up by a local contractor to cater to the new trade brought by the war, it was decorated in the Arabian Nights style, with spangles and stars on the ceiling and double love-seats at the back. These latter had brought down the wrath of Canon Kerr, the fiery old administrator of St John's, who described them in an Easter sermon as 'hot seats to Hell'.

Now, however, the Coliseum seemed the ideal solution. In the discreet, carpet-heavy hall, a queue was filing, supervised by a splendid commissionaire in sky-blue uniform and cap. It was a long queue, but unlike the tin-roofed cinema at the end of town, the atmosphere was orderly and the rate of absorption regular. Fenced in by plush ropes, we waited, stolid as oxen, whiling away the time by looking at publicity stills or testing the carpets in which, as Papa said, one could sink to the fetlocks. Finally, the commissionaire came over to us.

'Two first,' he said. 'Main film's begun.'

'What's that?' asked Henry anxiously.

'He means we'll have to separate,' Hugh explained.

'I'll take the caddy,' said Papa promptly. 'Where do we go now?'

Bumping through the darkness after the cinema attendant's torch, we found ourselves going down the vast shelving floor of the auditorium. Every row seemed filled, a sea of dark heads. Nearer and nearer loomed the screen until the usherette led the way across in front of it. As we followed, I saw a tiny box-shaped shadow rising and falling at the bottom of the screen: it was Papa's hat. At the far corner, underneath the double sign EXIT/GENTLEMEN, were two empty places. Seats banged as we sat down. 'They don't give you much room for your legs,' commented Papa, turning himself several times, like a dog, before settling.

Directly above us, high and insubstantial as cloud formations, reared the images of the film. A window opened like a gulf at the back of a modern apartment to reveal a vista of skyscrapers. A man crossed the screen, his legs, distorted by the angle of vision, grasshopper long. He was speaking angrily to a woman whose face suddenly swam up to us in close-up: beautiful, sad and as huge as a barn door.

'God,' said Papa, 'that's the living spit of young Barney Owen's wife. But I didn't know she wore make-up.'

In a street now, a yellow taxi speeding through the bright lights of the city.

'What's happening?' demanded Papa impatiently, rapping his ash plant against my legs. 'Where are we going?'

It was only then that the truth dawned on me. Despite his travelling, Papa had never been to the cinema. His journeys were in search of new listeners, not new sights, and once set down, he continued talking. I remembered with sudden horror a story of how he had gone with a party to the All-Ireland in Dublin and spent the day in a relative's house in Clontarf, listening to the game on the radio. This was the first time he had ever been in a picture house, the first time, indeed, he had ever been affronted by the idea of fiction. What he thought was happening on the screen, whether he regarded these images as real people or shadows, I could not say, since he struck straight through it to whatever everyday life he could recognize.

A man came hurrying down to greet the couple and bring them back through the stage-door.

'That fellow has a wee look of Micky Boyle about the eyes,' Papa announced.

'S-sh' came from behind us, the first indication that we had an audience.

Inside the theatre, some kind of rehearsal was in progress. Stagehands were moving in the shadows, shifting scenery, focusing lights. Standing with the couple in the wings, we saw the soprano spotlighted on the stage, her throat distended with sound, her bosom rising and falling.

'She has the right big udder,' said Papa admiringly.

The comment behind us had risen to an uproar. 'Disgusting,' I heard several times as I tried to sink lower in my seat.

As the singer spread her arms in one final throbbing note, a chorus came tumbling out onto the stage, drum majorettes wearing cartwheel cowboy hats and boots, and kicking their long white legs in the air. Papa leaned forward so as to inspect them more closely.

'Where did you say we were?' he asked.

'In New York – in America,' I said, my face flaming.

'By Jasus, they don't wear much in your country!'

It was this remark, delivered at the top of his voice, which finally provoked an intervention. From the row behind a soldier thrust his closely cropped head between us.

'Look 'ere, Grandad,' he said mildly, 'you're not the only one in this dump.'

For the first time, Papa became aware of his audience, but without understanding how he had gathered it.

'What the hell's wrong with you?' he said sharply to the head which had landed so unexpectedly in his lap.

'Put a cork in it, will you, please,' said the soldier with patient exasperation. And then, seeing that Papa still did not understand: 'Would you mind closing up?'

'Shut up yourself,' said Papa angrily, 'or I'll give you a belt.'

He raised his ash plant in the air: wavy as a spider it appeared on the screen, right across the face of the leading man.

That did it. Cries of protest came from every part of the house, including the balcony. Several people rose in their seats, craning to see what was happening, while the commissionaire came down the aisle, shining his torch directly into Papa's face.

'I'm afraid you'll have to leave, sir. You're creating a disturbance.'

190

'What hell disturbance do you mean?' said Papa. 'I'm danged comfortable. And the wee fellow's great: he's explaining it all to me.'

'People are complaining.'

'That's right,' said a hard voice. 'Put him out.'

'Come on,' I said, tugging at Papa's coat. 'We'd better leave.' But I
don't think he would have gone except that our three companions suddenly appeared beside us, having heard the row from the other side of the
hall.

'I think we'd better go,' said Henry Anderson, gravely.

Everyone turned to watch as we marched out, Papa in front, escorted by the commissionaire, myself last, thankful for the darkness which
hid my face. At the door the manager was waiting, a plump little man who
hovered around us in dismay.

'There's never been anything like this here before. But we'll refund
you your money if you insist.'

But Papa had understood finally and was disgusted.

'You can shove your auld cinema up your ass,' he said briefly and,
ramming his hat down on his head, led us out onto the pavement.

I remember one more thing about that evening in Laganbridge. As we
passed glumly down the street, a group of boys were standing outside the
sliding door of Lyons garage. Several of them wore boiler suits. They
watched us with interest and before we were out of earshot, one of them
gave a low incredulous whistle.

'That's a right crowd of country-looking idiots,' he said. I looked at
my companions. If they had heard him, they did not betray it by the flicker of an eye. Dark-faced and silent, they plunged down the street towards
the car.

*

By right, the story ends there, and anything further will only spoil it.
During the return journey, Papa sat at the back and Henry in the front. I
don't know what they talked of, or indeed, whether they talked at all,
because I soon fell asleep with my head sideways in Papa's lap, from
which I had to be lifted when I got home.

But life often adds a codicil; seventeen years later, I descended from
a Greyhound Bus in Oklahoma City. In the glaring cafeteria, the voice of
Elvis Presley was wolfing through 'Heartbreak Hotel'. Gene Fullmer had
just beaten Sugar Ray Robinson: the paper I had bought in Salt Lake City

the previous night was full of it, since Fullmer was a local man. Eating a sour mess of beef and hash, I entered into conversation with the man beside me. He seemed rather disreputable, his hat jammed on his head, his jaws masticating ceaselessly. Yet he also seemed somehow familiar – that great nose, that coppery tint (noticeable even under a day-old beard), those wise eyes of legend.

'I'm a Cherokee from Tulsa,' he said, with what I took to be both fatalism and pride. 'What part of Oklahoma do you come from?'

'From Oklahoma City,' I said, involuntarily, 'County Tyrone,' and choked with a mixture of joy, shame and ridiculous conceit.

16

Death of a Chieftain

•

Smith & Wesson in one hand, machete in the other, his T-shirt moist with sweat (except where the great raft of the sun hat kept a circle of white about his shoulders), he beat his way through the jungle around San Antonio. Behind him followed a retinue of peons, tangle-haired, liquid-eyed, carrying the inevitable burden of impedimenta. With their slow pace, their resigned gestures, they seemed less like human beings than like a column of ants, winding its way patiently over and around obstacles.

When they came to a clearing that satisfied him, he declared a halt, calling up his carriers in succession. The first put down the table he had been hugging across his shoulders, peering through its front legs for the path ahead. Around the table were piled various instruments and items of food with, to top the mound, a bottle of tequila and a neat six-pack of Budweiser beer. With the air of an acolyte bringing a ritual to its conclusion the last carrier approached, lugging a battered cane-chair. Bernard Corunna Coote sat down, breathing heavily.

Food came first. Like a bear let loose in a tuckshop, he ransacked the parcels, tearing the tinfoil or polythene bags open. Half an hour later, while the natives lay around, somnolent as stones after their brief meal of tacos, he was still fighting his way through a cold roast chicken, washed down by draughts of lukewarm beer. Finally, wiping his mouth, he turned to work.

Compass and sextant, lovingly consulted, pinpointed his position. Then he erected a triangular instrument, like a theodolite, and took readings, both horizontal and vertical. As though satisfied of where he stood, but not what he stood on, he produced a gleaming spade and began to sink holes around the clearing. From them he took 'samples', handfuls of red clay and stone, which he heaped on the table, to the height of a child's sandcastle.

By the time he was finished, the whole clearing looked as if it had been attacked by a regiment of moles. From under their conical hats the Indians watched: now it was their turn. Exasperated by their sleepy gaze, he dispatched runners into the forest to bring back further samples. When they returned to lay their spoils before him (curiously shaped fragments of flint, stones faintly resembling arrowheads, stones in which veins of mica flashed) he interrogated them about anything they might have seen, with an optimism that only gradually died into disappointment.

All these details were entered on a large roll-like map of the district. At the top of the chart, in a fair hand, was inscribed the Indian name of the region: *Coatlicue*, the land of the God of Death. At the bottom was the owner's name: *Bernard Corunna Coote, His Property*. In between, from the central axis of San Antonio, the ever-increasing lines of his excursions radiated outwards, like a spider's web.

*

If the centre of the spider's web was San Antonio, the centre of San Antonio, as far as Bernard Corunna Coote was concerned, was the Hotel Darien. It stood on a promontory overlooking the town, a great bathtub of a building whose peeling façade was only partly disguised by a fringe of palm trees. The disparity between its size and the adobe hovels gathered around its base would have been shocking, were it not for its enormously dilapidated appearance, like a rogue mosque. From whatever angle one approached, its grey dome was the first thing to become visible; a landmark to the market-going Indian, slumped on his burro, a surprise to the traveller, who felt as though he were arriving at Penn Station or St Pancras.

The history of the Hotel Darien combined mercantile greed with the despairing quality of romance. In the 1890s, after the failure of the de Lesseps Panama project, a group of Liverpool and New York businessmen (already linked by the golden chain of considerable shipping profits)

194

had been taken by the idea of cutting a railroad through the jungles of Central America. Such a railway would save ships the dangerous journey round Cape Horn: cargo could be shipped across the isthmus in a day. The tiny fishing villages at either end would become great ports, where the goods of half a continent were transferred from boat to rail and vice-versa. And so the Hotel Darien came into existence, a luxury hotel where top-hatted businessmen could relax, gazing proprietorially out onto the Pacific.

And then, in 1902, while the first cowcatcher was pushing its way through the jungle, news came that the United States had taken over the Panama Canal project. The Hotel Darien did not die immediately: one does not destroy a white elephant if it has been sufficiently expensive to construct. The railway came in due course and though the opening was less spectacular than planned (the President's speech was drowned in a tropical thunderstorm) there was a little light traffic, especially tourists attracted by the idea of travelling through savage country, with a stout pane of glass between them and the alligators. But gradually it degenerated into a jungle local, staggering from village to village, its opulent carriages white with bird-droppings.

Business picked up slightly in the 1920s with the planning of the Pan-American Highway. But even that passed about fifty miles away and only occasional parties deviated to San Antonio, drawn by the legend of the railway or by the few excavated archaeological remains in the area. Gradually the Hotel Darien sank to what seemed its place in the scheme of things, a remote limbo for remittance men, unwanted third sons, minor criminals, all those whose need for solitude was greater than their fear of boredom. And strays from nowhere that anyone had ever heard of, like Bernard Corunna Coote.

Bernard Corunna Coote came to San Antonio in the late summer of 1950, part of a guided tour from Boston. He looked out of place from the beginning, a large man, sweating it out in baggy flannels and tweed coat, with, perched incongruously on his forehead (like a snowcap on a tropical peak), the remains of a cricketer's cap. He stank of drink and had the edgy motions of someone who had not slept for days: black circles were packed under his eyes.

His companions skirted him as they descended from the bus. Only one person showed any interest in his arrival: from his niche under a pillar on the shady side of the square, Hautmoc, the town drunkard, opened an opportunistic eye. When the American matrons chattered off, armed with cameras, in search of the colourful town market, Hautmoc moved in. He found Bernard Corunna Coote sitting on the terrace of the town café, drinking tequila.

'Señor,' he said, with sweeping politeness, 'may I join you?'

When the main party of SUNLITE TOURS returned, Hautmoc and his companion were still deep in conversation. Originally spotted as a soft touch, something in the uneasy bulk of his victim had moved Hautmoc who was busily explaining to him his favourite subject: the ethnological basis of American civilization. His mahogany face, mystical with drink, leaned towards the white man.

'But in the mountains, beyond the Spaniards' reach, the poor people remained,' he oracled. 'They – we – I are still a pure race.'

Coote did not speak, but his eyes flickered interest.

'Spaniards, bah! a decadent syphilitic race from a dead continent, Mexicans, bah! a spawn of half-breeds. The true Indian…'

The SUNLITE TOURS bus was loading in the square. As the negro courier looked over, sounding his klaxon, his passenger ordered another tequila.

'You were saying?' he asked.

'The true Indian, *los hombres de la sierra*, are the aristocrats of this hemisphere, the purest people in the world.'

The courier came towards them, touching his hand to his yellow SUN LITE cap.

'Mr. Coote, we're leaving now, sir.'

Bernard Corunna Coote turned up a watery, but firm, eye.

'I have just discovered the purest people in the western world,' he said in Spanish. 'In such circumstances, one does not leave. *Yo me quedo aquí.*'

As the bus roared from the square, a surprised line of New England matrons saw their late travelling companion and an unknown Indian, their two heads together, roaring with laughter. Between them, like a third party, stood the new bottle of tequila.

'In the old days,' said Hautmoc, with a meaningful gesture toward the bus, 'we would have sacrificed them. A land must be irrigated with blood!'

And thus Bernard Corunna Coote became one of the permanent guests of the Hotel Darien, and as much a feature of the town in his own way as Hautmoc. Daily he padded down to the square for a morning drink, and to collect his mail. According to the postmaster, a quiet student of these matters, most of the letters bore a king's head and came from Inglaterra. But there was also a newspaper bearing the ugliest stamps he had ever seen, a pale hand clutching a phallic sword, and surrounded by what looked like (but was not, as he found when he consulted the dictionary) Old German script. It was all mildly puzzling, and he took the unusual step of being polite to Hautmoc when he next met him, hinting at a free drink if information was forthcoming. But as everyone had long ago agreed, the latter was a cracked vessel, returning little or no sound, except his pet theories about race and human sacrifice.

'I don't know,' he said, screwing his eyes like an animal dragged into the light. '*Es muy difícil*. He says he is from the oldest civilization in Europe, as old as the Indian. But it is not English.'

To the rest of the town he was *el Señor Doctor*, the brooding figure whose place at the café table no one ever took, even on market days. The schoolboy cap had given way to a widebrimmed sun hat, the tweed coat had disappeared, he wore floppy cotton drawers, and rope-soled sandals instead of Oxfords, but they could still recognize a learned man when they saw one. Even if mad: catching those large, watery eyes upon them, the women in the marketplace drew their *rebozos* over their heads and made a gesture of expiation as they bent to ruffle among their baskets of fruit and pottery.

II

The people in a position to know most about el Señor Doctor were those who appeared to care least: the three other permanent guests of the Hotel Darien. The oldest was not really a guest, being the hotel manager, but he had so little work to do (and that little he tended to leave to the servants) that only rarely were his companions reminded of their business relationship with him. A cadaverous Iowan, called Mitchell Witchbourne, his bony features had the asceticism of a Grant Wood painting: one looked behind him, expecting to see a clapboard barn and silo. This impression of weathered starkness was increased by his high-pitched voice. Night and day it creaked, like a weathervane, sending out stories, jokes, hints of what looked like hope and communication, but gradually took on the shrillness of signals of distress. At forty he had been manager of a chain of Midwestern hotels, from Chicago to Colorado: what had brought him, ten years later, to a decaying seaport on the Pacific coast?

No one knew either what had brought Jean Tarrou, the neatly moustached little Frenchman who spoke English with a slurred brokenness which grew more charming each year. A devotee of *la culture physique*, his room was full of mechanical contraptions upon which he practised nightly. (An American matron, hearing the sounds from the adjoining room, had burst indignantly in to find him squatting in black tights on the carpet, one hand held high, the other pointing sideways, a human semaphore. His legs were caught up in pulleys, towards the ceiling, at an angle of forty-five degrees.) Now and again he dropped hints of a distinguished past, a *licence ès-lettres* from the Sorbonne, consular service in the West Indies, but the trail came to an abrupt end with the last war. He had served under Vichy, but did not detest de Gaulle, a paradox which indicated that his troubles were as much private as political. In any case, like most French people, he did not discuss matters with people outside his family circle, even when, as in San Antonio, they were either far away, or nonexistent.

The person about whom most was known was Carlos Turbida, who was still young enough to derive satisfaction from the idea of being a black sheep. The son of a wealthy Mexican fish merchant, his father had retired him from the capital after his third paternity suit (it was not the behaviour he objected to, but the carelessness). Officially, he was in charge of the south-west section of the family fishing fleet, and, once a week, he roared away in his Porsche to the nearby harbour. Tarrou had seen him there, the distinctive olive-green machine parked among the fishing nets while a bored captain pretended to listen, as he strutted up and down the quay. He even cultivated a sailor's walk, but the effect was not so much athletic as sexual: he rolled his hips as though carrying a gun. But generally he lay in bed, eating sweets, reading movie magazines, and dreaming of Acapulco: the perfect portrait of the Latin-American *cicisbeo*.

Their main interest in Coote was mathematical: he made the necessary fourth for most card games, poker, bridge, gin rummy. To endure the silence of a place like San Antonio habit was indispensable. Five evenings a week they played, grouped around a table on the veranda, while the tropical night grew heavy outside, and the Indian waiter came, bringing a lamp, and fresh drinks. At first they played for pesos, but then, disdaining the effort of tossing coins on the baize, they turned to counters, using matchsticks as chips. As the sums involved mounted – from tens they progressed to hundreds and sometimes thousands – even that kind of tally became impossible. So each time the soberest of them (it was usually Tarrou) kept a record. Though their skills were roughly equal, it was necessary, to keep an edge on the game, to believe in some apocalyptic day of reckoning: in the meantime, there was the drug of ritual contest, with memory floating to the surface as the hands were occupied.

'I remember once,' said Turbida, 'driving from Monterey to Mexico City. You know the road?' He raised two fingers to indicate a bid.

'Up, up, up,' said Witchbourne, sawing an imaginary steering wheel. 'Then, down, down, down.' He clutched his stomach.

'I spent the night in a little hotel, high up in the Sierra Madre. In the corridor, outside my room, I see the, how you say, chambermaid. She has long black hair, down her back, a pure Huastecan Indian. As she pass, I take hold of it.'

'I pass,' said Tarrou, and poised his pencil over the white slip of paper at his side.

'Let me go, she cries, let me go. There were tears in her eyes. I say, I let you go, if you come back to stay. That night, I sleep with her six times. She cries again when I leave in the morning. What can you do with silly girls like that?'

'You can only eat them,' said Tarrou, pleasantly.

'I'll see you,' said Coote, hunching his shoulders across the table towards Turbida. The latter laid down his hand calmly: in the heart of his palm two dark queens lay, without embarrassment, beside two smiling red knaves.

'Damn,' said Coote.

There was silence while Tarrou shuffled the cards, laying them (with that pedantic precision he brought to every action) in a neat semi-circle before each man. If Turbida's stories were mainly sexual, his were more frightening, tasteful vignettes of people and places which only gradually revealed, under their smooth surface, an underlying terror.

'It is on that route, if I remember rightly,' he said, 'that the natives bring one glasses of freshly crushed orange juice. The bus stops by the groves just at midnight and the whole air is full of the smell of oranges.'

Both Witchbourne and Coote reached simultaneously for more whiskey.

'But it is not quite as gracious a custom as on the route to Vera Cruz,' he continued. 'There is a little station there, just before the railway descends from the mountains, where the women come, selling camellias laid out in hollow canes, like little coffins. It is only then that one notices that most of the women are crippled: one has no fingers, another no nose, a third a stump instead of a leg.'

'Heredo-syphilis,' said Witchbourne gruffly, 'the Spanish pox. These mountain villages, no water, no medical services, intermarriage: never get rid of it.' His moustaches were bright with whiskey.

'I bid you a hundred pesos.'

'I raise you fifty,' said Turbida excitedly.

As Coote threw in his hand, Tarrou leaned forward, delicately poised as a cat. 'I will raise you both fifty,' he stated. After a further flurry of bids, the others faltered, throwing in their hands. While Tarrou recorded his victory, Witchbourne swept up the cards for the next deal, glancing swiftly at the Frenchman's as he did so: three fours.

Of Witchbourne's conversation there was little to be said: the past for him was a devastated territory, a no-man's-land, through which he wandered, picking up fragments. Hardly anything he said could be added to anything else, the only recurrent factor being his practice of ending the evening by telling a joke. And his favourite was the story of *The Vicar and his Ass*. When he began, everyone tensed, assuming stares of interest, like executives on a board meeting.

'There was a parish in the mountains where the people had a long way to go to church. So they all went on their asses, and to pass the time, they played games, the boys pinching the girls' asses and the girls' asses biting the boys' asses. Then they tethered all the asses at the church door. One day during the revolution, a bomb fell in the graveyard. In the confusion, everyone jumped through the windows, the boys falling on the girls' asses, the girls on the boys' asses. As to the vicar, he missed his ass altogether and fell in the bomb hole. Which goes to show...' Witchbourne paused dramatically. Tarrou and Turbida seemed frozen, their features pale with insulted sensibility. Only Coote, who was hearing the story for the first time, gave the necessary prompt.

'What?' he asked.

'That the Vicar did not know his ass from a hole in the ground,' said Mitchell Witchbourne with satisfaction. As the waves of unease spread around the table, he gathered up the cards and rose to his feet. 'Beddy bye,' he said softly, disappearing off into the darkness. The others looked at each other with the expression of people who did not know what to think, and did not dare ask.

*

It was in this atmosphere – a harmony woven of night sounds: the warm darkness beyond the veranda, the tinkle of ice-cubes, the rise and fall of voices – that Bernard Corunna Coote felt impelled to his first confession. Having drunk more than usual one night, he announced, with sudden confidential exactness: 'I am a renegade Protestant!'

There was silence for a moment. Then Witchbourne, who was dealing, flicked an eyebrow upwards. 'Ach so,' he said, in guttural parody.

'We have few Protestants in Central America, as a such,' said Turbida. 'They do not seem to go with the climate.'

'You do not understand,' said Coote, beating the table with his glass. 'I am a renegade Ulster Protestant.'

'I have heard of the Huguenots,' said Tarrou politely. 'And, of course, the Hussites and Lutherans. But I do not know of your sect: is it interesting, perhaps, like the Catharists or Boggomils – Eros rather than Agape?'

'You still do not understand,' said Coote fiercely. 'I am a renegade Ulster Presbyterian; an Orangeman!'

'Ah, a regional form of Calvinism,' said Tarrou sweetly. 'We have had that too: the Jansenists of Port-Royal. But you should not let it worry you.' He studied his cards carefully before raising three fingers. 'Catholics, Protestants, Communists, *nous sommes tous des assassins*.'

A silence fell, heavy as the night outside. It was broken by the sound of Bernard Corunna Coote weeping: one tear fell, with a distinct plop, into his whiskey glass. His large head, flabby with drink, runnelled with tears, looked like a flayed vegetable marrow. The game continued.

After this rash beginning, Bernard Corunna Coote learned to offer his confidences with the same casualness as he played his cards. And though (unlike the latter) they lay without immediate comment, he knew that they were being picked up, one by one, gestures towards a portrait. Assembled, they made what Tarrou once smilingly called

Le Petite Testament de Bernard Corunna Coote.

Bernard Corunna Coote came from a distinguished Ulster family, descendants of Captain William Coote, who was rewarded for his skilful butchery in the Cromwellian campaign with a large grant of Papish land. Industrious in peace as war, he was the founder and first Provost of Laganbridge: an equestrian statue (brave, beetle-browed, a minor hammer of the Lord) still stands in the town square, on the site of an old palace of the O'Neills.

The family seat, however, was at Castlecoote, overlooking the river. At first, little more than a four-square grey farmhouse or 'Bawn' (fortified to prevent the sorties of dispossessed Catholic neighbours), it was redesigned by John Nash in 1755. As they watched the new building rise – the doorways flanked with fluted Doric columns, the noble rooms with elliptical designs on the ceilings, the terraces diminishing to the river – something seemed to happen to the family features. ('You could see it in the portraits,' said Bernard Corunna Coote, 'they felt easier, less predatory, more secure.')

In this handsome Georgian building, generations of Cootes grew up, the eldest managing the estate (and generally the county as well, being Grand Master of the Orange Lodge), the younger going into colonial service, the daughters marrying other Plantation squires, their equals in land and religion. The only break in this pattern came when war broke out: then, as one man, they rushed to the side of the King. Hardheaded, with the bravery of the Irish, but more sense, they made magnificent soldiers, especially when commanding a regiment of their own tenants. A Coote had led the crucial charge at Corunna, a Coote had been aide-de-camp to Wellington, a Coote had led the Ulster division on the Somme. Whenever the Empire was in danger, a Coote would take command, looking at the battlefield as though it were a few hundred acres of his own land and say, with a brisk return to the vernacular: 'WULL DRIVE THIM THRU THERE!'

To this tradition, compounded of the sword and the ploughshare, was born a son, Bernard Corunna Coote, a sore disappointment. His whole career seemed a demonstration of the principle of cultural reversion, i.e. the invasion of the conqueror by the culture of the conquered. His childhood was spent listening to old Ma Finnegan, the Catholic tenant in the lodge gate: she taught him the Rosary in Irish and the tests for entering the Fianna. His holidays from public school were spent roaming the hills in a kilt, with an Irish wolfhound at his heels. From these walks sprang his vocation: in his third year at Oxford he announced that he was going to be an archaeologist, an expert on the horned cairns of the Carlingford culture, the burial places of the chieftains of Uladh.

He was on a field trip, deciphering standing stones in the Highlands of Donegal, when war broke out in September 1939. Bernard Corunna Coote could no longer resist family tradition: he joined as a volunteer in the North Irish Horse and fought in both the African and Sicilian campaigns. But though he acquitted himself well (whatever else, he was no coward), the contrast between how he regarded himself and what was happening to him became too much to bear. The first his parents heard of it was when he was reported as refusing a decoration 'on the grounds that he did not recognize the present King of England'. A campaign for the use of Gaelic in Irish regiments also brought comment, coinciding as it did with the preparations for D-Day. Invalided out of the army in 1944, he did not (at his father's request) return to Castlecoote. After rattling around Dublin for a few years, he disappeared to America.

III

From these confidences, delivered so haltingly, heard so calmly, Bernard Corunna Coote received the peculiar form of comfort which was the secret of the Hotel Darien. His companions spoke rarely of what he had said (the only direct comment was Tarrou's puzzled remark that he did not see what all this had to do with religion), but he knew that it had been heard and, if not understood, accepted. He became one of the members of an invisible club, an enclosed order whose purpose was not so much contemplative as protective: behind these walls they seemed to say, you are safe, all things are equal, you may live as you like. He no longer sought Hautmoc (Lord High Muck, Witchbourne scornfully called him, his name being that of the last Aztec chieftain who tried to propitiate Cortez by a mass sacrifice) for long conferences, though Witchbourne still watched him from behind the pillars of the arcade as he went to collect his letters. Apart from that morning stroll, he had been assimilated into the world of the hotel.

It was some months, however, before he was introduced to the second ritual of the permanent residents: the visit to the town whorehouse.

Every Sunday afternoon, led by Mitchell Witchbourne, dazzlingly spruce in white ducks and embroidered shirt, they made their way to an old colonial house at the other end of the town. This spacious building belonged to Dona Anna, a mestizo matron whom Witchbourne – remembering some comic strip of his youth about an orphan girl – had nicknamed Obsidian Annie. She was not really an orphan, but the widow of an officer who had taken the wrong side in the Revolution. Finding herself stranded in San Antonio, she had applied her strong, practical nature to developing the primitive prostitution system of the area – the famous 'double-baths' of festival days – into a regular business. Under her care she had usually about half a dozen young ladies, ranging from sixteen to thirty, with the dusky, almost negroid beauty of the women of the peninsula.

Events at the Casa Anna always followed a definite order, the decorum of Sunday blending with the lady's desire to do her best for her most monied visitors. First, the girls appeared, wearing their holiday best, long flounced skirts, embroidered lace *huipls* or bodices, and heavy ear-rings made out of United States gold pieces. Dona Anna, of course, being one of *los correctos*, the people of good standing, wore a stiff dress of dark Spanish silk, to distinguish herself from such peasant finery.

They all had a social drink together while the men made their choice (there was usually a new recruit to spice routine). Then they withdrew to their rooms where, beside each *palias* stood the inevitable bottle of tequila. Through the long afternoon everyone loved or drank or watched through the windows the boys shinning the banana trees, like insects on a grass blade. Now and again there was a satisfying plop! as one fell into the undergrowth.

It seemed a good life.

As darkness gathered, everyone came together again for the evening meal. This took place in the dining hall, the largest room in the house, with fortress-like doors opening on to the patio. At the head of the table presided Obsidian Annie, a clapper by her side to summon the two white-coated Indian house boys. As the food piled higher (local delicacies like turtle eggs, or iguana roe, with purple yams and papayas), a kind of wild gaiety seized them, the girls shrieking as the men pinched them through their thin finery. Even Obsidian Annie relaxed her vigilant decorum, growing nostalgic as she drank from the stone jar of fresh *pulque* at her side. Tears trickled down her thick make-up as she remembered the days when she had been a young girl, the great days before the Revolution: Obsidian Annie was not a democrat.

'And on Sunday we all rode together in Chapultepec Park. Oh, you should have seen us, the girls sitting side-saddle, wearing black hats and skirts, and lovely Spanish leather boots. And the men, with their silver buttons and braids, in the *charro* style, as handsome as Cortez!'

It seemed a more than good life.

*

The delay in introducing Bernard Corunna Coote to the second ritual of the Hotel Darien was cautionary: they feared that the same forces which had pushed him to total confession would push him further, and that they would lose a hard-won recruit. But they need not have worried; he and Dona Anna got on together like a house on fire. Previously it had been Tarrou who had been her favourite, as coming closest to her aristocratic ideal; in moments of tenderness she called him Maximilian, remembering the blond prince who had tried to bring French civilization to her country.

But between a suave member of the middle-class and something approaching the real thing, there was no question. In clasping Bernard Corunna Coote to her firmly corseted bosom, she clasped her own youth, a bloated version of the *caballeros* who had escorted her through Chapultepec Park. And from her flatteringly warm embrace (a blend of fustian and volcano), he seemed to extract a maternal solace.

True, he had bouts of restlessness, but they were the 'thick head' of the novice, rather than real rebellion. Whenever he sulked, refusing to come to the banquets by which she set such store, she went to fetch him. Soon they were drinking and singing together, he calling her 'his favourite g-e-l' and teaching her the songs of the Continental Irish brigade:

> On Ramillies field we were forced to yield
> Before the clash of Clare's Dragoons

The only person upset by this arrangement was Tarrou, who discovered in himself vestiges of a jealousy he thought extinct. But having given up life *as a such* (to use Turbida's phrase), why quarrel with one aspect of it? His wit grew more strained, his stories more silkily sadistic, but his ill-humour did not seem to threaten the equilibrium of their communal life. Not, at least, until the night of the May Festival, several months later.

205

For the members of the Hotel Darien, the May Festival was the major trial of the year, the one day when the town broke in on their consciousness with an usurping rattle and roar. A famous local patriot had said that a Revolution should be as gay as a Carnival: in his memory, San Antonio made its carnivals as violent as revolutions. From the tolling of the cathedral bell in the morning, through the Blessing of the Goats at midday, to the processions in the evening and the Grand Ball at night, it was one long orgy of noise. Indians in gaudy finery pressed through the street, shouting and waving banners: by nightfall most of them were roaring drunk, challenging all-comers with their machetes.

In previous years the inhabitants of the hotel had made half-hearted attempts to join in the fun. But they could never relax or feel at home, the locals parting before them as they came to the wooden beer canteens in the square, their connoisseur's interest in the blind flute-player turned to mockery as they passed, the local matrons parting with relief from their embrace in the dance tent, with its flaring gasoline lamps. As they left, they heard the music spring up again, its vitality underlining their isolation:

> Woman is an apple
> Ripe upon a tree –
> He who least expects it
> May have her beauty free;
> And I pray to San Antonio
> *That it may be me*!

Their object became to close it out of their consciousness. They could not go to Dona Anna's establishment because (cupidity getting the better of her aristocratic inclinations), it was full of drunken Indians. Neither could they relax in the garden or on the terrace: the noise was too great. So they remained indoors, with all the windows and doors locked. But the heat became so intense that they felt they were drowning. Even under the fans there was no relief, the metal wings only stirring the thick air.

By nightfall they had gathered in the hotel lounge, in the vague hope of playing their customary game. But they were all drunk, with that peculiar restlessness, that draining of energy which a day's drinking brings. Together with a nervous irritation: Tarrou's voice was razor-sharp with menace.

'Shall we begin now?' he asked, for the third time.

No one spoke. There was a burst of cheering that made the windows rattle. A firework rose in the air, broke and fell, illuminating the room with a sudden glow.

'Shall we begin?' said Tarrou again, rapping the deck of cards on the table.

Still no one spoke. Another firework climbed within the square of the window. Coote watched it moodily: he felt isolated from the others and had the impression he was missing something.

'I see you are impressed by our peasant customs,' said Tarrou, with acidity.

'They do make a lot of noise,' Witchbourne interposed.

'You are not the only one, of course,' continued Tarrou. 'Dona Anna also likes them, although she pretends not to. It is easier to impress peasants.'

'But not so much noise as some city people do,' said Turbida, hastily joining Witchbourne's rescue operations. 'There is a rough night-club behind the Reforma where as soon as the girls appear everyone shouts . . . ' He expired in giggling lecherousness.

But Tarrou was not to be cheated of his prey so easily.

'The noisiest night-club I ever knew was on the borders of the Goutte d'Or district in Paris: you know, the Arab quarter. There was a fat Algerian tout there, a sort of barker. Now that I come to think of it, he resembled our friend there...' He gestured towards Coote, who shifted slightly in his chair. Like an animal entering a slaughterhouse, sensing the glint of steel hooks, he was becoming aware of the menace directed towards him.

'The only time there was silence in that club was during the act involving the Siamese twins. Some day I must tell you about that.'

'Some day,' said Witchbourne, gruffly.

'I remember—' said Turbida again.

'But the Siamese twins, though an interesting act, lacked the simplicity, the imaginative daring of the barker's own speciality. I have told you he was an Arab. He wore a long flowing burnous: at first I thought it was for local colour. But at the end of the evening, he removed it, slowly. It was only then that one realized – *on le soupçonne toujours d'ailleurs, avec les types gros comme ça...*'

'What?' asked Turbida, in spite of himself.

207

'That he was a woman. A big, fat, ugly, aged woman.'

There was silence. Mitchell Witchbourne's face was white. But it was Coote who spoke, finally, dragging his great bulk up.

'You go too far,' he said raspingly. 'Even in hell there are limits.'

IV

Happiness is a balance, precariously maintained: to achieve even its semblance requires training. While the others, with instincts geared to survival, swept the incident aside, Bernard Corunna Coote clearly could not. For days he avoided the hotel and news drifted back that he had been seen drinking with Hautmoc. After a while, he began coming again to meals, but when Witchbourne ostentatiously produced the card table he disappeared, and they heard him crunching down the avenue towards the town. He did not even return to the Casa Anna, though Obsidian Annie inquired after him, saying that she had seen him (again with Hautmoc) at the local café. It was agreed that Tarrou should speak to him. One night, as Coote was ploughing back through the darkness, the slim Frenchman presented himself at the door, his cold eyes taking – but not returning – the latter's surprised glare.

'We do not see you now,' he said pleasantly.

Coote did not answer, all his efforts absorbed in the task of breathing. But he moved forward as though to brush past Tarrou.

'Why do you not join us in the evenings any more?'

Coote stopped. 'You know why.'

'*Mais, mon ami,*' Tarrou spread his hands, gently. 'These things are unimportant. *Dans l'ivresse, comme dans l'amour, il faut tout pardonner.*'

Coote looked at him for a long time, and his eyes seemed to clear in the hallway light. Then he moved forward again, resolutely.

'May mwah, jenny pooh pah,' he said, in his harsh Ulster accent.

For his former companions of the Hotel Darien, however, no answer was final. They did not begin to despair of him even when he disappeared on his first 'expedition'. It looked so harmless, a large man with a morning-after face and stubble, going off into the jungle by himself, carrying a hammer. And the bag of samples he brought back, examining them for hours on the terrace, were like the coloured beads a child might play with. But when instruments and books began to arrive at the post office and the day's wanderings spread into weeks, they began to be alarmed: in the organized quality of these frenzies, they recognized an alien discipline. Swallowing his pride, Witchbourne went out of his way to speak to Hautmoc, and inquired as to their purpose. The latter graciously accepted the drink offered him, but was far from helpful.

'He is looking for something we have both lost,' he said mysteriously.

*

Smith & Wesson in one hand, machete in the other, his T-shirt moist with sweat (except where the great raft of the sun hat kept a circle of white about his shoulders) he beat his way through the jungle around San Antonio. Behind him followed a retinue of peons, tangle-haired, liquid-eyed, carrying the inevitable burden of impedimenta. With their slow pace, their resigned gestures, they seemed less like human beings than like a column of ants, winding its way patiently over and around obstacles.

Even the rainy season did not halt him, physical obstacles being only a drum-call to the military ardours of his ancestry. Coming to a flood-swollen river, he would plunge in, his weapons held high above his head: sometimes only the hand and the round circle of the hat could be seen as he sidestroked heavily across. If there was a current he would float with it, until he struck an outcrop. Then, like Excalibur, he broke to the surface and trampled ashore, water dripping from his bulk, as though down the side of a mountain. By the time his followers had crossed (going to a village for the loan of a pirogue, or wading downstream until they found a fording place) he had already blazed a trail into the pelvic rankness of the jungle on the other side.

What the Indians thought of their master – a comic gringo if ever there was one – was at first tactfully submerged in the fact that he paid well. Sufficiently well for them to want to humour him when, following some atavistic memory of a Victorian jungle trek, he insisted that they should carry their own packs and leave their burros behind. But as the months passed, something of his anxiety was communicated to them: just as they sped with eagerness on his errands, so they watched with increasing concern his disappointment as he turned over the stones they had brought. A man, they knew from their own lives, could bear only so much misfortune: in Bernard Corunna Coote's case they felt that some incongruous struggle was going on, an almost physical rending, as though a blind man were trying to see, or a cripple to walk.

Sometimes he would stop short in his tracks, as if struck by a blow from behind. The pale blue eyes would glaze and turn inwards, the shoulders hunch, until he looked like the oldest of earth's creatures, some grey mammoth embedded in ice or rock. And the cry that he gave, low at first, rose till it seemed beyond human pitch, a trumpeting that tore the heart with its animal abandon.

*

It was after one of these outbreaks (dutifully reported by the servants), that the inhabitants of the Hotel Darien decided that a last effort should be made to save Bernard Corunna Coote for themselves. For, to their surprise, they had discovered that they needed him. From selfish exasperation at the loss of a necessary companion, they had passed to real concern, and an emotion that only their long habits of reticence refused to recognize as love. It was as though their bluff had been called, and the suffering they had gradually relegated to the background of their own lives had suddenly reappeared before them, monstrous, dishevelled, wringing its hands.

But what was to be done? They had a formal meeting in the hotel lounge ('the scene of the crime' as Turbida said brightly, before Tarrou's coldly speculative eye fell upon him) to discuss the situation. Tarrou's attempt to apologize had failed. Witchbourne's efforts to elicit information from Hautmoc had been fruitless. There remained Turbida, the soiled innocent of the party, whom no one would ever suspect of any serious motive. Witchbourne's mild eye joined Tarrou's in resting upon him. Turbida must find out what Bernard Corunna Coote thought he was doing.

The opportunity came a few days later when Coote returned from a long absence in the jungle. He looked more exhausted than ever, with a rough growth of beard and a tear in his trousers which exposed long thin legs. But he did not seem surprised to find Turbida in his room, his expansive shape splayed over a cane chair.

'Good day—?' the latter asked, with the upward inflection of the hunting classes.

Bernard Corunna Coote snorted, but did not answer. After depositing a sack in a corner, he dragged off his clothes, and stepped under the shower. Through the yellow curtain Turbida could see his body, a whale under water.

'I have been looking at your books,' shouted Turbida, lifting up a volume, with a large painting of a pyramid on the cover.

Still no answer. The shower sank, a hand groped for a towel: Bernard Corunna Coote emerged, clean, spiky-haired, decently clothed in white.

'Interesting chaps, these Aztecs, when you get right down to it,' continued Turbida, turning the pages. 'Place like Monte Alban now, makes you think…'

Coote stopped pummelling himself. 'You have been to Monte Alban?' he asked incredulously.

'Why, yes,' said Turbida, trying desperately to remember the illustrations Tarrou had shown him, 'and to Mitla too.'

'Did you see the scrollwork at Mitla? The cruciform chambers?'

'Yes, yes…' encored Turbida.

'The spiral and lozenge pattern are the same as at Newgrange. It was a characteristic of the race, the delight in abstract pattern. But we were a thousand years before.'

Turbida was about to inquire where Newgrange was when he saw that Coote was no longer listening to him, his face contorted with fury and anguish.

'Think of it! When Cortez and his Spaniards came, they found the Maltese cross, and the Indians spoke of strange white men. Certainly it was Brendan—'

'Brendan?' echoed Turbida.

'Saint Brendan who discovered America. But what about even earlier? We know that the Celts were a widely dispersed people: traces of them have been found in Sardinia, Galicia, the valley of the Dordogne. We are the secret mother race of Europe. But if . . . ' He halted, as though transfixed by the daring of his thought.

'If,' prompted Turbida.

'We could prove that the Celts not merely discovered but founded America! Think of it—' He brought his face close to that of Turbida, who could smell the furnace blast of cheap spirits.

'Then, for the first time, the two halves of the world would fit together, into one, great, universal Celtic civilization.' He raised his arms high, then let them fall slowly again. 'All I need is a proof.'

'Like what?' asked Turbida in a hushed voice.

'Oh, there are minor ones. Character, for example. Hautmoc says that the original Indians were the purest race in the western hemisphere: we still place a great emphasis on purity. And physique; remember the beard-

ed statues of La Venta?' He tugged his own beard vehemently, to empha-
size each word. 'After us, there were no bearded men in South America.'

'But a major proof?'

Coote seemed to hesitate. It was months since he had spoken to anyone: should he now reveal his hopes to a comparative stranger? Only the
music of international renown could heal several generations of outraged
tradition: here, in San Antonio, Bernard Corunna Coote was staging his
last fight to restore himself not merely to his family, but to the whole history of human knowledge.

'I told you once of the cairns of Carlingford and the Boyne, the burial places of our early chieftains. From the decorative motifs I deduce a
connection between them and the pyramids of the lost civilizations of
Central America. But the pyramids, according to Hautmoc, were designed
for human sacrifice only, and not for ritual interment. If I could find...'

He hesitated again, drew a deep breath.

'Somewhere, in the most remote areas, probably in the thick of the
jungle, there must be traces of those earlier structures upon which Monte
Alban, Palenque, Chichen Itzi, were based. If I could find one single passage grave or burial chamber...'

'Like what?' asked Turbida again.

'Like this!' cried Bernard Corunna Coote, seizing and opening a large
green volume. 'Look!'

*

Carlos Turbida was still trembling when he joined the others an hour
later.

'But the man is mad,' he cried plaintively.

'The question is irrelevant,' said Witchbourne, with unaccustomed
severity. 'Which of us is even half sane?' His gaze swept across his companions, like a searchlight across rocky ground.

'Still, it is strange,' said Tarrou. 'I was sure he was cured. Who would
have thought the irrelevant could have such deep roots?'

'But nothing can be done. It is too late...' wailed Turbida again.

'It is never too late,' said Witchbourne sententiously. 'While there's
life there's hope. What do you think, Tarrou?'

'I think,' said Tarrou, 'that the time has come for our famous reckoning.' From his pocket he produced a sheaf of white dockets, neatly bound
with rubber: he ruffled it under their noses.

'A sum of money is always useful,' agreed Witchbourne.

'But then, what will you do?' asked Turbida.

Tarrou shrugged. 'We shall see. I will perhaps go and talk to our noble friend, Lord High Muck.'

'But what about?'

'About literature,' smiled Tarrou. 'Where is that book you say Coote gave you ?'

V

The rainy season passed. The mouth of the San Antonio River was no longer choked by floating vegetation, and the long dugout canoes could sail directly up to the market place. The mountain paths had dried and the peasants came down to the village in ox-carts, lined with layers of crushed sugar-cane. The few meagre crops were to be harvested, maize, sesame seeds, beans. Soon the first tourist bus would turn into the square, to halt for an hour or so before continuing its journey southward.

It was on the anniversary of their first meeting that Hautmoc came to Bernard Corunna Coote with unexpected news. The latter was sitting at his accustomed place on the terrace: he had not been on trek for over a week, and looked more than usually morose, his shoulders slouched over the café table. Behind him hovered the proprietor, fearful not that he would attack anyone (despite his noise, the gross foreigner was surprisingly gentle, not like the common-class of Indians who broke loose with their machetes when drunk) but that he should do himself harm: the day before he had fallen on his way to the lavatory. Now and again, from that seemingly quiescent mound of flesh, a hand would emerge, and grope around the table for the bottle which was poured, with many whistling sighs and groans, in and around his glass.

It was then that Hautmoc appeared on the far side of the square near the post-office. It was hard to miss him because, after several months of unaccustomed prosperity, he had deserted his trampish practices and dressed as befitted a descendant of kings, with an elegant *serape*, slashed in scarlet and black, and a white sombrero. Moreover he was walking briskly, almost running, with an abandon that surprised Bernard Corunna Coote, who had been talking to him only the night before. He came directly to the café table, but did not sit down, gazing at his friend and employer with a kind of tranced look:

'Master,' he said solemnly, 'we may have news.'

Bernard Corunna Coote stirred uneasily. 'What do you mean, you may have news?' he grated.

Hautmoc looked over his shoulder, towards the café owner, indicating that he did not feel free to speak. 'We may have important news,' he said.

With an effort, Coote threw out his arm towards the chair opposite him. 'Sit down and have a drink.'

'There is no time,' said Hautmoc, slowly. Then he leaned his head swiftly down towards the other's sunken face, and whispered into his ear: 'We have found what you were looking for.'

Bernard Corunna Coote started. Did Hautmoc know what he was saying? Like the shepherd boy suddenly face to face with the wolf, like the alchemist seeing a yellow liquid condense in his crucible, he gazed at him, slowly believing his eyes.

'Where ?' he asked, rising from the table, his face aglow.

*

The sun was low in the sky on their second day's march when they reached the area indicated by Hautmoc. It lay near the source of the San Antonio River, a region Coote had rarely explored, believing it already well known to the natives. But perhaps he had been wrong to ignore it: after all, river-beds were the traditional centres of civilization. But so high up? For hours they had climbed up the mountainside, through the thick forest of the lower slopes, where springs made the ground soggy and treacherous. Then they crossed a belt of shale and rock, where the river sank to a trickle, and they found animal skeletons bleaching in the sun. Finally, towards evening, they emerged onto a small plateau, set, like a shelf, against the steep incline.

A light wind was blowing. Below them, the valley fell away, a matted sea of vegetation, divided by the thin line of the river. There was no sign of a living thing, the smoke from the occasional village or clearing being absorbed in the transparent mist that lay above the trees. At the limit of their view the sun was sinking, like a coal at the heart of a dying fire.

'Is this the place?' said Bernard Corunna Coote, impatiently.

After easing off their packs, the Indians had gathered around him and Hautmoc, as though waiting for an order. The latter did not answer, but remained looking out, in melodramatic serenity.

'Is this the place?' asked Coote again. 'Where is it, or what is it called?'

'It is called Coatlicue,' said Hautmoc seriously. 'It is one of the most ancient of our sacrificial grounds. The people took refuge here during the Conquest. There used to be a temple.'

'But where—' demanded Coote fiercely.

'Behind,' said Hautmoc. Folding his *serape* around him, an elegant figure in scarlet and black, he turned to lead the way.

In his excitement at the view, Bernard Corunna Coote had not yet had time to look behind him. Now, following Hautmoc, he turned. Above them rose a rock face, sheer as a wall, making the area in which they stood seem artificially compact, like an apron stage. The outer edge of the plateau was covered with a hide of tough yellow grass, knotted so close that it made walking difficult. This yielded to a close undergrowth, where lichened boulders lay around like ruins: to Coote's astonishment there was the semblance of a path through it, stained with burro droppings. This lead to a clump of well-watered trees: was it the source of the river? Parting the damp oar-shaped leaves, Bernard Corunna Coote saw an open space ahead, a clearing at the entrance of which Hautmoc and his fellow-Indians had gathered to await him.

In the middle of the clearing stood a group of stones. As he drew closer – scattering the natives to right and left like ninepins – he saw that they formed a shape, the unmistakable humped outline of a tumulus. There were two stones on either side, with a closed passage at the far end. There was the great flagstone, resting on the five stones as smoothly as a table top. The whole thing was symmetrical, textbook perfect, even the dark quiet faces grouped around seemed in harmony – except for one thing. As Coote approached, his foot crushed something in the grass. Whoever had hoisted the flagstone had forgotten to remove the pulley rope. It wound imperceptibly down the crevice between the two nearest side stones until, like a snake, its end struck up at the sole of Coote's sandal.

He stood there, looking from the rope to the construction, and back again. Then he followed the rope to its source, under the top stone, and tugged. The stone shifted, audibly. He stepped back and gazed for a long time, until even the Indians – professionals of the steady gaze – felt uneasy. Their leader came over and touched him on the shoulder but Coote did not move.

'Master,' said Hautmoc gently, 'we meant no harm.'

Coote still did not reply, his eye rolling over the same square of space, like an eager student crazed for an answer.

'We would not have known how to build it, but for Señor Tarrou. He taught us. And Señors Witchbourne and Turbida provided the money for the workers.'

215

Coote looked at him, vaguely. 'But you, why did you do it? You told me you would have nothing to do with them.'

The dark face of the Indian seemed to crease and open, as though reliving a painful decision.

'They' – he pointed to his fellows around – 'did it because they wished to please you. I—' he hesitated.

'Yes?' demanded Coote.

'I did it because – because if the place you are searching for does not exist, then it should. Your dream and mine have much in common.'

Coote looked at his companion for a long time. Then a hint of a smile crossed his face.

'Hautmoc,' he said majestically, 'you are even madder than I am.'

But the other was not listening, his eyes resting fondly on the stones before him. 'There is still one thing lacking to prove us both right,' he said sadly. 'Such stones cry out to be used.'

For a long time Coote's expression did not change, as if he had not heard what Hautmoc had said. Then he straightened, his great back cracking, and looked at the Indians around. They returned his gaze with expectant, admiring eyes, as though his countenance reflected the pure bronze light of the dying solar god. Knowledge passed swiftly across his face, a spasm of lightning.

'I understand,' he said gravely.

Slowly, with the dignity of a military ceremony, he removed his large sun hat. His face was a hunk of meat, fiery red, but above it his bald head shone, the whitest thing they had ever seen. He stepped briskly forward, the Indians falling in line behind him. When he came to the passage grave he marched straight in, leaving them to file to one side, where the loose rope dangled.

'Pull,' he ordered, settling himself in the trough of red clay.

As he waited for the heavens to fall, his countenance became relaxed and pure, all provincial crudity refined to a patrician elegance, the ripe intensity of a soldier leader born of two great traditions. Softly on fields of history, Ramillies and El Alamein, Cremona and the Somme, the warpipes began to grieve. Closing ranks, silent regiments listened, Connaught Rangers and Clare's Dragoons, Dublin and Inniskilling Fusiliers, North Irish Horse and Sarsfield's Brigade. The stone started to creak.

'After all, it is a good way for a chieftain to die,' he thought contentedly.

216

PART V

17

An Occasion of Sin

About ten miles south of Dublin, not far from Blackrock, there is a small bathing place. You turn down a side road, cross a railway bridge, and there, below the wall, is a little bay with a pier running out into the sea on the left. The water is not deep, but much calmer and warmer than at many points further along the coast. When the tide comes in, it covers the expanse of green rocks on the right, lifting the seaweed like long hair. At its highest, one can dive from the ledge of the Martello Tower, which stands partly concealed between the pier and the sea wall.

Françoise O'Meara began coming there shortly after Easter of '56. A chubby, open-faced girl, at ease with herself and the world, she had arrived from France only six months before, after her marriage. At first she hated it: the damp mists of November seemed to eat into her spirit; but she kept quiet, for her husband's sake. And when winter began to wear into spring, and the days grew softer, she felt her heart expand; it was as simple as that.

Early in the new year, her husband bought her a car, to help her pass the time when he was at the office. It was nothing much, an old '47 Austin, with wide running boards, and a rust-streaked roof, but she cleaned and polished it till it shone. With it, she explored all the little villages around Dublin: Delgany, where a pack of beagles came streaming across the road; Howth, where she wandered for hours along the cliffs;

the roads above Rathfarnham. And Seacove, where she came to bathe as soon as her husband would allow her.

'But nobody bathes at this time of the year,' he said in astonishment, 'except the madmen at the Forty Foot!'

'But I want to!' she cried. 'What does it matter what people do? I won't melt!'

She stretched her arms wide as she spoke, and he had to admit that she didn't look as if she would; her breasts pushing her blouse, her stocky, firm hips, her wide grey eyes – he had never seen anyone look so positive in his life.

At first it was marvellous being on her own, feeling the icy shock of the water as she plunged in. It brought back a period of her childhood, spent at Etretat, on the Normandy coast: she had bathed through November, running along the deserted beach afterwards, the water drying on her body in the sharp wind. She doubted if she could do that at Seacove, but she found a corner of the wall which trapped whatever sun there was, and when the rain spat she went into the Martello Tower Café and had a bar of chocolate and a cup of tea. Sometimes it was so cold that her skin was goose-pimpled, but she loved it all; she felt she had never been so completely alive.

It was mid-May before anyone joined her along the sea wall. The earliest comer was a small fat man, who unpeeled to show a paunch carpeted with white hair. He waved to her before diving off the pier head, and trundling straight out to sea. When he came back, his face was lobster-red with exertion, and he pummelled himself savagely with a towel. He had surprisingly small, almost dainty feet, she noticed, as he danced up and down on the stones, blowing a white column of breath into the air. As he left, he always gave her a friendly wink or called (his words swallowed by the wind): 'That beats Banagher!'

She liked him a lot. She didn't feel as much at ease with the others. An English couple came down from the Stella Maris boarding house to eat a picnic lunch and read the *Daily Express*. Though sitting side by side, they rarely spoke, casting mournful glances at the sky which, even at its brightest, always had a faintly threatening aspect, like a chemical solution on the point of precipitation. And more and more local men came, mainly on bicycles. They swung to a halt along the sea wall, removing the clips from their trousers, removing their togs from the carrier, and tramping purposefully down towards the sea. One of them, who looked like a clerk (lean, bespectacled, his mouth cut into his face), carried equipment for underwater fishing, goggles, flippers and spear.

What troubled her was their method of undressing: she had never seen anything like it. First they spread a paper on the ground. Upon this they squatted, slowly unpeeling their outer garments. When they were down to shirt and trousers, they took a swift look round, and then gave a kind of convulsive wriggle, so that the lower half of the trousers hung limply. There was a brief glimpse of white before a towel was wrapped across the loins; gradually the full length of the trousers unwound, in a series of convulsive shudders. A further lunge and the togs went sliding up the thighs, until they struck the outcrop of the hipbone. A second look round, a swift pull of the towel with the left hand, a jerk of the togs with the right, and the job was done. Or nearly: creaking to their feet, they pulled their thigh-length shirts over their heads to reveal pallid torsoes.

At the beginning, this procedure amused her: it looked like a comedy sequence, especially as it had to be performed in reverse when they came out of the water. But then it began to worry her: why were they doing it? Was it because there were women present? But there were none apart from the Englishman's wife, who sat gazing out to sea, munching her sandwiches, and herself. But she had seen men undressing on beaches ever since she was a child and hardly even noticed it. In any case, the division of the human race into male and female was an interesting fact with which she had come to terms long ago: she did not need to have her attention called to it in such an extraordinary way.

What troubled her even more was the way they watched her when she was undressing. She usually had her togs on under her dress; when she hadn't, she sat on the edge of the sea wall, sliding the bathing suit swiftly up her body, before jumping down to pull the dress over her head: the speed and cleanness of the motion pleased her. But as she lifted the straps over her back she could feel eyes on her every move: she felt like an animal in a cage. And it was not either curiosity or admiration, because when she raised her eyes, they all looked swiftly away. The man with the goggles was the worst: she caught him gazing at her avidly, the black band pushed up around his ears, like a racing motorist. She smiled to cover her embarrassment but, to her surprise, he turned his head, with an angry snap. What was wrong with her?

221

Because there was something: it just wasn't right, and she wanted to leave. She mentioned her doubts to her husband, who laughed and then grew thoughtful.

'You're not very sympathetic,' he pointed out. 'After all, this is a cold country. People are not used to the sun.'

'Rubbish,' she replied. 'It's as warm as Normandy. It's something more than that.'

'Maybe it's just modesty.'

'Then why do they look at me like that? They're as lecherous as troopers but they won't admit it.'

'You don't understand,' he retreated.

*

It was mid-June when the clerical students appeared at Seacove. They came along the coast road from Dun Laoghaire on bicycles, black as a flock of crows. Their coats flapped in the sea-wind as they tried to pass each other out, rising on the pedals. Then they curved down the side-road towards the Martello Tower, where they piled their machines into the wooden racks, solemn-looking Raleighs and low-handled Hercules racers.

When they reappeared, some of them had started undressing, taking off their coats and hard clerical collars as they came. Most already had their togs on, stepping out of their trousers on the beach, to create a huddle of identical black clothes. The others undressed in a group under the shadow of the sea wall, and then came racing down; together they trooped towards the pierhead.

For the next quarter of an hour the sea was teeming with them, dense as a shoal of mackerel. They plunged, they plashed, they turned upside down. One who was timid kept retreating to the shallow water, but two others stole up and ducked him vigorously, only to be buffeted, from behind, in their turn. The surface of the water was cut into clouds of spray. Far out the arms of the three strongest swimmers flashed, in a race to the lighthouse point.

When they came out of the sea to dry and lie down, they generally found a space cleared around their clothes, the people having withdrawn to give them more room. But the clerical students did not seem to observe, or mind, plumping themselves down in whatever space offered. One or two had brought books, but the majority lay on their backs, talking and laughing. At first their chatter disturbed Françoise from the novel

222

she was reading, but it soon sank into her consciousness, like a litany.

'Father Dargan says that a strong swimmer should make the light-house point in ten minutes.'

'But Pius always had a great cult of the Virgin. They say he saw her in the Vatican gardens.'

'If Carlow had banged in that penalty, they'd be in the final Sunday.'

'Father Conroy says that after the second year in the bush you nearly forget home exists.'

While she was amused by their energy, Françoise would probably not have spoken to them, but for the accident of falling asleep one day, a yellow edition of Mauriac lying across her stomach. When she awoke, the students were settling around her. It was a warm day, and their usual place near the water had been taken by a group of English families with children, so they looked for the nearest free area. Although they pretended indifference, she could feel a current of curiosity running through them at finding her so close; now and again she caught a shy glance, or a chuckle, as one glanced at another meaningfully. Among their white skins and long shorts, she became suddenly conscious of her gay blue- and red-striped bathing suit, blazing like a flag in the sunshine. And of her already browning legs and arms.

'Is that French you're reading?' said one finally. Just back from a second plunge in the sea, he was towelling himself slowly, shaking drops of water over everyone. He had a coarse, friendly face, covered with blotches, and a shock of carroty hair, which stuck up in wet tufts.

She held up the volume in answer. '*Le Fleuve de Feu*,' she spelled; 'the river of fire, it's one of Mauriac's novels.'

'He's a Catholic writer, isn't he?' said another, with sudden interest. The other turned to look at him, and he flushed brick-red, sitting his ground.

'Well,' she grimaced, remembering certain episodes in the novel, 'he is and he isn't. He's very bleak, in an old-fashioned sort of way. The river of fire is meant to be,' she searched for the words, 'the flood of human passion.'

There was silence for a minute or two. 'Are you French?' said a wondering voice. 'Yes, I am,' she confessed, apologetically, 'but I'm married to an Irishman.'

'We thought you couldn't be from here,' said another voice, triumphantly. Everyone seemed more at ease, now that her national

223

identity had been established. They talked idly for a few minutes before the red-haired boy, who seemed to be in charge, looked at his watch and said it was time to go. They all dressed quickly, and as they sailed along the sea wall on their bicycles (she could only see their heads, like moving targets in a funfair) they waved to her.

'See you tomorrow,' they called gaily.

*

By early July the meetings between Françoise and the students had become a daily affair. As they rode up on their bicycles they would call out to her, 'Hello, Françoise.' And after they bathed, they came clambering up the rocks, to sit around her in a semicircle. Usually the big red-haired boy (called 'Ginger' by his companions) would start the conversation with a staccato demand: 'What part of France are you from?' or, 'Do ye like it here?' but the others soon took over, while he sank back into a satisfied silence, like a dog that had performed an expected trick.

At first the conversation was general: Françoise felt like a teacher as they questioned her about life in Paris. And whatever she told them seemed to take on such an air of unreality, more like a lesson than real life. They liked to hear about the Louvre, or Nôtre Dame, but when she tried to tell them of what she knew best, the student life around the Latin Quarter, their attention slid away. But it was not her fault, because when she questioned them about their own future life (they were going on to the Missions), they were equally vague. It was as though only what related to the present was real, and anything else exotic; unless one was plunged into it, when, of course, it became normal. Such torpidity angered her.

'But wouldn't you like to see Paris?' she exclaimed.

They looked at one another. Yes, they would like to see Paris, and might, some day, on the way back from Africa. But what they really wanted to do was to learn French: all they got was a few lessons a week from Father Dundee.

Another day they spoke of the worker priests. Fresh from the convent, a *jeune fille bien pensante*, Françoise had plunged into social work around the rue Belhomme and the fringes of Montmartre. And she had come to know several of the worker priests. One she knew had fallen in love with a prostitute and had to struggle to save his vocation: she thought him a wonderful man. But her story was received in silence; a

224

world where people did not go to mass, where passion was organized and dangerous, did not exist for them, except as a textbook vision of evil.

'Things must be very lax in France,' said Ginger, rising up. She could have brained him.

Still, she enjoyed their company, and felt quite disappointed whenever (because of examinations or some religious ceremony), they did not show up. And it was not just because they fulfilled a woman's dream to find herself surrounded by admiring men. Totally at ease with her, they offered no calculation of seduction or flattery, except a kind of friendly teasing. It reminded her of when she had played with her brothers (she was the only girl) through the long summer holidays; that their relationship might not seem as innocent to others never crossed her mind.

She was lying on the sea wall after her swim, one afternoon, when she felt a shadow move across her vision. At first she thought it was one of the students, though they had told her the day before that they might not be coming. But no; it was the small fat man who had been one of the first to join her at Seacove. She smiled up at him in welcome, shielding her eyes against the sun. But he did not smile back, sitting down beside her heavily, his usual cheery face set in an attempt at solemnity.

'Missing your little friends today?'

She laughed. 'Yes, a bit,' she confessed. 'I rather like them; they're very pleasant company.'

He remained silent for a moment. 'I'm not sure it's right for you to be talking to them,' he plunged.

She sat up, with a jerk. 'But what do you mean?'

'Lots of people on the beach' – he was obviously uncomfortable – 'are talking.'

'But they're only children!' Her shock was so deep that she was trembling: if such an inoffensive man believed this, what must the others be thinking?

'They're clerical students,' he said stubbornly. 'They're going to be priests.'

'But all the more reason: one can't,' she searched for the word, '*isolate* them.'

'That's not how we see it. You're giving bad example.'

'I'm giving what?'

'Bad example.'

Against her will, she felt tears prick the corners of her eyes.

'Do you believe that?' she asked, attempting to smile.

'I don't know,' he said seriously. 'It's a matter for your conscience. But it's not right for a single girl to be making free with clerical students.'

'But I'm not single!'

It was his turn to be shocked. 'You're a married woman! And you come—'

He did not end the sentence but she knew what he meant.

'Yes, I'm a married woman, and my husband lets me go to the beach on my own, and talk to whoever I like. You see, he trusts me.'

He rose slowly. 'Well, daughter,' he said, with a baffled return to kindliness, 'it's up to yourself. I only wanted to warn you.'

As he padded heavily away, she saw that the whole beach was watching her. This time she did not smile, but stared straight in front of her. There was a procession of yachts making towards Dun Laoghaire harbour, their white sails like butterflies. Turning over, she hid her face against the concrete, and began to cry.

*

But what was she going to do? As she drove back towards Dublin, Françoise was so absorbed that she nearly got into an accident, obeying an ancient reflex to turn on the right into the Georgian street where they lived. An oncoming Ford hooted loudly, and she swung her car up onto the pavement, just in time. She saw her husband's surprised face looking through the window: thank God he was home.

She did not mention the matter, however, until several hours later, when she was no longer as upset as she had been at the beach. And when she did come round to it, she tried to tell it as lightly as possible, hoping to distance it for herself, to see it clearly. But though her husband laughed a little at the beginning, his face became more serious, and she felt her nervousness rising again.

'But what right had he to say that to me?' she burst out, finally.

Kieran O'Meara did not answer, but kept turning the pages of the *Evening Press*.

'What right has anyone to accuse people like that?' she repeated.

'Obviously he thought he was doing the right thing.'

She hesitated. 'But surely you don't think…'

His face became a little red, as he answered. 'No, of course not. But don't deny that in certain circumstances you might be classed as an occasion of sin.'

She sat down with a bump in the armchair, a dishcloth in her hand. At first she felt like laughing, but after repeating the phrase 'an occasion of sin' to herself a few times, she no longer found it funny and felt like crying. Did everyone in this country measure things like this? At a party, a few nights before, one of her husband's friends had solemnly told her that 'sex was the worst sin because it was the most pleasant'. Another had gripped her arm, once, crossing the street: 'Be careful.' 'But you're in danger too!' she laughed, only to hear his answer: 'It's not myself I'm worried about, it's you. I'm in the state of sanctifying grace.' The face of the small fat man swam up before her, full of painful self-righteousness, as he told her she was 'giving bad example'. What in the name of God was he doing in this benighted place?

'Do you find me an occasion of sin?' she said, at last, in a strangled voice.

'It's different for me,' he said, impatiently. 'After all, we're married.'

It came as a complete surprise to him to see her rise from the chair, throw the dishcloth on the table, and vanish from the room. Soon he heard the front door bang, and her feet running down the steps.

*

Hands in the pockets of her white raincoat, Françoise O'Meara strode along the bank of the Grand Canal. There was a thin rain falling, but she ignored it, glad, if anything, of its damp imprint upon her face. Trees swam up to her, out of the haze: a pair of lovers were leaning against one of them, their faces blending. Neither of them had coats; they must be soaked through, but they did not seem to mind.

Well, there was a pair who were enjoying themselves, anyway. But why did they have to choose the dampest place in all Dublin, risking double pneumonia to add to their troubles? What was this instinct to seek darkness and discomfort, rather than the friendly light of day? She remembered the couples lying on the deck of the Holyhead boat when she had come over: she had to stumble over them in order to get down the stairs. It was like night-time in a bombed city, people hiding from the blows of fate; she had never had such a sense of desolation. And then, when she had negotiated the noise and porter stains of the Saloon and got to the

Ladies, she found that the paper was strewn across the floor and that someone had scrawled FUCK CAVAN in lipstick on the mirror.

Her husband had nearly split his sides laughing when she asked what that meant. And yet, despite his education and travel, he was as odd as any of them. From the outside, he looked completely normal, especially when he left for the office in the morning in his neat executive's suit. But inside he was a nest of superstition and stubbornness; it was like living with a Zulu tribesman. It emerged in all kinds of small things: the way he avoided walking under ladders, the way he always blessed himself during thunderstorms, the way he saluted every church he passed, a hand flying from the wheel to his forehead even in the thick of city traffic. And that wasn't the worst. One night she had woken up to see him sitting bolt upright in bed, his face tense and white.

'Do you hear it?' he managed to say.

Faintly, borne on the wind, she heard a crying sound, a sort of wail. It sounded weird all right, but it was probably only some animal locked out, or in heat, the kind of thing one hears in any garden, only magnified by the echo-chamber of the night.

'It's a banshee,' he said. 'They follow our family. Aunt Margaret must be going to die.'

And, strangely enough, Aunt Margaret did die, but several weeks later and from old age more than anything else: she was over eighty and could have toppled into the grave at any time. But all through the funeral Kieran kept looking at Françoise reproachfully, as if to say 'You see!' And now the disease was beginning to get at her, sending her to stalk through the night like a Mauriac heroine, melancholy eating at her heart. As she approached Leeson Street Bridge, she saw two swans, a cob and a pen, moving slowly down the current. Behind them, almost indistinguishable because of their grey feathers, came four young ones. The sight calmed her: it was time to go back. Though he deserved it, she did not want her husband to be worrying about her. In any case, she had more or less decided what she was going to do.

*

The important thing was not to show, by the least sign, that she was troubled by what they thought of her. Swinging her togs in her left hand, Françoise O'Meara sauntered down towards the beach at Seacove. It was already pretty full, but, as though by design, a little space had been left

228

directly under the sea wall, where she usually sat. So she was to be ostracized as well! She would show them: with a delicious sense of her audience she hoisted herself up onto the concrete and began to undress. But she was only halfway through changing when the students arrived. In an ordinary day, she would have taken this in her stride, but she saw the people watching them as they tramped over, and the clasp of her bra stuck, and she was left to greet them half in, half out of her dress. And when she did get the bathing suit straightened, she saw that, since they had all arrived more or less together, they were expecting her to join them in a swim. Laying his towel out carefully on the ground, like an altar-cloth, Ginger turned towards the sea: 'Coming?'

Scarlet-faced, she marched down with him to the pierhead. The tide was high, and just below the Martello Tower the man with the goggles broke surface, spluttering, as though on purpose to stare at her. A little way out, a group of clerical students were horse-playing: she wasn't going to join in that. Without speaking to her companion, she struck out towards the Lighthouse Point, cutting the water with a swift sidestroke. But before she had gone far, she found Ginger at her side: and another boy on the other. Passing (they both knew the crawl), falling back, repassing, they accompanied her out to the point, and back again. Were they never to leave her alone?

And afterwards, when they lay on the beach, they kept pestering her with questions. And not the usual ones, but much bolder, in an innocent sort of way: what had got into them? It was the boy who had asked about Mauriac who began it, wanting to know if she had ended the book, whether she knew any people like that, what she thought of its view of love. And then, out of the blue:

'What's it like, to be married?'

She rolled over on her stomach and looked at him. No, he was not being roguish, he was quite serious, gazing at her with interest, as were most of the others. But how could one answer such a question, before such an audience?

'Well, it's very important for a woman, naturally,' she began, feeling as ripe with clichés as a woman's-page columnist. 'And not just because people – society – imply that if a woman is not married, she's a failure: that's a terrible trap. And it is not merely living together, though–' (She looked at them: they were still intent.) '–that's pleasant enough, but in order to fulfil herself, in the process of giving. And that's the whole paradox, that if it's a true marriage, she feels freer, just because she has given.'

'Freer?'

'Yes, freer after marriage than before it. It's not like an affair, where, though the feeling may be as intense, one knows that one can escape. The freedom in marriage is the freedom of having committed oneself: at least that's true for the woman.' Her remarks were received in silence, but it was not the puzzled silence of their first meetings, but a thoughtful one, as though, while they could not quite understand what she meant, they were prepared to examine it. But she still could not quiet a nagging doubt in her mind, and demanded: 'What made you ask me that ?'

It was not her questioner, but Ginger, who had hardly been listening, who gave her her answer. 'Sure, it's well known,' he said pleasantly, gathering up his belongings, 'that French women think about nothing but love.'

He pronounced it 'luve', with a deep curl in the vowel. Before she could think of a reply, they were halfway across the beach.

*

She was still raging when she got home, all the more so since she knew she could not tell her husband about it. She was still raging when she went to bed, shifting so much that she made her husband grunt irritably. She was still raging when she woke up, from a dream in which the experience lay curdled.

She dreamt that she was at Seacove in the early morning. The sea was a deep running green, with small waves hitting the pierhead. There was no one in sight so she took off her clothes and slipped into the water. She was halfway across to the Lighthouse Point when she sensed something beneath her: it was the man with the goggles, his black flippers beating the water soundlessly as he surged up towards her. His eyes roved over her naked body as he reached out for her leg. She felt herself being pulled under, and kicked out strongly. She heard the glass of his goggles smash as she broke to the surface again; where her husband was drawing the blinds to let in the morning light.

Today, she decided, she must end the whole stupid affair: it had gone on too long, caused her too much worry. After all, the people who had protested were probably right: the fact that the boys were getting fresh with her proved it. She toyed with the idea of just not going back to the beach, but it seemed cowardly. Better to face the students directly, and tell them she could not see them again.

So when they arrived at the beach in the mid-afternoon they found her sitting stiffly against the sea wall, a book resting on her knees. Saluting her with their usual friendliness, they got hardly any reply. At the time, they passed no remarks, but lying on the beach after their swim they found the silence heavy and tried to coax her with questions. But she cut them short each time, ostentatiously returning to her book.

'Is there anything wrong?' one of them asked, at last.

Keeping her eyes fixed on the print, she nodded. 'More or less.'

'It wouldn't have anything to do with us?' This from Ginger, with sudden probing interest.

'As a matter of fact, it has.' Shyness slowly giving way to relief, she told about her conversation with the little fat man. 'But, of course, it's really my fault,' she ended lamely. 'I should have known better.'

Awaiting their judgement, she looked up. To her surprise, they were smiling at her, affectionately.

'Is that all?'

'Isn't it enough ?'

'But sure we knew all that before.'

'You know it!' she exclaimed in horror. 'But how…'

'Somebody came to the College a few days ago and complained to the Dean.'

'And what did he say?'

'He asked us what you were like.'

'And what did you say?' she breathed.

'We said' – the tone was teasing but sincere – 'we said you were a better French teacher than Father Dundee.'

The casual innocence of the remark, restoring the whole heart of their relationship, brought a shout of laughter from her. But as her surprise wore off, she could not resist picking at it, suspiciously, at least once more.

'But what about what the people said? Didn't it upset you?'

Ginger's gaze seemed to rest on her for a moment, and then moved away, bouncing like a rubber ball down the steps towards the sea.

'Ach, sure some people would see bad in anythin',' he said easily.

And that was all: no longer interested, they turned to talk about something else. They were going on their holidays soon (no wonder they were so frisky!) and wouldn't be seeing her much again. But they had enjoyed meeting her; maybe she would be there next year? She lay with her back against the warm sea wall, listening to them, her new book (it was Simone de Beauvoir's *Le Deuxième Sexe*) at her side. A movement caught her eye down the beach: someone was trying to climb on to the ledge of the Martello Tower. First came the spear, then the black goggles, then the flippers, like an emerging sea monster. Remembering her dream, she began to laugh again, so much so that her companions looked at her inquiringly. Yes, she said quickly, she might be at Seacove next year.

Though in her heart she knew that she wouldn't.

18

A CHANGE OF MANAGEMENT

John O'Shea groaned as he lifted the morning paper from the front of his desk, where his secretary, Nan Connor, had left it. He was already in a bad temper (for the second time that week he had got snarled in a traffic jam on his way in from Clontarf) but what he saw on the front page did not help. That bastard Clohessy was in the news again; chubby and smiling, an assuring blend of episcopal dignity and *bon viveur*'s charm, his face seemed to start out from the lead photograph with the immediacy of a film star's. Among the dignitaries at the blessing of the dried-vegetable factory were the Most Rev. Dr Martin, Bishop of Avoca, the Most Rev. Dr Nkomo, Vicar Apostolic of Katanga (a fine tall African, nurtured by Irish nuns) and Dr William Pearse Clohessy. At a dinner in the Leinster Hotel afterwards, Dr Clohessy, Chairman of Bord na h-Ath Breithe, the National Renaissance Board, said that this new factory, for which they had all worked so hard, represented another beam in the scaffolding of Ireland's future.

Another nail in its coffin, more likely, thought O'Shea, nearly disintegrating with rage as he gazed at the picture of the new factory which headed the Advertising Supplement. A long low building, it seemed to consist mainly of glass, acres of it, with intersecting ridges of concrete creating a pattern grid. Surely normal people would not be expected to work in a chilly barracks like that, which looked as if it were designed for Martians. He looked to the side for space vehicles, but all he could see was a car park, with the Tricolour flying, against a background of mountains. We congratulate the architect, said Dr Clohessy, on his revolutionary conception, which liberates the forces implicit in the building's environment, so that employees will have the sensation of working close to nature, without its disadvantages. The stark beauty of its outline challenges nature's ruggedness in the granite majesty of the Wicklow Mountains.

As O'Shea was dwelling with tortured relish on the idea of granite majesty, and wondering which of Clohessy's team of ghost-writers had dreamt it up, the door of his office opened and his secretary came in. 'Here are the letters, Mr O'Shea,' she said, placing a small pile of opened envelopes on the IN tray to the right of his desk. She stood back, smoothing her skirt with a broad hand, as he ruffled through them. 'Will you be wanting me?' she asked, at last, with unconscious generosity, gazing over his head through the window.

'Is there anything urgent?'

'The Chairman wants to see you at eleven; his secretary rang to confirm the appointment. I believe the Efficiency Experts are due soon.'

'Anything else?'

She hesitated. 'Mr Cronin called.'

'What did he want?'

'He said you were to meet him for lunch in the Anchor.'

As always she delivered the message with a disapproving air, as if she felt that he should not be going to places like the Anchor, especially with people like Tadgh Cronin. Nan Connor was a decent, middle-class Dublin woman, and there were certain classes of behaviour which she could not admire. Once when she had tried to stall Cronin, saying that Mr O'Shea was engaged, he had broken into a torrent of bad language. 'Will you get that bastard for me, or I'll come and wrap your guts around a lamppost,' he finished. The girls at the switchboard had laughed, but she had not found it amusing; and she never would.

John O'Shea smiled affectionately after her, as her masculine shoulders disappeared through the door. Whoever had dreamt up granite majesty should have known Nan Connor; there was something heart-warming about people who behaved according to form. He reached for the first file on his desk and began to turn its pages thoughtfully. It was ten-fifteen, and all across Claddagh House the typewriters took up their morning song.

MEMORANDUM: ON THE HISTORY OF CLADDAGH HOUSE

Claddagh House was a handsome building, of port-wine brick, standing on the South Side of Dublin, near the river Dodder. Formerly known as Kashmir House, it had been built by a retired Army Officer at the turn of the century. But the family had left after the Revolution, no longer finding life comfortable in Ireland, and the house had changed hands several times. After a period as divisional headquarters of the Boy Scouts (Dublin Brigade) it had caught the eye of a government minister, who was looking for somewhere to house an off-shoot of his department. Since money was scarce, no effort was made to remodel it: the stuffed tiger heads of the original owner still lined the entrance hall, and in the Chairman's room hung two crossed assegais, with the head of an eland between them.

What pleased John O'Shea about Claddagh House was its Victorian spaciousness; it was unashamedly designed to be lived in. A militant laurel hedge protected it from the road, too high for the curious, but just high enough for the occupants to command both directions. There were two pillared entrances, through which one could sweep, the car coming to a halt before the door with a satisfying spurt of gravel. A well-tended lawn began at the side of the house, coming to a climax in the treeshadowed expanse at the back.

The front was dominated by two enormous bay windows, a flight of steps between them mounting to the door, with its well Brassoed-knocker and official plaque. John O'Shea still remembered the first day he had penetrated the grave dignity of that façade. A junior civil servant, he had just been seconded to Claddagh House, and did not know what to expect. He stood at the empty reception desk in the hall, under the stuffed animals, with their bared teeth and eyeballs. The only sound in the building seemed to be coming from underneath the stairs.

When he opened the door and saw the crowd around a table he nearly backed out, thinking he had interrupted a conference. Then he recognized the object in the middle of the table: from a battered-looking radio rose the florid accents of a racing commentator.

They're coming into the bend now, King's Pin in front, Whistling Nun second, Richards nursing Champagne Paddy on the inside. *And* here we come into the straight. It's still King's Pin; but Whistling Nun is challenging. I say, this is something; King's Pin, Whistling Nun and Champagne Paddy neck and neck. *Two* furlongs to go and King's Pin is falling back; it's between Whistling Nun and Champagne Paddy. *One* furlong and Richards' mount is beginning to flag; it's Whistling Nun all the way now – *Whistling Nun by a length*!

11 AM

After ten years, John O'Shea still found that first view of Claddagh House prophetic. It was not that work did not get done, but that it took its own sweet pace, without the panic of a central department. Files accumulated and were dealt with before they simmered into urgency. Then they were tied in red folders and buried in cupboards as large as bank-vaults.

And there was always time for relaxation. Twice daily they assembled in the old kitchen under the stairs for tea. In the summer they could take their work out onto the lawn; O'Shea had been sitting under a lilac tree when a swallow dunged on a letter from the Department of Finance. Everyone contributed to the typists' Black Babies Fund; everyone went off sugar and milk during Lent; everyone joined in the Staff Dance and Annual Outing.

Which was why he found the timing of his appointment with the Chairman curious: if he was holding it during the teabreak, it was because he wanted no one to interrupt them. And that was unlike Jack Donovan, who gave the impression of conducting his business in public. His gregarious vagueness masked a veteran shrewdness; he might be late but he was rarely wrong in a decision. From ten-thirty, when he rolled in to consult the rain gauge, until he left for his game of golf in the afternoon, he refused to be hustled by or for anything.

As John O'Shea opened the door (after a polite knock) he caught the sharp odour of the cigars Donovan favoured. On one of the eland's horns a hat was hanging: it gave the animal a querulous, lopsided look. Donovan himself was at his desk, a plump tweed-suited man, who raised his head cordially to indicate a chair. Rejecting the open box of Will's Whiffs which his Chairman pushed towards him, O'Shea settled himself expectantly.

'You wanted to see me, sir?'

As usual, Donovan took his time to answer, tidying the papers on his desk before leaning back, his fingers joined.

'Yes, indeed,' he said. 'I have a job for you. Rather, I have two jobs; or one job with two aspects.'

O'Shea waited politely for clarification.

'There's a dinner tonight in' – he pulled a piece of paper towards him – 'the Royal Hotel, Carricklone, which I am supposed to attend: they're launching a local development plan. But…'

'You would rather I did.' Which was it, this time, yachting or golf? Since it was mid-week, it was probably golf, at his favourite seaside course, near Bray.

Donovan smiled. 'That's right. But not for the reason you think, though I do have a previous engagement. In any case, even if I was free, I think you should go. You see, Clohessy will be there.'

John O'Shea started. 'That…' he began automatically.

'I'm not sure that I don't share your impatience with Mr – Dr! – Clohessy: he seems a rather pushy fellow,' said Donovan judiciously. 'But one mustn't rely on spot judgements; he has the reputation of being very capable. Which brings me to the second part…'

'I hope it has nothing to do with Clohessy,' O'Shea burst in.

'Well, as a matter of fact, in a sort of a roundabout way, it has. You know that the Minister feels that perhaps we should be reorganized. It's partly a political thing, of course – we were founded by the previous government – but they also feel that perhaps we are a little old-fashioned. You've heard the efficiency experts are coming in…'

'Miss Connor said they were due next week.'

'They're only a front, of course. I don't mean that they won't do their – whatever they do – conscientiously, but their report will give an official reason for pointing out something that we all know already: that this is not a very modern organization, and that I'm not a very modern manager.'

'I don't think that's so important, sir,' said O'Shea loyally. Donovan wheeled his chair slightly, so that he was gazing through the window. On the green pelt of the lawn, a solitary blackbird was trying to extricate a worm; when it succeeded, it nearly fell backwards, the worm projecting like a typewriter ribbon from its beak.

'I'm a bumbler,' he said quietly, 'and the age of bumblers is past. But I was lucky; I managed to last until nearly retiring age. I'll be able to disappear without undue fuss.'

'Have you any idea of who might be replacing you?' asked O'Shea nervously.

It was a minute or two before Donovan answered. 'Yes,' he said heavily, 'I think I do. It's mainly guesswork on my part, coupled with one or two fairly obvious straws in the wind. But I think that not merely me, but also Claddagh House, are to be retired. There's going to be what the English papers call, I believe, a takeover bid.'

'By whom?'

'By Bord na h-Ath Breithe. They plan to pull down the house and set up a new joint building.'

'Under Clohessy?' breathed O'Shea.

'Under Clohessy.' Donovan swung the chair round so that he was facing O'Shea directly. 'That's why I want you to go to Carricklone. So that you can get a closer look at the man you may soon be working under.'

1 PM

Why did Tadgh Cronin always spend his lunch hour in the Anchor? As John O'Shea pushed open the heavy mahogany door, a hollow sound rose to greet him, like the sea booming in a cave. They were standing six deep at the bar, with waiters threading through the mass, carrying platters to the tables at the back. It was certainly not the food, because it was always cold, pallid thighs of chicken or rough cuts of ham and beef. It was certainly not the women because, although there were several presentable girls present, they seemed to accept that they were on sufferance and did their best to pass muster as men, sucking their pints slowly. A lecher would have had a field-day, provided he remained sober enough to remember his priorities.

No, the sole purpose of this draughty, uncomfortable high-ceilinged place was drink. And with that O'Shea caught sight of Tadgh Cronin, ensconced (his brooding posture demanded the word) in a corner, under a vine-leaved mirror advertising Guinness. His black steeple hat was on the chair beside him, flanked by a crumpled *Irish Times*. As O'Shea sat down opposite, he saw that his face looked heavy and flushed, and that the hand that reached out for the pint was shaking.

'Hard night?' he asked sympathetically.

Cronin turned an imploring eye towards heaven. 'Christ!' Then, step by step, he began to piece together (as much for his own sake as O'Shea's) the events of the previous night. They had all been having a quiet jar in the Anchor when that bastard Tomkins, the sculptor, barged in. A row had developed between him and Parsons, the stained-glass artist, and they had all been thrown out. When they moved to some girl's flat in Rathmines he, Cronin, had tried to make peace between Tomkins and Parsons, with the result that they both turned on him. A window had been broken, and when he got home at four o'clock, he found he had been cheated by the taxi man.

O'Shea made another sympathetic noise; he had heard the same story before but he had a connoisseur's taste for the gruesome detail. How much had the fare been from Rathmines to Ballsbridge?

'I got half a dollar outa quid: that makes seventeen and six for two miles. Over eight bob a fecking mile – you could fly cheaper!'

Together, in gloomy silence, they surveyed the bar and its customers. A well-known actor was leaning at the counter, surrounded by a circle of admiring young men. When he saw Cronin, he bowed gracefully so that they could see the dark, corrugated lines of his wig.

'Did you make it to the office, at least ?'

'I'm going in this afternoon. Old Brennan's beginning to get a bit narky.'

Brennan was Cronin's immediate superior in the Department of Woods and Lakes. A harmless, long-suffering man, he not merely over-looked the fact that Cronin spent most of his time in the office studying form, or writing reviews for the daily papers, but even countenanced his long absences, periods when he disappeared underground, only to turn up looking as if he had been passed through a mangle. It was a combina-tion of old-fashioned fidelity and the respect still paid in the community to the idea of the poet, half pure spirit, half biting satirist. But the latter excuse was beginning to wear thin; Cronin had not published a book of poems since his flamboyant post-university days.

'That reminds me,' said O'Shea, 'did you see Clohessy in the paper?'

Cronin's gesture combined dismissal and disgust. 'That smooth bas-tard!'

'He seems to be getting on,' said O'Shea carefully.

For a split second Cronin's lethargic eyes ignited with hatred.

'On!' he growled. 'Of course he's getting on. Hasn't he got what you need to get on in this country?'

'You mean energy?'

'I mean neck; pure, unadulterated, armour-plated, insensitive neck. The countryman's recipe for all occasions.'

O'Shea forbore from pointing out that like himself Cronin had been born in the country: having taken root in Dublin during his student days, he now saw himself as a city father, defending civilization against the barbarian.

'Still, he's a fine-looking fellow,' he insinuated.

A snort was regarded as sufficient answer to that remark. But Cronin seemed to turn the matter over, for a few minutes later he raised his pint and looked across it at O'Shea. 'I'll tell you what's really wrong with Clohessy.'

O'Shea waited expectantly. 'What?'

'It was one of the boys in his office put me on to it. He said that Clohessy whipped over to him at one of their new Press Conference do's and took the glass from his hand telling him he had had enough.'

'Well?'

'It's the old de Valera trick brought up to date: no one ever saw that sacerdotal heron under the influence. There is something fundamentally wrong with someone who has never been seen drunk. They can't be trusted.'

5.15 PM

South of the Liffey, on a late autumn evening. People are beginning to pour from offices, Government Buildings in Kildare and Upper Merrion Street, the Tourist Board in Mount Street Crescent, the Electricity Supply Board on Lower Fitzwilliam Street. The stone fronts of the Georgian houses look mournful, with bulbs already lit in ground floor and basement rooms. Above the shiny, wet rows of parked cars a light mist is gathering on the trees; a plume of smoke shows where leaves are being burned in a black-railed square. At the end of a wide street rises a vague blue shoulder of the Dublin Mountains…

The curious thing, O'Shea reflected, as he swung his Volkswagen along the canal leading towards the main Limerick road, was that he actually knew Clohessy. Or rather he had known him briefly years before, when they were both students. But why had he never mentioned the incident to anyone, not even to Cronin or Brennan? Especially when it would have made ideal material for pub gossip!

It had been a seaside resort in Donegal where O'Shea was in the habit of going for his holidays. Generally he went with a gang from the university who, to save money, camped in a field overlooking the bay. For a fortnight they racketed through the town, drinking, dancing, swimming. One year Clohessy had joined them for a few days, brought by one of O'Shea's friends. Although he moved in different circles from the rest at college (he was a member of the fencing team and secretary of something new called the Political Society), he seemed a decent enough chap, fresh-faced, rather silent. When they splashed in the diving pool or chased girls in the smoky dance hall, he tagged along, though somehow a little distant and separate.

Then, one evening, a group of them were sitting out on the cliffs. The air was cool, and they felt full of youthful idealism and sadness, watching the sun go down on the Atlantic. They were discussing what they would be after they left the university.

One had said he just wanted to be a good doctor, if he could get a practice. Carmody, O'Shea's bosom pal, had said (his arm looped around a girl as usual) that he wanted to see a bit of the world first: poor bastard, he had joined the Air Force and been shot down in a dog-fight over Benghazi. Another wanted to go back to teach in his home town in Tipperary. Then someone asked Clohessy what he wanted. He did not answer immediately and O'Shea remembered watching the fishing fleet sail slowly back towards the harbour. They seemed so frail and motionless and yet they kept edging imperceptibly towards their goal.

Then, in clear and precise tones, Clohessy outlined for them the shape he wished his career to follow. By twenty, he hoped to graduate with First Class Honours in Legal and Political Science; he would then enter a well-known Dublin firm as a junior executive. By twenty-two, he would be Fencing Champion of Ireland, but would give it up afterwards: it took too much time. By twenty-five, he should be Assistant Manager and have his Doctorate in Economics. By thirty, he would certainly be a section head, but since he could hardly hope to rise any further in Ireland for the moment, he would probably go abroad and work for one of the big economic organizations, to gain top managerial experience. It was difficult to get a proper salary in Ireland at that level, but he felt sure that the government would ask him back before he was forty, to take charge of a national or semi-state organization. Perhaps they would even create a new one, some man-sized job commensurate with his training and abilities.

O'Shea heard Carmody suck in his breath sharply, whether in astonishment or in anger he did not know. The others seemed struck numb: coming from farms and country pubs, they had probably never heard anyone reveal such ambition before. Perhaps it was meant to be a joke? Clohessy, unaware of the effect he had made, was squatting like a Buddha on the esparto grass, throwing pebbles over the edge. They could hear them fall from ledge to ledge, before striking the pool at the base of the cliff. It was getting cold: one of the girls suggested they should be going in. As they left, O'Shea saw that the others avoided Clohessy.

That scene had remained in O'Shea's mind ever since, a secret source of contemptuous amazement as, year by year, he saw Clohessy's career trace the rising arc of its fulfilment, less like a human than like some natural phenomenon. Would the great man remember their earlier meeting? He doubted it: he was hardly the type to bother with those who had not kept pace with him in the world. Nor was O'Shea the sort to remind him. Catching sight of the flat spaces of the Curragh, he accelerated: he still had a good distance to travel before Carricklone.

9.50 PM

It was the brandy-and-Irish-coffee stage; wreaths of cigar smoke drifted slowly upwards in the dining-room of the Royal Arms Hotel, Carricklone. In the foreground, balloon glasses caught and reflected light: in the background waiters were grouped in stylish impassivity. His Lordship the Bishop of Carricklone was speaking and he was well known to detest interruption. A small man, with bushy eyebrows incongruously grafted on an old woman's face, he was launched onto one of his favourite subjects – the impurity of modern life. It had nothing to do with the problems of local development but, somehow, it always seemed to crop up in His Lordship's speeches. His pectoral cross danced as he thundered into the home stretch of his peroration.

'Gentlemen, we must never betray this pearl! In this modern world of drinks and dance halls, of so-called progress and speed, our country should remain a solitary oasis. On all sides we are wooed by the sirens of lax living, but – remember this – if Ireland holds a special place in God's plan it will be due to the purity of her men and the modesty of her women.'

The bishop blew his nose with a large white handkerchief and sat down abruptly. As polite applause rippled down the table, John O'Shea looked at the faces of his companions for any response to this stirring call to arms. A dozen well-fed (Galway Oysters, Roast Kerry Lamb, Carrageen Moss) and well-wined (Chateauneuf Saint Patrice) faces reflected nothing but sensuous contentment. At least it was an audience of adults: the last time His Lordship had spoken it was to warn a Confirmation class in a remote country parish against the dangers of Communism.

As O'Shea's gaze reached the end of the table, it encountered the smooth full moon of Clohessy's face, sailing above an immaculate shirt front. Why did so many public figures come to look like that, as though moulded in wax? To O'Shea's surprise the left eyebrow appeared to flicker slightly in his direction, in a kind of conspiratorial schoolboy's wink. But before he could decide whether he was mistaken or not, a brandy glass rang, and he saw that Clohessy was getting to his feet to reply to the Bishop.

The voice was clear, but it took some time before O'Shea grasped the substance of the argument. It was not a dramatic speech, compared to the Bishop's, but it seemed an unobjectionable one, its points neatly tied together every now and then by a mild joke. What His Lordship had said showed his deep concern for the community, a concern they all echoed. There was often a bleakness about village life in Ireland due, not of course to our own faults, but to our sad history. The absence of trees and adjoining woods, the fact that the church was generally towards the outside of the town, the grimness of the public houses – all this made for a certain gloom. He did not mean to say that Carricklone was not a wonderful place, all Munster knew it was (this reference to the Hurling Championship brought cheers) but its charm was a trifle obscured by decayed houses and concrete run-ups. He looked forward to the day when the people of Carricklone would have the model town they obviously deserved.

It was a pity that the factory that was coming was a foreign one, but we were a little retarded in these matters, and besides it would restore Carricklone's ancient links with the Continent! After that, there should be a crafts and recreation centre: it was important, as the Bishop had said, to train the young for their place in modern life. And for the summer, a swimming pool, so that they could meet in the open air. These new buildings could form the nucleus of a true community; before long the people of Carricklone might be strolling around their piazza or village square in the evenings, while from the open door of every pub came the sound of colourful music and dancing.

As Clohessy sat down, to a thunder of applause, O'Shea turned to look at the other end of the table. Most of what Clohessy had said, it had slowly dawned on him, was an inversion of the Bishop's speech, using its emotional power as a springboard. On paper, it would have seemed the usual parade of clichés, but in its context, it was almost revolutionary; yet to O'Shea's surprise, His Lordship the Bishop of Carricklone was not merely smiling broadly, he was leading the applause.

After Clohessy, nearly everyone spoke. The Mayor of Carricklone promised his warm support for every worthwhile initiative. Several local merchants pledged not merely moral but financial assistance. The local architect and town clerk began to compare sites for the crafts and recreation centre. As the speeches gradually crumbled into specific discussion people changed places to keep up with them. In this excited buzz of proposal and counterproposal the bland mask seemed to have settled again over Clohessy's face. He was sitting between the Lord Mayor and the Bishop's Secretary, and the inclined head of the priest, redolent of discreet satisfaction, the way Clohessy curled his finger round his glass or raised his head briefly to smell his cigar before leaning confidentially towards his companions, seemed a paradigm of worldliness.

And then the dinner was breaking up, people rising and moving towards the door in little groups. O'Shea saw that, with the swiftness of long training, Clohessy had already shaken off the Lord Mayor and the Bishop's Secretary. Now he was cruising across the room, shaking hands as he went. Having worked his way almost to the door, he came level with O'Shea, who was still standing awkwardly behind his chair. There was an instant's delay, and then his face creased into its famous smile:

'John O'Shea!' he said. 'After all these years.'

11 PM

'Well, what did you think of the speeches?' asked Clohessy. He and O'Shea were sitting together in the comfortable, clublike atmosphere of the hotel lounge, with the two Martels that Clohessy had ordered before them.

'Do you mean yours or the Bishop's?' asked O'Shea carefully.

Clohesssy burst out laughing. 'Wasn't he wonderful! John of Carricklone is one of the last of the Old Guard: he ought to be in a museum. I heard him give the same speech two years ago in Mullingar; only there it was a sermon. I suppose,' his face became suddenly serious, 'he believes it's expected of him.'

'What do you mean?' demanded O'Shea. He was not used to this class of talk about bishops: satire, yes, he could appreciate, but friendly familiarity was a rather unsettling note.

'It's one of the troubles of being a public figure. What is the average bishop but an elderly man closed up in a palace, surrounded by people who tell him what he wants to know. Which he then tells back to them; there is nothing more corrupting than a captive audience.'

He spoke with some passion and O'Shea could not resist a probe.

'Is that how you feel?' he inserted quietly.

Clohessy started slightly and gave O'Shea a cautious side-long glance. But, though repenting of his outburst, he seemed willing to continue.

'Yes, a bit,' he admitted. 'But of course it's different for us.'

The 'us' was so unconsciously patronizing that O'Shea stung back before realizing it.

'You don't mean to say you don't like it?' he said with heavy sarcasm.

'Like what?' demanded Clohessy.

'You know – the fuss, the dinners, the photographs – what people call fame. Surely—'

Clohessy gave a controlled sigh. 'Oh yes, I know what people think: that I do all this for personal gain and glory. Clohessy the big-time executive, his right hand greeting a bishop, while his left robs the nation's till. And I know I do fairly well out of it, but I regard that as a reward—'

'Reward for what?' O'Shea burst out involuntarily. Then, catching himself in time: 'What do you mean, sir?'

'You know bloody well what I mean. It's not the board meetings that kill. It's going from cocktail party to cocktail party every evening; eating chicken and ham at public banquets three times a week; never once getting angry or dropping a wrong word. How much stamina do you think that takes?'

There was such a note of sincerity, almost of agony, in his voice that O'Shea was embarrassed into silence.

'And that's not the worst. Going down the country to try and put across the merit of some project – the county councillors – Christ, man, it's like being thrown to wild animals.'

'So you mean to say you don't enjoy it!' repeated O'Shea incredulously.

'Enjoy it! There's nothing I loathe more. Nowhere else in the world is a top executive at the mercy of every self-important little fart with a grievance.'

'Then, why do you do it?' O'Shea burst out.

Clohessy revolved the brandy glass slowly between his podgy, well-manicured hands.

'I suppose you'd call it patriotism,' he said, with some sadness.

'Patriotism!'

'Look, Seán.' At the lapse into the vernacular, O'Shea felt his spine stiffen, but Clohessy was only leaning forward with confidential eagerness.

'When I came back to this country after the war, I saw that it had no future. My first instinct was to clear out again, and to hell with it: with my background and training I could have a comfortable life anywhere in the world. You'll admit that…'

O'Shea nodded. There was no denying that just as some men bore the marks of sanctity, so Clohessy had the credentials for worldly success stamped on his brow.

'Then I thought that was a bit cowardly. Why not come back and try and create a future for the country at the same time as I was creating my own? As you know, we've had a lot of patriots.'

'You can say that again,' said O'Shea fervently.

'But what it has never had are a group of practical, hardheaded people who would try to put it back on its feet, like any business. People not afraid to face the priests, the politicians, the whole vast bog of the Irish middle-class, and woo something positive out of it. One would have to give up a lot, of course…'

'Like what?'

'Oh,' said Clohessy expansively, waving his hand in the air, 'it's not easy to define; the fleshpots of high commerce – the knighthood, the

Tour d'Argent and Claridge's, the yacht at Cannes. The mistresses, even, if you like. The really big stuff never comes to Ireland. I know: I've seen it.'

O'Shea was silent.

'But there would be the satisfaction of being one of the first in a new line of well-trained – eh — '

'Patriots,' finished O'Shea.

'Yes.'

There was the awkwardness which often follows an unexpected burst of intimacy: the two men sat side by side, without speaking, in the curved leather armchairs. O'Shea glanced covertly once or twice at his companion, but now that urgency had left it, his face had resumed its usual bland, immobile expression. The skull was full and round, with a light fringe of silver hair on the edge of the Roman brow. The cheeks, in particular, were smooth and ruddy as though he had been born only that morning. Ten thousand mornings of close shaving, and Yardley's Lotion, had left the skin as polished as wood; even the wrinkles seemed deliberate, the necessary fine grain of maturity. It only required a Papal Cross or the panoply of an honorary degree to complete the picture of what Cronin had once called 'His Royal Emptiness'. Could such a man be sincere?

'Do you see Cronin much now?' asked Clohessy suddenly, as though divining O'Shea's thoughts.

'Now and again.'

'God, poor Cronin! The original Stone-Age Bohemian; in any other country he would have been remaindered years ago. I wouldn't mind if he did his own work, but as it is, he just mucks up both jobs. And to think that we all admired him so much at college! The pity is…' (thoughtfully).

'What?' asked O'Shea with some wariness.

'We could still use a man like that. Business has broadened, you know, become more intellectual, more of a science.'

'He would probably think Public Relations corrupting,' said O'Shea feebly.

Clohessy's nostrils flared. 'I hate irresponsibility like that! People like Cronin think they are the salt of the country, but what did they ever do for it? This is not Dark Rosaleen, the Silk of the Kine, but a little country trying to make its way in the world: why can't Cronin get down and push like the rest of us?'

There was an answer to that, but O'Shea couldn't think of it at the moment. Instead he finally asked the question that had been bothering him all night.

'Tell me, sir, why did you tell me all this?'

There was a pause during which O'Shea was made to feel his tactlessness. Then Clohessy rose to his feet, buttoning his short coat briskly.

'Well, you know,' he said slowly, 'there aren't really very many people one can talk to. And we are old school chums, in a manner of speaking. Besides' – O'Shea had never encountered a glance which combined affability and threat in such proportions before – 'we'll soon be working together, and I felt we should have a little talk first; on neutral ground.'

After Clohessy had gone (his chauffeur stepping smartly from the corner of the bar, where he had been waiting over a bottle of stout, to open the door for him), O'Shea remained sitting for several minutes. What Clohessy told him differed very little from what he remembered of their boyhood meeting, except for the note of idealism. Was the latter only an afterthought, to disguise the thrust of naked ambition? The fact that their talk had been planned, not spontaneous, argued as much, but he couldn't be sure. For the first time, O'Shea realized why he had never retold that original encounter: despite his surface scorn, he had never really made his mind up about Clohessy. Now he would have to make it up pretty soon.

9.50 AM

'Can he not wait?' asked O'Shea fretfully.

The hysteria in Nan Connor's voice came through the intercom as a sort of flat shriek. 'He just won't. He says he must speak to you. And he's beginning to use bad language.'

O'Shea looked despairingly at the litter of papers on his desk. 'All right, put him through.'

There was a crackle, a silence and then he heard Tadgh Cronin's voice intoning angrily: '*Will you for Christ's sake put me through to John O'Shea or I'll—*'

'O'Shea here.'

'Jesus, John, is that you, at last. I had a hell of a job trying to get past that female full-back you call your secretary.'

O'Shea was going to remark that after all she was only doing her duty, but all he said was: 'Well, what's on your mind?'

'I'm going to resign.'

'You're what?'

'I'm going to resign. Old Brennan told me yesterday afternoon that the Secretary had informed him that my behaviour was a disgrace to the Department and that if I didn't pull my socks up drastic action would have to be taken. Very well, says I, if it's a case of pushing or being pushed, I know my position. I'll resign!'

There was a dramatic pause, but before O'Shea could venture a comment, Cronin was away again.

'Of course, I told Brennan that it wasn't his fault, he isn't a bad old bugger. But do you know what they introduced last week: *all latecomers to sign the book in the boss's room.* No man with any pride could stand for that class of nonsense. Next thing they'll be having management classes during the tea break. Still, old Brennan looked surprised: you shoulda seen his gob drop.'

'I'll bet he was,' muttered O'Shea fervently. He would have said more, but there was a peculiar note in his friend's voice, a kind of forced complacency that warned him.

'Well, there you are, I showed them. I'd have told you last night but I couldn't find you. Where were you, by the way?'

'In Carricklone. With Clohessy,' he could not help adding.

'With Clohessy!'

Gratified by Cronin's surprise, O'Shea found himself, almost without thinking, giving an account of the previous night. At first he only described the dinner and Clohessy's speech but as he warmed up to his subject, he could not help including a (discreetly tempered) version of their interview as well. It was partly that he wanted to speak of it, partly also because he could not resist rubbing in that he had news of his own.

'You don't mean to say you swallowed that?' said Cronin incredulously.

'I don't know,' said O'Shea uneasily. 'What do you think?'

There was a pause at the other end of the line and then Cronin's voice came through, triumphant, low, almost a snarl.

'I was right!'

'What do you mean you were right?'

'To resign. The hour has come. *The bastards are on the march.*'

'What!'

'Listen.' O'Shea could nearly see Cronin grasping the receiver at the other end, in his excitement. 'Since this country was founded we've had two waves of chancers. The first were easy to spot; the gunmen turned gombeen: they were so ignorant that they practically ruined themselves. But this second lot are a tougher proposition. In fifty years they'll have made this country just like every place else.'

'And what's so wrong with that?'

'You know damn well what's wrong with that: they'll murder us with activity! Factories owned by Germans, posh hotels catering to the international set, computers instead of dacent pen-pushers: do you call that progress? Well, by Jesus, I don't, and I'll fight it tooth and nail. If this country becomes a chancer's paradise, it will be over my dead body. Over my dead body, do you hear?'

And that (repeated several times with increasing vehemence) was Cronin's parting shot. After vaguely agreeing to meet him for lunch in the Anchor sometime during the week, John O'Shea put down the phone, and turned to pick up the uppermost of his files. But he found it hard to concentrate, Cronin's words ringing in his ears. They had been friends for years, drawing an odd comfort from their differences of temperament, but of late O'Shea had begun to feel the strain. It was all right for Cronin to feel so defiantly about things; if the rhythm of drinking had not already corroded his faculties, his resignation might be the spur his talent needed. But for people like himself, there was no real escape left, not even here: the most they could hope to find was someone under whose direction they might give of their best. Besides, was it such a criminal thing to wish to lead an ordinary life?

Somewhere, on the banks of the Liffey, or overlooking a Georgian square, a great new building would rise, a glass house against which the world might, at first, throw stones, but would gradually accept. Inside, in a large, discreetly lighted room, with Tintawn carpeting and an abstract on the wall, would be Clohessy. And in one of the adjoining cubicles, perhaps, a file open before him, just as it was now... Half-surprised, as though looking into a mirror, John O'Shea greeted his own future.

19

A Ball of Fire

It was on the first of November that Michael Gorman first saw the old man. He remembered the exact day because, with a revival of piety that surprised him, he had been praying in the hideous imitation Gothic church of St Philomena's, Harrington Road. As a boy, he had been fascinated by the ceremony of remembrance – going from the village chapel to the rust-eaten rail of the family plot, and back again – and he recaptured enough of the experience to feel a warm fulfilment. Did he believe? After several years away he had put such considerations aside. If one was fortunate enough to find oneself in the last city in the world where faith was an element, like water or light, questioning seemed churlish. The bicycles streaming across Baggot Street Bridge on a Sunday morning was a nearly mystical sight.

He was coming back along the canal towpath. It was a walk that he liked, particularly in winter when everything emphasized the process of disintegration. The canal had not been cleaned for years, and all kinds of oddments came sailing gaily by: hingeless buckets, dead animals, a skeletal pram. On the far bank there was a disused barge which sank lower into the mud each year: was it an illusion, or did its greening planks sag visibly as he watched? He halted under the dripping trees to inhale the viscous odour of a Dublin winter twilight.

It was then that the man appeared. At first he was only a shape, a vague sensation of someone at the far end of the towpath. Then it came closer and closer, a growing point on the rim of his consciousness, an affirmation of movement against the heavy stillness. As he turned to continue his walk, the figure came almost abreast. It was a small man, about five foot high, wearing a cloth cap, pulled low, and an open-necked shirt. He was moving so fast that his boots drummed on the hard clay of the path. He passed Michael Gorman without a look, striking him with his shoulder so that he nearly pushed him into the water. 'Where in blazes do you think you're going,' the latter called angrily. But the little man was already halfway down towards the bridge. Above his dwindling figure, as at the end of a tunnel, the setting sun tried to burn its way through the fog, which was gradually smothering it.

He told his wife about it later that evening. She was sitting at the fire sewing a pillowcase, and he was reading aloud extracts from the evening papers. The Government was sending an Aberdeen-Angus bull to the Pope. A gang of thieves who had been terrorizing the Northside were caught when they stopped to drink a case of stout in a kitchen. There was also a warm correspondence as to whether fathers should chastise their teenage daughters when they came home late. RESPONSIBLE PARENT urged the use of a supple leather strap but he was outdone by SERIOUS LASS who suggested that delinquent fathers should be beaten by their daughters. Not for the first time Michael Gorman noticed how strange his world was becoming: were there really so many sadists in Kimmage?

'That reminds me,' he said. 'I met a funny little man today. No, met's not the word – bumped into.'

'I know.'

'What do you mean, you know?' Her calm authority often irritated him. 'You weren't there.'

'I know because it's probably our next-door neighbour.'

Three months before, it seemed, the small man had turned up next door and asked to rent the basement flat. The two old Protestant ladies who owned the house – living on the second floor in a surrealist confusion of faded draperies, ironwork and old furniture, the debris of their country home – had not seen him as a threat either to their virtue or their money, their two rival preoccupations. Nor, since they rarely went out themselves, were they troubled by his habits, spending all day in his room, to emerge at dusk and speed like a bullet to the nearest pub. Beyond the elementary needs of shopping, he spoke to no one in the area, though once when Deirdre Gorman was coming home she had found him fumbling drunkenly at his door, and had opened it for him. Whereupon he had said, with sudden distinctness: 'Thank you,' and lifted his cap.

'I think he's had a hard life,' she said contentedly.

'What do you mean?' he jeered.

'One doesn't avoid people without some good reason. He feels betrayed; I imagine he must have had an unsuccessful marriage or something like that.'

'What you mean is that if he had married someone understanding like you he might have done better, I suppose. Christ, what sentimentality! As a matter of fact, we don't even know if he was married: all we know is that he is a bloody crank.'

Deirdre Gorman laid down her sewing for a moment, and transfixed her husband with a calm blue eye. 'Why I do believe you're jealous. Of a little old man!'

It was, oddly enough, true; though he couldn't admit it. There was only one thing to do: drop the subject. Letting the papers slide to the floor in a heap, he rose to go to his studio in the adjoining room.

Michael Gorman never went willingly to his studio: he always wanted for something to give him impetus, a kick from outside. He had got a prize for drawing in the Intermediate, and vaguely thought of going to art school; but it hadn't worked out, and he soon forgot about the whole business. A decade later the impetus returned, but in a rather different form. He found himself making compulsively elaborate doodles in the office, and, to safeguard his job, began to draw a little at home. But even that did not satisfy his curiosity, and he started to paint, crudely at first but then (it was amazing how quickly one learned to use oils) with a bit more polish. A handful of these appeared in a local exhibition and, almost against his will, he found himself regarded as a promising young painter.

And expected to produce more when he was not even sure why he had done the first. For the second evening that week he found himself contemplating the meaningless white square of the canvas with something like hatred. Even the smell of the paints (and the brushes snugly reposing in their jam jar) nauseated him. Besides, some of them, like white lead and prussian blue, were actually poisonous. Picking up a brush, he smeared it in the palette he had just prepared (delicious!) and began to trail it along the edge of the canvas.

What appeared at first was a kind of rough sketch of the canal, a streak of water and low sky: he could almost smell the rotting leaves. But with a rapidity that frightened him, this faint likeness began to submerge under a series of dark, slashing brush-strokes. Once again, something was happening; and he found himself fighting to keep the flow, but control it, make it run between invisible banks like a river in spate. Within an hour the canvas was covered with sticky, messy, almost intractable paint, a maelstrom of pitchy colour into which he plunged deeper and deeper. He was so exhausted that he felt like slipping to the ground; with a last, accusing look at the picture (what under heaven was this?) he reeled off to bed.

In the following weeks Michael Gorman saw the little man quite frequently, like a feature of the landscape one has overlooked, which then becomes obtrusive. As he came home from work in the evenings he would meet him scudding through the dusk, a small parcel – loaves, eggs, a pot of jam? – under his arm. If he went out with his wife for a walk before going to bed they were sure to cross him lurching home from the pub. No matter how drunk he was he always made a clutching gesture with his cap towards Mrs Gorman, a token of respect which clearly did not include her husband.

'I told you he was sweet,' she remarked serenely.

'Like Prussic acid, I suppose.'

'Bogman!' she smiled, moving away.

But the worst was when he appeared in The Eagle's Nest, the pub which Michael Gorman frequented. Not that he drank as much as he used to: the double needs of his office and studio kept him pretty well drained of surplus energy. But when a painting wasn't going well he would call on a sculptor friend of his who lived across the bridge, and accompany him for a few jars. Sometimes his wife came, but more generally not; she had never got used to the peculiar rhythm, the alternations of sluggishness and vitality, of public house drinking.

He was in the act of downing his third pint one late November evening when he saw the little man. At first he thought he was mistaken (Christ, the bastard couldn't be following him!) but sure enough, there he was, standing on his own at the end of the bar, his cap so low that it seemed part of the pint glass before him. He was going to go over and speak to him, but thought better of it, turning to the barman instead.

'Do you know who that scruffy leprechaun is at the end of the bar? The one gathered up into a ball, by himself.'

It took a minute or so, before the barman finally understood whom he meant.

'Oh, that,' he said, with relief. 'That's Mr Daly. He comes in quite often.'

'Do you think I could offer him a drink?'

The barman wiped the counter around Gorman's glass before answering. 'Well, now,' he said, 'the way it is, I wouldn't be too sure. He's a very quiet class of a man (a mechanic of some kind, I believe) and I don't think he likes to be disturbed. Do you know, like?' Whether Gorman knew or not he had to accept. What kind of protection society was there forming around this pocket misanthrope? At least, he wasn't going to be part of it; turning to his sculptor friend, he announced abruptly that he was clearing off home.

December came, and the weather changed, drenching the city in pale sheets of rain. His dealer had asked him for a further batch of paintings for a group exhibition, so Michael Gorman spent most of his evenings in his studio, touching up his more recent works and trying to choose between them.

That was the hardest task. He had them arranged, in varying lights, around the walls, and kept trying to come back on them quickly, as though he were a stranger. Certain pleased him immediately because of their increasing technical skill; there was an elementary artisan's pride in doing difficult, tricky things. But when he returned to them later, they looked oddly empty, despite their attractive surface: the eye rebounded from them, soothed but unsatisfied. Surely paint was only a thing to be

255

used, like a pen or knife and fork, not an end in itself?

There were others in which there was a kind of movement, a threatening darkness, but it was so undefined as to be almost mawkish. Surely people would laugh at him if he presented things that he could not explain, or justify, even to himself? Among them was the painting he had begun over a month ago, on the first of November, and to which he had never been able to come back. Not merely did he not understand it, but it made him slightly sick to look at; so he finally turned its face to the wall.

During all that time he had nearly forgotten about his troublesome neighbour. Now and again he heard noises next door, a clanking sound, as though an old washing machine was being turned. And one night he could have sworn he heard a lorry drawing up, but in order to be sure he would have had to tiptoe through the front bedroom and pull back the blind, and he did not want to give the old man the satisfaction of spotting him. Perhaps he was moving? That would be a blessing.

Dublin at Christmas! You could sing that, Michael Gorman felt, if you had an air to it. Halfway through the month came the first party, a muffled drum-tap presaging dissolution. Then the rhythm quickened. The only real obstacle to party-going is distance; in a city of moderate size the same cast could be indefinitely reshuffled. Night and day the Gormans' phone kept ringing with invitations.

After an initial stand for sanity, Michael gave in. Instead of working in the evening, he found himself bolting a meal when he came home, and changing his clothes, before going to some party. He even began to convince himself he liked it when he found himself driving back at three in the morning for the third time in succession; and then waking to the retching consciousness of another workday dawn. He also found himself slipping out of the office during the day, to replenish the alcohol in his bloodstream.

It was on one of these outings that he absentmindedly made his way back to The Eagle's Nest. He entered through the long dark passage-way at the back to discover that, at four o'clock in the afternoon, it was as full as on a Saturday night. It was foggy, the lights had already been switched on, and there in a far corner, he spied his neighbour, Mr Daly.

This time he did not wait to ask the barman's advice. The little man's whole attitude, the silence which he spread around where he was mournfully sucking his pint, was an insult to the convivial spirit with which Michael Gorman felt himself imbued. Taking his drink in his hand he went over, and tapped him aggressively on the shoulder.

'Will you have a pint?' he said thickly.

Mr Daly did not seem to hear, so Gorman leaned his face down.

'I said will you have a drink with me,' he bellowed.

As Daly raised his head, Michael Gorman saw his face clearly for the first time. He had a pale, but neat forehead, deeply indented with lines and so thin that the bones stood out clearly under the skin. And his mouth and eyes were mild; not fearful, but curiously passive.

Of course I'll have a drink with you,' he said clearly. 'As long as you don't shout.'

When Michael Gorman brought back the two Jamesons from the counter, the little man had cleared a space for him. But though he thanked him politely for the drink, he showed little inclination to talk any further. And to his surprise Michael Gorman found himself falling in with the faint melancholy of his companion's mood. Only when he was preparing to go back to the office did Daly speak to him again.

'Give my respects to your wife.'

'I will.'

'You know,' said the little man hesitantly, 'you're lucky. You have a very good woman.'

Generally Michael Gorman managed to find a brickbat buried in this remark, but this time he let it pass.

'And your own wife, sir: how is she?'

The old man looked steadily at his glass. 'Boy,' he said reminiscently, 'she was a stinger!'

The climax of the season was the party on Christmas Eve. It was held in a florid Victorian barn of a house belonging to a merchant prince who collected paintings, and liked to surround himself with artists. At first Michael Gorman objected to going, on the grounds that it would be a chilly, boring affair but he swiftly found out that his host had a simple recipe for a party: pour drink and music over the assembly until their faculties disintegrate. Even ten days before the result would have horrified him: now he found himself greeting the familiar uproar with quickened pulse.

As distance is measured in relation to one chosen point, so Michael Gorman determined to measure the progress of the party by observing the behaviour of the principal guest. He was an Irish writer just back from lecturing in Upsala, and for some reason he wore a deerstalker hat, in which three artificial flies were impaled, a Bloody Butcher, a Tup's Indispensable, and a Connemara Black. He looked like Christian Dior's idea of a countryman, and as Michael passed he heard a single stentorian phrase rise and float away: 'When I knew Yeats…'

It will be a long time till that bastard is drunk, he thought grimly. Three hours later, however, as he descended the stairs (negotiating with elaborate tact the corner where a Harvard student was trying to pinion his wife) he saw the writer slumped against the wall. His eyes were nearly closed, but he clutched Michael in an effort to convey some message.

'Plaster,' he seemed to say.

'The wall, you mean? Yes, it is pretty well done,' said Michael. The writer shook his head angrily. 'Plastered,' he said with an effort.

'Oh, you mean you're drunk,' said Michael. 'Never mind: we aren't far behind you.'

Straightening up, his companion managed to shaft his bow for the last time. '*Bastards*,' he said, and in case there should be any mistake: '*Those who have money*.'

With a rush of fellow-feeling Michael assisted him to a nearby sofa, where he fell asleep with his head on a pile of coats. Then he went to claim his wife: it was time to be going home.

As they drove down the mountainside in the early morning, Michael Gorman sang softly to himself. Although he had drunk a lot, he was in one of those rare moods when drink brings an intense clarity, and the thin, pure dawn on the moors (more like water than light) invaded his mind gently. Now and again he cast an affectionate glance down to where his wife lay curled up, her head nudging his side.

When he had been a young man, tackling the Chinese Wall of chastity of the average Irish maiden, he had thought vitality the supreme virtue. He had dreamt that love, when it appeared, would be a wild flame. In his late twenties, when sexual success became easier, he had discovered to his surprise that vitality was a deceptive and dangerous thing. Now and again his relationship with his wife blazed with the passion of their first meetings, but its basis lay elsewhere, in the persistent tenderness, not spasmodic but continuous, which flooded every aspect of their lives like a calm wave.

As though she felt he had been thinking of her, Deirdre Gorman straightened up. After yawning a few times, she pressed her nose against the window-pane.

'Do you know what?' she said.

'What?'

'I've been thinking about it, why I feel so sympathetic to that old man, Mr Daly I mean, our neighbour.'

'Why?'

'I think the reason is that, in some curious way, he reminds me of you. I mean, I could see you becoming like that, if everything went wrong, and there was no one to look after you.'

Michael Gorman received this news without comment: he did not feel up to digesting its implications at that hour of the morning. All he remarked was: 'Maybe we should have a look when we get back to see if he is up, and wish him a Happy Christmas.'

It was when they drew the Prefect up opposite his flat that they saw the line of milk bottles. It must have been growing on the basement ledge for days, but they had not noticed, in the confusion of party-going. After rattling down the staircase, and hammering at the door for a few minutes without answer, Michael Gorman decided to go round to the back. It probably only meant that the little man had gone away for the holidays, but it was as well to be sure.

It look him quite some time to climb laboriously over the wall separating the two gardens: in the end he had to look for a bucket to hoist his feet on. And as he let himself down on the other side, his hands scraping on the cement, he nearly stepped on a cat, which sprinted away, like a thin shadow.

The walled-in area at the back of the house was gloomy with neglect. A pool of rain-water had formed where the grill of a drain was clogged with dead leaves. The door was firmly locked, but there was a small barred window to the left. Raising himself with his elbow on the sill, he peered through, rubbing his sleeve against the glass. The room was dark, but he could make out some details. There was a fireplace, stuffed with old papers, which spilled onto the floor. Beyond it was a filthy mattress across which – his legs dangling over the edge, his mouth open in the unseemly rictus of death – lay Mr Daly.

The police came an hour later, a sergeant and a chubby-faced young guard. They propped their bicycles against the railings, ceremoniously removed their clips, and clattered down the stairwell to the basement. After examining the premises, they decided that the only way to enter was by breaking down the door.

They took it in turns, moving to the back wall of the tiny courtyard, and then coming with a rush. They seemed puzzled at the resistance it offered, and after the fifth charge the young guard rubbed the thick wad of his serge uniform.

'Tis a killer, dat one,' he said, as though he had been breaking down doors all his life.

Finally it gave. Not at the lock, but at the centre, the whole heart of the door opening in with a rending crash as they charged, one, two, in quick succession. Stepping through the splintered remains, they found why the bolts had not given way. There were four of them, one for each quarter of the door: seen from the inside it looked like a fortress.

That was the first surprise. The second came when they entered the main room. In the old days it would have been the kitchen, but now it was dark and cold, and as the light came on, a rat scampered across the blue expanse of stove which occupied the far wall. But it was not that which took them aback. Across the stone-flagged floor, orderly as a regiment on parade, stood row upon row of slot machines. Some were without handles, some had lost their symbols, some were completely disembowelled but all were waiting, patiently in line, for the hand of the repairer.

'Jumping Jesus!' said the Sergeant.

Nor was that all. After a tour of the back rooms ('Death by natural causes, I'd say,' said the Sergeant, looking gravely down) it was decided that the young guard should remain in charge until morning. As he settled himself in with a detective story he had found in a corner, the idea occurred to him to make himself and Michael Gorman some tea. There was no gas, so he went to the meter in the hall. The shilling entered, the gas spurted; and then the coin came ringing back again, through the neat hole that had been made to facilitate its exit from the meter.

When Michael Gorman returned to his own house, instead of going immediately to bed, he went straight to his studio. Although exhausted, he felt full of a hard, flickering energy of a kind he had rarely experienced before. But as yet it was undirected, so he prepared his paints, hoping to begin a new canvas.

And then, on an impulse, he crossed the room to where his only uncompleted painting, the one of the first of November, stood with its face to the wall. He placed it on the easel: its livid spaces stared back at him, a chaos of unfulfilment. Then he reached for a brush, and began to work.

Across the dark expanse of the canvas, a line began to develop. At first frail, like an electric wire, it grew stronger, more defined. It became a dancing, independent line, full of a weird energy, and softly radiating light. It ran right across the canvas until, completing and culminating the picture, it finished in a smothered explosion of colour, like a ball of fire.

20

THE THREE LAST THINGS

Mrs Hanger was dying. In the whole village everyone knew it; but then she (and her taciturn, gloomy husband) had been there ten years. And during that decade she had entered into the ordinary life of the community, chatting to the old, playing with the young, sipping an occasional sherry in Sheila's pub. If she was not one of their own, something no outsider could ever hope to be, she was certainly no 'blow in', as an angry Irish leader had once defined it; she was as close to being accepted as anyone had come. They loved her openness, her warmth and lack of malice, the cheerfulness of her brown American face: *God love her*.

Besides, Castlehobble was not an ordinary town. It was beside the sea, but it was not a resort. You might cycle or drive out to some quiet cove, or boat out to one of the islands, but it did not have the garish, sun-worshipping life of the modern seaside. People went to fish, people swam (naked even, when they found a deserted island beach) but Castlehobble was not especially interested in bronzed summer visitors, speaking strange languages, and striding half-nude down the main street, garlanded with dangling cameras, tentacled Walkmans. They might drink in the one fashionable pub, or buy out the new delicatessen line in the grocery store, but Castlehobble only smiled at them, from an incurious distance. It had its own way of life, its own gait of going, to which they were irrelevant, as unreal as tropical birds that had blundered onto a chilly coast.

That was why Martha's dying meant so much to them – she was the one foreigner they had nearly taken to their bosom, so to speak. For if the Hangers were not natives, born and bred to the bare rock, neither were they migrants, who might up and disappear when the first cold tipped their wings. Had she (and again, as an afterthought, they added her husband) not lived out the long winter months when the town was swathed in a constant mist, or squalls of rain, and the foghorn on the point could be heard, wailing like some disconsolate beast? Then they became a real community, living in and through each other, organising whist drives, dinners, dances, Old People's Evenings and children's games, usually in the splendid Community Hall which her husband had helped design for them. A local wit had dubbed it Happiness Hanger, a description that would hardly apply to the glum, lean face of its designer. The son of a clergyman, legend had it, in which case he was living proof that, like their own priests (Father Ger, for example), servants of God should remain celibate, offer it up.

Ten winters she had endured with them, weaving spells of friendship and gossip against the driving wind and wet, the claustrophobia of that remote Western coast. And now, when she was dying, they were forbidden the house – well, not quite forbidden but not expected to call too often, or without warning. For that was the practice of the community, dropping in on each other with the latest news, a pregnancy, a marriage, an impending law case. But this simplicity had its own strictness, an order in disorder, which could be violated.

The town had a new police officer, for example, a zealous young man just out of training school, whom they nicknamed the Sheriff, because of the way he kept his thumbs hooked in his regulation belt. He also had broken the unspoken rules of Castlehobble by checking driving licences, or, worse, waiting in the darkness outside public houses or private parties to arrest stumbling citizens sleepwalking towards their cars. There had rarely been an accident in Castlehobble where people knew their way home, even in the blackest nights of winter, by a kind of alcoholic radar, the seventh sense of drunkenness. To fail to understand this showed that the young guard, Seán Wayne, as they derisively called him, was only a city slicker who had confused the real and the Wild West.

All this Martha understood, for she was a real and sympathetic listener, who fathomed how small, homely details should be woven into a saga. And there were the more intimate problems of health; only a desert father or Himalayan fakir would have endured the insidious chills of winter in Castlehobble without murmur. Colds, chilblains, rheumatics, arthritis, hacking coughs and constant flus with all their attendant remedies – did she not know about them all? She had become a dab hand at their favourite anodyne for all ills: the white lightning of illegal alcohol served up hot with cloves and home-made honey. Yes, they had become accustomed to telling, even showing, their troubles to her, swollen veins and cracking joints, shingles and ringworm, yet now, in her hardest hour, they were expected not to share her own sufferings.

The wise women of the village all decided, in a close session in Sheila's snug, that it must be the fault of her husband, but it was not as simple as that. Knute Hanger might be a tall, lean foreigner who spoke to no one unless his wife was present to warm the occasion, but that was not the reason for the sudden withdrawal. Nor was it a clash of custom; the Irish habit of *céillithe*, of dropping in unexpectedly for a chat and a jar, against the formality of European manners: pre- and postprandial drinks, the carefully maintained fortress of the family circle. No, the real reason was religion; but the kind of religion Castlehobble was least able to understand – the Hangers were both, by conviction and choice, practising atheists.

Castlehobble was an easy-going community, and proud of being so; it was definitely not one of the old priest-ridden parishes of the West, where the sins of the flesh were excoriated regularly from the altar, blasted, then beaten from the hedges by the parish priest's blackthorn. There was a small Protestant community treated as near normal by their Catholic neighbours: all farmers, sharing the vagaries of wind and weather; had they not endured the Famine together? There was a large artists' colony (potters, painters, an Australian poet with bog-Irish ancestors, who preferred Cork and Kerry to Canberra, a sculptor who hammered out large erotic abstracts, massive lingams of steel that people preferred not to comprehend) but most of these 'blow ins' were Irish, and had presumably started off life as Catholics, like everybody else. So they knew the code of their neighbours, and if they had long, friendly arguments with them, playing cards or drinking, they still knew how to watch their words, not to cross the tactful threshold of religious belief.

Only a few miles away, at Ballylicken, superstition flourished, and religion reigned. A statue of the Virgin in the roadside grotto had been seen to move, though as the crowds swelled through one summer her mobility became less obvious. Then a gravedigger had discovered an uncorrupted body in the local cemetery, 'the two eyes smiling straight up at me,' he explained emphatically in the public house that evening. The young corpse, it seemed, had been a living saint, a sweet-tempered child who died early, consumed by innumerable maladies, yet with the name of God always on her lips. Or so claimed her now elderly remaining sister who had all but forgotten her existence until she rose up again, so to speak, in the graveyard.

Castlehobble had no such special favours from the Almighty but it kept an open mind; there was an annual pilgrimage to Lourdes, which was greatly enjoyed, but as much for the wine and the *craic* as for the religious consolation. But to ignore both church and chapel and declare that God could not, did not, exist was something else. In the long memory of the village it had happened only the once, when someone had harmlessly asked Knute Hanger which church he favoured, what religion his country or region practised.

'None, thank God,' he had answered curtly and then, in case there should be any misunderstanding, added with a wrathful urgency which belied his usual sullenness and silence: 'I do not hold with such rubbish. Why should we invent a Being to blame for our own beastliness?' And as his interlocutor shrank away before this sudden explosion, Knute advanced on his hapless victim. 'If he does exist, then he is, as you say here, *a right bastard*,' was Knute's final salute, mistaking an expression of total shock for one of religious anguish, an emotion not prevalent in Castlehobble, or indeed in the whole country.

So in Sheila's pub they discussed the situation in whispers. 'She's not well at all,' said Sheila, 'and sinking daily.'

'I don't like the look of her; she's not long for this world,' echoed her sister; between them they laid out all the female corpses of the village and would, it seemed, lay out Martha before long, with all the ancient and impassive skill of their kind. In preparation for which they had been admitted to the bedside; but the astonishing thing was that they had gone, not on some tiptoeing errand, but at Martha's specific request, as old friends from whom she would shortly be requiring a last service. Such lack of mystery or false modesty, such matter-of-fact clarity about death was something totally unexpected and alien to Castlehobble, more accustomed to the solemn tones of the panegyric or the wakehouse eulogy. Surely the end was not like closing down a shopfront, or shutting a gap;

just a formality, a shade harsher than most because of the pain involved? But even that seemed to be scanted, for as Sheila said, 'She won't talk much about her sickness at all, and when she does speak, she's clear as a bell.'

And her sister added: 'You'd never guess from her face what she was going through, although of course she's nearly grey and light as a ghost. Talk about soldiers – she'd show them how to die any day. The bold Knute wouldn't face the firing squad as lightly.'

The other women listening agreed, with secret pangs of envy and admiration, for, after all, the sisters had been allowed to see such a paragon of their sex's proverbial powers of endurance. And they swallowed hungrily any scraps of information about Martha's state, both of body and mind, while feeling terribly cheated. Like actors summoned to a modern version of a classical tragedy, relegated from the solemn and mournful responses of the chorus to the sideline, they felt oddly useless, somehow insulted in their final, traditional role as sympathetic witnesses of human destiny. Funerals had changed since the old days when whole families would pray the dying into the next world, preparing the wake while waiting for the last gasp, soothing the brow while setting out the whiskey and snuff, but such hygienic death, such a clinical withdrawal, like a curtain drawn in a hospital ward, was more like New York than Castlehobble. Why had the Hangers decided to live there if they chose to ignore its most cherished feelings about what an old Irish poet had described as the three last things?

'And how is Knute taking it?' they enquired with carefully phrased indifference. As far as they were concerned, he was the real stumbling block, the spanner in the works, who must ultimately be to blame for his wife's sudden severity of attitude. For he defeated all their expectations, in looks, dress and behaviour: dignified as a senior clergyman, like his father probably; they still did not know what to make of him, especially when he had dropped his guard so abruptly once, shown his savagely secular hand. That such a serious man should deny the existence of God was impossible; most of the educated men of their world, priests and teachers, were specifically dedicated to upholding religion. And Knute looked more like them than they did themselves – never a breath of scandal, never a savage bout of drunkenness, but always so soberly dressed, with his neat beard and dark clothes. And so courteous, bowing to every

woman he met on the street, all the assembled friends or least acquaintances of Martha, as if they were ladies from some dignified past. How
could you have the manners of a gentleman and not believe in the
Supreme Being? And behave with such deference to womankind if you
were not prepared to recognise, to accept their humble, centuries-old
effort to share His suffering, under the banner of the one true God, who
had shown us how to accept death?

If He had hung in shame and pain on the good wood, bared his man's
body to the savagery of the Roman soldiers, and the taunts of the Jews,
then they should bring his consolation to their dying friend, defy the terrible paganism of her husband, speed another soul towards heaven.

*

In Ralph's (pronounced 'Raife's') American Bar the menfolk gathered to
discuss the situation, in the intervals of watching a re-run of a World
Championship fight on the television.

'It's not right, it's not natural, it's not how things are done,' said the
boss, a squat, close-cropped man who had spent years in the NYPD, New
York's Finest. Ralph's was a good pub, with a sophisticated range of
drinks, a diversity of taste the owner had brought back with him. Tequila,
Cretan Raki, Bastida de Cao, Cassis, Cinzano, Saint Raphael, Pastis,
Vermouth, Ricard, Metaxa, Ouzo and Floc de Gascoigne - you could find
them all lining the higher shelves of the bar, behind the usual chubby
Paddy or Powers whiskey bottles. People rarely asked for them but Ralph
liked to have them there, to remind him of his wilder days in New York,
and they made good opening gambits in casual conversation with
impressed visitors.

But if there was a touch of cosmopolitan ease about Ralph's Bar
there was also an atmosphere of subdued hostility: you either agreed with
the owner or you got out; he did not like, could not bear, to be contradicted.

'She should have a proper wake, and a proper funeral,' he declared,
pulling a slow luxurious pint, with its priestly collar of froth. 'It's the way
it was always done here, for saint or sinner.' His listeners did not query his
knowledge of either state, for the flare of his temper was feared and
famous. When his dander was up, he would have struck a saint, or emp-
tied a pint over a priest. Meanwhile, oblivious to Ralph's theological

views, George Foreman was sinking to the canvas on that hot night in Zaire, surely never to rise in glory again, psyched out by Cassius Clay, now known as Mohammed Ali.

*

Knute Hanger gazed out through his dining room window at the light dying on the Atlantic. He had always loved the sea, its squalls and smiles, that continually changing presence, which he could see from every window of the house in which he had chosen· to live. Rather he and Martha, the son of a German pastor and the daughter of a German Jewish survivor of the pogroms.

For years after the war they had searched the world for some outpost of uncomplicated kindness. Southern Mexico had seemed right for a time, but they got tired of being called 'gringo' by the children in the marketplace, and Martha had discovered that prices doubled when she entered the local shops, and although she addressed them in fluent Spanish, they always answered in broken English, forcing them back to the Yankee ghetto.

And so they tried Ireland, moving further and further west, until they found this harbour home. Here in this damp extremity of Europe, they had found a haven, the paradoxical ideal of a gregarious isolation. The town of Castlehobble received them, but also left them discreetly alone. There were the long conversations with the locals in the shops and public houses but no one intruded, while responding cheerfully to any overture. And there were enough artists to ensure a minimum of technical exchange, if Knute was going through a bad period. Yes, on the whole, it had been fruitful; for a decade of loving peace, during which he had painted some of his best pictures, and Martha had raised their children, and come to know and love the village, warily at first, but with a gathering appreciation of the web the locals spun around every incident in the endless saga of Castlehobble.

And now their union was being broken up, by the dictates of a cruel fate, their love was being extinguished. There were only a few gleams of light left, far out at sea, as Knute softly quoted to himself famous lines from *King Lear*: 'As flies to wanton boys are we to the gods; they kill us for their sport.' There could not be a God, whatever historians said about our advance from polytheism, the multitudinous deities of the Greeks and Indians, because if there was one central Being, then he was a blind monster, whom one could only loathe.

Take his most intelligent, loving, but now dying wife. Why create such a delicate, affectionate, thinking creature only to destroy it? Such a death was the ultimate absurdity, an affront to life. If God existed, he was to blame for having devised this cruel charade, and not only for single human beings, however valuable, but on a grand scale. Contemplating the full horror of the twentieth century – death camps and atomic bombs – if God existed, he must be a sadist, for allowing such things to happen. Bad enough that mankind should die, as Martha was now doing, but not stripped, humiliated, broken down by pain or torture.

That was the dilemma of free will, of course, but Knute agreed that it was better to blame the bestiality of some men than invent some all-powerful Aztec entity who sat back, accepting these rivers of blood as homage, or reclined on his golden throne, deaf to the cries of suffering beneath him. Instead of a medieval vision of Christ the King, who would separate the sheep from the goats, the Elect from the Damned, Knute Hanger, son of Pastor Hanger, heard these cries of anguish, saw the stumbling hordes of victims, whose supplications ascended endlessly into the void. The twentieth century was an Inferno with no hint of a Paradiso; why kid yourself, as the Americans said, when with fire and brimstone, as in the Old Testament, man blasted his fellow man, was, indeed, prepared to blast the very earth itself? If the Christian God of these Irish peasants, and his learned father, really existed, then he was to be hated and dethroned immediately. Any so-called parent would step in if he saw his child mistreating even a dog; the way Martha had tended a whole zoo of ailing animals, cats, mongrels, donkeys beaten or deserted by their owners. But God the Father showed no compassion, only the blind face of indifference; the latest example being the way Knute's beloved wife was being broken down, cell by dying cell. He was right to have declared war against the Christian fallacy as early as he could, disbelieving for the same reasons his father had believed.

*

Knute Hanger's father had been a Lutheran pastor in an industrial town in north Germany, near the Baltic. He remembered his study, its deep stillness, like a cellar or a well, the simple cross on the table, the few Durer etchings on the walls. But mainly books, the complete works of the great philosophers, like Emmanuel Kant, the poets like Goethe and Schiller, a copy of Luther's *Heilige Schrift* on a lectern. He had browsed there for hours when he was a boy, devouring the Old Testament for its wonderful stories of war and lust and high adventure, Daniel in the Lions' Den, or the boy David defying Goliath.

Yet it was in that tranquil atmosphere that he had at last to confront his pastor father. It had begun at school where so many of his schoolmates had joined the Hitler Jugend. Knute was against it but his father felt it would be wiser not to make a fuss. Young and all as he was, Knute discovered in himself a rage that he did not know he was capable of; he ended up shouting at the pastor.

'You believe, Father, that I should follow these puppets, as they strut like their stupid fathers. Little bullies, in a few years they will be swilling beer, and boasting, like that horrible fatso Goering. Surely your son should behave better? I am proud to be a scholar, like you, and besides, I loathe uniforms.'

His father tried to explain that there were historical reasons for what was happening.

'It's that Treaty is to blame, and the shame of Weimar. Germans feel humiliated; they want to show that they are not broken, they are still men.'

'A uniform doesn't make a man better; do we respect a postman or ticket collector more than others? No, the Nazis want to march together like maniacs, saluting that little counter-jumping lunatic from Austria, with the false name.'

'You are unfair: the Nazi Party has helped to give Germany back its pride. Versailles was an act of revenge, not a peace pact. We raise an army again, and the world respects Germany again.'

'Respect, my eye, he will lead us to Wagnerian perdition, your Chancellor. Look how he has already cowed your people; are you proud of the Reich Church? Have you heard of Pastor Bonhoeffer's professorship at his seminary being terminated? Or does he not count, because he is not an Orthodox Lutheran? Maybe he should learn Luther's gift for abuse.'

His father went silent, gazing around at his library, so proudly accumulated from Gymnasium days. He was a fine man, but the theological works he loved to peruse – Busching, Bauer, Kaehler on the Historical Jesus – were of no use to him now, confronting his brilliant son, an

270

adolescent hurled into harsh maturity. It was only the first of many sharp exchanges, the last being when Knute announced his decision not to come to church any more, because of what he regarded as his father's cowardice. It was after the service and the *kapellmeister* was running through a fugue in the background. The pastor had timidly suggested that instead of denouncing *Mein Kampf*, as his son wished him to do, one should consider the good ideas in it.

'Like his views on the Jews, written largely by Streicher? Are they alone to be blamed for the inequality of the German economy? We should be our own scapegoat.'

But his father still prevaricated and Knute could stand it no longer.

'If good men like you stand by, then we are lost. Or maybe your Church is at fault: I've been reading Luther in your library, and he abused the Jews because they didn't convert.'

'That was late in his life. The Jews have always suffered: it is their race's destiny. But you know Psalm 126 quoted in Brahms' *Deutsches Requiem*: "they that sow in tears shall reap in joy." There is a larger pattern which you are too young to discern.'

Joy indeed. He saw the stormtroopers at work in the Jewish ghetto, prodding a bearded Hasidic rabbi forwards with a bayonet, reviling children, smashing old shop windows. Should the old Christ-killers have turned the other cheek, like true Christians?

Some dark cloud now hung over the world, deforming men into Bosch-like creatures, fanged wolves, murderous insects, drinkers of blood who showed a cannibalistic delight in mangling human flesh and bone. In the Middle Ages there had been the dreaded Plague; during the Reformation the Wars of Religion. But neither malady nor religion could be produced as an excuse for what was happening in their own fatherland. So there and then he had decided that the God his father prayed to could not, did not, exist, if he were to make any sense out of contemporary life, which violently proclaimed God's absence, his desertion, his disappearance. Knute Hanger left home, slipping across the border into Denmark, then making his way to England when the war broke out. In due course, as his reward, he would be amongst the first Allied soldiers to enter Dachau. He still kept a photograph on his desk as a souvenir of that day, the final incontrovertible proof of man's latent savagery, contradicted only by the sweetness of generous spirits like his now bravely dying wife.

*

Martha Hanger had arranged to be alone, one hour in the morning, one in the afternoon, one after dinner, so that she could compose her declining energies to face her problem. Her problem, she thought ironically, her demise, her sudden disappearance, an abrupt leaving of all the small details of her life; daily she wrote goodbye notes to distant friends. Her favourite books surrounded her on the bed, mainly poetry, because she would never again have time to immerse herself in the structure of a novel, to interest herself in the loves and hates of fictional characters. Poetry lay in small piles on either side of her, or at the foot of the bed, the thick bulk of a *Collected*, single volumes as slim as devotional or political pamphlets. Which, of course, they were, in a sense, manifestos about living and loving, from the darkness of Paul Celan to the quivering self-regard of Rilke, the thunder of Thomas. Each one offered her a different vision and, according as she weakened or wavered, she could reach for the psychic shock of their particular truth. How could you reconcile the measured tones of the vice-president of the Hartford Insurance Company intoning that 'life contracts and death is expected, / As in a season of autumn. / The Soldier falls' with the angry outcry of Dylan (they had met him in the White Horse in 1952, dishevelled but full of aggressive grief for his dying father) that we should 'not go gentle into that good night'? If she raged against her fate, she did it, as she had done most things in her life, gently, calmly, with consideration for others. She admired the fury of the drunken Welsh gnome but her upbringing gave her more in common with the Connecticut recluse.

Tiring of poetry, or writing last letters, she could look up to contemplate the pictures she had chosen to keep as lifetime companions on the walls of her bedroom. There were the Irish works acquired during the last decade, mostly traditional glimpses of Castlehobble life, an old man battering his stubborn donkey along, a proud fisherman holding up a gleaming fish, a study of a sparrowhawk or kestrel swooping over a small animal. There was a hint of menace in some of these studies by local artists, the teeming hedge life that went on relentlessly under the lichened stones and dripping, cloudy skies when the warm evening was full of owl calls, the rustle of fleeing prey.

But they were meek, almost soothing beside the strange abstracts of her husband, canvases covered with slashes of dark paint, or dripping

272

with colours like tears running down a raddled face. How well she knew the brooding that had gone into them, days, weeks, months on end as Knute wrestled with the void which, for him, underlay the living world. He could not sleep, he prowled the house talking and crying to himself until the tension eased, with some temporary victory or stay against the cannibal darkness. She did not feel as strongly about things as he did, but she accepted his views: was she not the daughter of someone who had nearly died in the camps he had helped to liberate?

His cartoons were now famous, a post-Holocaust version of George Grosz, an assembly line of black humour with small men being savaged by giant spouses, who were subjugated in their turn by phallic machines: the sexual cruelty of modern war and modern life was systematically exploited in a horrifying but palatable way. The very people who were being satirised – gaunt American hostesses with rings sparkling on every finger – rushed to buy them, in an extravagant act of self-castigation. The baby seal bleeding on the ice with a New York Maenad standing over his tiny carcass, screaming, 'I want that fur for Tuesday's party at the Strumpfs', hubby!' had become a signature for the Conservation Lobby. And the divorcing couple slicing everything in two, their palatial house, their car, their pets, and finally their children, with war cries of: 'And now are you satisfied?'

She preferred less obvious drawings, which detailed the little cruelties of nature, a heron stilting with a still-living fish in his slender beak, the heron which lived in a misty pool where the river debouched in the sea. They went by to see him on clear evenings and were rewarded sometimes to see His Eminence, as they called him, gain the rewards of his patience. And there was a clutch of gannets offshore which would dive past the boat with that undeviating marvellous line of speed, striking the still water (for they could not spy their target otherwise) with their beaks, with a sound like a quick clap. Observing nature, he was unparalleled in his loving exactness: a spiky whirl of evening swallows, all beaks and claws and tiny wingbeats, a badger they had met on the road, loping along, head low, all hunched up. And the hedgehogs he brought home, to feed with a spoon and scraps from the table, as he did the baby birds. How could this tenderness coexist with his stridency, his satirical harshness: perhaps because he could not harm a butterfly himself, he was horrified by the nonchalance of those who did?

He was a loving, caring but most complicated man, and perhaps the loneliness of the abstracts was closest to his real self. She knew how deep they came from inside her husband's psyche, an attempt to describe where no description was possible, to sound the rhythm of darkness that beat all night under the skies and seas of the world. Done in rage, vexation, near despair, they were the testimonies of a supremely honest spirit. If Nihil, even Satan, or Lucifer, the fiery fallen, was in charge of this universe, then every work of art was a gesture against its black power, a throw of the dice in a game that had no meaning. It could not be denied, but must be fought, to the bitter end.

How much of the old Protestant pastor still lay within him, with unbelief as his belief! It was a position that God, if he existed, would pity and understand – the God of the New Testament. There had to be genuine unbelievers, people whom the apparently useless appendix of belief was missing. She had never forgotten his description of entering Dachau, the yellow smoke from miles away, the sudden hush of the jubilant troops, the figures scrabbling at the wire; the ultimate insult to the nostrils, the smell of the charnel house. Heartsick, fumbling, their marching pride reduced to silence, the liberating troops had offered presents to their skeletal greeting party but the bodies rejected even C-rations immediately.

She could see all this behind his paintings and in their dark way they brought her some comfort. For it was into the darkness she was sinking. Each day she sank a little bit further away from it all, like a waterlogged boat. The disease had already reached her lower limbs; she had never thought she would see the day when she could not wiggle her toes but it was already there and climbing towards her knees. The doctor and the specialists had said that the whole process would take a month and that it was irreversible; she would die slowly upwards, her brain wearily clear until the poisons engulfed her whole system.

There is nothing clears the mind like a sentence of death; she had found the old Johnsonian cliché true for her. For what could she do to distract herself from the anguish, the pitiless facts? She did not drink much, and although the doctor offered her drugs, she took them only when the pain was devouring; it was constant and inexorable but not unbearable. The last few days might be difficult: she had discussed with her Irish doctor a special cocktail of drugs which would, he said, make St Lawrence hornpipe on his gridiron, and at that ultimate point between death and life, dissolution and reality, she felt she might be allowed some hilarity. In the meantime, she set herself as bravely as she could, for the sake of her husband as well, to die the way they had lived, with the stern humility of rational humanism. Sweetened, in her case, by poetry; she reached down for one of her favourite volumes and began to chant to herself the slight but singing lines she already knew so well. 'What answer but endurance, kindness / Against her choice, I still affirm / That nothing dies…'

Consoling words, but were they true? She would soon be in a position to find out. She heard the murmur of voices through the door, the voice of her husband, the voice of the local parish priest, Father Gerard O'Driscoll, Ger for short. He had called up Knute early in the month, with tentative courtesy. He had not been officially informed but the whole village was following her rapid descent with such fascination that he could not help knowing about it. So he proceeded with all due ceremony, phoning beforehand, setting an exact hour for his visit. And he arrived with a bottle under his arm, a bottle of Schnapps from Ralph's Bar, for he knew his host's taste. Many's the winter evening they had spent, playing chess, and drinking quietly, as the waves lapped against the harbour wall, the light died from the porthole windows, and the winds strained the rafters, until the room creaked like the cabin of a ship at sea.

Knute Hanger received the gift in silence and set out two neat glasses. After the third application of the dry, sharp spirits, the priest felt free to speak.

'There is no hope, then?'

'None.'

'How long does she have?'

'Four, five days, maybe a week. It goes fast in the final stages.'

'May I see her?'

Knute was silent for a while, then he threw back, rather than swallowed, a swift Schnapps.

'As long as you don't try to sneak in any prayers. She should die as she has lived. No fooling around with rosary beads or holy water; absolutely no false promises about the next life, compassionate judges and flapping angels. It is not our style.'

It was the priest's turn to be silent and apply himself to the Schnapps. He liked Knute, with whom he had spent so many pleasant evenings (they were now equally matched in chess, Knute's early skill grown rusty in the

Irish air, the priest using long, lonely hours to practise in his presbytery). And he liked his directness, so bracingly different from the calculated vagueness of so many of his Irish parishioners, who approached a subject as if it were a hare hidden in a thicket. But this evening Knute was more brusque than ever, under the pressure of this new trial, this new proof, the priest realised, of all the worst that he feared and felt about life. They had discussed that too, near the end of the bottle, but theological exchange was not in order, when simple human compassion was needed.

'Of course not,' he said, draining his glass. 'I just want to say a straight goodbye. We worked together a lot, you know, in the charity area. A very genuine woman, always glad to help, no matter what our differences of opinion might have been. We were always open with each other.'

He could not prevent an embarrassed sharpness creeping into his own comments.

Knute hung his head, hopelessly.

'In you go. She's expecting you. When she heard you had telephoned, she particularly asked to see you. I said it would be pointless, that you couldn't help but try and lure her, that it was your bounden duty to twitch the thread, that you were a priest first, and a friend afterwards. I know your sort.'

Father O'Driscoll was silent. The diagnosis was not far from the mark and, once again, as in many previous exchanges, he had to register the man's honesty. It came hard to Knute to speak harshly, the priest could see, but he said what he felt had to be said, no matter what the circumstances. Would to God – there he went again – his parishioners could manage such probity. But Knute had already read his silence as hurt.

'I know,' he said flatly, 'I know because of my father; he had to preach, too. He believed, against all the evidence, that even I had a Christian soul which had to be saved, against my will. He thought that all suffering could be explained if it led us to Christ: that even the poor tortured victims of Nazidom might achieve baptism by desire, expire in such pain that it brought them close to what the Portuguese call The Man. You remind me of him sometimes, when you speak of your straying parishioners. In a good-humoured way, of course, Father, but I can feel the hunter, the heavenly fisherman, biding his time, and I resent him. That baited hook hung over my childhood soul. There have been tyrants before, and bad times, but there is only one God. I despise and resent such single-minded sophistry. My soul, immortal or mortal, is not a fish, nor am I a brand to be plucked from the burning; your God loves cruel metaphors.'

And you have been squirming on his hook ever since, thought Father O'Driscoll, but he withheld his comment. What in heaven – there he went again – did he know about the whole process, despite what they had taught him in the seminary? He learned from his life, with the staff of his belief to help him. With a last swift snort of Schnapps he headed for the sickroom, and for the strangest deathbed exchange of his pastoral life so far.

*

Father Ger O'Driscoll was used to death, and deathbeds; they were as much part of his daily rounds as of a doctor's. Confessions at the week-end were not as regular as they used to be and even Mass attendance had dwindled a little. At first he had been inclined to blame the influx of artists into the community, which was becoming an Irish branch of St Ives, but he knew they had very little effect on his flock, most of whom were blind to them, even the erotic sculptures of John Lucy, with their oriental application to the details of lovemaking.

It was more likely to be mere laziness, staying up at night to look at 'The Late Late Show' on television, or some horrible Hollywood soap opera. How often had he dropped into a farmhouse and found them sitting in darkness, not facing the heat of the stove, or murmuring the rosary, but watching two TV stars grapple on the coloured screen. Teenage sex, lust, abortion, homosexuality, incest: they knew about all now, in theory at least, as it washed into their own kitchens all the way from Los Angeles. They turned it off for him, but the conversation was stiff, until he indicated he was keeping up with Gay Byrne and Jackie Collins and the other real stars of their nightly firmament. Even the ads exposed breasts and crotches to old bachelors who had never seen either; why did they never mention them in confession?

Still, he was always called for at the end, even by the most hardened. As a matter of fact, he thought grimly, his hand on the doorknob, it is nearly my most successful role, a sort of Holy Meals on Wheels, the Oils. And with a start, he remembered that he had automatically brought along his reticule (what a local quilter called his 'heavenly sewing basket') in the car, in case it might come in handy. He opened the sickroom door.

After all his years tending the sick, he was still not prepared for what he saw. Martha was propped up in bed, reading the *Collected Poems* of an Irish poet, which he had given her shortly after they had installed themselves in Castlehobble, and realised that they shared common interests. She looked weary, waxen, but her eyes were bright.

'How are you, Martha?' he asked and could have cursed his blatant stupidity.

'Surprisingly well,' she said. 'Although I have, of course, lost the control of my lower body. No feeling in my toes, none in my legs, and now it is creeping inch by inch, strictly on schedule. But as deaths go, it is an easy enough one, I suppose. At least I can keep my head, say goodbye to my friends forever, and observe death's progress. An easier journey outward than many you will have seen, Father; poor people.'

Even dying, her thought was of others who had suffered more. Automatically he found himself looking around for holy pictures, as in the majority of the sickrooms he visited. But instead there were drawings and paintings, particularly the strange, dark visions of her husband. He could not profess to understand the large, weeping abstracts, Veronica's veils with no divinity shadowed in them, but they had a powerful aura, which always made the priest shiver, as if contemplating slivers of the stricken psyche, the Godhead in pieces.

'So this is our last meeting,' Martha Hanger said, almost with a laugh as she saw Father O'Driscoll start with dismay before her brisk honesty. 'Unless there is one of your miracles, of course, as in dear Ballylicken. But I doubt if I will be singled out for such an honour. And I hope you have not come to convert me. Knute has probably warned you off. As the tree falls, so should it lie: I should die as I have lived.' She corrected herself. 'As we have lived.'

Ger O'Driscoll was silent. Nothing in his seminary training or his pastorate had prepared him for this; it was certainly the most direct deathbed exchange he had ever had, with the victim more convinced than the Christian pastor who had come to succour her. And yet, he knew from his experience, she must be afraid. He had tended all sorts, old mountainy men and women whose faith was as simple as spring water, notorious drunks who had craved oblivion, but nearly all died hard, till he brought them to some kind of resignation before the inevitable. He still remembered the wail of a tough old crone from the back of beyond, with the rosary beads clamped around her fist, as she rocked to and fro, crying into the winter night: 'There's a cold wind and a long road before me, and me not knowing where I go.'

'And don't you feel afraid?' he ventured, finally.

'Doesn't everyone?' countered Martha briskly. 'I have seen many of my family die, and now it is my turn. I must not cry out against our common fate. I die at home, with my husband, not butchered by the roadside, or tortured, or gassed, like so many of my people. I should be grateful.'

Out of his depth, Father Ger still blundered duly on.

'I think I know what you mean. Many of our people must have felt stricken after the Famine that laid this country waste. But we did survive. Yet sometimes, surely, you have felt something, a whiff of infinity, a sense of some larger pattern that envelops all poor human accidents into meaning, even the crudity attendant on death?'

'Of God, you mean,' she interjected, curtly enough. 'Oh yes, after making love properly, perhaps, and not only with Knute, but earlier, with Nathan, a young Talmudic student who was killed. For wars create tenderness as well, you know. Do you know the Indian doctrine of *mithuna*, that the act of love can be an insight into the process of creation? Knute can show you those wonderful sculptures from Konarak, executed about the same time as Chartres. Strange how the West celebrated celibacy, the East physical love, both in the name of religion.'

But the priest had buried his head in his hands and she was immediately concerned for him: 'Poor Father Ger, it is not fair to speak of such things to you; the flesh was probably a heresy in your young days. I am very stupid. But there have been other moments.'

'When?' he managed, almost through tears.

'Oh, sailing, when the sea was at force five. In a yacht, however small, one is so conscious of all those tensions, the wind shifting, the waves lurching. The forces of life are so close to one, the danger and the excitement.'

'The forces of life,' he said weakly, 'perhaps we are giving different names to the same thing. God can be both benign and angry, like the sea.'

'And he sends storms, of course, that drown people. One of our most gifted friends was plucked off a rock where he was fishing by a sudden wind. He had already been stricken by polio and didn't swim very well and the sea was high. Maybe he should not have been there, but he was resting from his work and the day was bright. I prefer not to blame anybody: it is the blind structure of life itself, sometimes kind, more often cruel . . . My husband may be extreme but he is right; you only begin to make sense of it all when you cease to believe. In sense, in a pattern, in a meaning. Senselessness may be the meaning, the acceptance of the void the beginning of true wisdom. You may call that God if you want to, of course; Nathan spoke of the great Jewish mystic, Isaac the Blind, who saw God in the depths of His nothingness.'

The priest was silent as a stunned bullock. Instead of bringing spiritual aid, he was being instructed by someone much more experienced in the diverse ways of the world, of religion, than himself. How could he answer her, when a part of his spirit was in sympathy with her point of view? But before he tried anything more, she came again to his rescue.

'Father Ger,' she said, affectionately, 'you must not heed too much. I may be feeling bitter. But you came to say goodbye to me, as a good friend. And you feel you have a job to do, in relation to your community, and. my extinction. So how can I help you? I'm ready. Then we can say farewell.'

Emaciated, but still full of purpose, Martha Hanger braced herself against her pillows to face the priest. He, in his turn, turned to confront her level, pain-consumed gaze, powerful as an open furnace. And in a few minutes they came to some agreement as to the arrangements of her approaching death, and the ceremonies that could, and could not, be allowed. A bargain was struck between them, down-to-earth as the old-fashioned slapping of palms in the marketplace, Jew and Christian, non-believer and believer, foreigner and native seeking common ground. Knute was not to be insulted; neither was the community that had welcomed them; and Father O'Driscoll was the custodian of that delicate balance. Her last variant made him reel a little, but she had already granted him so much ground that he could only give in, laughing grimly a little at how it might be received. He emerged from the room to where the silent Knute awaited them. Together they finished the bottle of Schnapps.

*

From that day forward, the people of Castlehobble came to pay their respects. Knute greeted them briefly but warmly, offering them a glass before they went in to see his wife. The great wooden dining table, the table of his father, and his father's father before him, was laden with Murphy and Guinness, beer of all kinds, large yellow bottles of Paddy and Powers whiskey, a harmless-looking bottle of poteen.

In and out they trooped, consoling, but also, he was surprised to see, especially when they returned from the sickbed, openly smiling. It was as if death were their element, something they could swim in more easily than the vast Atlantic that beat at their doors. They did not get mouldy drunk, they did not overstay their welcome; only Ralph of Ralph's American Bar waxed a little maudlin, remembering his own mother. 'She reminds me of her, you know, Knute, leaving with everything in place, thinking only of those left behind, on this hard earth. After my mother's death I found little notes everywhere, where she had stored things. And I cried to see them: it was as if she had never left us, and was smiling down from Heaven's Gate.' And he wept, draining another glass.

But he was the exception to a most considerate and orderly procession. As it wound on, day after wearing day, Knute began to wonder about its effects. Was it wearing out Martha, that fount of goodness? No matter how many visitors came, he found her exhausted, but smiling, afterwards. And no one came back: it was a final farewell, which left the bed heaped with flowers, little souvenirs like white heather, four-leafed clover. Peasants though they might be, they were to be congratulated on their courtesy and infinite tact. Deep in some forgotten part of his psyche he felt something stirring, the embers of a religious emotion, which their reverence and respect before the brute fact of death fanned a little. He too bent his head, humbly, before the unknowable, felt briefly the fiercely touching power of simple faith, with its uncomplicated response to the mysterious sorrow we all share. And he thought of Flaubert in his old age looking down at a cradle in the house of his favourite niece and saying sadly: *Ils sont dans le vrai.* The sentimentality of the old, certainly, but perhaps these seemingly simple yokels were right in their way of dealing with death. So he felt for the moment, after they had left and he and his exhausted sleeping wife were alone once more. After he had made the evening meal perhaps he would feel more himself.

*

A fortnight later, the day of the funeral dawned, chilly but bright. And now Knute was definitely in poor humour, agitated as a monkey before the many details involved. The last week had been hard, seeing his brave and beloved Martha begin to drift in and out of insensibility. He kept a nightly vigil by her bed, but she no longer knew him, and as he watched the spirit he had loved fade from her eyes, and all the avenues of her wasted body close down, he felt a disconsolate longing for some kind of ceremony, after all.

Although there was always something to keep him occupied, to bring him back to what, normally, he would have called reality. When the doctor confirmed death, there was the ceremony of laying out, and the final funeral arrangements. And now the hearse was standing, dark and shining as a beetle, before the door. And his own old friends had come, the few who lived in Ireland, driving through the early dawn to pay homage to a spirit that they admired, that had influenced their own lives. There were a few embassy officials, for after all, recluse though he might be, Knute Hanger had an international reputation. And some members of the nearest Jewish community, Martha's family being of the older faith.

Discreetly, cars turned and churned before the hall door; instinct and the sight of the gleaming hearse seemed to have brought them out of hiding. On a terrace overlooking the sea, Knute dispensed glasses of dry white wine to his distant guests with a numb but practised politeness that reminded him of his own father. How was he going to get through this of all days? A half of his life had gone, the better half, the dear creature who had endured his bitter moods, now disintegrated into something worse than dust. He could not say if he had loved his wife; he and she had been one, and yet half of that entity was now an extinct and rotting body. Gloomily, he gestured towards the door; after all, he was the master of ceremonies.

Never had he seen his courtyard so full; the bonnets of the cars shone like a shoal of glistening fish. He nodded here and there, recognising Sheila, looking very dignified, Ralph, whom he always had difficulty disassociating from the wooden frame of his bar, the faces of all the people from whom he had bought his goods, the shopkeeper class who seemed to be the backbone of all small Irish towns; a Famine atavism surely?

It did not take long to manage the coffin through the door and then, to his surprise, he was expected to lead in lifting it into the hearse, balanced by other strong, silent men. How absurd all this formality was: there was a corpse, which might just as well be shoved out to sea, or buried in the garden, instead of all this public exploitation of grief, by funeral homes and clergy and so many others! Even work had stopped.

With Martha's coffin safely stowed, under a surprising inundation of flowers, he headed back to the lead black car. In all the teeming mackerel shoal, no one moved, or showed a sign of impatience, waiting with silent understanding for his signal. When he gave it, they began to fall in line, discreetly, deliberately, behind the hearse. As the cortege swung through the narrow streets of Castlehobble, a whole cluster of church bells began to ring out, Protestant and Catholic, ding and dong. If Martha Hanger did not believe in one God, she was being saluted, sent off, by two versions of him.

Along the coast road the cortege sped towards the new graveyard overlooking the sea. Then they climbed out of their cars, stumbling over graves, to where the fresh earth of a newly opened one gaped. Then the ceremony began, in unseasonably bright sunlight.

Usually in Castlehobble all such ceremony was conducted by the priest or parson, both of whom were there. But now Knute stepped forward, speaking rapidly in German. It sounded like poetry, but he paraphrased only a few lines for his audience.

'Today we realise the total absurdity of human existence. One day we are here; tomorrow, gone. We are but butterflies, doomed mayflies dancing on a summer lake. The ultimate proof of the meaninglessness of existence for me is the death of this fine being whom we all admired; she died as bravely as a condemned prisoner. She was an angel but her wings shrivelled in the fire of death. Nothing…absurd.'

He paused but the inhabitants of Castlehobble were already in a state of shock: such language had never been heard in the graveyard. What was Father O'Driscoll doing? He was listening intently to this stream of pagan gibberish. 'From Nietzsche to Sartre, men have tried to face the harsh facts of nothingness but I cannot believe. Only a week or so ago I spoke for the last time to Martha: she said how good our life had been. But now it is annihilated, as if she had never lived, we had never loved, and I am angry, angry with this Nobadaddy in the sky.'

Stunned, the folk of Castlehobble saw Knute Hanger shake his fist at the sky. And then another figure stepped forward, not Father Ger, but led by him. It was the cantor of the dwindling Jewish community of Cork, a venerable-looking gentleman with a small skullcap, like the Pope's, only black.

With Father Ger at his side he launched into the noble cadences of the Jewish Office for the Dead, the 'Kaddish'.

He who maketh peace in his high places, may he make peace
for us and for all Israel and say ye, Amen.

This time there was no translation. Stiff in the sunlight, the Castlehobble mourners let the waves of language break over them. Some of them had heard at one time or another that Martha was Jewish but they did not really associate it with this strange language, far stranger even to their ears than the German that had marched before it. Were they never to get a look in, be allowed to say a Christian word over an old friend in a Catholic graveyard which sheltered their doubtless outraged own?

At last Father Ger stepped forward. As the gravediggers began to reach for their spades, he started the 'Our Father'. The whole congregation, Catholic and Protestant, joined in, although they noticed that Knute did not. After it was over, he gestured towards the gravediggers again. But Castlehobble was not done yet: one 'Our Father' had not slaked their need to express their grief, to affirm their theological existence. From the depths of the crowd rose the unexpected sound of a prayer in Irish, guttural syllables soon taken up by the waiting throng.

Knute looked up, startled; it was his turn not to understand a word. But for the people of the islands, for whom it was their native tongue, it was still not half enough. They had heard poetry and prayer in every language except the ancient language of the place, the language still heard on the islands that glimmered in the bay, the language of the mountains, the language that had defied English, the language of the faith. If Martha Hanger had chosen to live in Castlehobble and had loved the area above all others in the world, then it would mourn for her in its own way. On that sunny hillside, the ragged keen of the rosary, 'The Sorrowful Mysteries', swelled to break, slow strophe after strophe, with the heavy stresses of the Gaelic.

*

At the post-mortem in Ralph's Bar it was generally agreed that things had gone well, the way they should, the proper way. 'We won,' said the boss, gloatingly; 'that last blast of the Irish, of the old Gaelic, finished them off. It sounded far better than that other old *ráiméis*. What was it, anyway?'

'Hebrew,' said a visitor, sharply. He was an American professor of Jewish ancestry on a sabbatical in Ireland, with a research project on

'Place in Irish Literature'. Castlehobble certainly was a place but it had recently begun to confound him. If it was so welcoming, with refugees from all kinds of different cultures, why this almost simultaneous insistence on the one true faith? He had tagged along to the funeral and found it impressive, the way all the traditions had found their natural place, even atheism. Then why this sudden triumphalism, this small-town piety?

He need not have worried: Martha Hanger had not played her last card. Through the week word got round, as rumour could travel only in Castlehobble, that Father O'Driscoll was going to say something on Sunday about the funeral, preach a sermon about his dear friend Martha's death. Even the late Saturday-night card school, artists, and determined alcoholics, all roused themselves that morning, waiting through, shivering through the length of the Mass for the final statement on Martha's death.

When, after the tinkle of the Mass server's bell had subsided, the priest turned to face his congregation, there was a stir of suspense. For the respectable citizens of Castlehobble, *les bien-pensants* or Holy Marys, still hoped that, despite all evidence to the contrary, the old truth would conquer, converting Martha into an unexpected proof of God's existence, despite that unheard-of behaviour in the graveyard. Maybe there had even been a deathbed conversion? God's ways were often strange, and Father O'Driscoll was as bright as they came, a seminary star who had once won an All-Ireland Medal for the county in Croke Park.

Remembering how often he had slipped past the wiles of players like Mick Mackey and Christy Ring and that this time he was playing for eternal stakes, they would not put it past him to outmanoeuvre a foreigner on the way to his goal.

They were certainly not prepared for what they heard. Row after row of Castlehobble Catholics sat in stiff disbelief as Father Ger warmed to his theme:

'A woman has died amongst us, an extraordinary woman. A woman whom we all loved, generous, charitable, and as she proved at the end, brave. There was a difference between us. She sincerely believed, like her husband, that God did not exist. You may think that this is because they lived in the great world, and saw things that we are spared in our green isle.'

Was Father Ger going to turn his argument around, to show how blessed we were in our geographical isolation; had Saint Patrick not said that Ireland would be drowned, not burned, at the end of the world? But

285

no – he continued, with fire and fervour, to defend Martha Hanger for not believing in God.

'A great English poet and laureate declared "There lives more faith in honest doubt,/ Believe me, than in half the creeds": that was the convinced position of Martha Hanger and her husband.' Whatever bargain had been struck in that sickroom, Father Ger kept to it with a vengeance; as well as a swingeing defence of atheism, he used Martha's example to lash his incredulous flock.

'You may think they disbelieved because they had seen the cruelty of man in far places. But our own brand of small-scale evil exists here: the butcher who slaughters the trembling lamb without thinking, the merchant who systematically overcharges, the factory farmer who despoils the fields, the drunkards on the farmer's dole, the ruthless property developer, the brutal schoolmaster, our association of unreformed alcoholics, who sometimes beat their wives and children when they are hauled home; the list is endless. And I have not included the mistreatment of animals for sport, for which this country is famous; remember the great lines of another English poet and, dare I say it again, saint? What would Blake have thought of coursing? "Each outcry of the hunted Hare/ A fibre from the brain does tear".

'So don't think for a moment that any victory was gained at this good woman's funeral. The ills that the Hangers have fought against all their lives are present in miniature in this village, painted over with piety. And it is that lesson we must learn from her death, endured so humbly. I say to all of you that if you were as sincere in your beliefs, as brave in your end, as Martha Hanger, then Castlehobble would indeed be a wonderful place. Her presence is still amongst us because she is as near as I have seen to . . . '

He paused while his dumbfounded flock waited for those final words which would ring in their minds for years.

'Martha Hanger, in her simplicity and dedication, to her family and to others, was as near as I have seen to what you call a saint. She was self-less, free from our corrosive malice, a giving spirit. She had that charity of which Saint Paul speaks: today she stands in the presence of God – or his absence, as she would have seen it. May we all strive to do as well in this world. I know that I will always try to follow her example.'

With tears in his eyes, but pride in his voice, Father Gerard O'Driscoll turned his back to the altar. The church was silent.

ACKNOWLEDGEMENTS

THE LOST NOTEBOOK

Mercier Press, 1987
A version of 'The Lost Notebook' appeared as 'Pilgrim's Pad' in *A Love Present* (Wolfhound Press, 1997) and in the Canadian journal *Exile*. It has also been translated into Italian and German.

A LOVE PRESENT

Wolfhound Press, 1997
'The Letters' in *Born in Brooklyn* (1990) (White Pine, Fredonia, New York, 1990); 'Mother Superiors' in *Fortnight*; 'A Prize Giving' in the *Irish Times*; 'Off the Page' in *Planet* in Wales and *Tracks* in Ireland; 'Above Board' in the *Irish Press*; 'The Parish of the Dead' in *Oberlin Quarterly* (1964); 'The Three Last Things' in *Shenandoah* (1997) in the United States.

DEATH OF A CHIEFTAIN

MacGibbon and Kee, 1964
Poolbeg, 1978
Wolfhound Press, 1998
Stories have appeared in the following magazines: *Arena*, *Elegance* (Amsterdam), *Diogenes*, *Gentleman's Quarterly*, *Kilkenny Magazine*, *Les Lettres Nouvelles* and *Threshold*. Acknowledgements are also made to the *Faber Book of Irish Short Stories* and the *Oxford Book of Irish Short Stories*. This collection has been translated into German: *Anlass zur Sünde* (Diogenes Verlag).